ARKAPELIGO
RISING

MA WEST

To My Lord and Savior

Jesus

PART 1
Chapter 1: No Tip   1
Chapter 2: Big M   9
Chapter 3: The Fog   21
Chapter 4: Emilia   33
Chapter 5: Family and Fog   41
Chapter 6: Hashmore   51
PART 2
Chapter 7: Begin Genesis Undone   63
Chapter 8: First Contact   67
Chapter 9: Intro the Doctors   83
Chapter 10: Aragmell   99
Chapter 11: Captain Calling   111
Chapter 12: Enter the Empire   123
Chapter 13: Time to Shine   129
Chapter 14: No Pain, No Gain   145
Chapter 15: Warrior See, Warrior Do   159
Chapter 16: To Make One's Bed   169
Chapter 17: Science, Schmience   177
Chapter 18: A Trip in Time   191
Chapter 19: Tallyho   209
Chapter 20: The Most Powerful Force in the Universe Chapter   221
PART 3
Chapter 21: Girl Time   229
Chapter 22: Prisoner Lift   237
Chapter 23: The Morning   245
Chapter 24: Shei Yao Yi Bei Shui?   255
Chapter 25: Cold Dawn   267
Chapter 26: Round and Round   279
Chapter 27: In the Name Of   289
Chapter 28: Blue Dawn   295
Chapter 29: Love's Need   305
Chapter 30: Angels and Demons   313
Chapter 31: The Briefing   325
Chapter 32: Omens and Comas   341
Chapter 33: I Say Hello, You Say Goodbye   357
Chapter 34: When Doves Eat   371
PART 4
Chapter 35: My Soul, My Soul, an Eternity for My Soul   385
Chapter 36: To Pray or Not to Pray   399
Chapter 37: Ascent of the Faithful   407
Chapter 38: Flight of the Faithful   415
Chapter 39: An Angel's Choice   431
Chapter 40: You Are What "What You Eat" Eats   441
Chapter 41: March to Victory   451
Chapter 42: Who Dares to Question the Lord?   465
Chapter 43: Fight or Flight   479
PART 5
Chapter 44: The Final Battle   489
Chapter 45: Rise of Captain Zeros   499

PART 1

1: No Tip

At last, the moment had arrived. Her lips moistened, her shoulders perched, and her thighs tightened. This was what made it all worthwhile. The control, the mastery, and the excitement were all hers to command. When she said go, the one would go. When she said come, the one would come. To the baroness, all the people here were her play toys—such was the power of this place.

They came in with the money, the fantasy, and the desire, but it was she who held the reins. The authority to decide who, which, and when was her untenable ace in the hole. The toughest, most decisive man would drop to his knees and beg when she held the fantasy so tantalizingly close yet so far out of reach. That was the experience she craved above all others. The leverage to conduct people, their purposes, and their methods was the strongest of all climaxes. Like a play written and performed live in her domain, the action flowed, with scenes being altered, edited, expanded, and revised in ways that she deemed fit until, at last, she released her dominance and sent them on their way.

There were, of course, always exceptions, and she took a deep breath as she watched one of those exceptions walk in her front door. In truth, he wasn't any different than the other johns who visited her establishment, well other than the fact he never tipped. Yet to her, there was something unspeakable, almost alien about him. It was more than just his spacey innocent look, but it was too hard to put into words what it was about him.

He lounged about, waiting patiently to be tended to, wearing that dopey aloof expression. She pushed the call button for the girls she thought would be suitable. These girls were more than her employees; they were her family. It was only with their collective help that she was able to rise to her position. However, as she pressed each button now, she felt herself cursing them. It was this man—this loser of a man—who excited her emotions and genitals, and she hated herself for it. But she shoved her irrational jealousy aside, slipped into character, and headed toward the lobby.

At last, the moment had arrived. His lips moistened, his mouth salivated, and his pants bulged. This was the experience he desired above all others. The so-called climax was nothing more than an ending and a transition on to the next. No, the physical enjoyments were nothing but a follow-through to the climax of the mind—a climax brought on not by touch but by power. The power to control people, their purpose, and their methods was the strongest of all hormones. Like a play written and performed live in his mind, the action flowed, with scenes being altered, edited, expanded, and revised in a battle between the actors and writers until, finally, the culmination erupted into the ejaculation of a perfect moment.

He downed the last of his drink and grabbed another from a passing waitress, who flirtatiously slid her hips into him. As a routine, alcohol was not on the agenda, but he needed to loosen up. There had been occasions in the past when, as the fantasy was building, an outside thought imposed itself and destroyed that perfect moment, which could be quite an expensive embarrassment. The thoughts about his daughter were most deadly—the fact that she would have been the same age as the employees, had she still been around, sometimes acted as such a trigger. Alcohol, he had found through trial and error, proved the best at subduing these intruders. And the positive physical effect also added value to the evening.

The baroness, a tightly shaped woman with a sharp face and a commanding posture, approached and wrapped her arms around him. Grabbing the back of the head, she pulled him in and passionately kissed him. "You are going to like these girls. They know how to please a man," she looked deep into his eyes, "as dignified as such."

This was why he had come here. Other establishments had mistaken his preferences, recruiting unfortunately young employees. Those places never saw his business, or any business, ever again. The baroness knew—she understood. It was never about the physical. Youthful optimism was his aphrodisiac. It was about the trains of thought, the curiosity to explore and see everything, and the arrogance to believe it could be done. The baroness only recruited professionals, girls not only smart enough to hold a conversation but perceptive enough to shift moods and emotions to match the situation. Their professionalism brought confidence, which was an adequate replacement for youthful arrogance and curiosity, and having an explorative nature was easy enough to fake, if so instructed.

Just as easy to fake, he thought, were power and status. That's what this place was, an adult playground—one full of role-playing children seeking out the exploration of a life lived only in a dream. He was no stranger to this, and neither were the employees. Every client had a backstory, a tale of sorrow for the self-pitying, a tale of adventure for the insecure, a web of deception and betrayal for those who had betrayed. As for the employees, money had always been seen as the quick street out of their childhood neighborhoods, a replacement for a missing father figure, or the next hit of addiction, whether it be physical or emotional.

His story, well he just made sure not to tell his story.

The lighting in the room shifted as if calling them to attention. A group of nine women walked in a chaotic cluster, as schoolchildren might do after their lessons on a summer day. Some of the girls held hands and whispered into an adjoining ear. It was well choreographed, as none went too far with it. There was no chasing or childish behavior. It was erotic.

The baroness found him sometime later. He sat alone in the locker adjacent to the shower, his back toward her. Her eyes carefully examined him—for what, she wasn't sure. She took a deep breath and nearly wondered aloud what it was about him that made her so interested. He was like most other men, scared and unaware of what they really wanted. She had seen it in his eyes as well as in a hundred others', the reflection of emptiness, an emptiness that they tried and failed to fill with shallow pursuits.

She waved off the two security guards who were accompanying her. They protested with a stern glance, as it was a strict matter of protocol that she be escorted during all collections. Again she waved them off, using her shoulder and hips to reinforce the message. It would be her job if something were to happen, as her bosses were very unforgiving people. Yet she was still unable to stop herself. She closed her eyes, put herself into character, and stepped forward.

"You must be quite the man. It's not often the girls ask me about a customer. Seems you have made an impression." If she startled him, he gave no impression. She approached quickly, wrapped her legs around his waist, and sat firmly on his crotch. It was a move she had performed many times. In addition to distracting the customers, who usually didn't take well to security, it placed her in a position of control. She grabbed his shirt and worked on the buttons.

"Only you, my dear, could make me so happy to hand over all my money." He spoke in a playful tone, but his words always seemed to carry a deeper message just outside her grasp. He ran his hands up her back, exciting parts that should not be.

She smelled his neck, sucking in his aroma. The lusty leftover pheromones from the girls snapped her back into work mode. It was a smell she was quite familiar with. No matter how hard they washed afterward, she could still always find the smell. Normally it didn't bother her, but on him, now it bothered her greatly.

"It's not money, dear. It's just a median. We scratch a little of yours. You scratch a little of ours. You wouldn't want your girls going itchy now, would you?"

"No, have to take care of the girls." He paused, giving her a look that shot straight through her. "So we all get what we need."

She knew exactly what he needed. He needed to be making love to a woman, not fucking these sluts. The word "slut" surprised her. Even if it was her own thought, how could she refer to the people she cared for and managed that way? "How much more do you need?"

"It's not how much—it's who. The perfect girl doesn't come along very often."

"And where are you going to find yourself one of those?" she asked, trying to be as cool and sexy as her emotions would allow.

"Find? No, found. Now it's just landing her." Something about the way he still lusted for her even after being pleasured was so enticing.

"Well you are sure scouting all the landing pads around here." She hoped her voice didn't reflect any of the jealously she was feeling as she said it.

He let out a little chuckle. "You keep sending bad directions."

He was not the first to flirt with her when she came to collect, but he seemed to be the most sincere. She ran her hands down his back and along his arms, grabbed his hands, one of which was holding the payment for tonight, and brought them close to her heart. Slipping the money—devoid of any tip—from his hand, she softly whispered, "Some flights never land."

What a woman! He consciously controlled his hands. Touching the girls was a paid privilege, but touching a baroness, now that could get a guy thrown out or even trespassed. Security or not, he wasn't about to lay a stray finger on her. Yet she made it so tempting. Her legs squeezed with just enough force to still feel smooth and powerful. Her smell drifted into his nose, and he felt intoxicated.

While not erect, he was fully aroused. This was a woman who knew how to build suspense. "Come with me." The sound excited him in a way no girl ever had before.

She led him down the main hall, and they entered the elevator. She pushed in a code on a keypad above the elevator controls, and the machine began its ascent. She said nothing, made no eye contact, but continued to hold his hand. Not knowing quite what this was, he decided it better to say nothing than to say something wrong. Determining what or how a woman was thinking was never in his deck of cards.

They got out on the roof floor of the three-story building. It was a cold New Jersey morning. Some of the city's high-rises could be seen reaching into the sky, out from behind the adjoining buildings. The smell of spring lilacs filled the early-morning air. It was a living roof—vegetables, herbs, and plants he didn't know the names of, because cooking wasn't really his thing. The lilacs next to the elevator were the biggest of the plants. Large raised beds filled the center of the roof, while tomato cages lined the sides.

Still, she said nothing but led him to the corner overlooking the front entrance. A chair sat on a small deck, where she motioned for him to sit. He complied, not sure what was about to happen. His heart raced, his hands sweat, and something between a tingle and a shiver ran up his spine. She sat on his lap but this time kept both legs to one side. He became very nervous. He had just performed—twice, in fact—that night. She would have known this. She couldn't be expecting him to perform again, could she?

She closed her eyes and wrapped her arms around his neck. He felt helpless in her presence, too nervous to touch, too unsure of what was happening to guess. A warm freeze stiffened him into place. She ran her hands down his back and lay her head against his chest. Then, for a long time, she did nothing.

2: Big M

The trained familiarity of her work phone's sounds interrupted them. The baroness hopped off his lap, strode toward the elevator, signaled security via the camera, and looked at the message. "Big M," it read. Her mood soured fast. Big M was one of the most annoying, arrogant, aristocratic fuckheads of a john. She pushed the lobby button, closed her eyes, and shifted into character.

She scrolled through the girls on duty in her mind's eye. Big M was difficult. She needed to use girls who could handle his personality. As she ran through them, she kept matching the girls up not with Big M but with him. Two thoughts followed the distraction. First, what the hell was his name? He always paid in cash, and it would be too revealing to ask one of the girls. Second, what the hell was she doing? She'd broken every rule just to toss it away at the ding of a ringtone.

The elevator door opened to the hallway, where Big M's security detachment had taken up various positions. There he was, all five feet eight of a mean little fuck. He had on a light-brown suit that was sloppily worn, unbuttoned. He had a handsome face, smooth skin, and a short well-trimmed mustache. He wore the lightening black of his hair to the side, as if it were a comb-over, with the sparse hair running down too far to one side of his head.

He was perched up against Melody, the front-desk girl, rubbing his genitals through his pants. "My cock's getting fuckin' lonely here," he yelled in a loud, drunken stupor.

The baroness's gut twisted. "Well my my, Big M, you know that's our specialty."

"Here is a fuckin' woman!" He placed his hand flat against Melody's face and gently pushed off, shifting his body to face the baroness. She sent Melody a glance of apology and solidarity. Big M came toward her, grabbing her breasts and moving in close. The smell of alcohol covered him like nasty cologne. She instinctively slapped his hand away and stepped to the side.

She took a commanding tone. "First we need to review the ground rules. We don't want a repeat of last time's misunderstanding." She grabbed him by the tie and pulled him toward her as she extended the last word. The elevator chimed, and she noticed the movement of bodies in her peripheral vision.

Big M reasserted himself, placing his fingers a bit too forcefully on her cheeks, and cupped her jaw. "Well find me some bitches that know how to treat a cock right." He pulled back in both tone and force. She could tell he was in a worse-than-normal mood tonight. This could mean trouble. He was a very rich and established client. Losing him would likely mean losing her job as well.

"We are ready for you. Come wash and prepare." She used her best business voice and gestured with her hands.

"I didn't come here for that. Now start sucking and get me a beautiful ass to fuck."

His impatience worried her, and she signaled for the on-deck girl. While the majority of the clientele were upper-class regulars, there was enough demand for instant gratification that the on-deck system had been implemented for weekend and holiday nights. She checked to see who it was. The girl's name was Terresa— young, inexperienced, troubled background, and new to the team all spelled trouble. Shit, why hadn't she bussed one of her go-to girls, damn it? She had slipped up in the elevator and let herself get distracted by whoever the hell that guy was.

"This here is Terresa, and she will get you started. I'll fetch some of your favorite girls and send them in." She grabbed Terresa's hand and placed it directly on the bulge in the pants. It was a signal not meant to be subtle. She also whispered into her ear, "Do exactly as he says, and I will get you some help as soon as I can." She looked earnestly into Terresa's eyes.

Big M put his hand down the back of Terresa's skirt, moved his hand around underneath the clothes, pulled it out, smelled it, smiled, and said, "Now that I can fuck."

The words surprised "No Tip" even though he was the one speaking them. "Now that is a man I want to buy a drink for!" He had already startled security by coming off the elevator. Now he was their absolute center of attention. "This, this is a man who knows how to treat a fuckin' lady. So where are those drinks?" He slapped Big M on the ass as he finished the sentence. Security was close, within arms' distance, but they were cool, obviously used to dealings in such settings.

"Damn right, treat 'em right and they fuck you over. Fuck

'em right and they bend over for you." Big M laughed and offered a high five that was childishly returned.

"You sure picked a nice one. Join me and make her squirm a little while." Big M paused at the invitation. "We cockmasters get to decide not only when they have had enough but also how much and when they get it." No Tip raised his finger, portraying a sense of deep thought from a drunk.

Big M looked over Terresa as if inspecting a product. The baroness had shifted her position so that Terresa could still see her while looking in the direction of her client, and she almost looked like a base coach signaling a runner. After an instant's delay, Terresa gave a pouty look and leaned into him. "Don't make me wait."

The performance was enough. Big M yelled for the waitress, who in all the cluster of bodies still managed to arrive as if on cue.

No Tip put a slight crook in his lips and proudly ordered two cosmos. After pausing for effect, he broke out laughing like a boy on a playground and threw a few gentle jabs into Big M's stomach. The joke hit the right tone with Big M, but he quickly switched the drink order to scotch on the rocks.

The two enjoyed their drinks and shuffled over to the lobby. No Tip told some more casual jokes as he began searching his pockets. The worried look on his face was enough to signal a woman as intuitive as the baroness, and she sent the waitress up to collect.

Big M was happy to oblige and called over one of the guards, who put his hand into an inside jacket pocket and drew near. The process was interrupted by No Tip's discovery of his wallet in a forgotten pocket. He put some cash on the tray and grabbed the two glasses that had been prepared in anticipation of another round. The two raised their glasses and downed them. No Tip reacted strongly to the drink, coughed, and spurted out, "I'll let you get to that little lady now."

He stood up straight and stumbled into the guard who had stepped forward when summoned for money. Sure enough, as was common in the industry, there was a clip in the upper breast pocket, attached with a small retractable string. He cut the string with a tiny blade he had surgically installed under his thumb and palmed the clip. Two different security guards grabbed him by the upper arms and wrists, escorted him to the door, and less than gently threw him out.

The baroness thought to herself, did he just fucking do that? What kind of balls must that guy have to go around fucking pick-pocketing the security of someone as powerful as Big M? That scam never would work on her. She'd picked up on it from the first line, pretty classic approach and technique. She had to admit, the execution was flawless, but what balls. An inner part of her felt drawn to him as security escorted him out. It was the bravest gesture she had ever seen, and it pissed her off greatly. Now she no longer had a problem she could control. It was no longer a matter of shifting players and positions. The bar had been set much higher. She had the means to attain a higher goal, a legitimate method to permanently get rid of a huge problem. She could ask for money up front, allow the discovery, and simply end the night, hopefully. Or—and the thought ached her—she could allow Big

M to do what he was prone to do, get too worked up, beat Terresa, and try to pay it off. This time, however, he wouldn't have the money and she would enforce his permanent dismissal. She took a deep breath and thought to herself, that man, what a beautiful asshole. Then she made her decision.

The look on Terresa's face showed her that it didn't take long for Big M's hand to find its way back into her skirt, and the bulge from behind indicated penetration, but not which hole. She watched the front door and took note as the guards threw No Tip to the left and directed Big M and Terresa toward an open room. That devilish smile on Big M's face made her sick to her stomach.

"Benson, clip now," Big M barked. The same guard as before obliged, only to discover en route that it had gone missing. Not missing a beat, Big M issued orders to the remaining guards, using his hands, and then focused all his attention on the baroness. "Who was he?" His eyes cased the room.

An icy shiver shot down her spine. Big M's advance was fast. His hands were on her face, and now she knew which hole it had been. She fought the impulse to flee, calming herself as best she could. "Now, sir, we are a business. If I disclosed another customer's identity to you, would you trust me not to disclose yours to another?"

Big M scared her with his raging eyes, but after a few moments of his penetrating stare, he turned around and went to Benson.

The baroness took advantage of the change in attention by calling the waitress over. "Find him. Check east alley first. Hide him." The words were chalky and rough as she spat them out.

"Find who?" the waitress asked.

The baroness paused for a second. "No Tip."

The waitress nodded and departed.

Big M spoke the words in a clear, cold, and crisp manner "You're fired." The guard bowed his head and turned to a petite man dressed in all black and wearing an earpiece. The guard, now unemployed, handed over his sidearm, his wallet, and a few other miscellaneous items before he departed. Big M tilted his head toward the petite man. "Do we have him yet?"

The petite man spoke into his wrist, put his finger to his ear with the piece in, and then nodded. "They will be bringing him around now, Mr. M."

Two guards dressed in black suits brought in the man the baroness knew only as No Tip by the arms and placed him before Big M.

With barely enough time between his ejection from the establishment and his return in custody to stash the billfold, it was unclear if they had seen him drop it in the planter. Once again, the man known as No Tip was in the clutches of armed men. The guards brought him before Big M, restraining his arms behind his back.

Big M's tone was much friendlier than he had anticipated, and that made everyone nervous. "Forgive the roughness, but there seems to be a misunderstanding."

"Happy to help clear up any confusion." He looked to the

right and left, making eye contact with the guards and hoping to get released, but they held firm.

"Good, then give it back."

"Give what back?"

"And you were doing so well. I thought for a second we might not have to go this route, but I'm happy we are." Big M smiled and then placed his hand directly to the right of his prisoner's groin. Big M pressed hard, and it hurt. It took everything not to scream. Big M placed his other hand on No Tip's shoulder and dug his finger in deep. Had the guards not been holding him, he would have collapsed.

The baroness approached. "Gentleman this is a place of business. If there is a problem, I suggest you take it down the block, where you won't draw attention here."

"Shut your mouth, whore," said Big M. "I'm attending to my business." Big M then made a hand gesture to the guards, who promptly chained and shackled No Tip's hands and feet.

"You going to arrest me?"

"No, I'm not an idiot. You, however, just might be. Search him." Several hands began a thorough search of all his pockets.

"Now, I get charged when the girls do this. Am I going to have to pay you too?"

"Glad to see you're keeping your spirits up, but I know how to deal with you, scum. Petty little suckball, you fucking leech off the good portions of society, spreading your seed through wretched whores, expanding the useless class. No, laws and rules don't mean anything to you. Your kind only knows one thing, dominance by superiority just like animals. Now let me demonstrate to you what happens when you fuck with me and the domination I can show." The petite guard handed Big M something as he came over. He ripped open No Tip's shirt, grabbed his nipple, pulled on it, and then sliced it off.

No Tip screamed out in pain as Big M continued to carve away. One of the waitresses hurried over to the baroness. The two engaged in hushed conversation, and then the waitress walked toward the group.

"Big M, sir, I'm sorry to interrupt, but one of the girls found this in the bathroom. It's got your picture on it, see, right there." She handed the billfold to one of the guards and backed off.

The baroness stepped in. "Whore or not, this is my establishment, and I don't welcome patrons who victimize my customers. You, Big M, will never be allowed in this establishment again, and any attempt to do so will result in a very public humiliation for you."

The speed of the baroness's demand threw Big M off. His anger immense, he put his face into No Tip's. "I don't know how you accomplished this trick, but you won't fool me. I own this town. There is nothing you can do. Are you and your little bitches going to kick us out?"

"Yes, yes we are." The baroness spoke with confidence. She raised her arms, and what must have been her entire staff filled the room, crowding out all of Big M's security detail. It was a masterful piece of coordination by the employees, from doormen to cleaners, the girls themselves, and maybe even a few stray johns mixed in to shore up the numbers.

"These whores are not worthy of our business. Expect a visit from the police. Your place is shut the fuck down now!"

The baroness smiled as if she had the upper hand. "Do that and YouTube just might find itself a new celebrity dirtbag."

The short man scowled at the baroness and then signaled for the group's departure, while Big M looked deep into the eyes of his new enemy and slammed his forehead into him, knocking him unconscious. As No Tip lay unconscious and bleeding from the chest, Big M snorted and left at a forced natural pace.

He awoke to find her side of the bed empty. He shouldn't have been surprised, but he was, and he was also saddened by it some too. He lifted the covers and looked at the bandages covering his nipple. Some pads had been placed directly over the wound, and tape wrapped across his body, keeping it in place. Some blood had seeped through the dressing overnight.

"Just in the nip of time for some tea." The baroness entered wearing a plush, billowy robe tied tightly, along with some tights or leggings—he wasn't quite sure. She held two cups in her hands.

He pretended not to hear the "nip" comment and stretched, trying to flex some muscle, and let out a deep "Hell—" but as the word began, his nipple ripped open again, causing his tongue to roll the "l" and drop the "o."

"Did you nip well last night?" The baroness smiled, sounding carefree like a teenager enjoying her first romance. "You will need a new nipple bandage." She put down the cups on a dresser near the bed, opened the drawer, and took out a little white box that contained bandages and other first-aid materials.

"I'm not sure if it's a turn-on or not that you need a first aid kit near your bed. What kinda stuff you into?"

"Nipples, mostly. Sorry, guess that means you're not my type." The baroness climbed on the bed and came close to him, placed her arms under his, and sat him up at an intimate range.

He tried to grab the end of the lace tying the robe shut but was redirected as the baroness pulled his bloody nipple patch off. She giggled childishly at his attempt to play off the pain.

"So it's nurse by day, baroness by night. Alter egos can have dangerous repercussions, young lady."

"And the nipple calls the rose red."

"Not me, just one ego too big for the universe and too small for myself."

"If only you had the skill set to match."

"Slip off that robe and I'll show you my skill."

The baroness couldn't hold back a laugh at the line. "Ain't no bedroom move going to get you into these pants."

"So how do I share your pants?"

The baroness grabbed his hands and placed them over her heart. "The right way."

3: The Fog

The pounding, the fog, the murmuring voices—they all signaled a bad day ahead. The voices' chattering echoes ricocheted throughout the girl's skull. She tried to move her arm, but restraints kept it in place. She looked carefully, but the fog hadn't cleared yet and was too thick to see through. Morning fog never brought good news.

"She's foggy again. I can't believe this." The words took a while to catch as they bounced unpredictably around her cranial cavity. Assembling them into a thought would still take some effort in the mist.

A cold wave permeated the fog, turning it blue. She rested for a minute, taking in the beauty of what she was seeing. The fog started to dance, and clumps gathered together as if they were being collected by huge invisible hands molding them to their whim. She felt like she could reach out and touch them, but it was an illusion created by the clumps, for as they continued to amass together, each time was farther and farther out of reach.

Slowly, a scene formed in front of her. Two people, a man in a uniform and a pretty—if not past her prime—woman stood in a doorway, speaking together. The straightforward body language suggested an intense and engaging conversation, but it was a distraction, and experience had taught her that once she lost to the clouds, it was all over.

"Look, look, she's slouching forward. She's coming around." The woman in uniform rushed to her side, yelled something, and then left the room in a hurry.

She turned her focus toward the man as he approached at her side. His voice sent a cascade of echoing bullets into her skull. They came too fast and screechy to be caught, leaving only chaos in their wake.

The woman in uniform returned with two others, whose uniforms were a different color, and they rushed to her side. They grabbed her, but she resisted, found her leg, and kicked it fervently out and up. It struck something, although she couldn't tell what. Her arms had been restrained, and as hard as she might try, they weren't letting go. No wonder, she soon realized, she was strapped down good.

"Who am I?" The words came loudly and were easy to catch, if not painful. "Who am I?" The words came again. "Who am I?" Again the words came, demanding an answer. "Who am I?" The words came again, and again, and again. The answer, while in her possession, still eluded her. "Who am I?" The words were softer, more patient this time. "Who am I?" The words were almost a whisper. "Who am I?" Then there was an answer: "Daddy."

⟨⟩

Today was twenty years. For three years, Drexter had assisted the design team, and for seventeen, he had been in charge of development, but now it was judgment day. His stomach twisted, and his heart sank as he watched her get out of the chair. Project Sasha consumed his entire existence, not allowing for a single day off, nor a day of sick leave. Sometimes he envied others, both parents and officers. Officers got to take their leave, and he often heard of exciting debauchery or pleasant, relaxing days with loved ones. Even parents got to take advantage of babysitters, grandparents, and date nights, yet there was none of that for him.

During the early years, it was especially stressful. There was always some political desk jockey vying for the project's termination, objecting on some John Lennon idiomatic fantasy ideal. It had cost him his career, and his rank, to save the project, which was all he ever had in his life. Now she was all he had—well her and one other, a secret other. Whenever his desires started to outweigh his resolve, he would find a bit of personal space and escape in a cloud of green smoke or enjoy a special sweet.

"Sasha, Sasha." He waited for her eyes to meet his. "Today is the day, Sasha. Today is the day we make that movie I've been talking about." He continued to watch her eyes. The fog was clearing, and he began to see the scared little girl trapped inside. "Sasha, tell me you remember."

A faint whisper came from her lips. "Yes."

"Good, good. So you remember what you agreed to. You agreed to wear the headband."

A monstrous, almost-evil roar erupted from within. "NO."

"Yes, Sasha. Yes, you agreed."

She again exploded in disagreement.

"Sasha, I won't play this game with you, not today. Now you agreed to wear it." He played an audiotape of the girl's voice agreeing to wear the headband.

A much milder sound came from the girl this time. "No."

"I am going to put it down here on your side table. Place it on correctly and I will remove the waist restraint. Complete your exercises, eat your nutrition, and then I think we can find some time for fun this afternoon." He watched her eyes carefully. The answers always lay in her eyes. The fog was her fuse, not designed or built in, just nature's ways. She would comply. He felt the twist in his stomach start to relax. Attaining the desired performance goals was never difficult. Sasha was the perfect athlete, agile and alert, and she possessed a gracefulness unmatched in the universe. However, getting the desired actions from her was an entirely different matter. Fun was not something she was accustomed to. It was a luxury he kept in reserve for big events, and this morning's evaluation was such an event.

She put on the headband and assumed the correct posture to indicate to the operator that she was ready and that the remaining restraints could be released. She stood up, walked over to an exposed closet, and grabbed her exercise suit. "Daddy, I know what I want to do for fun today. I have been thinking about it for a long time, Daddy."

"What is it you would like to do today, Sasha?" It was important he continue to use her name. It was a form of control, and Sasha was a girl who needed to be controlled.

"I want to make a friend today, Daddy."

The knot in his stomach came back with a vengeance.

Thanks to a little delay in the recording, the event was going spectacularly. They were on the base's rifle range, with Sasha currently demonstrating her superior marksmanship skills. She was responding in accordance with the commands, and as predicted, her test results proved astounding. Of course, she was well practiced in each of the drills. Sasha was not a girl made for schooling in the traditional sense. She had instructors, herself, and her classmates, all developed under the same program.

Drexter had been a rising star, an Ivy League graduate with an enlisted background. As much as he would never admit it in public, being black certainly helped his cause. White politicians were always anxious to be seen with so-called successful minorities, and he used that to his full advantage.

Initially, this program was supposed to be a stepping stone, but some problems arose with the classmates. An instructor was killed in cold blood. When instructed to terminate the offending classmate, a second broke ranks, terminating a third. It was a massive black eye for an expensive and secret program. Deaths were not easy to keep quiet, and a breach would mean the end of the program. They offered him a nice easy job at the academy. No more a shining star, he pushed and pushed, called in favors, and finally, after talking to the chief of staff himself, won a small victory. The program would be wound down rather than dismantled wholesale—no more classes, no more instructors, no outside contact, just keep the girl from becoming a problem.

There had already been long discussions over the issue.

Social contact was limited to the doctors, his boss, and him. It was a safety issue and would not be negotiated further. Yet he still wanted, wanted to give her just this one. His mind tussled back and forth between following orders and risking it for her. He had a plan, one he had come up with long ago. There was an old VIP shelter in a basement in Manhattan. There was also a girl Sasha's age in Manhattan, a girl who might be able to relate a little bit to Sasha.

He remembered the recording as Sasha hit another bull's-eye. Speaking into it, he explained to the viewing audience: "The initial fear that the subject would lack fine motor skill has not come to fruition. In fact, the subject has shown an extreme increase in her ability to control her fine motor skills." He barked out a command: "Sasha, flying crane."

The girl changed her shooting position to a well-rehearsed pose. Sasha arched her back and threw her left leg up and back, her right arm out, and while facing downrange, fired off a shot that hit the outer ring of the bull's-eye. She then swung her entire body around and, arching her back with seemingly inhuman flexibility, now faced downrange upside down and fired off another shot.

"As you can see," he spoke into the recorder, "Sasha is able to maintain near-perfect steadiness even while in a pose most of us are unable to enter at all. Even more than that, and the true greatness of this project, is Sasha's ability to process and react faster than any human on earth." He hoped that his nervousness didn't come across in his voice, but this was a part in the demonstration that tended to bring about the fog, as it was so termed. He barked another command: "Sasha, identify and engage only blue targets with red centers, and catch."

He pushed a button that engaged a string of ten multicolored targets at the far end of the range, moving them at moderate speed from left to right. He also picked up five hackie sacks. He underarmed the first hackie sack, placing it within easy range of Sasha's free hand. A shot fired just as she caught the small sack. He threw the second one, also underarm, near her outstretched leg. She caught the bag with her foot and fired another shot. A second shot rang out almost immediately afterward. He threw the third bag directly at her, hoping the rapid fire didn't reveal the much rehearsed aspect of the drill. Amazingly, Sasha raised the weapon out of the way in order to catch the bag with her mouth. She then re-aimed the weapon in her shoulder and fired almost as quickly as her eyes could get downrange. He threw the fourth bag high and fast, uncatchable, except for Sasha, who broke pose and extended the rifle into the air at maximum range. With the rifle butt stock, she intercepted the bag, allowing it to fall into her open hand as she retook her pose. He stretched out his arm and dropped the final bag.

Two shots rang out as Sasha grabbed the rifle barrel and swung it and her body around. She tossed the rifle forward, landing it softly on the ground. The bag dropped gently on top of the rifle butt stock. Years, actual years, he had spent on this demonstration. It was a delicate matter to find a right setting to avoid bringing on the fog. Leaving her disarmed was also a lesson quickly learned in the experimentation phase of development.

He swallowed hard and turned his back to Sasha. It was a risk for sure. Normally, he would go through the fog protocol, but today was demonstration day, and he took the risk. "As you can see, the Sasha program has created the world's most potentially lethal weapon. Sasha correctly identified seven of the ten targets as blue with red in the center." He moved the camera to zoom in on the targets. "A quick tally shows two shots in the red, three in the black, one shot high, and another one low and left. Clearly, the desired physical attributes have been accomplished, but as we all know, the crux of the matter is of course control." He brought the camera back and approached Sasha.

"Sasha, mission accomplished. Report." He barked the order.

Sasha exited her pose. Her chest was heaving, and she was perspiring. He looked into her eyes. The fog was there, but still light. He muscled about his best reassuring smile and reissued the order. For a long stretch, nothing happened. Damn, he thought. He was too slow. The fog must have set in while he was doing the wrap-up. He issued the command one more time: "Sasha, mission accomplished. Report."

Sasha took a deep breath. "Ten of twelve objectives completed, ready for instructions."

"Hydrate and standby." He moved back to the recorder and finished his well-prepared speech, urging the continuation of the program.

⟨⊐⟩

Daddy was pleased. She could always read that hidden smile. Sure, he had gotten better at hiding it, but Sasha could still read him like an open book. He was worried—he had gotten worse at hiding that. She didn't think it was the testing or going off base that bothered him. It was her. That was why he was trying so hard to hide it.

"Sasha, today was . . . is a very . . . important day in the, um, growth of a . . . young adult."

He was so nervous, and he only stammered when it was something he didn't want to talk about.

They were on the highway now, approaching the city. The skylight beamed as tall in life as it had in heart. Her thoughts of just how many ordinary people were out there distracted her from Father's relentless verbal roundabouts. "Special people, special adults, special young adults are isolated, I mean, trained. I mean, special, trained, young special adults . . ." What could all those ordinary people be doing? She pictured a man saying goodbye to his coworkers, walking out of the building on his way to hop on the subway toward home. Maybe the wife called and said she had a hard day and wanted him to pick up dinner. A variety of food choices circulated through the image in her head before the man decided and moved on.

"And that special training is what makes you special. So special that you had to be specially trained individually."

Tonight, she imagined on, the man bought some Chinese. The base Chinese was always awful, but she thought it could have been so tasty if cooked by a real Chinese. Her mind's eye could see him sitting on the subway, with two Styrofoam containers and a small pouch in a plastic bag resting in his lap. He had to bring his computer home today, no escaping work tonight.

"Now it's important that we have some . . . unique conditions and, um, unique experiences that make you unique."

Father had changed keywords. This could be a long speech.

Her daydream continued with a beggar sitting just close enough to make the man feel uncomfortable. She could see the man wrestling with the morality of the situation. He wanted the wontons, at least one, since he was going to have to work late tonight. The thought of offering the poor man half of the wontons crossed his mind, but he couldn't think of a way to divide the food in a way that wouldn't be rude.

"Now don't let your uniqueness bother you. Just be . . . aware of others' uniqueness too. Aware, yes, aware that they are unique too."

They were approaching the bridge to take them into the city. The traffic had slowed, as volume was building. She imagined the sub car again. Handing over the whole bag of wontons would of course be the easiest way, for the man had been putting on a few extra pounds lately, and spring was coming. Luckily, his stop arrived before any action was taken, and he was able to disembark with wontons still intact.

"Awareness is the key, awareness of uniqueness and the, um, special unique awareness of that uniqueness."

She saw the man adjust his bag as he trudged down the hallway and up the stairs, out onto the street level. Her mind imagined him taking a deep breath, smelling the flavors of his impending dinner. Then, out of nowhere, a public bus flew in off the street and smashed the man dead center into a light post behind where he was standing. The sudden turn to violence startled Sasha.

"What, what'd I say?" Father had obviously noticed the startle.

"It's nothing. Would you just get to the point, already?"

"The point is, you need to be aware of yourself and how uniquely different your experience has been. Your new friend will reference many things you haven't been exposed to yet, and I don't want you to feel bad about that. It's just the way it had to be because of the incident and the fog."

Father had stressed that word many times before: the "fog." It wasn't her fault it happened. It's just that when things happened, they got foggy, and then she woke up somewhere new. Whether only a few feet away or a few hours later, she never knew how long it was going to last or where it was going to take her. Nor did she know what was causing it. Father had said it was the brain's way of dealing with the requirements of her job. Well too bad it didn't come with an off switch, she thought to herself.

"Seriously, keep things very relaxed. If, if, IF you sense any—and I mean ANY—fog, you go to the bathroom and call me. Do you understand?"

She understood, and understood it was important too. Why couldn't he just understand that it was important to her as well and that she wasn't going to do anything to screw it up? This conversation was starting to bother her. She looked forward and sat still.

"Young lady, do you understand?" This time, Father waited for an answer. He looked at her. "Sasha, do you understand?"

Again she stood still, motionless. She didn't mean to start out this way, but she figured humor was the best choice for this occasion, and she waited for the right tone in his questioning.

"Sasha, Sasha, what happened? Is it happening now?"

That was the tone, so she slowly turned her head toward Father, stared blankly, and yelled, "Boo."

4: Emilia

For a military establishment, it was very nice, a VIP fallout shelter built in the forties as a WWII bomb shelter, converted over to offices and storage in the sixties. The government had only reestablished occupancy when Synied, a military research contractor, took over the building. Being in a post–9/11 world, it was decided that Manhattan would need increased VIP sheltering capacity. For now, however, nobody needed sheltering, so only a minimal staff of private security were occupying the premises.

Emilia was six feet one of pure mixed-blood beauty. An early base subject, she was the product of genetic marriage but was denied the enhancements after scoring too low on the ability test. Her knowledge of the program, while limited, kept her under the military umbrella, with assigned caretakers and on-base education. Emilia was a girl who could understand the desperately lonely situation Sasha was coming from.

Emilia had been escorted in prior to their arrival, and she sat thumbing a magazine as the elevator door opened. A strange tension built up between them as if the overripe nature of the thing had spoiled it. Drexter and Sasha approached Emilia, and she began to rise in greeting. Emilia's cleavage was unmistakable as she rose, and it was the first time in quite a while that Drexter had felt anything of a libidinous nature.

He skimmed the top sheet of paper in his right hand and began reading aloud: "Emilia Echoheart and Sasha are hereby granted twelve hours' leave with the following restrictions. There are no off-base privileges, no weapon privileges, no vehicle privileges. Both of you are to report back to me at no later than," he looked at his watch, "2030 hours. Any questions?" Both girls looked rather blankly at him like children watching TV in another room.

Rather than press the issue, he decided to retire to his own rest and relaxation. He peeked into all the rooms before choosing a couch in a study at the far end of the corridor that connected the rooms, similar to an office building. The smell of his feet, while not pleasant to the nose, was soothing to the soul. This must be what it is like for single parents on the outside, he thought, always looking to pawn their children off on a playmate or trustworthy adult so as to find that peace-of-mind time.

For several minutes, he let his mind wander, from past memories to future dreams and back again. A burst of girlish laughter brought a smile to his face. Children having a good time and, via extension, the parent getting credit for that fun while not actually having to be physically involved—that's a win-win. He thought back to the one and only attempt the program had made to throw a birthday party for one of the program subjects. The idea of children's games seemed appropriate, and in the right spirit, but placing balloons around genetically engineered warriors showed bad judgment. The administrators were forced to use their last resort in order to get the situation under control. They had to gas the whole lot. Developing social skills, they thought, could be done later in the program. Developing loyalty, obedience, and courage was a higher priority. The birthday-party fiasco was one of many examples disproving their first thoughts.

〈ㄷ〉

Daddy left the room, and Sasha stood there not quite knowing what to say or what to do. After a second, she walked up and hugged Emilia. "Thank you for being my friend." Even to Sasha, it sounded a little desperate, but she didn't care. For so long, she had been lonely, longing for companionship. Daddy had always been good, but when it came to socializing, he was a poor example. She remembered playing Barbies with him. Time after time, the tea party or big date would always get redirected to a mission or be interrupted by some villain. Daddy was the king of trying, but often the king of failing too. How she longed to play dress up, wear makeup, or even go on a date. Now there was someone to do all those things with. Sasha imagined herself and Emilia laughing together as they tried on elegant dresses and talked about impossible futures. She had no idea how to make that happen. Luckily, Emilia broke the ice by offering Sasha some soda and cookies.

The two sat in awkward silence for a few long minutes, staring at the cookies. A thousand thoughts ran through Sasha's mind. Long before the birthday-party incident had left her completely isolated from anyone her own age, much less female, she would daydream about this moment. She would imagine holding hands, whispering secrets, and giggling. Her thoughts raced faster as the nervousness over the silence grew. This was nothing like what she had imagined, and a sense of panic grew inside her. She blurted out the first question that came to mind. "Can you tell if your boobs are still getting bigger?"

The sheer bluntness and personal nature clearly caught Emilia off guard. Her face expressed surprise and disbelief, yet she took her time and smiled before answering. "I know, isn't it the most annoying thing in the world? It's like, please don't stop, please don't stop, but then they don't, and suddenly they just get in the way whenever you're trying to do anything." Emilia wiggled her arms around her chest. "Then," she stressed the word, "there is the boob sweat. As if the new hormones and smells weren't enough, now I have to worry about boob sweat too. It's like, give me a break."

Sasha laughed more genuinely than ever before, now relieved of the emotional and physical tension. The hair along her back stood up, and a shiver ran down her spine and even lower, as she realized that they would be close friends—close not because of her but because of Emilia.

The sound of cupboards opening and closing stirred Drexter back to life. Expecting to see teenagers on the prowl for food, he instead found Emilia in a slightly bewildered hunt, for despite searching the pantries, she was moving too fast to consider any of the options. "How is it going?"

"First I thought it was kinda childish for her to want to play hide-and-seek, but she is actually kinda hard to find."

He chuckled. "I know from firsthand knowledge how true that can be. How are you two getting along?"

Her lips suggested she was about to speak, when she pulled back and changed her facial expression. "Fine," her voice dropped off a little, "sir."

"Relax, Emilia, this isn't some sort of test, trial, or exam. There are no cameras, no examiners. The program you knew is long gone. Sasha is just a ruminant fighting to survive in a world not yet ready for her."

"So she will be fighting, then?"

"Life is a battle, Emilia. But some battlefields are easier to see than others. Somewhere down inside Sasha is a young woman engaged in battle, fighting her situation, her conditioning, her upbringing. All of that fighting just to be the young woman she is supposed to be. You, Emilia, I'm counting on you to be the catalyst that desperate young girl needs to flourish. So let me ask you again, how is it going?"

Emilia's hard look softened. She still measured her words, but they felt more honest. "She has all the hallmarks of a homeschooled child. Some private things she just can't wait to tell me, despite the newness of our relationship, and many common things she wants to avoid as if deeply personal in nature."

The thoughtfulness of her answer impressed him, and he was about to express it when she came back with more. "Which is an indication that she longs to connect with someone on a deep basis and has no selective judgment on whom to form that relationship with, while actually fearing that same relationship because she knows the difference in frames of reference will be so great that the relationship may flounder."

He wasn't quite sure he got her meaning. "That sounds fairly clinical and rehearsed."

"Well that's because it is. It's from my own chart. Why are you asking me if she is normal? How the hell should I know? My whole life, kids have looked to me as the normal one. They were always like, wow, you lived here your whole life, so you must be so normal. But I couldn't be! Every time I would make a friend, they would leave the next year. Then, again, make a friend and they leave, make another friend and they leave. No, normal is having a mother, a father, and a home. All I had was a place. Why did you bring Sasha here? Did you think we would become best friends? We will probably never see each other again. How close do you think we should get?" Pent-up anger flared through her voice.

He stepped back and quivered. "I just thought the two of you could have some fun. I'm sorry I put too much pressure on you."

A tear swelled in Emilia's eye, and her jaw shook a little. "I really can't find her."

He held out his arms to hug her. "Don't worry, I will help you find her."

It was somewhat touching, and Sasha wiped away the beginnings of a tear. Emilia was a confusing girl to Sasha, but it was more than just figuring out a new person. Whenever Sasha looked at Emilia, she became stricken with feelings. Most of their early conversations had been awkward, like two virgins groping in the dark, hoping to find something they both liked. Nervousness overcame her whenever there arose a pause in conversation or action. She longed for Emilia's approval and attention.

"Sasha dear, have you been listening?" Daddy spoke the question, not sure where to direct the sound.

This game of hide-and-seek no longer seemed appropriate, so she announced her presence as she climbed down from the upper corner of the ceiling. A small hallway extended out from the kitchen, where Sasha had wedged herself into the upper corner. "Yes, Daddy, I have."

Emilia's stunned look brought a certain self-confidence to Sasha, and she liked the feeling. In fact, she liked most of the feelings she got from Emilia.

Daddy offered to order some pizza, but she wasn't hungry. "Daddy, I want to go shopping."

His face twisted, revealing the answer long before any words came out. "Now, Sasha, I am very proud of what you accomplished this morning, but I am afraid we are not ready for a shopping trip."

"We or you? You are the one who's not ready!" Hostility arose in her voice.

"Don't you take up a tone with me, little lady."

Emilia broke in, calming things down. "Ooh, really, what did you accomplish this morning, Sasha?"

Sasha and her father stared at each other for a long, hard moment. Then, taking Emilia's lead, they each backed off.

"Sasha is the world's best athlete, dexterous beyond belief, extremely well coordinated and balanced like a cat, and all Sasha did this morning was prove it."

Sasha's cheeks blushed, not so much because of what was

said but because of who heard it.

"Wish I could have seen that. How does one prove such a thing?"

"Sasha, how about giving us a demonstration? What about running man?" Daddy asked.

Sasha nodded, and Daddy moved Emilia over into the middle of the kitchen, about ten feet away from the wall. Sasha moved to the entryway and began sizing up the maneuver.

Father yelled, "You have a nine-foot ceiling, so be mindful of your clearance."

She took a deep breath, ran three strides, and jumped forward, clearing Emilia's head and stretching out her entire body in midair. She landed into a summersault and used her momentum to jump out and up. She made sure to keep her speed up as she ran up the wall, rotating her body so as to run back across the room, perpendicular to the floor, above Emilia's head. The move worked as it was designed to do, and Sasha ended up behind Emilia, who had turned around to see the spectacle. Emilia was clearly impressed. "So don't play against you in basketball, got it."

Sasha smiled, happy that she had been able to impress her new friend.

5: Family and Fog

His heart sank a little when he saw the phone number. It would be Major Brandett. "Yes, Major, this is Drexter." He tried to sound normal as his mind searched for what could be the matter. It was much too early for a program decision, unless it was to be terminated.

"Major, yes, hello, where are you?"

"Yes, sir, you see, I filled out the leave statements. I put them on Lorine's desk."

"I don't have time, Major, to go looking for some damn piece of paper. Just tell me where the hell you are!"

"Manhattan, sir, the Synied building, military research lab." He had always found it difficult to develop a rapport with the major. They had a history, in fact. Drexter had been promoted to major before Brandett. Brandett had maintained that grudge despite having had much more second-half career success than Drexter. Even after losing his rank, the major still held it against him.

"What the hell are you doing there?" The major waited just long enough to make him think he wanted a response. "Well it doesn't matter. Out of the way is where I need you. The president has made some considerable moves, and we are prepping for something big. Can't tell you what because I don't know. What

I do know is that we are expecting domestic deployment, which means to us that Project Sasha will not be deployable. Again, your mission is to keep her under control and out of the way. Now give me a real assessment, no politicking. I'm going to need all the manpower and officers I can get. Can Project Sasha be left unattended and still be controlled?"

This was a new tone for the major. Drexter scanned it for traps. Then, deciding that it was a genuine request, he gave it a genuine answer. "For how long a time frame, sir? If we are talking hours, then yes, I would say this location can be made to accommodate those conditions safely. But there is a time limit on that, sir. This young girl has many PTSD triggers, and sooner or later, she will run across one. She does not yet have the proper internal controls to manipulate the fog."

"How far out are you? I need you here and her out there, tucked away. Make it happen."

"Yes, sir, it's a few hours' commute, so I can't give you an exact ETA, but I will report to your office. Is this about the project, sir?"

"Negative, uniform of the day is dress alphas. Make sure you look sharp. General Jones will be on deck, so for God's sake, don't do anything to embarrass me. Oh, and hurry the hell up!"

Had Sasha been able to view herself from outside, even she would have to concede the remarkable emotional transformation that had just occurred. He was going to leave. It was a routine they had been through a hundred times a year. First the phone calls and then the scramble to organize and assemble gear, and as she called it, the question checklist. Do you have contact phone numbers? Money for dinner? Homework done? Truth is, he never even really listened to the answers, only covering his bases so she had one less excuse. It was never really about her, always giving orders, always being the good soldier. Sometimes she wished he wasn't such a good soldier. Then, that way, he could abandon her just as she'd always expected.

She and Emilia sat on the couch. She was unaware of how much her body language had changed since the phone call. Hardly a word had been spoken until she started the "called into work" speech for Emilia. "Watch this," Sasha said. "Now, Sasha, I know we have been through this routine so many times before, so think of it as something I need from you more than something you need to have done." Her arms and legs were crossed now, and her top leg began a nervous bounce.

Daddy entered the room, came over, and sat down next to the girls. His hurried and frantic pace had now been intentionally slowed. Daddy shifted his weight and extremities in an attempt to look like he wanted to be comfortable. Then, after a long breath, he verbatim quoted Sasha's imitation: "Now, Sasha, I know we have been through this routine so many times before, so think of it as something I need from you more than something you need to have done."

Emilia let out a little snicker. Its meaning registered with Daddy. "Fine, fine, I get it, you know the routine. Listen, I don't know what's up, but I can tell you it's not about the program, so you can relax. I will leave money with the guards upstairs, for them to order you two dinner. Emilia, I contacted your program director, and he wants you to stay here as well. We trust you guys to keep each other in line. Don't let us down. Sounds like we will be busy, so all scheduled activities for tomorrow are now TBD. Report in to me when you have awoken in the morning." He moved in as if he was going to give Sasha a hug. Then he stopped and left the room.

Sasha sat still for a moment and then looked at Emilia. "Let's get drunk tonight." Then they both smiled and laughed.

Drexter hated it when the major called him in like this, mostly because he knew that the major hated him. He was able to keep a healthy distance most of the time, but when certain events came up, whether it was a drill, parade, or VIP guest, he was forced to participate in the chain-of-command games.

Early in his career, he didn't mind it so much. In fact, he remembered being a young lieutenant, staying up late and reviewing invoices so that he could report a savings at the budget meeting. Those times and his zeal for the job had gone long ago. Now the thought of being an armory officer, a safety officer, or whatever other crappy assignment just annoyed him.

He paused before starting the engine and looked around the parking garage. He had parked in a dark corner, far back in the underground garage, right next to the air vent. He looked carefully for any cameras. Then he reached under the seat, unbuttoned a secret compartment, and brought out a small box and opened it. Inside was his oldest companion, his most reliable shoulder to cry on, and his getaway from it all.

Storage and procurement were always a problem. Buying in quantity meant storage, while frequent trips meant more opportunities for discovery. He had, on several occasions, considered requesting a transfer to Fort Lewis, where it was at least legal in the civilian world. However, coming up with a legitimate context proved too difficult, and for all the difficulties associated with the major, he was at least a supporter of the project. At one time, he even considered experimenting with it on Sasha, hoping to help her with the fog. But he could picture the meeting now, as he stood there arguing for a dopey drug to help a patient with a foggy condition. They would laugh him out of the room. So for now, it was just his little secret and his little buddy. The major and his parade could wait another hour. Besides, this was his leave day anyway.

He leaned the seat back and held that precious smoke deep inside his lungs. He slowly exhaled through his nose, feeling it roll to the front of his mind as he got himself into complete relaxation and let his mind wander. It passed back and forth between real and imaginary, past and present. Still, his thoughts traced back to her over and over again. Those legs, those beautiful legs gave him needs. He knew he should try to purge them from his mind, yet even with the smoking, they always came back to her. He inhaled again, keeping the smoke in the vehicle. There would be plenty of time to air out on the drive to base. He turned the radio on, hoping for a distraction. After several minutes, he knew there would be only one way.

He searched the area. Finding it deserted, he unzipped his pants and satisfied his needs.

His body finally reached full relaxation after climax, and he lay motionless, enjoying his moment to himself. The slamming of a door startled him, and he checked his mirrors. It was one of the bunker guards, a young guy, private security. He never trusted private security. They always proved either incompetent, dirty, or just plain violent. He tracked the man as he got into a small, black truck, started it, and sped out of the parking garage with urgency.

Propelled by fatherly intuition, Drexter followed the vehicle. Judging from the manner in which he drove his vehicle, this guy was aggressive and disrespectful. The vehicle pulled into a newly opened meter, and the guard jumped out and walked with purpose down the street. Drexter wasn't able to pull over till halfway down the block, yet he was able to get a glimpse of the guard going into a storefront about halfway back.

Walking back to the approximate area, he was able to narrow it down to two storefronts. One was a pizza joint, and the other opened into a small strip mall located on the ground floor of the high-rise. He scanned the immediate area inside the food court but failed to spot the guard. Surveying the stores, he found mostly fast food, a Walgreens, a temporary tax store, and a liquor store. Frustrated and unsure of himself, he returned to the vehicle. Was he just being paranoid? Weed had done that to him before. Synied was a reputable contractor, he told himself, and driving like a jerk doesn't make one a jerk. He took a deep breath, realized he was in uniform and might smell like marijuana, started the vehicle, and began his drive to base.

Her head was beginning to spin and her stomach starting to squeeze. It was not Sasha's first time getting drunk. In the military, there was never a shortage of boys looking to get some girls alcohol in the hopes of gaining some physical access via mental deficiency.

She took another sip and sat close to her friend Emilia. Strange feelings overcame her when she looked at her friend. She tried to fight off the impulses, but Emilia would shift or move and a piece of skin would be exposed. Sasha wanted to kiss the parts of her friend, the parts she knew she shouldn't or couldn't.

The girls broke out in a burst of laughter after Emilia finished a story about growing up. They shared so much in common, Sasha thought. When Emilia would talk about the isolation, the wonder of the outside, and even what she hoped for her future, it felt like they were in lockstep. Emilia was a girl who understood her like nobody before ever had. Emilia was a girl she wanted to be around.

The elevator into the facility chimed, indicating that someone was on their way down. Two young men, one of whom had been the procurer of the alcohol, stepped out wobbly and yelled, "Where the party at?"

His presence in the room greatly annoyed Sasha, her body tensing up as the two men arrived.

"See, here the girls I was tellin' you about, my man. Told you they hot. I want the black one." The smell of heavy drink filled Sasha's nostrils as the two men sat down on the couch. The one who sat next to Emilia put his arm around her. Anger started to fill Sasha, but she focused, keeping the fog at bay.

"Thanks, fellas, but we are looking forward to a girls-only night, thanks." Emilia tried to remove the man's arm from around her.

"Well it wouldn't be a party without us, now. Don't worry, we'll make you feel real nice," the man sitting next to Sasha said as he put his hand on her leg. She closed her eyes and went to her happy place and fought off the fog.

Emilia struggled with the guard next to her as he moved in closer and closer. He sat down on her lap, preventing her from standing. "Now, girl, don't be like that. This will be a good time, a really good time, with that body of yours."

"That's right, asshole, my body, not yours!" Emilia yelled at him, trying with all her might to get him off.

"Now knock it off. Your black bitch friend knows what to do. Just sit there and enjoy it like the slut you are."

The man sitting next to Sasha aggressively moved his hand upward. There was no way to hold back the fog anymore. Her arm reached out with lightning speed, grabbed her assailant by the neck, and squeezed. The man pulled his arms back, desperately trying to break her grasp. Sasha spun over his lap, grabbed him by a shoulder pressure point, adjusted her free arm around his neck, and squeezed even harder. The second man lunged off of Emilia, taking the three people to the floor. Sasha landed hard on her back and released her grip. The two men were now on top of her, wrestling her, fighting for control. Emilia screamed.

The fog prevented Sasha from seeing anything other than the danger. In some ways, it acted like a guide focusing her attention. The fog would clear to her left, and she would roll there, dodging a blow. The fog turned red and guided her anger as she attacked. There was no conscious thought of action or reaction—it was follow or fail. The fog commanded total obedience, for its control was safety, its hazy embrace was comforting, and in the worst of times, it was a gift from above.

Slowly, the fog lifted. Emilia's screams echoed through it. Sasha listened again, listened hard. Emilia's voice was out there somewhere, and she had to help her, she just had to. "Stop, please stop," came Emilia's voice. What were those men doing to her? Sasha had to find her, but the harder she looked, the denser the fog got.

"Sasha, please stop. Sasha what are you doing? Please stop, Sasha." Emilia's voice was filled with sobs. She was asking Sasha to stop? Sasha didn't know what she was doing, so how could she stop? The fog near her feet began to clear as she focused on the sounds. A body lay at her feet, a man's body. Blood covered the man's face as he lay motionless except for a gentle bounce in his chest. His nose was off to the side and was making a hissing sound with each breath.

Sasha took several deep breaths, pushing the fog out farther with each one. The man who lay at her feet was the man who had brought the alcohol. His buddy, who was also much bloodied, grabbed him by the collar and dragged him to the elevator. He sat there cowering as he waited for the ding and an open door to safety.

Sasha looked back now at Emilia, her face filled with horror. Sasha feared the worst, but Emilia's clothes had barely been ruffled. Sasha walked over and hugged Emilia. She didn't return the hug, instead keeping her arms in tight to her torso as tears streamed onto Sasha's chest. Sasha looked down at her hands as she held Emilia, and guilt suddenly overcame her. She had just gotten blood on Emilia's beautiful clothes.

6: Hashmore

Where the hell was the mayor? A nice, relaxing second career, he'd said, a desk job, a nine-to-five. This was the final straw. It was time resign. Well, after the current crisis was over, then Hashmore would resign.

Where the fuck was the mayor? "Fuck" was probably more appropriate as a verb, concerning where the mayor really was. Politics had never been on Hashmore's radar, but after his partner from the force and best friend had actually won a damn election, how could he turn him down? His friend was a different man back then—a man of character, loyalty. Now he was just another politician swimming in the forbidden fruits of power.

Of all the worst times to be a no show, this was top of the damn list. Albany wasn't in a waiting mood, and apparently the feds were breathing down their necks too. Whatever the hell it was, it was about to become his problem, alone.

In all honesty, it was the control room that sealed the deal. This place was unbelievable. Sheltered in the deepest basement, wired to the highest point, not only was it super futuristic in appearance, but it was also top of the line. Installed, funded, and hidden, all after the September attacks. This room could monitor any public location on the island. It could track up to five thousand individuals or vehicles simultaneously. Image recognition, filters for infrared, X-ray radio and communication-interception equipment, city-management interfaces—it all gave him a strong sense of connection to an avenue of influence. Hell, there were even four small flower gardens surrounding the conference table in the middle. This was a cool room, and it even had an attached dormitory and kitchen.

Being a Christian man, Hashmore would never outwardly admit that it was the power the room brought that was the real allure. The power to enforce God's justice, that's what he told himself, and that's what was true. He'd spent a career tracking down and bearing down on the devil's henchmen, protecting society. Now, however, he had a different responsibility, and it was a much greater responsibility than simply handing out God's vengeance. It was time to retire.

He looked down at the blinking lights. Every line was waiting, waiting for the man in charge. He thought about where some of the mayor's favorite romantic hideaways were. Damn him, this was not a relaxing second career! He looked at his watch—ten seconds, he would give it, and pray for ten more seconds. The time passed. He took a deep breath and pushed the button on the intercom. "This is Hashmore, city emergency manager, and I will be handling things here on our end."

Four words into the briefing and he was already regretting not quitting before this assignment. Four words that shook him, four words only whispered in private contingency-planning meetings had now slammed their way into the forefront of the world. "Prepare for martial law" was the order of the day. The president himself was scheduling a press event to announce it.

Where the hell was the mayor? The question bothered him because now, instead of focusing on the most important task at hand, he had to do political things. Damn, this was why Hashmore didn't want a public-office job. Speed of execution was of some importance. He felt a surge of power click his mind into gear. He liked to refer to it as an alacrity shot, a chemical cocktail for the brain, made up of adrenaline, testosterone, and epinephrine—like rats in an experiment, every emergency responder gets it trained in the brain to take the shot when the tones drop. He would have to tamp that down, however, if he was to adequately substitute for the mayor. The mayor—where the hell was that cheating, lazy, lying bastard?

He pushed the intercom. "Linda, get all the senior staff together, ten minutes. Then start recruiting yourself some help, screw the overtime." He took a short pause to think. "Patch me through to Colonel Major."

He grabbed a pen and started jotting down notes of things that had to be done. Experience had taught him it was easier to prioritize an existing list than to write and prioritize at the same time. His mind was jumping, chasing, and running from thought to thought. Rather than try to control it, he wrote it, filling yellow note after yellow note. By the time his eight sticky notes were covered, the intercom buzzed and Linda's voice came over: "Colonel Major parked on line 204."

"Colonel M, how the hell are ya?"

"Fine, Mr. Hashmore. Mayor out in the field again?"

"Tell you what, fucking handcuff that guy to his desk and they'll both go missing."

"Well maybe he isn't the one needing to be handcuffed to the desk in order for him to stick around it," the colonel said with a chuckle. "Now what the hell is going on? The fed channels are going absolutely haywire."

"Only tell ya what I know. Something fucking big is coming down the pipe from the highest level. No indication if it was doomsday-type shit, riot-worthy scandal-type shit, government takeover, or what the fuck. Marching orders were to prepare for martial law. Albany is going to be handling the guard and working with the boroughs, including oversight of the bridges. However, we will not be getting any assistance from the guard or adjoining agency. Let me pause there. What sort of manpower can we possibly gather in the next eighteen hours?"

The colonel grunted as if clearing his throat. "Either you're a very different man than the mayor or shit is very serious indeed. I could have my men at full strength in eighteen hours, a man force of over eighteen thousand officers. However, sir, if we want to maximize deployment time over an extended period of time, as I do believe this sort of situation might require, then I suggest a deployment number closer to twelve thousand, with officers in reserve to replace due to injury and fatigue, and trust me, sir, you do not want tired officers armed and grumpy."

"I will defer to your knowledge and judgment so long as you feel you have what you need to control the street if things get a little ugly."

"Understood, sir, what are your running assumptions as to the cause of such large-scale social disturbance."

"Damn if I know. Here's a direct quote from my briefing that might help—'We expect a very fluid and volatile situation to commence from as soon as now to the president's address to the nation at 9:15 a.m. Begin immediate ramp-up operations, and prepare for martial law if necessary.' So that, Colonel, is about the most detailed thing they said."

There was a serious pause before the colonel spoke up. "In all my years, I have never heard anything like that. Mr. Hashmore, how do we proceed?"

It was nearly a half hour before Linda buzzed him with what he wanted to hear. "Mayor on line one, Mr. H."

He started to speak the same instant his finger pressed the phone button. "Where the hell have you been?"

The mayor said, "I thought I was your boss. I overslept a little bit. Anyway, what's tonight's crisis? Traffic, have you ever tried to get into the city during rush hour, forget about it. Somebody should fucking do something about this shit."

"Wish I could be so lazy about a little thing called martial law."

"What the fuck you talking about? Martial law for what? Nothing on morning news about riots or shit. Who the hell tell you that?"

"Albany, and yes, let me quote for you." He picked up his notes from the briefing. "'External factors beyond human control may induce unnecessary fear and confusion among the masses. Preparations must be made in advance to control messaging, give reassurance, and quickly respond and put down any innocents before they can escalate.'"

After a short pause, the mayor came back. "Hot damn, finally some action. I was starting to think pussy was the only exciting part of this job."

"Where you at? I'll send an escort."

"J turnpike, and make her a blonde today."

⟨T⟩

Things went so much smoother with the mayor back in the office. Hashmore looked down at his interactive map. The table-sized interface device was used to interact with RUDY, the computer software program that controlled the whole command center. Each field unit was issued a cell phone with automated GPS equipment that could relay that unit's position. When used in conjunction with the Bluetooth visor and headset, it could make each unit a real-world extension of the command center—often also referred to as RUDY.

Currently, he was scrolling through the list of units available. For now, the number was abnormally low. He and the major had agreed that officers with children would be given immediate leave to secure them at appropriate locations, but no leave could be granted if shit started hitting the fan. Second, they activated all reserve and volunteer units. He was overseeing a group of these units right now.

"No, no, the barricades just need to be off to the side, ready for deployment." He listened as the voice on the other end asked a question. "Well now I don't know how we will need to deploy them yet." Another pause. "Hey, watch the tone. Truth is, we don't know what to expect. It may even be necessary to alter the deployment mid-event, so just do what you can, damn it!" Hashmore ripped off his headset. "Damn retired think-they-know-it-alls."

The orders were pretty vague. External factors, beyond human control—those words sounded like political cover to him. A green check mark appeared on the map interface, a unit checking in as available. Normally there was a clear purpose, like protesters converging on the police station or a high-speed pursuit, but this time, he had no idea. He decided to focus on larger food stores, ports of entry or exit, and the subway. The transit authority would help with the latter, but clearing the subway system, if necessary, would be a monumental undertaking as a sole priority, much less a third.

The conference room started to fill as the mayor continued to "do the rounds over the phones." Bankers, investors, rich and annoying, all of them thinking that they were God's prize to this world. Personally, he couldn't wait till the rapture would take these bastards down to their rightful place. The mayor didn't seem to mind kissing their asses, but for him, it was out of the question. As a man of talents and morals, he deserved to be in charge, making sure shit got done right. That's why the mayor hired him.

Sure, his long friendship with the mayor would have gotten him a job somewhere, but it was his God-given talents that put him in this position now, in charge. The rush of adrenaline that came with every decision, every outcome, flooded away any regret or remorse over accepting the job. His whole life had led up to this moment, this challenge, and all of it God's will. Now, as he prepared to walk into a room and issue orders to some of the most powerful men in the world's greatest city, a smile broke across his face and he thanked God.

The mayor ended his phone call, walked up to Hashmore, and placed his arm around his friend. "It's good to have you by my side in such times. I've missed this, you and me, in the heat of the cause, striving for better."

"How do you do it, Biggo? Putting up with these bastards, consensus building? Don't you just miss the days when all we had to do was nap and slap?"

"Of course, but the challenge must grow. How many hours did we spend pissing away, complaining about those jackasses before us? Did you forget the dream, the frustration and the passion? Before, we helped the individuals—now we help the masses. If a little ego stroking is necessary to make that happen, well then I must remember that it is not about these bastard or us bastards. It's about those bastards out there. The more we better our society, the better reward we deserve."

Hashmore let out a big breath. "Biggo, you always did know just the right thing to say. I only wish your rewards weren't so . . . tempting. Now, if you will excuse me, I see some egos that need readjustment and tasks that need to be completed." The mayor nodded his head and left as Hashmore closed his eyes and approached the briefing room door.

⟨⌐⟩

Oh, Lord, thank you for this glory. Thank you for this power.

I can feel your strength. I can feel your confidence. I can feel your will flowing out of me. It has been a long time, my Lord, too long. Once, you wielded me like a dagger, capturing or destroying demons infesting your garden. Wield me now again! Let me once again be your hammer! Let me reign down your vengeance upon the evil.

Yes, Lord, show me the way. Show me how to wield your sword. I am eager to please. But, Lord, I find no demon to smite, no villain to chase. What am I to do, Lord? Why give me this power and nothing to wield with it? Is evil approaching? Is this the call to arms? I am ready to answer, Lord. Yet, Lord, where will the evil come from? I see no evil in front of me, nor behind me. I see only men, not demons. What would you want me to do to man? Perhaps, Lord, this power is to ready my fellow man. Shall I lead the battle against the devil's own brood? I am ready, Lord, lead me to your victory.

The briefing went smoothly enough. Despite their overflowing arrogance, the group managed to maintain composure, and hell, they might have even understood what Hashmore told them. Now that he'd had his fun, it was time to get to some real work. While the mayor had to do his bullshit with the "elite" who only thought they were the most important, he now had to do real work with the truly important people.

Linda had already convened the people who ran this city: Colonel Major, head of the island police force; Commander Thomas, head of fire, rescue, and EMS; Buck Houltwater, the city services coordinator; Lisa Stevens, the water systems supervisor;

Bent Anderson, the city's technical head; and of course the most annoying man in the world, Dane Cook, head of transit authority.

Dane Cook was a man who failed to see his place in the world, a bureaucrat who fancied himself a detective. On more than one occasion during his career, Cook had interfered with an investigation simply in the hopes of claiming it for himself. Now all that leeching had paid off, when Cook landed a cushy job where he could leech off subordinates.

Hashmore got right to business. "All right, everyone, game time is quickly approaching, and we haven't installed a game plan yet."

Of course Cook was the first to respond. "What the hell are you talking about? You need to fill us in on what's going on first before we can game plan."

Grinding his teeth, Hashmore continued. "All we know is that the president is going to say something today that will create a lot of panic and/or anger, and let's just hope it's the first. The president speaks at 9:15 a.m. eastern. That means I want us at maximum staffing and potential by 7:30 a.m. Let's start by saying that I don't know what's going to happen, but I do know that we are going to be the ones responsible for dealing with it. Now let's sit down and quickly get on the same page about our goals and priorities." Keeping a commanding tone was important in a room like this. Display weakness, even a little, and these alpha personalities would jump on it instantly.

He wasn't worried though. If God be for him, who dare be against him?

PART 2

7: Begin Genesis Undone

The sky screamed out in that universally unmistakable tone of pain. Oddly rolled clouds billowed across the sky. The pitch of the scream rose to a wretch. Then silence followed. No traffic, no machinery, no birds, just total silence. One, two, three, No Tip counted in his head, and then came the wave.

The wave brought back with it the sound, which only added to the confusion and misery. He was thrown several feet and landed a foot away from the rooftop edge. Many of the plants had been flung over the side as well. He would have prayed for anyone down below, but as suddenly as the wave came, the air seemed to leave. He began to panic, feeling as if the wind had been knocked out of him underwater. His body flinched and convulsed, desperately seeking air but finding none.

A hot breeze delivered the foulest, most wonderful oxygen-filled air he had ever consumed. A bright flash filled the sky, but he was in no position to see what was occurring. He lay there for several seconds, breathing hungrily, seeking to blow off built-up CO_2 and return his body to equilibrium. The pitch of the scream in the sky had lowered and ended with the sound of erupting water. He gathered himself and rose to his knees. Surrounding the great city were four enormous tethers reaching out into the sky and passing through deep, lightning-filled clouds.

A small bird now reacquainted with the skill of flight took off from one of the remaining brushes on the rooftop.

There, at the bottom of the skyline, he saw it. A wall of water multiple stories high was descending on his location. The building began to shake and sway. Lunging from his kneeling position, he grabbed hold of a pipework protruding from the top of the building. The wave was not quite as high as the building, but great amounts of seawater splashed and doused the roof, as if the flush of a toilet had pounded the building and collapsed the edge of the roof. His feet scrambled wildly away from the crumbling edge while his arms held on to the pipework as if it were a falling baby.

The building remained upright, but a large portion of the front had now been washed away. The pipework stayed in place as the seaboard side of the building and floors started to collapse around him. He slid like a fireman down two floors, to where he was able to jump onto solid flooring. A small group of people gathered around him, one of them pointing to the sky. Dozens of smaller UFOs zipped overhead, but he focused on one just above the water. Ten meters in length and three in height, it had a polished looked but gave no reflection or shine. A white, pulsating halo emitted from its undercarriage and penetrated deep into the sea.

Loud screams proved ineffective, forcing the baroness to physically touch each member of the group. Entranced by the unexpected and unfathomable nature of the scene that lay before them, she wrapped her hands firmly around No Tip's waist and tried to pull him in the direction of the stairs, but he resisted. Again she pulled him, mistakenly interpreting his disagreement for disillusionment. This time, he pointed to the sky, but she still misunderstood. On her third attempt, she placed him in a pressure-point hold.

"Aggggh, let go of me, are you trying to get everyone killed?" His cognitive response surprised the baroness, and his accusation even more so, suspending any immediate response from her. He reached out with his free arm—"free" being a relative term—and yelled, "Look, damn it."

$$\gg$$

What was this idiot doing now? He just said what? Look where? The baroness's mind searched for answers in the face of so many unexpected events. By the time her brain caught up, her body was inexplicably being dragged up the stairs, trying to resist but still bending to his will. His will, what the hell was his name? "Nip the Kid" sprang into her head, and she let out a tiny giggle.

The pitch of the whistling had changed again and was slowly rising in scale. Dozens upon dozens of alien craft swarmed the sky. One of the giant tethers had landed just offshore from her building. Well technically she didn't own the building, but for all intents and purposes, it was her home more often than not. How many nights had she slept here instead of at her home?

She looked skyward as it darkened behind rolling, energetic, expanding clouds. Using the tethers as tracks, black slits raced down from the sky, one after another, on each side of the city, encompassing it in a ring that splashed down deep into the waters, hurling gigantic waves out in every direction. She was in the path of one of those waves. The thought struck her again: she was in the path of a huge wave. Her instinct was to run, but he pulled her back. What was that fool doing, anyway, counting? His free hand was moving in a rhythmic motion as if keeping time. He wasn't even looking at the wave of impending death barreling down upon them—it was time to ditch this guy. She yanked her arm, trying to pull away, but this time, he barked back. "I know what I'm doing. On the count of three."

"Count of three? What are we doing on the count of three?"

He smiled an ominous smile. "Three."

$$\gg$$

Her legs were numb yet moving as if willed from an external source. Her breath left her as the horizon rose, only a split second, and then collapsed. The baroness concentrated on adjusting to the freefall. Her arms rose out in desperation but found no anchor. She forced out a breath and saw the ship. The relief came only as a precursor to the realization that he had been wrong. The ship was going to pass them. This fool had just killed her, and she didn't even know his damn name.

8: First Contact

It was impossible to remember which came first, the headache or the blurry vision. No Tip tried to move but was restrained. He looked left and right, but the blurs only changed in tone and pigment, never clarity. There was no sound, due to a soft, cushy gel that had been placed around his ears, preventing him from hearing anything. After attempting several variations of movement, he discovered that slow, gentle motions allowed some freedom for his upper body, but from the thighs down, he was stuck firm.

Several questions ran through his mind, but his last memory of jumping from the roof with the baroness only allotted for speculation. Purgatory was his guess. Seemed right, kind of like a time out. He smiled. Purgatory, he thought, heaven is at the end of the road.

A thick, moist tentacle grabbed his arm while several tingly pricks, as if a bug were walking along his skin, crossed from his forearm down to his fist. He held tight as long as he could, but the sensation became too much and he had to open his hand. A warm, polished stone was placed in it, and the entire hue turned black. His vision escaped him.

"Species from third plant from the Sol star system, identify yourself!" Powerful and demanding, the voice rang out from all directions as if inside his head.

He responded verbally. "What?"

A solar map appeared in front of him. It zoomed in a few layers, where a map of this solar system lay before him. The display highlighted Earth. The voice rang out again. "Identify yourself, species, or we will do it for you."

What an unusual question for purgatory. "Are you God?"

The voice responded. "No, I am the one asking the questions. What is your species identification name?"

"Why, am I being interrogated?"

"You are being cataloged."

"By who?"

"By the ones who saved your life. Now quit being ungrateful, and answer the questions."

"Why did you save me?"

"To catalog you."

"Did you save my companion?"

"She will be cataloged too. Are you satisfied? May we finally proceed on to catalog? We do it with every patient."

"How are we communicating?"

He felt a strong "ughhhh" sensation before the answer. "Through a translator stone."

"Why can't I see or hear anything?"

"Standard first-contact procedure. Now I insist, we must get on to cataloging. How does your species identify itself?"

"Human, are you not?"

"Have you not ever met another species before? Have you not ever been to other planets before?"

"No."

"Well I'm not an information booth. I'm a cataloger. Save your questions for some poor sucker in the waiting room. Now let's get back to the questions. Are there only the two variations of humans, or are there more?"

"Oh no, I don't go for any other kind, just women, thank you."

"So there are other variations? Please describe?"

"Wow there, missy, some doors I just have no interest in going behind. If someone wants to have a doc attach or remove a dingy, well that's just not something I want any part of. Keep those doors closed is what I say is best."

There was a pause before the alien continued. "The translator interprets your meaning to be no variation by natural occurrence. Is this a correct interpretation of what you just said?"

"Yes?"

Again came a pause before the questions resumed. "Are humans the only sentient species on this planet?"

"I saw a monkey drive a car once."

Another audible sigh echoed in his mind. "Please, I am not a politician. I am not a scientist. I'm a data collector, so please just answer the questions I ask. We have many to get through."

"Dolphins. Gotta say dolphins. Did you know I was sexually assaulted by a dolphin at SeaWorld?"

The questions came rapid fire, as if the being on the other side had stopped caring and accepted any answer given. Their nature was as disarming as the lack of quality control until they reached a most unexpected question: "Who is your Lord?"

$$\gg$$

A white haze filled her vision while a gel-like substance covered her ears. Two senses eliminated, the baroness thought to herself. All she could smell was her own breath, and no need to taste that. She moved cautiously and slowly. Her movement was challenged but not hampered, like walking underwater. Her legs had significantly less mobility, enough to find a comfortable sitting position.

Something touched her right forearm. She pulled it back, startled. The gripping object held, but only strongly enough to follow, not to control. It was a signal—it was trying to comfort her, and she relaxed. The tentacle's grip slid lower, and she understood it to mean that she should release her fist. A polished rock was placed in her hand, and it quickly warmed.

A voice emanated in her head. "Being from the third planet of the star known as Sol, identify your species."

She paused for a minute, gathered her thoughts, and focused them into the stone.

"My name is Veronica Mars, and I am human. Now I request

you answer a question."

There was a slight hesitation. "Request denied. Are there only two variations of human, or are there more?"

"Then answer denied. Now please let us not get off on the wrong foot. I feel like a cornered animal right now. I'm sure you can appreciate that, so please answer some questions to make that corner just a little bigger."

"You humans drive me crazy! I'm very busy. Someone else can answer your questions after I have finished cataloging you."

"Humans, how many others have you seen?"

"Just the idiot who pulled you off the roof, my dear. Now, my species has males too, and if you don't keep them in line, they start jumping off of idiocy and into infidelity."

"You saw us?"

"It made evening news after . . ." She felt a subtle warmth in an inner part of her brain before the voice finished the thought. "Going viral."

"Where am I?"

"Ok, please let me finish my job after this question. I imagine there will be someone to answer your questions later. You are on the welfare ship." An untranslatable alien sound crossed her mind. "You and your mate were brought here after one of the Arkapeligo scout ships caught you during your less-than-flawless escape from the surface. Now please answer the question. Are there only the two variations of the human species?"

Her thoughts swirled about. For the moment, they centered

on him. That stupid idiot almost got her killed. Son of a bitch, she was glad he was alive so that now she could kill him. She calmed down and focused on the stone, answering the question. "Only the two, male and female, now please answer just one more question?"

"Fine, last one."

"How do I look?"

"Why do you only say two types when clearly there is a third?"

"What do you mean?"

"A third type of human. It isn't male or female yet. It's," she felt that warming in her brain again, "in your uterus."

$$\gg$$

The questions were extensive and exhausting, many of which he simply didn't know the answer to. They were specifically biological in nature, with an occasional cultural one mixed in. While No Tip was a prisoner, he didn't quite feel like one. His senses had been hampered, his body invaded. Yet they demanded nothing from him other than what seemed to be required for medical treatment. His emotions were playing havoc with him. He found it hard to process and believe what he had just witnessed, yet he couldn't deny his current state either.

Upon completion, or "close enough" as the cataloger put it, the thigh clamps released and a visual filter displayed a pathway for him to follow. The gelled substance acted as an escort, stiffening every time he tried to stray off the displayed path. He still had yet to see his captors, and that made him nervous. He needed to size them up, assess what kind of natural capabilities they had.

They obviously possessed superior technology, but what they offered in natural capabilities would be much more telling.

The display arrows led him to a black wall with a panel on it. He tried to slide the panel, but it wouldn't budge. He tried pushing on the panel; he tried pulling on the panel. He even tried to turn away, but his gel suit hardened. "Ok, I don't get it." He spoke the words out loud but received no reply. "Ok, computer . . . activate . . . on . . . interface." Now he was getting frustrated. He felt his sides for objects that might be hidden in any pockets.

He cursed and tried kicking but only ended up hurting his shin on the hardened gel. He tried sitting down, hoping that the gel would harden as he neared the floor, but it didn't, and he fell on his ass. His feet remained pinned to the ground as he tried to stand, but it was unmanageable with the placement of his feet and the restrictions of the gel. His thighs were burning, and he was sweating profusely. He gave one last thrust upward, at maximum allowable speed. He was approaching the top of his stance when a slight shift in his torso reopened his nipple wound, and he screamed, lost his upward movement, and fell backward. The gel supported him just enough at the thighs to bend his back, making it the most uncomfortable position possible.

His screams called attention, and several blobs of light began to move around him. Great, he thought, spectators, first human in space killed by equipment made for the handicapped. A warm, oily tentacle applied pressure to his back, slowly raising him to a standing position. The relief was immense. He moved close to the blob, and yet still his vision wouldn't clear. He was unable to get a better sense of anything other than their outlines. These were tentacle creatures. His impression was of dozens upon dozens of tentacles extended from the top and bottom of its central barrel complex.

The tentacle slid down to his hand and wrapped around one time. He fought the temptation to pull away. He breathed and allowed his hand to be placed against the wall. The tentacle shifted its position farther up the forearm and then abruptly thrust his arm inside the wall. A warm beam scanned his palm, and a display on the wall lit up, showing some of his biometric data. Several shapes were displayed in boxes scattered across the monitor. He waited a minute for something to happen, but nothing did, so he looked at the shapes. One looked like a box, one like a chair. One looked like a coffin. One was a circle. He didn't understand. He looked around, and several blobs were in the area, yet he couldn't hear or see them. After a while, a tentacle grabbed his other hand and brought it to the monitor, where he touched a shape of a circle. The machine hummed and vibrated as it released his hand. Smoke lightly fluttered out, and after a long minute's wait, there was a tone, and a smaller door opened along the bottom of the big door.

He bent down in order to go through it but was struck in the head and shoulder as he did so. The object smacked him in the head and stopped. He pulled back and discovered that the object that had hit him was circular, with two flat sides, about two-foot diameter, and soft on one side, hard on the other.

The visual display now highlighted a new route. Finally, he tried to walk it but was denied movement without the presence of his new object. The displays led him to a wall, where a cube area was highlighted. He couldn't tell if there was an actual physical presence or if it was entirely visual. He stared at his new location, wondering what sort of stupid task he was going to have to perform with this, stool, he guessed. He hesitated before entering the cube—his prison, more likely, he thought. He tried to walk away, but his feet held firm.

After several attempts to get away, he ran out of ideas and simply walked into the cube. Again his feet would move him to where they wanted him, but nowhere else. The display changed, revealing another layer of clarity concerning his surroundings. A new message flashed across his eyes as he was assigned a patient number, followed by a smaller number, which he assumed was the patient-being-seen number.

He seemed to have free movement within the cube but was denied movement outside the cube. He began by searching the rear wall, physical enough. Maybe there was a control panel like the last location—nothing. Then he tried the floor—nothing but a cold, hard surface, like smooth black concrete. Nothing composed the side walls, just an inability to walk into or past them. His torso was free for all movement, but his feet were firmly planted on the ground and required force to move. He stood on his new stool and examined the ceiling, only to discover it was made of the same material as the floor.

Next he tried removing his gel restraints. Simply learning how to grab hold of the gel was difficult enough, and it took dozens of attempts just to get it right for the first time, and hundreds to become proficient. Although he'd accomplished grabbing hold of the gel, applying the pull-twist, tear, or pinch maneuver proved impossible. Every sudden movement was met with rigid force, every maneuver met with loss of grip. Even his thumb blade was useless in the gel-like substance, for it would immediately repair itself even as he cut. This was a prison he wasn't sure he could escape from.

$$\gimel\mkern-8mu y$$

The thought consumed her, infected her mind. All thoughts of the new universe the baroness had entered were merely distractions. Thoughts of what had happened to her girls, her business, and her life never surfaced. She felt them though, like an elephant in a room full of elephants held back by the doors of life. Was she pregnant? Couldn't be? No, she told herself, more out of hope and denial than circumstance.

The questioner ceased to answer any of her questions, but she answered theirs to the best of her ability. All of hers were answered with the standard reply: "I'm a cataloger, not a healer. Please direct that question to a healer." Her thigh clamps released, and a new visual filter engaged.

She had a much better picture of her surroundings now, but still all persons were blurred, and nothing was completely clear. A yellow highlight displayed her requested route of travel, to which she acquiesced and followed obligingly. It led her to a display on a wall, next to a large outlet. A highlighted box appeared on the wall, and she pressed it with her left hand, which passed right through it. A warm beam scanned her hand, and a new display showed on the screen. She waited for a minute, trying to ascertain what the shapes meant. She scanned the room and noticed several of the blurred people scattered about, each with what appeared to be an object to lounge with. She got the idea that this was a waiting room and the shapes were a selection of possible furniture. Each guest had their own preferences, so each alien must have had their own as well. The choices on the display seemed to correlate to a chair, a foot stool, a bench, and a hammock—she was guessing on that one.

She pressed the bench, and the machinery behind the wall began to churn. She took her new bench, surprising lightweight, along the highlighted route. It led her to a cube in between two other occupied cubes. She gave her surroundings a quick once-over and then resumed her quest to find a healer. How she would recognize the correct blob was yet to be determined.

First she attended to her gel suit. It was too difficult to maneuver the substance, but it proved easy enough to hold in place while she moved out of it. The cold air on her naked legs made her thankful there were no other humans around. A long scar, well into the healing process, now appeared, running along both of her legs. She ran her finger along the scar, and a flashback of her legs snapping against the roof of the alien vessel flashed before her mind's eye.

She left the headpiece on but was able to remove another filter by fiddling with it. While people were still blurred, their shapes were much more clearly defined. Most of the beings aboard seemed to belong to a race of tentacled blobs. Long, wavy tentacles bobbed innocently about above their silhouettes until called upon to perform some requested action. Others were much thicker and closer to the ground. At one point, she swore a flying cat passed her, right at eye level.

The waiting room was very large, with slatted walls running across at intervals so as to allow cubes to fill the entirety of the floor. She picked up on a small group of blobs traveling together and followed them for some time, until they arrived at a huge, towering shaft with large, slanted walkways speeding along the interior. The group traveled down, but her instincts told her that the healers would be up, more archetypal.

She tried speaking with a few of the blobs, but they acted disinterested, and without a stone, she couldn't understand any of the sounds they made. None of the doors restricted her access, and most of the levels were filled with blobs simply waiting in their cubes.

She was feeling frustrated when her instincts picked up on something. It was a single blob, sitting alone along a wall of cubes. This would have been the floor below hers from her initial starting point, but at this point, it was the sixth floor she had visited. She hoped it would communicate with her, lead her to a healer, lead her to an answer.

She approached the blob carefully, slowly. It was alone, and she had no idea why. She considered how to begin, what to say, and opened her mouth to speak, but all her thoughts came out as a loud, weeping cry.

$$\sum\!\!y$$

It felt like hours he had been sitting there, stuck stewing in his own thoughts, a toxic place if ever there was one. The only excitement had been when a blob a few blocks down and across went crazy. The alien pushed something along the wall, when a toner buzzed, bringing several new blobs to tend to the wigged-out one.

No Tip's back was really bothering him now. First there were the girls, and then Big M, jumping from a building, and that stupid foot-stool machine—all in all, a pretty exhausting day.

His arm hair awakened, and his senses stretched out. Something was coming. It was moving fast, too fast to be another prisoner. He shifted his weight to his toes and slid his ass forward to the edge of his seat. If it entered, this would be an opportunity, an opportunity that shouldn't be passed up. He extended his thumb blade. The creature was moving directly toward him—this was it. His heart pounded. As the creature neared, he noticed that it was bipedal—a surprising advantage for me, he thought. Familiarity would be where he struck. Four steps, three steps, lunge.

The sudden reversal in fortunes probably precipitated the action, slowing him down just enough to move at max gel velocity. The cry was distinctly human, and the voice familiar, even if he couldn't place it immediately. It was too late, however. The cry was sharply cut off as his leg swept hers out from under her and caused her to fall hard on the floor. "Baroness?" he asked, bending down to help her up. "Is that you?" A warm, soft hand touched his shoulder and pulled, attempting to rise. He placed his hands under her legs and lifted. Soft, gentle lips touched his, and she kissed him passionately.

It was an amazing kiss. He couldn't say that about many in his lifetime, but that would be one. Too bad it didn't last very long, because before he knew it, she had jumped out of his arms and was pulling him down by the ear. Several open-palmed slaps followed. There must have been a slap following each of the seven words not allowed on TV. The baroness tried to say something more, but only tears and sobs came out, and she held him close, in the most loving way he had ever been held before.

$$\overline{)y}$$

Now that he was there, the need for a healer didn't seem so urgent. Her fury came in like waves upon the shore. Something about this man evoked such emotion from her. She couldn't explain it but just hated it.

"Baroness, is that you? How did you escape?" No Tip asked her.

"Escape what?" she asked through tears.

"Never mind, help me out of these restraints. How did you do it?"

Without words, she came in close and pressed against him. He pulled back on his injured-nipple side but otherwise stood anxiously still. Her arms touched his bare skin as she held his waist in place and tilted her head for him to kiss her. Their lips embraced, their skin touched, and her body warmed deep inside. Something touched her leg, and she jerked back. Her face flushed, for while she still had her panties and top on, he did not.

For all her professional experience, she couldn't stifle a little giggle. She felt like a virgin schoolgirl. She helped him out of his leg and shoulder restraints, and now kept a greater distance. He still seemed to have more visual filters on, and she wasn't about to help him there, as it had been a week or so since she last shaved her legs. Then she helped him take off the ear gels.

He said, "Thanks, now tell me, what do you know? How big is the ship? How many guards, prisoners? Are you ok? What happened?"

"What are you talking about? My god, we almost died. My god, you almost killed us!" This time, she punched his arm. Then she thought about who "us" meant, and it made her nervous and anxious again.

"Stop that. Now let's find a way out of here. And I might add, if you are so fine, how do you explain that scar on your leg? It runs pretty high."

She hadn't even noticed that he touched her leg, and the worry about her unshaven status returned. Between that and the new scar, she had never felt less attractive.

"What do you think, are we on a spaceship in space, on land, or in an alien world, or in an alien building on Earth?"

"My god, what happened to my leg?" It felt fully functional and normal, despite the long scar running down the entirety of her right leg and down the thigh of her left. She ran her fingers up and down along the scar. For several long seconds, she stayed motionless, staring into space. Thoughts of everything that had happened to her over the past few, well, what felt like hours came gushing out in large, uncontrollable waves of tears.

He stood there dumbfounded for a moment before closing in and hugging her gently. She struggled to hold back the tears, but the harder she tried, the more she failed and the worse she felt. She promised herself she could be strong, that she would never lose control again. Yet here she stood in the arms of a strange man, sobbing as thoughts of life overpowered her.

It took a while before she regained her composure and looked up at him. "Is this all really happening? Can we go back to yesterday? I like yesterday so much more." She blinked the remaining tears from her eyes and gazed at his face.

Finally, he replied. "Yesterday was fine, and today is interesting, but I live only to avoid tomorrow." He paused. Whether he was giving her time to think about it or didn't know what to say next, she couldn't tell. "For now, I think we should scout around, use this new mobility to get some bearings. Whatever happened, or is happening, we can't affect it right now, so let's move forward."

It took a few breaths for the words to come out, but she felt relief after their departure. "I need a healer." He looked her over thoroughly, leaning in close to examine her backside as well.

"Looks good to me. Of course, there is one more place to look, and I just happen to have the proper tool." His face twisted in an awful attempt to look seductive, a look made all the more unattainable by the alien device still covering his eyes.

She couldn't contain her look of revolt as he spoke. "Never speak to me like that again." Her voice was sharp and commanding, filled will a forcefulness of will, and his face reflected understanding and reverted to that of a guilty puppy getting caught red-handed. She took a deep breath. "Now, I agree with your choice of action, but not purpose. We will scout the area, but our intention is to find and interact with a healer." She nodded her head and began to turn.

"Uggh. Baroness, if it is of so much importance, I will assist you." He bowed a sarcastic bow. "If I may have permission." He moved his arms back toward the wall.

She debated about responding with anger but knew from past employee encounters that it was better to let heat-of-the-moment comments pass. So she chose the least confrontational response. "You may."

He raised his arms up, approached the wall, and pressed against it. The cube lighting turned yellow, and an audible ding sounded. He walked back to her position. "You're welcome."

9: Intro the Doctors

The gel-like patches around his eyes still heavily filtered what No Tip was seeing, especially in terms of the other life-forms. A dark, heavy blob—no, it was two dark, heavy blobs connected thinly together at the top—approached swiftly. They seemed to hover more than walk, yet there was still a gentle swaying that indicated moving extremities. The attachment at the top separated into several independent fraying tentacles. They would often connect with the partner's tentacles for a short time and then disconnect, pull back, and find a new partner.

The baroness stood in place and waited for them. He leaned against the wall, looking as nonchalant as possible but also observing as much as possible. The now-distinctly two blobs zipped past the baroness and came to him. Several of the tentacles reached out and placed sticky pads on his skin. He tried to brush them off, but the two insisted, using spare limbs to subdue him. After all the pads had been attached, a transparent display appeared, with an outline of his body, his vitals, alien writing, and various charts and graphs he couldn't understand.

A translation stone was placed in his hands, and a voice came across. "How are you feeling?"

He responded with his own questions, finding these stones quite easy to use, very intuitive. "Where are we? Are we in a ship?

Are we still on Earth?"

The stone was pulled away, and several bursts of various perfumes erupted in an allergenic nightmare of smells too intense and foreign for his nose to process. Like adjusting to an unpleasant order, he got over this new experience too. The tone of the conversation seemed to change as each smell seeped in, until the brain had time to counterfilter.

After the smells subsided, the stone was returned to his hand. "Please, sir, we are very busy. Please only use the installed summon devices for medical emergencies."

"My apologies," he replied in thought, "but it is my partner there who wanted you summoned." He walked next to the baroness, who had turned but stood with her hands on her hips. The tentacles reached out once again, covering their new patient with their sensors until the screen came up. He still held on to the translation stone and lifted it up.

One of the doctors reached out to touch the stone. "It says that there are only two types of humans. Are you sure of that?"

The baroness whirled around, grasped the stone, and tugged it out from his control. Her face hardened. "You mind?"

He smiled. "No, I don't mind."

She hit him on the arm, forcibly turned him, and gently kicked him in the ass.

$$\mathbb{Y}$$

Now that she had the stone and some privacy, maybe she could get some answers. She took a deep breath and held out the stone. "Am I pregnant?"

She received a question in reply. "Are there only two types of humans?"

"Why do I keep getting asked that? What's wrong? Am I pregnant?" A tear spilled from her tightly clenched face.

The two beings, their exact appearance still shrouded in haze, cycled through several charts, graphs, and images. Random smells enveloped the area from time to time as the information being displayed and evaluated changed. At last, after a very sour smell had come and gone, she received a message through the stone. "Yes, yes you are pregnant. However, alien biology isn't our area of expertise." A chart now appeared on the display. Several tentacles moved and swiped the listed items around in a manner that was incomprehensible to her. "We have scheduled you for a visit with Dr. Fengie. Now please stay in your assigned cubical." A new display appeared, one that looked like a map. She tried to understand and memorize it, but it proved too difficult. A light in the cubical next to his lit up. "We have reassigned you to this location so you may be together until the doctor calls for you." The two blobs then rejoined tentacles and departed as quickly as they had come.

No Tip had returned to his wall and was leaning sloppily against it with his arms crossed. Something about his mannerisms, the way he did things, was so teenager-ish and yet so enchanting. She tried to picture him as a father, but the only image that came to her mind was that of him smoking weed with a teenage son and his friends. She could see him telling wild stories, encouraging terrible behaviors, and being a real pain-in-the-ass husband.

Shit, she thought to herself. The look on his face showed that she had been caught thinking about him, and that made her very upset. She approached him and focused all of her energy, all of her passion, on him. He was the cause of all this. She raised her hand and prepared to lash out and attack him. Her blood started to boil, and she felt sweat forming across her body. She neared him now, but he took no defensive action.

She raised her arm high and brought it down hard on his chest, followed by a blow from the side of her head. There she kept it, with her arms now wrapped around him, holding and squeezing him until the tears came. Her mighty tears soaked his chest. He was the most infuriating man she had ever met. He gave her such power with all that anger, yet in his presence, she had never been weaker.

$$\lambda$$

It was an hour or more before anything happened, and compared to the events of the past few days, they were a slog of dead time and doldrums. They sat leaning against the wall in the adjoining corners. While they were not constrained into the cells, a visual red hue would blink across their vision, with an arrow pointing back toward the cell if they left. Outside the cell was also little activity. No other cells nearby were in use, and only sporadically would a blob moving with a destination pass by.

It was a striking contrast in the baroness. Formally, she was so strong, commanding, and secure. However, now that she had relaxed, she came across so much more like—he hated to think it—a woman. She was flighty, multitasking, given unto fear-driven trains of thought, and unpredictable—a true woman.

Whatever the doctors had said to her certainly made her relax some. He had tried to get a glance at something useful but had come up dry. The baroness's conversation certainly didn't seem too revealing, but then again, he wasn't privy to its content. At one point, he tried to talk her into going exploring around the ship, but she would have none of it.

The baroness's conversations were full of questions, but he quickly learned that she wasn't necessarily soliciting answers, and after a brief pause, she would either answer the question herself or move on to the next topic. Occasionally, she would tell a story or interject some life lesson into her trains of thought. Once "weary" started approaching "annoying," he lay his head down on her shoulder and closed his eyes. Half expecting a slap to the face, he was greeted with silence and a gentle hand against his cheek. She helped him use her lap as a pillow and rubbed his back. Whatever annoyance had built up was soon washed away, and he melted to sleep right there.

⅄

It was quite the contrast in him too. When he was "on," he was so confident, secure, and manly. Now, as the baroness looked down at him while he lay in her lap, he looked so innocent, weak, and needy. This was someone who needed her looking after him. She felt closer to him now than she had felt to anybody in her entire life. She pushed the fear into adrenaline and felt her heart flutter at the realization of her feelings for him. He was such a terrible talker. His conversation skills were lacking, to say the least. Did he, she wondered to herself, return her feelings?

A tone dinged, and an alien neared the cell. This alien had a different configuration—tall, skinny, and lanky. It stood very tall, nearly touching the ceiling as it lumbered forward.

No Tip jumped to his feet and took a protective stance in front of her. His paranoia was also something she would have to improve on. She touched his shoulder and pushed him off to the side. The alien held out his hand, and a transparent display appeared. The display contained a picture of an alien. It was the first unfiltered image of an alien either of them had seen. The creature was barrel shaped, with numerous long tentacles extending from the top of the barrel shape and dozens of thicker tentacles protruding out from the bottom. The alien's skin was an orange-red leather-like substance. The words and information were still unintelligible, but the graphs showed a very high percent—neither of them was certain what it was a percentage of. After a few minutes, the display disappeared, and the creature turned ninety degrees.

"Where are you taking her?" He used a commanding voice.

"It's time for my appointment. Would you just relax?" She brushed her hand against his neck and then walked out of the cell. The alien proceeded immediately as she exited the cell. It led her across a great hall of cells, nearly twenty or more, she thought to herself. Most were empty, but some held what she thought were animals. At last, they entered a hallway. The tall alien approached a barrel-shaped blob form and handed something over as well. The alien turned ninety degrees again and stayed motionless.

The blob who had taken control of the item was now moving down the hall until it noticed that she had not followed. The barrel shape returned, and she felt a tentacle grab her by the hand. She was led down a hall and into a room where the alien from the picture display now stood. A translation stone was placed into her hand, and the blob forms exchanged tentacles for several seconds before the one stepped aside.

It was hard to tell if the constant tentacle motion was controlled like breathing or more like a cat's tail, possessing freedom till called upon. Several large pieces of equipment were scattered about the room. A large rectangular pillar rose out of the middle of the room. Several displays flickered and transmitted their foreign knowledge.

"Please, please come in, come in." The voice was audible despite a lack of physical contact with the translation stone. The baroness cautiously moved forward. She felt safe, but unfamiliarity and stress kept her wits at bay. "My my my, what a lovely specimen. You have the radiant glow of life in and about you. My name is Dr. Fergundimite Exquestobar—please call me Fergie. That beautiful female who brought you in here is my mate, Ferunditime Fresuestobar, or Fengie for short. Please do sit down on the examination table so we might have a better look at you."

The visual filter had let her see the doctor clearly, but his mate was still nothing more than a blob. The baroness held up the stone and spoke verbally, even if a little nervously. "Where am I?"

The reply came loudly after a deep-hearted chuckle. "What an excellent question. Always, always be aware of your surroundings, a very good rule to follow, indeed. Now, please come sit down." Several tentacles held the side of the table, clearly indicating where he would like her to go.

A new voice entered her mind. This one sounded distinctly female. "Once again my husband manages to say so little with so much. Please do sit down. This ship is the mother ship to the scout ship the two of you were so unsuccessfully trying to jump onto.

Congratulations, my dear."

As the baroness sat on the table, the displays jumped to new images. The image of her and No Tip jumping off her building and starting to fall cut off to display new graphs, and various pictures of her body.

Fengie's voice came across." I see you were able to remove the assist devices. Shall I assume that the legs are feeling well?" He came over and removed the last of the gel pads, and her vision cleared.

The baroness held up the stone. "Yes, my legs and body feel fine. I am here for a separate reason." The last few words were hard to spit out.

Fengie's voice came again. "She hides her assertiveness behind a cloud of tepidness."

Fergie responded with a deep laugh. "Yes, yes I am very interested in observing social interactions, but please, my dear, let us meet our quota before we dive into our own curiosities and projects."

"Yes, dear, you are right, of course, and she is an expecting mother, I see. Tell me, are there only the two types of humans, male and female?"

The conversation and question made her nervous and scared, and she couldn't hold back some tears as she raised the stone and spoke. "Why does everyone keep asking that? What's wrong with my baby?" Hearing herself actually ask the question hit her hard. She had never imagined being a mother. "I, I, I can't be pregnant, can I?"

A strange, moldy smell entered the room. Fengie's voice replied. "I'm sorry, dear, the order of your questions confused us. Yes, you are indeed pregnant. As for the health, that's what we are here to examine."

Fergie spoke next. "Yes, yes, exciting business here." Several tentacles manipulated the displays, zooming in on her abdomen. An image of several hundred cells clumping together appeared on the monitor closest to the doctors.

The baroness held up the stone again and spoke with a stutter. "Is that my baby?"

One of Fengie's tentacles reached out and slowly lowered the stone. "Yes, my dear, isn't it beautiful?"

Fergie commented next. "From the cell growth, I would say this child is roughly," he trailed off as he entered data into one of the displays, "one and one-eighteenths planetary rotations old."

The baroness's hands rose to her face, and she both smiled and cried with a fierce intensity. One of Fengie's tentacles grabbed the translation stone. "My dear, you were leaking your thoughts out all over the place. Please take your time, and communicate normally." Fengie held on to the stone and stepped back. "Perhaps we need to educate you on proper usage of the translation stone before we go any further. Then, my dear, we can discuss some of the particulars as to exactly how you became pregnant."

⅄

God, he was bored, and damn if his nipple didn't sting. The baroness was convinced that this ship was a place of refuge and healing, but his gut and nipple told him otherwise. It just didn't make any sense to him. Why attack a planet but save some of its individuals? The whole situation was making less and less sense to him, and his frustration was growing.

At least the baroness had gone off to her meeting or whatever. She was a distraction, and even now here alone, he could still feel her presence. Faint vapors of her perfume would break free from their crevices, float into the receptors, and trigger her in his brain. The past few hours with the woman had been more than ever before, but it was still a far cry away from being a relationship, and he struggled to push her out of his mind.

Thus far, he had gleaned at least four different alien types. They would stroll past his location at seemingly random times, as singles, pairs, and one group of three. It was nothing that would indicate a patrol, nor did any of the aliens appear to be holding or transporting anything. The aliens who moved from his right to his left moved with a greater sense of urgency, but with the vision impairment of the gel glasses, details were impossible to come by.

After some time, he came to the conclusion that perhaps the end of the hallway held a lounge or dining facility, but he wanted to wait for the baroness's return before he started exploring. Two figures moved in from the left in a hurry. He took note, hopping to his feet. The shapes indicated that one was of the same type that took the baroness away, and the other was the same as the cataloger. They came to the center of the cell and held up a translation stone.

He slowly approached, drawing the annoyance of the tentacle holding the stone, which then shook it up and down. The voices were in his head as soon as he physically touched the stone. "Sorry for the informality, but we are in a significant hurry. Please answer the questions as accurately and thoroughly as possible." A transparent display appeared out from a wrist device on the being. It showed an image he had seen before on the TV, but it was TV-doctor script talk, as far as he could understand it.

A new voice entered his head. "Identify this genome." There was a long pause as they obviously waited for his answer. He shrugged his shoulders and raised his eyebrows.

The first voice returned. "Identify the origin of this genome."

He replied with a long, slow, drawn-out, "Blood." Despite his hampered vision, there was a clear disbelief in their body language.

The voice returned. "I told you, try the DNA strain." A new image appeared from the wrist console. This time, it was another image he had seen on the TV before, a circular wire of balls. "Please, to which creature does this DNA strain belong to?"

His hand rose to the back of his head and scratched. "I have no idea. Can I have you zoom out some more?"

A sharp response came back. "Please, this is very important. Your child has this genome strain in its DNA, yet neither you nor your mate has it. Please identify the source."

"What? First off, I don't have a mate, much less a child. I'm not a doctor or even a medical hobbyist. I have no idea what the hell you are talking about. Now, how about you start answering some of my questions?" He crossed his arms and stood with his feet shoulder-width apart.

The second voice, belonging to the taller being, came across. "Please, are humans the only sentient being on your planet?"

"What does 'sentient' mean?"

An unmistakably angry tone entered the cataloger's voice. "You humans, why do you have to be so stubborn? We're trying to save your pathetic little civilization here, and you're giving us attitude. Why not help those trying to save your species while the rest of your kind gets ready for death?"

The taller being came across now as she gently put her extremities around the barrel shape of the cataloger. "Calm down, calm down. Let me have another try, ok?" The being then entered the cell.

No Tip backed up and entered a combat stance, but to his surprise, after entering the cell, the alien lowered itself as if dropping to a knee. The gesture caught him off guard but wasn't enough to reduce his rushing adrenaline.

"Please, we must know if humans are the only creatures on Earth capable of upper-level thoughts."

He answered quickly, keeping his body on alert and at the ready. "What, like a degree or something?"

A groan came across. "Sure, or even something like self-awareness, ability to think and interact with other species?"

"I had a dog once, taught it to ambush the mailman."

Again, another groan. "No, not like that, not an animal you domesticate but an animal that can have, say, free will."

"Free will, you mean like when that bastard dog bit me, or my ex decided to cheat—or me, for keeping the dog?"

The two aliens shifted to face each other better. "Is his translation stone broken?" asked the taller alien.

The cataloger said, "No, these humans just don't get it. They can't see beyond themselves. So caught up in their little existence that they can't see we are trying to help." The anger and frustration were clearly transmitted.

No Tip tweaked an old saying of his uncle's: "The blind must be taught to see. Navigation by feel is a slow and painful process."

The taller alien knelt. "To use your analogy, crossing the street is a bad time for a first lesson. Sometimes you just have to grab hold of the nearest hand and trust the universe to lead you to safety."

He paused a moment, considering. "Dolphins."

The cataloger excitedly responded. "Yes, yes, dolphins, what habitat does this create live in?"

"The ocean?" The display from the console changed again, this time displaying several sea creatures. He recognized many of them, including squids, whales, sharks, and a few others.

"Please approach and identify the creature known as dolphin."

He waved his hand, indicating which one was the dolphin. Upon receiving his input, the two aliens began interfacing on both sides of the transparent display. For several minutes, the two were deeply engaged in their computer work before the taller alien turned back toward him. "Now, you are sure that these dolphins are sentient? We have just invested significant resources into their capture."

"Yeah, sure, I guess. I don't know."

The two aliens exited the cell, and their thoughts crept across. "Humans, annoying as hell."

$$\mathcal{Y}$$

The translation stones were amazing devices, not quite technology, more than geology, and a little bit psychic, with some intuition. Fengie proved to be an adept teacher, if not a little condescending at times. She explained the stone's ability to project and absorb not only one's own but others' thoughts and feelings too. She also explained that despite the stone's advantages, many races forbade its usage, and a great many others had enacted usage protocols. She didn't fail to wish the baroness luck on learning Emottocon, the universal basic language.

After a few practice exercises, they returned to the doctor, who was working furiously at his station. A noticeable change had occurred in both scent and body language. The air here was filled with a clean smell of laundry detergent, and Fergie's tentacles had stopped swaying.

A shudder passed through the baroness's body. Fengie went to Fergie, and the two exchanged tentacle embraces. Hissing noises filled the room with a wild array of odors so strong the baroness was forced to back away.

"Ahh, yes, please sit down." Fergie must have activated a fan, because the smells soon dissipated. "Smell is an integral part of how our species communicate. In fact, it wasn't until after our own first contact, many generations ago, that we developed verbal thoughts. Chemical commutation proved more effective on our home world, as it is a world with a very dense sky and minimal visibility, with frequent rains. So much so that the animal life has adapted to non-sight navigation."

"Fergie, my dear, please, there are important matters to attend to. You can babble on later. Let us get to your discovery."

The word jolted the baroness's heart. "Discovery?"

A new image filled every display in the room, and Fergie turned to face the baroness. "Can you identify this genome?"

Having heard the word before was no substitute for actual knowledge of its meaning. "What is a genome?"

A musky smell accompanied Fengie's reply. "Dear, did the stone not translate, or do you not possess this level of knowledge?"

"I'm not a doctor. How am I supposed to know? What does it mean about my baby? Does my baby have this? Is it good? Tell me something about my baby that I can understand."

Fengie's tentacle wrapped around the baroness's shoulders, and several pads massaged her skin, but Fergie was next to speak. "My dear, your baby is perfectly healthy." His tone was comforting. "A genome is like an instruction booklet. It tells the body how and even when to develop. Each genome comes in a pair, but they only control one specific trait or characteristic. Both you and your mate have 352 genome pairs, yet your child has 353 genome pairs. This is a most unusual development. Evolution doesn't occur with additions of genome but by alteration.

"My dear, you could be the mother of the next evolution in humankind. Then again, it might be a hidden trait longing for discovery, or your child will be some kind of freak, but either way, it is very exciting."

The baroness's heart sank. The word "freak" fixated in her mind, and images, feelings, and fears rolled through her. "Freak," the word rattled around her head, and emotions consumed her. Words she had heard many times from girls at the shop and vowed never to utter herself came out unfiltered and raw. "I don't want this baby. Get it out of me."

The stench of burning rubber filled the air. Both Fengie's and Fergie's skin tones darkened. Fengie removed her tentacle and stepped back as a wave of furious thoughts basted across the baroness's body. "This is a place of healing! You will leave your murderous, barbaric practices behind. Life is the most precious of all currencies. This is the Arkapeligo, the greatest mission undertaken by life, for life. We are its stewards, healing its injured and curing its diseased, and catalogers of its essence. We will have no more of such talk."

The lecture extracted the internal conflict within her, and the baroness bawled for several minutes. Then the smell returned to normal, and Fengie placed a tentacle on her shoulder. The baroness's words came out in babbles. "Everything is just changing so fast. I'm so scared I don't know what to do."

10: Aragmell

The prospect of food was enticing. The baroness was still away, and No Tip debated whether to seek out food and have it ready for her or await her return and seek it out together. This debate eventually led to a compromise. He would scout out the nearby area to minimize his time away.

He had gone no more than eight steps when one of the taller, more slender aliens approached him and handed him a tiny stone, the diameter of a pen cap, covered in a sticky substance, and indicated that he should put it in his ear. The thought of putting this alien object in his ear churned his stomach, and he tried to wave it off. The alien insisted, grabbed his arms, and forcibly rolled the stone into his right ear. "You will come with me," the voice commanded.

Obviously the alien possessed superior strength, but he never liked being manhandled and was in no mood for this kind of treatment. "I will NOT!"

"You have an appointment with a specialist. I am here to escort you. Now please come this way." The alien began to walk but became frustrated by the inaction of his patient. "I apologize for forcing the stone into your ear, but we have a strict time crunch, and the other sectors of the operation are demanding information critical to the success of this mission."

The softening of tone again caught him off guard. This place was never quite what he expected. "What kind of specialist? What mission are you talking about?"

There was a short pause. "I will answer your question, but only as we walk." The alien turned and moved at a rapid pace. "You have an appointment with an assessment officer who will collect information that I will disperse to the other sectors as they scramble to collect and save as much as necessary to preserve the existence of your race and other sentient life."

"What other sectors?"

"Please, sir, I am not an operations specialist. I am an administrative adjunct. I get individuals to where they are supposed to be and disperse the knowledge gained by the specialists, nothing more."

There was no time for any follow-up questions, for they had arrived at a large door, and the alien stepped to the side. The alien reached out and removed the gel pads around No Tip's eyes. The sight of the alien unfiltered filled him with an instinctual fear.

The alien's body was like that of a thick hide, evolved from a hunter species, its eyes, ears, and nose all designed to track and attack its prey. It had a humanoid form with four limbs, but it appeared to have additional joints. A long, slender tail headed by a sharp nail coursed across the floor behind him.

Opening the door, the alien signaled for him to enter. The room inside was vast, open, and dark. A single light shined on an alien standing in the middle of the room. He crept closer, and as he did, a new light appeared, illuminating a long staff. The alien spoke in a thundering voice. "I am Aragmell, and you will defend yourself."

After several minutes, Fengie returned her tentacle to the baroness's shoulders. "My dear, my dear, please don't panic. Just because I say that there is the possibility of your child being a freak doesn't mean that it will come to pass. Everything we see here indicates a healthy child. This genome is interfering with our normal algorithms, so we can't determine the sex of the child yet. Now, please, take a deep breath and look around. This is a place of healing and recovery. You are not alone. We are the Adrinoleen, one of the first five races to be integrated into the Arkapeligo. We mostly function as doctors, healers, and catalogers. Now there are over thirteen races here, each one of them committed to others' survival, so please, my dear, you are not alone."

The words calmed her, and the massaging tentacles warmed her. "Where is he? The one you call my mate?"

Dr. Fergie pushed several buttons on the console to bring up a map display. "Aw, looks like he is in with the assessment officers. Rough business there, but it is unfortunately very necessary. A lesson learned through costly mistakes. Mistakes that could have been easily avoided had those darn administrators—"

A tone of anger came across with his words, when Fengie interrupted him. "My dear, there you go, off on another one of your tangents. Please let us focus on our patient, not politics."

"What do you mean, rough business? Is he ok?"

"There should be no lasting damage, but it is a trying and difficult assessment designed to test each race's ability to integrate into the Arkapeligo. They will not only test his physical capabilities but also push his emotions to the limit. Should he fail, you will be tested. Should you fail, your race will most likely face nonacceptance and shortly perish."

Fengie carried on. "Too bad you chose such an inferior specimen as a mate, but I have much confidence in your ability to pass. Now, please, we have another specialist to see."

$$\sum$$

Aragmell charged forward with incredible speed and agility. Only by instinct did No Tip raise his staff in time. The blow still came with enough force to knock him backward several feet, nearly causing him to lose balance. The third strike came vertically. Each time, he simply reacted, barely positioning the staff in time to receive the blow. He was on the defensive, with no time to formulate a plan. It wasn't even ten seconds before he was on the ground. Aragmell's tail had him tripped up without notice.

"Few creatures this weak rise to the top of a world's evolution. Are the females of your species the warriors? Perhaps it's a question of motivation." A transparent display arose from his wristband. The room's vast interior now lit up, a great classism opened, and in the middle of it was the baroness. She stood motionless, her hands tied behind her and around a pillar. Her feet were perched on a platform that extended no farther than a foot radius out from it.

A console appeared several feet to his left, a large red button placed in its center. "This is the Arkapeligo, and only the strong may live here. I am its defender, its purifier. If I am allowed to press that button, your mate's restraints will be released and she will perish. You will then perish by my hand, and this whole endeavor will cease as we continue our search for the strong." Aragmell spun his staff and entered a warrior's stance.

"Baroness! Baroness! Baroness!" Each call was met with no response. His blood boiled. Outmatched or not, he would defend the baroness. "What have you done to her?"

"She proved inferior. She has been cataloged."

A tear slipped from his eye. That stupid girl, trusting this was some sort of hospital ship. His anger rose at the aliens' betrayal. He lunged forward, using his anger to launch an attack. He struck hard, going straight at Aragmell, who easily sidestepped and slammed his own staff into the side of his human opponent. The blow hurt, and it hurt bad, knocking him to his knees and the wind from lungs.

Aragmell stretched and turned his back toward his opponent, shifting in the direction of the button. "Perhaps I was wrong. Maybe the female sex is the warrior sex. It often happens that the ranks of soldiers are filled by the weaker sex. No creature as weak as you could ever rise to the top of a food chain."

The desire to breathe took precedence. No Tip fought through the pain in his side and hurled his staff at Aragmell. The blow seemed to do little more than annoy him, and he continued his slow walk. The pain still ravaged No Tip, but he forced one leg up and then the other. Soon, with the return of some air to his lungs, he dove at Aragmell's feet.

He extended his nail blade and aimed for what he thought was a tendon in Aragmell's foot. The creature howled, kicking his leg out and launching his opponent across the room. "For that, I will destroy you with my bare hands." By the end of the sentence,

Aragmell was on him, landing blow after blow after painful blow.

No Tip's vision was blurry, his mind numb to its surroundings. He felt his limbs flailing with the force of the impacts, but he had no more control. He wasn't sure how long he lay there, but once his mind cleared, he saw the beast tending to his wound. When he tried to move, the nerves reactivated and his entire body screamed.

Aragmell's voice boomed in his head. "For that little stunt, I think I will invest a little more into this." His display showed the baroness. "Yes, I see here, her sexual organs are compatible. Maybe I will make you watch as I pleasure myself." Aragmell pulled out a blade and set it next to the console before walking to the edge of the classism. The platform holding the baroness moved toward Aragmell.

Anger overrode all his nerves, and No Tip hollered in pain and forced his legs to move. He walked toward the console and gathered his breath. "Baroness, I can't save you from death, but I can save you from hell." Then he pushed the button. The baroness's limp body fell as the platform retracted and dropped deep into the darkness.

Unable to stand fully erect, he grabbed the blade with his left hand. Dragging his right leg behind him, he moved as quickly and stealthily as possible. Pain had no recourse against the anger flowing through his veins. Fever gripped his mind, singularly focused. He sprang at Aragmell. The creature knelt and laughed, rejoicing in his prey's decision, regaling at its agony.

Together, surprise and position of favor were enough to topple the beast. Aragmell twisted and caught his opponent's arm, but not before the knife drew blood. The force was enough to knock Aragmell onto his back. His opponent, No Tip, landed in a position of power above him. Aragmell screamed out in a horrible roar of pain as the sharp steel slowly pressed through the beast's skin.

He could feel the laboring of Aragmell's chest beneath him. Blood ran out from his wound and weakened his resistance to his blade. Something had changed, but No Tip's anger pushed him on without thought. He pulled the knife out and placed it at the neck of the great beast. With every labored breath, his blade moved closer.

$$\gtrless$$

Dr. Fergie excused himself and asked for leave so he could prepare a report for the administrators. Dr. Fengie escorted the baroness back out into the common area and across a row of large cells, most of which were empty, but the baroness could have sworn she heard an elephant as they traveled. She was led into a long, narrow room. Several objects, she guessed chairs, were placed in a row on the near side. Fengie indicated for the baroness to sit and then left to inform the specialist of their arrival.

A large bulk of a beast entered the room. The baroness jumped at the sight of his predator face, leather skin, and intimidating stature. The beast's mouth moved, and unintelligible sounds emanated from his mouth. Several seconds passed before the baroness picked up a translation stone. The sound level rose as the words crossed her mind. "Must I repeat myself?"

Her body froze. She had been sitting comfortably, processing everything she just went through, but now she was filled with horror and dread.

With angry snarls, the beast asked again, "Must I repeat myself?"

Fear coursed through her body, but she wasn't alone and had to constantly remind herself of that. She repeated Dr. Fengie's words over and over again in her head, and to her great surprise, she spoke them out loud. "This is a place of healing and recovery. This is a place of healing and recovery. This is a place of healing and recovery!"

"Yes, it is indeed. Now must I repeat myself?" The beast again snarled.

Encouraged by her ability to say anything at all, she took a deep breath and believed. "Yes, yes, you will have to repeat yourself. I wasn't holding my translation stone."

"Very well. Know this, I am Aramethel, assistant to Aragmell, and should your mate fail, I will be conducting your evaluation."

The baroness found a named beast much less intimidating. "Evaluation of what?"

"Your race's ability to integrate peacefully into the Arkapeligo. We will have the ability to watch your mate's evaluation. This room is adjacent to the examination room. Now, please sit. Dr. Fengie should be back soon. Her species requires that each mated or parental pair exchange pheromones every thirty hours or so. To miss an exchange would prove harmful, and missing two would be fatal." The beast then entered the room, jumped up onto a ledge, and lay like a dog.

⟩⟩

"Please, stop." The words came with blood from the creature's mouth. "Please, you victor . . . poison from tail."

The blade now touched the skin of the beast, his anger boiled, and he prepared to do something he vowed never to do again.

"My family . . . just goodbye . . . poison . . . please."

No Tip pressed the blade firmly against skin, but some internal force held him back. The rise and fall of the creature's chest was struggling, and a dark-blue drip formed around his mouth. "Please." Rise, pause, fall, pause, rise—the rhythm indicated he was dying.

"It's better than you fucking deserve." He released the beast.

Aragmell brought his wrist to his mouth and spoke into a small device. "End evaluation."

⟩⟩

For the second time in as many days, she saw herself plummet to her death, both times at the hands of the man she feared she may have fallen in love with. The baroness's stomach churned as she saw herself tumble from the pillar. Emotions so mixed and confused overcame her senses. The first sights of him being beaten had already worked her into a tizzy. The sight of her own death boiled the pot over, and now as she watched him prepare to kill her imaginary assailant, something clicked in her heart and all went numb.

The lights in the area lit up, illuminating a large dome shape. The beast Aragmell, once near death, transformed and rose, holding his opponent in place as he did. It was all too apparent that the beast was in no real danger at all. A shiver of anger ran through her as she thought to herself, some protector.

She was startled by Fengie's tentacles rubbing her shoulders again. Aramethel announced that her mate had passed the test and she would not be tested. Then, after wishing her a good day, the beast left.

The baroness turned to Fengie. "What just happened? I feel so numb."

Fengie smiled and let out a sweet smell, like hickory and lavender. "Something wonderful. Your race has just been chosen for salvation, and who would have thought a being with so many obvious deficiencies could pass a test of such inner strength?"

A hissing sound drew the baroness's attention, and she saw Aragmell enter the viewing room holding a limp, pale body as if it were a dirty diaper. She panicked and rushed to his side. Aragmell brought him over and dropped his limp arm over the baroness's shoulder. She jumped as he cringed in pain at the placement of her hand upon his side. She helped him lie down on the piece of furniture Aramethel had occupied. He was obviously concussed, and his now-misshapen face brought out tears of compassion from her. She ran her hand through his hair and couldn't be sure, but his head felt lumpier now. Her eyes met his as he stared blankly at her, and in that moment, she felt more sympathy than she had thought herself capable of. Then he spoke. "I'll have the blonde tonight, mistress." Then she simply wanted to kill him again.

Fengie grabbed a tool out of a pocket and began shining a dual-layered laser with a blue interior light surrounded by a ring of red. Touching her wrist display, she summoned two small, black robots. Each rode an inch off the ground and was the size of a loaf of bread. The only noticeable sensor system was a round eye, which seemed to have limited independent mobility. Fengie commanded the bots as they entered. "MOPs, bring me the MendelaScope." The two almost-cute little bots scrambled off with a chirp.

Fengie spoke with a tone that was unmistakably like that of a mother catching her child being naughty. "Mr. Aragmell, it was not necessary to cause this much discomfort to this being. Really, have you no self-control? We are trying to save these pitiful creatures, not beat what little intelligence they have out of them. Now leave before I decide to file a report!"

Aragmell's chest expanded, nearly doubling in circumference. His face snarled furiously, his legs widened in stance, and with a slight hunch, he let out the most intimidating growl. Aragmell slid his left foot back, causing the baroness to jump behind Fengie, brought his left foot forward, and left the room.

"Pay no mind to him. They always get aggressive after a fight, but don't you worry, they know their role as guardians of the fleet very well."

The machine Fengie had summoned was now being towed in by the two MOP bots and placed beside the patient. A cap ejected out from the top of the machine, and Dr. Fengie put it on the patient's head.

"There isn't any permanent damage to brain tissue. However, I can't say the same about the eye socket. I am afraid there will be quite a bit of short-term discomfort and longer-term cosmetic damage." Then Dr. Fengie turned to the baroness. "My dear, I am so sorry you had to endure all this, but believe me that it really is in the majority's interests that we thoroughly vet all new races into the Arkapeligo."

After several minutes of scanning, buzzing, and even some clicking, the cap ejected itself off of the patient's head. Dr. Fengie stepped forward and looked deep into his eyes, examining before she stepped back and allowed the patient to see the baroness.

"Oh my god, Baroness, thank God you're alive! But how?" The words seemed heartfelt, but now that he had his right mind back, the baroness's sympathy morphed into rage.

"Twice, that's twice in two fucking days you have killed me!" The baroness's palm struck him hard. Then came another and another, and for the second time that day, she kissed him passionately.

11: Captain Calling

Dr. Fergie rushed into the room. "Quickly, quickly, my friends." He rotated his body toward the bed, where the baroness stood holding "Patient 00" in her arms. "Bravo, patient double-zero, well done, but I am afraid there will be no time to celebrate, for we have been summoned to the captain's quarters."

Fengie hurried to exchange tentacles with her mate. "What does it mean? We have never been summoned before." A look almost reminiscent of worry accompanied by the reek of melting plastic gave the room an ominous feel.

Fergie said, "Apparently my report has gotten the administrators all up in a tizzy."

With the tentacle exchange completed, Dr Fengie again summoned the MOP bots. The group then hurried into something called a "shaft lift," which sped them up several flights and into the bridge of the ship.

The room expanded outward in another dome shape, making the ship feel a bit like bubble wrap folded over itself. This was also the first room they had been in with permanent work stations installed. There were two new alien species operating interfaces in a cubical that adjoined a central circular platform.

As the group exited the platform, a slick command room

extended around and above them. Atop the platform stood a larger, duller Adrinoleen. His height was about the same, but his diameter was noticeably larger, and his tentacles, while longer, displayed little movement. He spoke with a slow, clear, monotone voice. "Patients 00, 01, and 02 of the human species, primary sentient species of your world, congratulations on successfully completing Aragmell's tests. Now we must attend to business. Dr. Exquestobar, anything you hear in this room is on a need-to-know basis. No one outside this room will ever need to know. Do you understand?"

While there was no audible reply, a mix of yeast and laundry detergent scented the room. The captain then looked directly at the baroness. "Patient 01, you are with child, a child with extraordinary potential. Never before have we encountered an additional genome, absent from the parents." The captain then turned toward Dr. Fergie. "Doctor, summarize your finding for our patients."

A nervous-sounding Dr. Fergie said, "Due to the very young age of Patient 02 and the method of conception, we must assume that there are other forces at work."

The doctor continued talking, but Patient 00 bent over to whisper into the baroness's ear. "Did that dog bastard touch you? I swear to God—"

The baroness spoke when he swore. "It's not exactly what you think. Just be happy for me, ok?" A tear fell, and a whimper shook her voice.

Patient 00 grabbed her hand and said, "I'm sure you will be a wonderful mother."

Three large bangs sounded, and they looked at the captain, who was still speaking. "What Dr. Fergie was saying was for your sake, not mine. If you have no wish to understand, then you will answer." Two large beast-like dogs entered from either side, and while they simply stood there, their presence felt tangible.

The baroness wrapped her arm around Patient 00. "Don't you dare get me killed for a third fucking time."

The captain continued. "We, meaning the Arkapeligo administration, have an urgent need to know, one, how this happened, two, what will be the result of this happening, and three, can we replicate this? Unfortunately, there are forces at work that are greatly rushing the entire process. So instead of completing our cataloging, we have been ordered to immediately escort you back to the Arkapeligo."

Dr. Fergie, with some confidence in his voice, asked, "What, sir, will happen to my research after the patients have been transferred?"

The captain, still quite lifeless in his mannerisms, said, "Doctor, you will not be transferred with the patients. I can only assume they will bring you in for debriefing."

The assertiveness in Dr. Fergie's voice was noticeable. "Sir, I must protest. As the discoverer of this genome, I claim my founding rights."

"Doctor, this goes beyond any sort of possible financial considerations. The Arkapeligians are proposing that this could lead to the total transformation of the political universe. It's too early to say if this could be used as a weapon against the Wilde, but it has more potential than any discovery to date."

The baroness leaned over and whispered into Patient 00's ear.

"What are they saying about the baby? I can't understand anything in this place."

Patient 00 spoke up. "Just a damn minute here, you are talking about things outside our frame of reference. We don't give a damn about your administration, your Arkapeligo. What we care about is this right here." He pointed toward the baroness and himself. "Now the only place we are going is back home, to Earth."

The captain's color seemed to return a little. "Earth. I am afraid that won't be possible. A Wilde ship is heading this way. Our transverse gates can allow us to travel great distances between destinations at near-instantaneous speeds, but we have no way of preventing their attack. You see, once that Wilde ship arrives, everything will be destroyed. You are now way too precious a cargo to ever let be destroyed. So we must therefore ensure your continued safety. In order to help accomplish this task, Patients 01 and 02 have each been assigned a private bodyguard. I believe you are familiar with Aragmell and Aramethel."

Both beasts turned and bowed toward the baroness. Then, pounding their fists against their chests, they let out a deep howl. "For the mission of life, so we gladly lay down our own!"

"And what say do we have in this?" the baroness asked.

The captain, while still idle, was slowly becoming more animated. "My dear Patient 01, you have the most important say in everything, for no noise can quiet a mother's call."

The overhead light suddenly turned red, and a buzzing noise toned twice as the air filled with a humid itch. The group's body language transformed to alert and focused. One of the aliens sitting in the cubical next to the captain spoke. "Arkapeligo has gone to battle stance. They are issuing an immediate recall of all vessels, launching the defense forces."

The adjoining alien continued as if finishing the other's sentence. "Incoming slip stream, massive in scale, opening directly in front of us, one hundred thousand kilometers."

The captain twirled toward a console on the right side of the room. The cubical had several types of maps displayed, some celestial and others local, with specific items actually moving in real time. "Navigator, get us away from that slip gate." The captain's podium then spun to the other side of the room, where he issued a command. "Defense force, prepare for boarding party."

A large image was projected along the top of the dome. Its spherical dimensions, upon study, revealed that each object was a ship, and the solid area around the edge appeared to be Earth. Patient 00 studied the image. It cast a spell on his eyes and built excitement inside him. The baroness held him tight, and he felt an awkward closeness to her. The feeling motivated him, encouraged his intuition, and expanded his perceptions.

While much of what was occurring around him eluded his conscious grasp, he understood a ship at work. The captain was running, and the image of a large, intimidating vessel emerging from a circular formation in the center of the projected image told him why. One of the aliens in the cubical adjoining the captain's platform announced the ship as an Imperial dreadnought, and the additional slip gates were forming, marking the locations on the map.

The area map changed into an image of a humanoid alien,

its face reptilian in appearance. Three tubular shafts ran several inches off the top of an arched bone outlining its forehead. Its eyes were that of a predator. A single piece of cloth ran from a pair of golden-leafed shoulder pads and down the center of its body.

The alien image spoke its words, consuming the whole of the room's attention: "This is Commodore Gaganious. I now claim this world and all of its inhabitants as property of the Xendorian Imperium. All subjects and information gathered by others from this world are to be relinquished at once. Noncompliance will result in penalties." Then, just as quickly, the image reverted back to the area map.

Complete silence deafened the room. The once-present energy now lay hidden beneath a shrub of fear. Patient 00 felt it—the call, the actors, and the roles—all unfolding in his mind. The baroness pulled on his arm, and he thought, what the hell do I know about what we're witnessing anyway?

The captain turned to the two aliens. "Instructions from the ark?" No, it was too early for that. There was still information out there, needing to be known before a decision could be made. And it didn't take long for that information to arrive. Several new images appeared on the map, and a steady stream of ships flowed, filling the screen with an image too full to be useful anymore.

The reply came: "Captain, instructions from the ark are to comply and surrender, but to do it as slowly as possible. Sir, they want us to provide the distraction as they finish the transverse gate." And then the energy of the moment burst.

The captain, now showing signs of animation, barked a furious string of commands. "Navigator, set course for the Imperial ship farthest from our position. Defense force, begin sabotage of all external hatchways' entrances, collapse hallways outside the bridge, and take the shaft lift out of commission. Communicator, tie up the comm channels and try to prevent any new messages from getting in." He paused briefly. "Medical, start gathering all data associated with the human into a single file."

The captain then twisted to look at the patients, doctors, and protectors. "I regret to inform you that the empire has claimed you as its property. Despite the enormous unknown potential of your child, we do not have the capability of claiming it from such a large force." He turned his back to them and focused his attention elsewhere.

The baroness grabbed Patient 00's hand. "What's happening now? This place is all so strange."

He took her other hand, held it in his, and looked into her eyes. "I promise you, I don't want to die either, and I will find out for you." The baroness looked less than impressed and pulled away from him. He asked Dr. Fengie, "What is going on, in terms we can understand please?"

Dr. Fergie responded instead. "My dear boy, we have been sacrificed. Oh, what a tragic and merciless universe. As last, we find a great hope in a universe awash in despair and it's snatched away mere moments afterward, so the last of our days will be full of dread and the knowledge that we were but an hour away from victory."

Patient 00 glanced at the baroness and raised his finger. "Let's just try that one more time. Dr. Fengie, in terms I can understand, what is going on?"

Dr. Fengie smiled. "You poor, ignorant fool, how I envy you in such a moment. I am torn as to whether or not I should rob you of such a gift, for the next few minutes will be the longest in our existence."

Again Patient 00 looked at the baroness and raised his finger. "Really, just one more time, be patient." He floated his palms down and then turned back to Dr. Fengie. "Doctor, ignorance is a state of mind, not a way of life. Now answer the question!"

A lavender smell accompanied the doctor's response. "We are going to be handed over to the empire. We will be interrogated and executed. The two of you will be given to their medical experiments division and almost certainly face a painful death as they extract every possible detail from your DNA. I shall pray for a quick death for the three of you."

Patient 00 looked back at the baroness. "See, told you I would find out what was going on." He then nodded his head and smiled like a proud child. Again the baroness stepped back and issued a message of disbelief with her face and body language. He marveled at how, the more awkward he felt, the closer and more comfortable she seemed with him, yet the more he tried to lighten up around her, the more she pulled away. He turned back to the doctors, who were comingling tentacles. "Doctors, you have to give us a weapon."

Dr. Fergie looked at them. "You already have two of our greatest warriors at your side. What good would a weapon do you?"

Excitement started growing in him. "No, we need a weapon to smuggle aboard their ship for use later."

Dr. Fergie said, "This is a medical ship! We have only basic firearms and ship defenses."

That sparked an idea. "Doctor, exactly, this is a medical ship, a medical ship that must have lots of germs and whatnot aboard it."

Dr. Fengie grabbed her mate with her tentacles, and they rushed off to the platform the captain was standing on. The platform lowered, and with a flurried exchange and flapping of tentacles, the captain's color grew to a glow. The platform rose again, and the captain issued a gust of new instructions. Dr. Fergie began accessing one of the terminals in the cubical next to the captain's platform. Dr. Fengie returned to the humans and their guardians.

Dr. Fengie issued Patient 00 orders into a terminal and then took the baroness off to the terminal Dr. Fergie was using. Patient 00's mission was to help delay the empire as long as possible while the rest of the crew developed and deployed a biological weapon. He was directed to the comm station, where a very active Adrinoleen controlled a litany of interfaces in an awe-inspiring display of multitasking. The Adrinoleen faced him and awaited instructions but finally had to ask him what the plan was.

Patient 00 hesitated. "I don't quite know yet. Uh, just patch me through to the commander of the enemy fleet."

A tentacle rose in question, releasing with it a smell both musky and moldy. "What does 'patch through' mean?"

"It just means let me talk to him, put him somewhere I can see him." The largest of the nearby displays immediately altered to solid black, and soon the reptilian face of a Xendorian stared back at him. He took a shallow breath, focused on the excitement, and tried to release his mind, giving a slightly annoyed attitude. "May I help you? Please keep in mind that I am very busy. As you can see, we have ourselves quite the project."

The reptile hissed his first syllable. "Human, you dare talk to your new master in such a tone. You will be taught quickly."

He kept the tone and talked without a plan. "Who do you think you are?"

The beast paused for a moment, just long enough to twang his excitement string. "I am the decider of fates, your master."

Patient 00 signaled for the transmission to end.

The Adrinoleen extended a tentacle and grabbed his hand. "Never have I heard anyone be so brave as to speak that way to such an overpowering force. 'Stall,' 'delay,' and 'procrastinate' I understand, but 'irritate' and 'enrage' are new for me."

A very nervous and urgent voice came across as a light on the panel ignited. "Patient 00, we are now being contacted by the Xendorians."

The pieces in his mind shifted, and new images rolled out in his mind's eyes. The Adrinoleen asked if they should respond, and with each negative response he gave, the Adrinoleen became more and more anxious. It was several long minutes before the first volley came close—so close, in fact, the power of the enemy ship's weapons rocked their vessel like a dingy caught in a heavy wake.

Patient 00 now signaled for communication, began speaking the moment the connection was established, and didn't finishing talking till he had overpowered the reptile's lambasting. "I already dealt with you. Do you see who I am? I am human. You see that planet down there? It's a human fucking planet. So I don't give a damn how many battleships, tinker toys, or misfits you think you have. It's time for you to leave now. I have Wilde to prepare for, so leave me before I decide to come over there and teach you some damn manners." Again he signaled for the communications termination.

The Adrinoleen turned back toward the console and shrank down low. Puzzlement crossed Patient 00's face as he failed to understand the alien's demeanor.

12: Enter the Empire

While the words were directed at her, they clearly failed to relay any meaning. "Baroness . . ." More often than not, she had spent the last two days confused, frustrated, tired, and hungry. Now, whatever this place was, it had everyone scrambling to stop it from changing again.

She liked Dr. Fengie, or at least she thought she did. Sometimes it was hard for her to tell. Dr. Fergie was always so jovial and kind, but there was still so much the baroness didn't know that handing over trust was a long leap. Then there were the two giant dog beasts that, shortly after having killed her, now pledged to protect her and her unborn child. Unborn child—the notion gave her a chill. How unfair, she thought, to have to discover her pregnancy mere hours after conception with a man she felt foggy about, at best.

Now she faced yet another difficult decision. Focusing helped keep her from becoming dizzy, but facing the full impact of the words proved too difficult and put her in a state of thought paralysis. The explanation, and anything that came afterward, was simply lost—or rejected, rather, by a brain too busy to accept new information.

She wasn't sure how long she stood there, but his lips brought her around. Blood pulsed through her lips, across her face, and back into her brain. His arms wrapped around her, and his warmth radiated through her. He looked deep into her eyes. "Don't be afraid. You are not alone. This is what we need to do."

She didn't understand, but his confidence pushed her thoughts forward, and her brain finally processed the words Dr. Fergie had spoken to her: "I am going to make you very sick now. I'm so sorry, but this is the least awful of our choices." The voice carried with it the most oddly coupled smell of lavender and rotten egg.

$$\gtrdot$$

The captain, now more animated than ever, stood manipulating a 3-D map of the local area. His tentacles twisted, rotated, and zoomed the map with precision. Constantly bantering orders, questions, and information, he demonstrated his multitasking skills.

"Captain, new slip gate opening, placing it on the map now," one of the aliens at the defense-forces cubical called out.

A station that had so far eluded Patient 00's attention added, "Sir, the size of the gate is normal, but the energy readings are far beyond any we have seen before. Sir, this could be a new ship class and/or a new slip technology."

Dr. Fengie grabbed hold of the humans, physically demanding Patient 00's attention and massaging the baroness's back. Dr. Fergie, now done at the console, loaded something into the device brought out by the MOP bots, approached the patients, and said, "My dear friends, how short a time to have known each other to be placed in a position requiring such absolute trust." He paused for a second. "We have prepared the weapon you asked for, but we beseech you not to carry out such an action, for it will take a great toll. Patient 00, we must confess that, of the options available to us, the best one will still leave you with about a one-in-a-thousand chance of death and a certainty of days full of agony."

Patient 00 nodded. "What about the baroness?"

Dr. Fengie talked this time. "We will be giving her a much milder virus. While she won't enjoy it, there is little chance of injury to mother or child."

Patient 00 rolled up his sleeve in a gesture that perplexed the doctors, but it did bring about a change of face in the baroness, who graciously explained its meaning.

Dr. Fergie continued. "Additionally, there are a few things you need to know. In order to make a virus that would be debilitating to the Xendorians, the two of you will have to mix your viruses together. Normally it would take days for the virus to grow properly, but we have not the time, so to make your body a better cultivator, we will have to artificially put you into a state of arousal."

The baroness hid her blushing cheek behind her hand. "Which one of us are you talking to?"

Dr. Fengie's hue grew brighter as she released the smell of a musky man. "Both of you, my dears. Now, do include Dr. Fergie in on any mating rituals you might engage in. He is always so fascinated by other species' mating habits." Then Dr. Fengie leaned in and spoke gently. "Then he always comes home with the strangest desires. Men, find one worth pleasing, and be grateful if you get pleased." She chuckled. The baroness only replied with a befuddled look.

Dr. Fergie continued the briefing. "Additionally, once the viruses are mixed and the new virus forms, it will still have to be disseminated quickly to as many Xendorians as possible in order for it to spread faster than they can quarantine. I imagine that you are high value enough that you will mostly encounter Xendorians, but be aware that other species may or may not have any effects from the virus. Once you have successfully distributed the virus, you will have somewhere between hours and days before they discover an antidote of their own or before their immune systems start to fight it and they gradually recover."

Patient 00 asked, "What are you giving us? I don't understand yet, how do we mix the viruses?"

Dr. Fergie jumped in. "What excellent questions. You see, in order to hide the virus, we modified a virus found right here on your home world." Dr. Fergie tapped a display. "Something called HIV, it has an excellent ability to hide from a body's natural immune system. So that one will be administered to the baroness. For you, Patient 00, I'm afraid we had to go a bit more brutish and nasty. This virus is a spinal infector. It will greatly affect your reflexes, and you may notice that your breathing and other nonconscious functions may start to behave erratically. While there is a larger window to cure and save the baroness, you will need to receive medical care in no less than three cycles of your planet or perish on the fourth."

Patient 00 swallowed hard and then repeated the question. "Well, doc, you sold me on brutish and nasty, but I still don't understand how we mix the two."

Turning a brighter hue and smelling like the gym, Dr. Fergie continued. "Well, yes, you see, your part is spread through saliva."

Now the baroness openly blushed, yet Patient 00 still seemed not to get it.

Dr. Fengie finished the conversation as only she could. "And we believe you're capable of rising above your numerous limitations."

>)/

Screaming is a universal sound, and when the lights dimmed and sparks zapped out of the walls, the shouts of terror echoed in, around, and from all directions. The captain proudly barked orders and regained the crew's composure. "Engineering, report."

An additional advantage of the translation stone was that focusing on a sound made its clarity rise dramatically, as well as the underlying emotional content. And in this case, the crew was scared and nervous. Patient 00 focused on the bridge and captain while Dr. Fengie examined his extremities. "Warnings across the board, we are dead in the water, captain. No actual contact with engineering."

"Medical, report."

"All life-support systems are offline. Gravity will lose momentum in seven minutes. No numbers yet, but we expect casualties."

With a loud thud, the spinning ceased. The display map turned into a view screen, which exhibited a slick, green, circular spacecraft. Waves in the hull raced around and around, giving it a sporty, suped-up feel. The view zoomed out, revealing that the ship on the display was barreling toward a stationary object: their ship.

"Captain, new class of Imperial starship is on a direct intercept, traveling at an amazing half light speed, sir, intercept in thirty seconds."

"Darn it, Patient 00, I asked you to delay them. Instead you just pissed them off? What kind of delay was that?" The captain turned back toward the assembled doctors. "Dr. Fergie, how much time do you need?"

Dr. Fengie, having collected something out of the machine brought out by the MOP bots, approached and inserted it with a stabbing motion directly into Patient 00's left thigh, inducing a dog-like yelp. Dr. Fengie then informed the captain that Patient 00 was ready, yet Patients 01 and 02 would need special equipment from a lab on a lower deck.

Without a word, the great beasts who had been silent now gathered up the baroness and her doctors, as a parent would a toddler, and trotted out of the room. The captain lowered his platform and signaled for Patient 00 to join him. As the platform lifted, the captain spoke. "She will need you very much, the baroness. In her is a great hope for the future. A hope that is nearly extinguished might yet still burn bright in her womb. Only, I won't be there to witness it, so I am going to ask you to be more than you are. Whatever your ceiling is, it must now be higher. That which you can accomplish must now be more. I have faith in you, father of hope."

The ship screamed in pain as its metal flesh was punctured. The ceiling crumbled, replaced by the body of a new ship. An extension reached to the floor, a door opened, and a single Xendorian emerged. He examined the room, faced the captain, brought out a weapon, and fired quickly, dropping the captain's body to the platform floor.

"We are the Xendorians, your masters. You will comply immediately, or you will face the consequences."

13: Time to Shine

It was both comforting and humiliating to be carried like a toddler. Yet the baroness tried to embrace the moment by taking deep breaths and clearing her mind. While new circumstances required much thought time to analyze her situation, she presently had only minutes. So instead of starting something she couldn't finish, she pushed it all out, felt around for a good feeling, and then focused on it.

She thought to herself, why did it have to be him? Patient 00—God, she didn't even know his real name. Yet her memory of his embrace on the rooftop was warming. He had been so nervous at first, but she'd stayed with it and let him come around. Once his primal urges were satisfied, she felt him free to express emotion. Now that he was no longer confined to a secondary need, she could feel Patient 00's heart and soul creep along her limbs as he let down his walls.

The baroness was jostled by a shift in terrain as Aragmell now leaped from ledge to ledge while they circled a vertical tubular passageway. The Annomites displayed absolute grace, agility, and perceptional acuity, so it was clear how and why this species had become the physical guardians of this culture.

Aramethel carried both doctors with him as he matched Aragmell step for step. The doctors' tentacles became a wild jumble of weaving mass, bouncing with the force of their hosts' movements. Coming to a halt, the great beast Aragmell announced that the next few ledges had been damaged in the attack and that they would need a moment to secure equipment. Aramethel tapped on his wrist console, and the baroness talked with the doctors. "You can cure us of anything you give me, right? When you said HIV, my heart nearly stopped."

Dr. Fengie smiled. "My dear, your species' primitive knowledge of medicine is already far inferior to our own knowledge of your species."

Dr. Fergie snickered, filling the area with a scent of baking cookies. "Our foremost job is to protect life. If circumstances weren't so dire, we wouldn't have weaponized you at all."

The ship rocked as screaming metal wailed from the top of the passageway. The baroness fell against the wall, only to see both the doctors tumble off the ledge. She yelled for her guardian to save them. "We protect you, my mistress. New doctors can be found along the way."

"Could they be saved?"

"Yes."

The baroness immediately jumped over the edge.

It was more than a moment before she asked herself why she had jumped. The baroness had no plan, no knowledge or justification, only fear—fear of being alone, fear of so much unknown, and fear of going forward through the unknown.

The rush of air across her face brought back her sense, if only long enough to be pushed away in fear of understanding the impending consequences. The doctors were falling much slower than the baroness, and she was closing the gap. Bright-red lights illuminated their deathbed as they neared the floor.

The cold came much too fast, long before the impact. A bone-chilling, breath-stealing, heart-stopping ice of a wind surrounded her body, filled her pores, and froze her breath. Then, as she prepared for the impact, the falling slowed even more. Two meters more, a meter for the doctors, and it would have been death. The cold froze them midair, and then—like a hand made of ice—it pulled them back up.

The baroness's lungs gasped for air but found none. Her body shivered for warmth but created none, and as she rose higher and higher in the passageway, she readied for death. She felt nothing from the blow. The great beast had collided hard, first with her and then with the passage door going back into the ship. Roaring alarms and tentacles prodding her everywhere were not enough to fight off the cold, so she closed her eyes and waited for death.

The dread felt as thick as frozen butter. The Xendorian walked to the captain's platform, kicked aside the captain's carcass, and came toward Patient 00.

"Captains are not cheap, repairs will require docking, and I expect to be reimbursed generously. And God help you if you cause me to miss my deadline." Patient 00 bluffed as he approached the Xendorian, using as much false bravado as he could muster. He launched his finger directly at the alien's midsection. "Your piddlin' little empire don't mean shit out here, bud, other than I now know you got the backing to fully reimburse me."

The burning came as instantly as the movement when a small, dark pus ball ejected from the Xendorian's tongue and immediately ignited the side of Patient 00's head in a wall of pain. Patient 00 tried to reach for it, but his entire body hit the ground, wrenching in pain, with his extremities locked behind his back. No longer in physical control, he was being manipulated like a child-sized toy. The Xendorian drew its face in close to his and hissed painful spits of pus as it spoke. "Where is your mate? Bring her to me now."

The mention of the baroness brought back a flicker of excitement. "You killed her, you idiot."

The Xendorian gave another hiss, this time very pronounced and elongated, as it visually scanned the room. Spewing more painful pellets of pus, it squeezed Patient 00 tightly. "Liar."

Something about the underlying emotion of the Xendorian filled Patient 00 with more confidence. "You will release me, NOW!"

The Xendorian grabbed Patient 00 and held him like a folded box under his arm. He began searching the room and, after a quick survey, raised his weapon and killed an unfortunate and randomly chosen Adrinoleen. "No more delays, I don't accept your answer."

"Accept it or not, isn't my problem. Procuring another human with that genome is my problem. Now, thanks to your reckless privateering, I am behind schedule and understaffed. I demand to speak to your supervisor immediately!" His bluff had obviously been called. "Four, only fucking four humans did we find with that genome, and now a quarter of them are dead. Dead! Thanks to you."

On the verge of despair, Patient 00 finally got a sign of hope as the Xendorian raised one of his extremities and spoke. "Begin planetary survey. Check all humans."

$$\bar{\jmath} y$$

"Terrified" would only express the beginning of what the baroness felt as water rose and submersed her. She threw out her arms, only to make contact with a hard, clear surface. Drowning— she felt as if she was drowning in ice water. Her body seized and contracted, her lungs expelled the last of their air, and as the baroness expected the rush of water into her lungs, she felt only air. A terrible chill slowed her body as she took in deep breaths of stale air. Her skin was sweating, and her memory returned with the calming of her mind. Now she understood that the cold was inside her and the water was warm.

Both doctors, the guardians, and several new Adrinoleens surrounded her as the water drained. The baroness's skin color had returned, and the room relaxed as she sat up and asked for some clothes.

With the passion of a mother, thankful after a child's close call, Dr. Fengie moved toward the baroness. "What do you think you were doing? Do you have any idea how close you were to death? You need to start understanding something right now. You are more important than any of us. We are all now expendable— you are not. You are never, never, never to endanger yourself again." Then, bursting with the smell of asparagus, Fengie thanked the baroness and hugged her tightly.

Dr. Fergie now closed in. "How are you feeling, my dear?"

While the cold had left her body, the baroness still spoke

with a shiver. "I've never come close to experiencing anything that cold before. I'm not quite sure how I'm feeling. I guess I feel like I would like a blanket."

After the baroness had finished with her clothes, she approached the great beast Aramethel and held out her hands like a toddler summoning a parent to hold them. "For such a physically inferior species, I am finding you and your mate to be surprisingly durable. I am yet uncertain how to ascertain which sex is the dominant sex." Then he scooped her up in one hand and marched out into the hallway with her.

Aragmell could be heard as they followed behind. "Doctor, as this is no longer a medical operation, I am assuming command. Do you acknowledge?"

Dr. Fergie made a gesture with his tentacles and then addressed the beast. "I most certainly do not. This is a hospital ship on a mission of rescue."

Aragmell growled. "This is a shipwreck, and we are on a mission of survival. Our best chance of avoiding the empire is to take a lifeboat to the surface and hide out until we can procure passage to the ark."

The doctors released a smell of burning rubber. "No, we have not yet administered the weapon. We must continue on with the plan and head for containment bay."

The two snarled and closed ranks, staring each other down. Dr. Fergie's tentacles thrashed about wildly above him. Aragmell's body seemed to grow slightly in all dimensions. The snarls and hisses reverberated through the corridors.

The baroness bent toward Dr. Fengie. "Isn't this the containment bay?"

"Oh no, my dear, no. This is the animal wash station."

The baroness stared blankly for a moment before hopping out of Aramethel's arms. She stretched, stood tall, and walked out of the room.

"Mistress Baroness, where are you going?" Aragmell asked.

"To the containment bay. Now, if someone who knows the way would lead, it might be faster."

The corridor was dark, but they moved with a coordinated effort, Aragmell taking up the lead while Aramethel came up last. The path zigged and zagged across a broad array of labs and holding cells, and they even passed a large water reservoir teeming with fish. An occasional flickering light or raised red lamp provided their only visual support.

Aragmell came to a stop at what appeared to be a dead end. "Mistress Baroness, I will have to force the door open. This will delay us by some time. Do you wish to alter your instructions?"

The baroness approached the wall and slid her fingers across it. She never would have known it to be a passageway. "Compared to traveling another route, which would be more efficient?"

Aragmell grunted. "Difficult to say, alternate route would delay us by at least a third of the total."

Not quite understanding the time reference, the baroness nodded, indicating to proceed with the door, and then sat next to the doctors along the corridor wall. She leaned back, rested her eyes, and waited.

She wasn't sure how long she had waited when what felt like a paw pressed down on her thigh, and then another one on her other thigh. Startled, she felt fur press against her body as she jumped with surprise. The weight of the paw kept her in place as it finished walking across her. All she saw was some movement that looked like a big bouncy ball rolling down the corridor.

Feeling her heartbeat quicken, she looked for the others, all of whom were engrossed in a panel that had been taken off the wall. None of them seemed frightened by the creature as it walked to the center of their group and, with authority, took control of the panel.

Its fuzzy round body, about the size of a warthog, wiggled and giggled as it manipulated the panel. The creature wore something around its girth, and it turned its head around to fumble inside for something. The creature was actually very cute, and the baroness held back the urge to pick it up and start cuddling. It brought out a long, slender rod from its bag. Glimpsing its paws, the baroness saw a large pad on the bottom of the foot rise, exposing nimble fingers underneath.

She didn't realize her staring had been observed. Dr. Fergie approached the baroness, causing a mild start, and said, "They are called Dognosis, or dogs for short. They were one of the first ten species to join the Arkapeligo project. Their world has a harsh surface, so they evolved as underground livers, and surface hunters. Their world had the most intricate tunnel system you could imagine. Rivers and seas have less power over the rocks of their world than the dogs. Alas, it is no more, destroyed along with all the other wonders of the universe at the hands of the Wilde or the empire."

The baroness composed herself. "Doctor, it all seems so strange, like I'm really in a dream. I hear and can maybe even feel a little bit about these things you talk about, empires, something called the Wilde, but they don't mean anything to me. Mere hours ago, I thought Aramethel was going to kill me. Now he swears to protect me. Doctor, really, I just don't know if what I am doing is right or wrong, or a crazy dream I can't seem to wake from. All I am sure of is that I am scared, very scared."

Dr. Fergie wrapped a tentacle around the baroness's shoulder. "My dear, I can certainly understand, so let me give you one concrete thing to concentrate on." Dr. Fergie paused as if to clear his throat. "You are the mother of a very special child, and that child is going to need your protection for a long, long time. Keep yourself safe, and keep yourself healthy." The doctor abruptly changed gears, indicating that the dog had repaired the door, and the group was ready to proceed.

The animal referred to as a dog began in the opposite direction, when the baroness knelt down and spoke to it. She still had a translation stone on her, but she had no idea if she could communicate with it. "Thank you, my friend, won't you please accompany us to our destination?"

Pausing, the dog turned its head and blinked several times before letting out a little yelp.

"Now, what shall we call you, my cute little friend? Do you like Mittens?" The baroness bent over as she spoke.

Raising a paw, the creature reached out and touched the

baroness's translation stone. The words, while inaudible, came across clearly. "Mittens, are you serious? Mittens? That's the stupidest . . ."

The baroness jumped back, causing the creature to lose physical contact with the stone. The creature yelped at her and continued on, but now in the same direction as the group.

The confusion and slight sense of horror must have been transparent, for Dr. Fergie answered her unasked question. "I believe that one is referred to as Logging, and it's usually best not to engage the Dognosis. They are not known for their manners, but they are excellent engineers, electricians, and miners."

Patient 00 dangled in the air like a rat held aloft by its tail.

"I have been robbed of my ultimate victory, but I shall still have my total victory." The Xendorian hissed with its tongue as it spoke. It then spoke into a wrist device "Commander Lymphod, I need a search party to board and locate the specimen, and what is the current posturing of the Arkapeligo?" No audible response came, but the body movements of the Xendorian suggested acknowledgment of a message. "Send covert ops to test the humans they have already acquired. Have them focus on high-security and military locations. For the current time, plan B is massive force, but I want an update before you execute." He ended the conversation with his wrist and grabbed his weapon.

"I am Commodore Gaganious. The lot of you will address me only as master, and from here on, you are now my property. As such, it is now my right to forfeit your lives as I please." In another needless display of violence, the commodore fired his weapon, killing an anonymous Adrinoleen.

The platform extension again opened. This time, four Xendorian soldiers marched in unison, awaiting instructions from their superior. The commodore held Patient 00 up as a specimen. "Search the ship. Find this one's mate. I want her and the unborn fetus alive, no exceptions." He waved his hand and aimed at another Adrinoleen before addressing Patient 00. "Where is she?"

It was the targeted victim who responded, with noticeable wavering in its voice. "Please, master, spare me. They went down the shaft. Please let me take you. Spare me, my master."

Patient 00 jumped in and marched on with his plan. "You might want to check his salary first. Let's just say it's commensurate with his skill. Now I'm a businessman, and I can see you are having a bad day, so why don't you let me help you?"

The commodore hissed again, misting Patient 00 with a sting, and fired his weapon, killing the Adrinoleen. "Deceit is in your species. I shall enjoy the day when we can cleanse the universe of your kind. My species is far superior to yours."

Patient 00 blinked through the stinging. "Yes, but so is greed, and greed is a universal language. Now, I might not be able to get you what you have already destroyed, but I can give you a lead on the other three." The Xendorian squeezed Patient 00 so tightly that his breath seemed to escape permanently. "But it will cost you."

The group scurried down the passageways, Aragmell taking the lead, followed by the baroness—with her new furry friend—and the doctors and Aramethel. The corridors were dark, yet light emanated from the fur of their new Dognosis companion. Dr. Fergie had explained that these creatures generated their own electrical power, a highly unique ability but one very well suited to a cave-dwelling species.

The group dutifully carried on, until Aramethel made an announcement. "We are not alone."

Turning around, the baroness squinted in the dark but failed to see anything. The Dognosis growled and stood on his hind legs, while the doctors moved closer together and more off to the side.

"I don't see anything," whispered the baroness. "What is it?"

Shaking his body and moving his masses of hair, the dog began to spark lightning, illuminating the area well enough to reveal a large, man-sized, upright Xendorian. Three circular protrusions extended out of the creature's head. His dark reptilian skin barely reflected enough light to show the outline of his body. The alien held a long staff upright, away from his body, and ignited his weapon.

Without consultation or orders, or to anyone's expectation, Aramethel charged, lunging first at an angle and then directly at the reptile. A bright burst of light filled the corridor as a stream of yellow tubes, reaching out like arms, bear hugged the beast, trapping him. The arms finished wrapping themselves around the guardian as he fell to the floor. Again they flashed brightly and then hardened as they darkened. Aramethel grunted and struggled but failed to move.

The baroness stepped back and spoke to Aragmell. "Don't try that. It didn't work, so don't try that."

Ahead of them, another alien reptile raised his weapon. "Beast of Atone, lay down your arms. We come only for the girl and her doctors."

Growling fiercely, Aragmell gave a reassuring answer. "Never."

Igniting great sparks of energy on each end of their staffs, the two Xendorians took up fighting positions and slowly moved in. The baroness and the doctors huddled together while their new dog friend continued to light the area. The staffs moved with gusts of wind as pangs of colliding metal rang throughout the halls. Aragmell dodged, struck, and avoided with absolute grace and power, yet it was obviously too much for him to handle.

Fengie pulled on the baroness's arm and sounded worried. "We must protect you. We must flee while we can. Aragmell cannot protect us forever."

The baroness was awestruck by the devastating beauty of the weapons as they searched for prey. "No, that is not the way. The safest way is together. How will you protect me after Aragmell is slain? Solving problems together is the safest way forward." She snapped her fingers to get Logging's attention and spoke softly but firmly. "My friend, you must free the guardian from his trap." She turned to the doctors. "I am going to place myself behind the closest reptile, at knee level. When Aragmell understands, he will push the reptile backward, tripping him over me. When that happens, I need you two to jump on the creature and help me hold him down."

Dr. Fengie grimaced. "That's the plan I would have expected from your mate. Are you serious?"

The baroness made her move without waiting for Fengie to finish. Hopping left and right like a boxer, she readied for what she hoped was an opportunity. When the moment came, she lunged forward to her knees, landing mere feet behind the nearest reptile. She whispered a prayer under her breath and felt contact. It had worked. The Xendorian was off balance, falling backward, and then his legs wrapped tightly around the baroness. The doctors beat the reptile with their tentacles, yet his grip on the baroness got tighter and tighter.

Acid spewed from the face of the reptile, and one of the doctors turned and screamed in pain. Snagging a striking tentacle, the Xendorian grabbed the other doctor and flung them both across the hallway. The Xendorian gripped the baroness by the back of the neck and lifted her as a dog would its young. "Guardian, once again, our species has been proven superior in battle."

Aragmell stepped back, obviously struggling to fight just the one Xendorian. His breast labored with intense rises and falls. "Release her, or you shall die, Imperial scum."

"Brave words, too bad they shall be your last. Finish him!" The Xendorian closest to Aragmell brought his weapon up high for a powerful blow. Able to block the attack but unable to withstand the force, Aragmell flew backward, against the wall. Approaching the beast, the Xendorian held his weapon against Aragmell's chest.

The sound of a weapon cutting flesh was followed by the baroness's scream and fall. The Xendorian grunted with his last breath as Aramethel lifted it high enough into the air to draw the partner's attention.

Anger filled the reptile's voice as he witnessed the dark death of his comrade. "You will die, beast." Taking advantage of the distraction, Aragmell shifted positions so that as the reptile drove its weapon deep into his chest, it missed vital organs.

Aramethel charged, striking the Xendorian and sending it back several feet. As if he'd lost no momentum during the attack, Aramethel executed a series of strong attacks, each one skillfully deflected by the Imperial at the cost of several feet. Aragmell grabbed a smaller weapon from his pouch and, from a seated position, threw the weapon into the reptilian's leg. The creature twisted and reacted in pain, creating an opening. Aramethel lunged, landed on top of the creature, and stuck his weapon into the pit of his enemy. Aramethel lay there, squeezing every last bit of life out of his victim.

The baroness ran to the doctors, both of whom were still alive, if not injured. Aragmell removed the weapon and covered the wound with his hand as he returned to the group. "That, baroness, is the empire. Take great care to avoid finding yourself in their care. Now, our destination is right around the corner."

14: No Pain, No Gain

The commodore reached out, grabbed Patient 00's injured nipple, and twisted it. Pain yelped from Patient 00's mouth, and his head wobbled with dizzying pain.

"Where is she? No more delays."

With his head flailing, Patient 00 closed his eyes. "In my heart." He drooped as lifelessly as possible, but something in his fall must have given away his consciousness.

Bending down close to examine him, the commodore cackled. "You beautiful fool, you have a translation stone. Now you will see the true superiority of my species over yours."

The commodore knelt on top of Patient 00. The center tubular shaft extended an organ that looked like a funnel, with a smaller circular opening at the top. The organ shifted and swiveled its end as if to make two fingers. The breath of the alien moistened Patient 00's face, and as the organ reached out and touched the stone, Patient 00 howled.

The pain started deep in his spine, and his body jolted and writhed as it traveled up his back. Patient 00's eyes rolled back into his head, and the burning crossed his brain, searching and hurting, burning and searching. At last, the commodore stood up, hissing in disgust. "Your primitive species hasn't even developed a telepathic node." He picked up Patient 00 and shook him like a baby. "You will tell me what I need to know." The commodore then dropped him back on the floor, where his victim truly lay unconscious this time.

By now, the rest of the crew had managed to sneak themselves off the bridge. The commodore addressed his wrist device. "Search team 1, report." After a short pause, he said, "Search team 2, report."

This time, the response came through. "Approaching target. Location, lower-level containment bay. Last contact with team 1 reported engaging target."

Rubbing his organ back into place, the Xendorian commodore spoke to himself. "How can such an underdeveloped species be so infuriating?" Then he addressed his wrist again. "Commander Lymphod, report."

Commander Lymphod's sound and tone were very uniform with his commodore. "Moments ago, contact with infiltration team was lost. Approximate five percent scanned with zero positive results."

"Cause of loss of team?"

"Warrior, sir, the humans have a guardian."

"Dognosis?"

"Negative, sir, a human guardian. She nearly single-handedly took down our entire team."

"Impossible! Prepare the assault team, and contact the emperor. I need to give him an unfortunate update."

"Understood, sir, for your information with the planetary assault underway, I will be using ship's crew for the assault."

"Fine, make sure to leave at least one warrior as rear guard. How is the planetary assault progressing?"

"As expected, the southern hemisphere will be under control shortly, and the rest of the planet within one planet cycle. Thirty percent of humans have been tested, with zero positive results."

"Acquisition of the artifacts?"

"Progressing smoothly, science teams have already begun excavation and should be concluded well before we recall the troops."

"Very well, continue as planned, and get me the emperor."

$$\searrow\!\!\!\!\!y$$

The twitching had started, and with it he had regained some awareness. The throbbing in his head prevented any conscious thoughts from passing through, but at least he was now able to see his surroundings again.

An image of a family seal projected from the commodore's wrist communicator. After several seconds, the commodore knelt as the image of another Xendorian, this one laced with gold elegantly wrapped around his tubular extensions, spoke. "Ah, Commodore, I didn't expect to hear so soon. I trust, then, that all went smoothly."

Staying in the kneeling position, the commodore spoke loudly and clearly. "I regret to inform you that a supreme victory was not attained. I am confident we can still achieve a total victory."

"That is disappointing indeed." The emperor hissed as he spoke.

"I am a simple soldier, sir. I am contacting you to seek your permission to engage the Arkapeligo, should they offer resistance to our objectives."

"You were right to contact me, General. This matter does involve political matters, at least for the short term. Your orders, General, are to use all force necessary to accomplish your objectives, but your new objectives are to avoid and minimize all loss of life outside of the human, Annomite, and Pergenese species. Societies move on fast when soldiers die in battle. They ingrain hatred of marauding invaders who kill innocents."

The commodore rose, smashed his chest, and was about to thank the emperor before his wrist was pulled to the side by Patient 00. "Finally, are you the man in charge around here? I have some serious damages to my equipment, facilities, and personnel, and we need to start talking about reimbursement."

Again with the hiss, the emperor responded. "Who is this? When the empire claims something, it belongs to us. Commodore, why have you not executed this creature?"

Pushing Patient 00 down to the ground, the commodore quickly regained his position of attention. "That was father to Patient 02. The scientists have deemed him a high-priority target. I apologize for the interruption. I shall contact your office upon completion of objectives." The image faded, and the commodore walked over to Patient 00. Grabbing him by the throat, he lifted him several feet into the air.

Coughing out the words, Patient 00 seemed to smile as he spoke. "Happen to have a cigar?"

$$\gg$$

The group limped its way to the containment-bay entrance. Dr. Fergie, now blinded from the attack, was being led by his wife. Aramethel took the lead as a battered and injured Aragmell took the rear. The group's new companion, the Dognosis Logging, also followed along. The baroness tried hard not to think of the creature as a pet. His attitude assured the baroness of his sentience, yet she still had a strong urge to pick up the creature and cuddle him.

Upon arrival, their dog friend rose to his hind legs and, lifting the pads under his feet, used his nimble fingers to remove the panel and begin fumbling inside. After several seconds, he walked over to a wall and removed another panel. Behind that panel was a large tube with a white fluid running through it. The tube hummed with the rhythm of great electrical power. Logging grabbed a tool out of his pouch, reached out with both arms, and completed the circuit with his body. He lit up, with small sparks emanating off his fur, and his body shook violently.

The baroness screamed and attempted to advance but was held back by Aragmell. "He will be fine, Baroness. Look, he has activated the bay for us. While he is in discomfort, he is in no danger."

Dr. Fengie manipulated the panel and activated a green light above the entrance door. "As expected, one hundred physical containment is still in place, yet unfortunately with the system in safe mode, I will have to make the inoculation by hand." Dr.

Fengie then came to her mate. "I'm sorry, my dear, but you will have to wait. Why don't you tell the baroness one of your stories as I ready?"

With a grunt, Dr. Fergie spoke. "Yes, yes, I guess you are right, my dear. Now, whatever shall I talk about?"

Aramethel waited outside with Logging as Aragmell tended to his wounds. The baroness, with nothing else to do, turned to Dr. Fergie. "Tell me about your abduction by the Arkapeligo."

The doctor perked up. "Wonderful, wonderful suggestion. I couldn't have picked a better topic. But, my dear, my species wasn't abducted, as you phrased it. You see, I was head physician of a prestigious exobiology hospital on my home world of Migan. While not the most esthetically pleasing planet, it is a world of many wonders of beauty. Canyon City is a mega-metropolis built in something like your Grand Canyon, but on a scale you couldn't image.

"As I worked in my office one day, in Canyon City as it were, this petite squirrel-sized aliens appeared out of nowhere on my desk. To this day, I have no idea how he got past security, but what he had to say to me changed the course of my life dramatically. This little fellow was quite amazing, full of technology beyond my comprehension. He spoke with a wisdom far beyond my own, and he radiated a powerful warmth that both intimated and comforted.

"'A project for life, by life' is what he called it. It was a mission to gather, collect, and—after the appearance of the Wilde—save sentient life. What doctor wouldn't be intrigued by a mission like that? It took time, a significant amount of my prime years. It was only with age that I was relegated to such a menial position as ship's doctor. I digress. With much pioneering, I was able to convince my kind to build a colony aboard this project ship. Initially I was head of the project, but as politics and skill sets applied themselves, I was happy to accept head doctor of the colony.

"I never saw that little guy again. I figured he would have been involved with the process, but he mysteriously vanished as easily as he had appeared. I do hope someday to meet him again, but I have no idea how long his life span would be, and it has already been so very, very long."

The baroness smiled, happy for the distraction of such a fantastic story. "So what are you saying, your species built the ark?"

Dr. Fergie chuckled. "No, no, no, my dearie me. We built our colony for life here on the ark. You see, the beauty of our story is that we are the only species to seek out the ark."

As the story ended, Dr. Fengie arrived, and with the baroness's permission, she administered the serum. The group began to move on, when the room went dark. No sound carried. Only the baroness's breathing filled the room.

"Aramethel has fallen. We must flee." Aragmell moved as he spoke. He scooped up the baroness and deftly navigated the dark corridors out and away from their original entrance.

⅀𝓎

His entire body hurt, his head spun, and Patient 00 felt like he was about to puke. He lay there underfoot, too sore to move and too concussed to think. So he did the only thing he could do—he farted.

The door opened, and in stepped a Xendorian holding an Annomite and something that kinda looked like a dog. "Commodore, team lead has sent me with a report, sir." The Xendorian effortlessly held his capture high in the air.

The commodore turned his attention to the soldier. "Report."

"Team lead is pursuing primary objective and her injured guardian. I have brought you one of her guardians and another one of her companions. This soldier requests the pleasure of executing his captures."

"Is that pleasure not the right of team lead?"

"Of course, Commodore, my apologies. This soldier is just anxious for battle and bloodshed."

"That is understandable. I, too, must restrain myself from terminating such inferior beings. What of search team 1, did this guardian not present you with an adequate challenge?"

"Team lead suggested a more stealth acquisition. This guardian was captured without conflict."

"A very wise move by team lead. Brute force is more fun but less efficient." The commodore approached the Xendorian. "I sense great power in you, soldier, but mind your place, and apprentice close to team lead. Now, as for these two, if this guardian was no match, then they shall be fed to the warrior. Let the weak be eaten by the strong."

The Xendorian soldier banged each of his captures against his chest and began to exit, when a scream interrupted him.

"Put down my crew, or I shall destroy you." Patient 00 had managed to stand, fueled by the knowledge that the baroness still lived and that these aliens had helped her. Yet the twitching was becoming more noticeable, and he looked less than intimating with his now-slightly misshapen face and bloody nipple. His hands bounced and flopped.

The Xendorian lowered his trophies and faced the commodore. "Commodore, I have been challenged. This soldier seeks permission to set obedience objective on this lowly creature."

The commodore almost seemed to sigh in disappointment. "Denied, this creature is an objective, but perhaps a demonstration is in order. Perhaps, once the scientists are done, we shall force Patient 00 to watch as you feed his friends to our warrior."

Relifting his trophy catches, the Xendorian came over to Patient 00 and, with little resistance, squished him between the two and carried them off, up into the commodore's ship.

$$\sum$$

The group moved with impressive speed. It was obvious that the doctors had other senses that allowed them to much more readily navigate the dark and narrow passageway. At last, they entered a long, tall room with several corridors breaking off on either side. A dim light came from the ceiling, creating a dusk-like ambience.

"Stop, stop here, Aragmell." The baroness shifted her body as she spoke.

"No time, we must flee." Aragmell slowed but didn't stop.

Pointing, the baroness said two words: "Ambush. Bait."

"It's amazing that a species with such little regard for self-preservation can rise to the top of its ecological food chain." Aragmell reached back and, with a tear and a howl, pulled off the sharp end of his tail and handed it to the baroness. The baroness clenched it between her teeth and then had Aragmell lift her up. Extending her arms and legs, she braced herself at the top of a corridor adjacent to where Aragmell would set the trap.

The two doctors stood there, helplessly watching as the Xendorian team lead approached with haste. With each opening, it scouted and prepared, as no assault from the sides could catch it off guard. As the alien neared Aragmell's corner, the beast's assault utterly failed. Deflected, but with an astounding recovery time, the Xendorian launched his own counterattack, knocking Aragmell backward to the ground.

Charging with great bravery, the two doctors were scooped up with a single grasp and raised high in the air. The Xendorian held out his staff weapon and prepared to finish his prey, but the baroness lunged forward and downward, aiming her knife deep into the neck of the Xendorian. Grimacing in pain, the alien fired his staff weapon uselessly against the wall. Injured or not, Aragmell once again showed his natural grace as he tore his teeth into the Xendorian's shoulder area and ripped off a substantial hunk of flesh.

The baroness dropped and ran. She hoped she had done enough, but it was now guardian versus soldier, and she was the prize.

The fur of the dog-like creature felt soft and comforting as it pressed along Patient 00's backside. Aramethel's shoulder made a nice headrest, but a quick look showed that the great beast's hands were bound together, and a silver cover prevented him from speaking. His body hung limp as if unconscious, but the swelling and leakage from his eye told Patient 00 otherwise, like a dog who had just been caught in the act.

The three bounced and jostled as they were carried into a new, strange environment. The commodore's ship was hot and muggy, and smelled of mold. The walls were green and leafy, the air misty. Strange, yet not totally foreign, plant life grew at various intersections, often even acting as a hedge or barrier. Their Xendorian captor held them high and proceeded to tilt them in what felt like the equivalent of a head nod each time they passed another Xendorian. Other creatures inhabited the vessel, but none seemed to merit their captor's attention.

As they bobbed along, Patient 00 found it too difficult to track their path or concentrate much, but as they moved, his hands made contact with something on Aramethel's backside. He had no clue what he was touching or doing but found a pouch hidden under the beast's clothing. He fumbled inside and felt several objects, randomly grabbed the first one, and—careful not to make large body movements—took it out and secured it.

The action alerted Aramethel, who now repeatedly banged his leg against Patient 00's. The two worked in disharmony, nearly dropping the device as they tilted and twirled through the air as if they were a trophy being hoisted by a drunk after winning a sporting event. With a little luck and patience, the device—nothing more than a small rectangular box the size of a mini iPad—fell onto Aramethel's thigh, and he was able to scoop it up and hold it between his forearms.

They had reached their destination. A large arena circled a massive pit filled with debris and vegetation. The area was largely free of other life-forms. A small, fuzzy creature rolled past, obviously more interested in its destination than the current situation.

The arena wall rose dozens of feet into the air. One large entryway lay at the far end, with its door currently down. Comparable to the size of a football field, the arena had a dirt floor with living vegetation scattered about. Several fallen trees dotted the center.

The Xendorian spoke to his captures without really addressing them. "The circle of heroes. Many noble deeds have been done in this arena, not by your species of course. I was here when Ramsheshian of Huban single-handedly captured a female warrior. I was here when the commodore defeated General Martisian. And I, too, one day will have my glorious day of battle. Now, for today, it will simply be your grave. I request that you do try to survive long enough for me to sit down. Most won't make it more than a few minutes. Do try to impress me."

The Xendorian pulled the three apart, allowing Patient 00 to fall to the ground. Logging and Aramethel were then placed over the wall and dropped into the arena. Aramethel ably landed and caught Logging as he neared the ground. Aramethel put Logging on the ground, sighed deeply, and watched as the arena door opened and pure terror walked out.

$$\sum$$

There was no scream, no wincing in agony or pain. The Xendorian, one arm now rendered useless by injury, regained a defensive position. Aragmell circled and moved like a boxer, also limited by injury. There were no wasted movements. The combatants struck purposefully and powerfully.

Sparks showered like fountains on the Chinese New Year as the two smashed weapons in mortal combat. The great beast Aragmell's breast rose and fell like mountains to trenches, and back again. The Xendorian's skin lifted in little flaps as its body rushed to cool the heating reptile.

It was fatigue, like a fighter who waits for the safety of the bell and discovers that no such bell will arrive. Aragmell, in desperation, lunged out with a last striking blow. The Xendorian leaped forward, striking down hard on the beast below. Aragmell howled in pain and dropped to the floor.

The Xendorian paused, kneeling for several seconds. Aragmell lay motionless except for his laboring breast, rising and falling. The victorious Xendorian stood over his opponent, sparked his spear, and raised it in preparation.

The baroness's guardians had failed, and she now had to do something about it. "Stop, spare him and I shall surrender to you. If you take his life, I shall attempt to avenge him, and if I fail in that task, I shall destroy myself."

The Xendorian placed his foot directly on the back of Aragmell's head, lowered his weapon, and stared at the baroness. "You humans are easy to underestimate. I make no assurance what the commodore will decide. Only that he will live till that point." The alien jolted Aragmell's body until it lay nearly motionless, and then he pointed his spear directly at the baroness. "Now surrender yourself."

15: Warrior See, Warrior Do

There he stood, hopeless to help, battered to submission, and concussed to confusion. Patient 00 could only hold his breath as what the Xendorian referred to as a warrior slowly entered the arena. Ducking through the entrance, the warrior stood high, nearly a story and a half. With two distinct sections, the creature had insect characteristics. The lower half was the size of a long room and rose eight feet off the ground. Six spiked legs scuttled about as it searched for nourishment. Two longer limbs extended horizontally on the upper section. The limbs looked fearsome, with sharp chainsaw-like knobs running down the bottom half. Smaller graspers lined the end of the limbs, and the tops appeared to have a natural armor plate.

Logging had taken cover behind a larger rock and was feverishly digging. Aramethel, his hands still bound in front, took small, patient steps, limiting his upper body movement as he moved in the direction of a vegetation patch nearly thirty feet away. The tactics seemed to at least bide some time as the warrior took a moment to groom itself. Long mantis-like limbs scraped over the warrior's back as it performed some instinctual ritual of pre-conscious grooming that ended with a shaking that sent spiky skin flakes out in all directions.

The Xendorian sighed. "Must not be hungry yet. Not to

worry, it will only take the scent of live flesh to ignite its unquenchable appetite."

Finding it difficult to gather his thoughts, Patient 00 focused on a detail, searching for clarity. "How did one man defeat such a beast?"

The Xendorian's sounds vibrated through Patient 00's head, intensifying the pounding and forcing him to close his eyes.

"Not a man, a Xendorian—a Xendorian guardian. Revered for his cunning strength of mettle and leadership, Ramsheshian was a living god. To be compared to something as pitiful as you, man, is a grave insult. A single warrior could wipe out your entire population. I hope the commodore won't be too merciful in deciding your fate. "

"Mercy is not for those who decide the fate of others."

The Xendorian appeared as if he was going to respond but instead turned his attention toward his wrist communicator, which now displayed a blinking button. "Soldier at the ready, team leader."

"I have captured the objective and her companions. The commodore and I are en route to your location. See if you can save the festivities for our arrival."

"Yes, team leader!" The Xendorian gave a salute, and once the communication was cut, he sighed and accessed his wrist communicator. "Well, human, since we have the time, let me enlighten you on just how superior a species we are to you. Our race, in the span of only three generations, has gone from first space flight to controlling an empire of thousands of worlds spanning hundreds of thousands of lights years. We have conquered so many worlds that each Xendorian citizen is entitled to their own city. Your race is so inferiorly developed that you still fight each other over things that could be acquired elsewhere. Your culture devotes the majority of its resources to the old and neglects the development of its young. You claim monogamy but practice polygamy." The Xendorian soldier leaned in close to Patient 00 and spoke with the hatred of a killer. "Your kind disgusts me."

After a short pause, the soldier looked down into the arena, where Logging had dug himself a shelter underneath a large boulder and Aramethel was frantically fiddling with his hands while taking cover behind a large shrub of vegetation. "Every Xendorian child is fully developed to reach their maximum potential, in whatever field that might be. Our state exists to develop, support, and organize its citizens. Your species operates in chaos."

Patient 00 responded only to the last line, as that was as far as his concentration would allow. "Chaos is the sound of freedom."

"Philosophical points only count when you have the means to enforce them." The Xendorian soldier again manipulated his wrist communicator. However, this time, Patient 00 noticed that he was changing the vegetation arrangements so as to keep the alien warrior on the far side of the arena. "Human, do not take the inferiority personally. We have conquered many species much more advanced technologically, evolutionarily, and telepathically than our own, so a pathetic race like yours is nothing more than practice."

Just when the pounding of the Xendorian's bantering had passed through, Patient 00 heard the sound of changing pressures that accompanied the opening of a huge door. He turned his head and felt his heart sink as the baroness, now in restraints, followed behind her limping guardian and her sighted doctor leading her injured companion.

A familiar voice rang out from the far side of the room. "Very well done, team leader, I do believe we have made it in time for the show. Now we shall add to the pot." The commodore's voice felt lighthearted and relaxed. He approached the new arrivals and looked them over as a master would his hound dog who brought in a fresh kill.

Then the commodore faced Aragmell and smiled. "No, it couldn't be. Team lead, have you any idea whom you have captured? This here Annomite is the once-great-and-powerful Aragmell—defender of Atone, sole survivor of the battle of Midus, most fearsome of the beasts. Look now, how the mighty have fallen to this pitiful excuse for a guardian." The commodore grabbed Aragmell as a dog would its pup. "You deserve a noble death, but being eaten alive will have to do." Grasping with two hands, the commodore flung the beast deep into the heart of the arena.

The commodore stopped at the doctors and activated his wrist communicator. "Science lead, I have acquired the primary objectives alive. Update the objective status of the human caretakers." There was a momentary pause. Then, after a sound pinged from his wrist, the commodore grabbed the two doctors and threw them into the arena, where they landed with a loud crash and a big dust ball.

The baroness screamed as her eyes now focused on the large, carnivorous alien warrior whose full attention was now on the doctors' landing spot. The large alien warrior was slowed significantly, as it had to clear vegetation while it worked its way directly toward the doctors. The baroness squirmed and wiggled but failed to get even the slightest release from her restraints.

The Xendorian known as the team lead picked up the baroness and placed her on the opposite side of Patient 00, leaving the lowest-ranking Xendorian in between. The team leader and the commodore took seats and activated their wrist devices to see additional viewpoints of the arena.

The commodore's first view was of Aragmell. The beast had landed without any noticeable new injuries and appeared to be taking shelter in a hollowed-out tree. "Bridge, relay image throughout fleet and to ground forces, over under will be set at ninety seconds, and event will commence in one minute. Soldier, how many you take to be alive at the mark?"

The Xendorian standing along the arena wall and guarding his human captures glanced back. "These pitiful creatures? Zero, Commodore, zero."

"And what say you, team leader. How does the captor view its prey?"

"The over, Commodore, the over" was all the team leader said, till the commodore gave the look of an annoyed drunk. "Tell you what, Commodore, I want to make it really interesting and take the prey to win."

A loud hiss rolled out of the commodore as his body vibrated. "My oh my, soldier, did you hear that? Team leader is smarting a bit from his wounds, or he has great faith in the gods of greed. Either way, we are going to have a good time." Then the commodore activated his wrist device and lowered the vegetation hedge, and a display scrolled through symbols.

$$\sum\!\!\rangle$$

The baroness tried to get his attention, but with his twitching and blank stare, she decided to come up with another tactic. For the immediate moment, she watched as her new friends scurried and fled for their lives. The creature was, except in scale, something more earthlike than the rest of the creatures she had so far encountered. The speed of the warrior was impressive as it made a beeline for the doctors. Her pulse quickened, her eyes scavenged, and her brain twisted, but the baroness was at a loss for how to help.

As loyal a mate as ever, Dr. Fengie bravely hid behind her blind husband, one unable to see and the other unwilling. "At least she will go down with her man, even if she can't bear to watch it." Yet like an angel, Aramethel, in full stride, knocked them several yards as he blasted into them, clearing them of the warrior's limb as it crashed down directly where the doctors had been standing.

The doctors took no time in fleeing, but Aramethel, with his front hands still bound, was slower and ended up in the grasps of the second limb.

The baroness felt more helpless than ever, desperate to help creatures whose actual existence she still questioned. So she pursued a course of action she hadn't anticipated: she turned to prayer. Yet as soon as her prayers were answered, she shifted back to old thoughts.

A boulder the size of a football smacked the alien warrior against the side of its head. The warrior turned its head and hissed but only paused as it brought the young Aramethel closer to its mouth. But Aramethel didn't let his youth deter his will to live or lose his cool, and using the alien's pause, he now opened the box Patient 00 had given him earlier.

The image of a nude, female Annomite appeared and began dancing above the device. Surprised by the abrupt arrival of a new enemy, the warrior threw Aramethel as it lifted up its giant mantle and attempted to strike the 3-D display. Several slashes went through the hollow image before it hit the ground, bouncing the device high into the air before it landed upside down, canceling the image.

Aragmell bent close to Logging's hole for several seconds before grabbing the large boulder and hurling it at the charging warrior insect.

A buzzer sounded, and the Xendorian soldier flinched its body as if to show frustration. The commodore called out in laughter. "Zero at ninety seconds. Well, team lead, looks like you still have something to play for. All right, soldier, who do you take to be last prey alive?"

The Xendorian surveyed the arena before answering. "Commodore, I'll take the digger."

"Team lead, what say you? Still have faith in your captures?"

"The greater their prowess, the greater my capture becomes. I believe both the Annomites and the digger survive."

The commodore chuckled again. "I shall have to include you the next time I play games of chance. The wife has been asking for a new ship."

𝄐

The baroness had never much liked sports, and now that she was watching alien overlords play them with her friends' lives, she was furious and desperate. As the gambler prays for a miracle and celebrates its arrival with sin, so did the baroness as she watched the fate of her friends.

The two Annomites worked in a well-coordinated effort as mentor and apprentice. One would flee as prey while the other rested and worked to free themselves of their restraints. Aramethel was the first to get his restraints off. Skipping in great leaps to the left and right as he fled, the young Annomite slid feetfirst, holding out his arms. The warrior's limb crashed down in a plume of dirt as it attempted to spear its fleeing prey. Aramethel burst out from the dust cloud and ran directly under the beast.

Aragmell leaped off a nearby shrub and landed on the back of the creature. The giant bug flung its torso back like a horse, but despite the restraints, he was able to hang on. The distraction provided an opportunity for Aramethel, who was now attached to the underside of the lower torso. The alien bug jumped, wriggled, and squirmed in an attempt to dislodge its prey.

Aramethel grabbed a rock off the ground and pounded a hole in the bug's mandible. Green pus poured out of the wound and covered the young Annomite in a stinky mess.

Aragmell diligently worked his way higher and higher up the insect. As he reached the top, he was able to take some control of the warrior as he manipulated the tentacles and organs that came out of the insect's head. It was slow and imprecise, but as the bug approached a section of the wall closer to the spectators, the ground beneath the bug collapsed, and it fell several feet into a pit.

"Oh ho ho, team leader is looking mightier and mightier. I must say, I didn't expect the beast to come even this close to matching his reputation." The commodore spoke with more joy in his voice than the baroness had expected, considering the circumstances. "This should prove entertaining now that they have enraged the warrior. No longer will it simply hunt its prey. With its injury, it's not a hunt—it's a battle for survival."

The baroness's relief didn't last long. Just when she thought they might finally catch a break, the reality burst her bubble. The alien warrior let out a screech of anger and pain, and physically changed color, now glowing red. Large plates lifted off the top of its mandible and extended into large wings. With three sweeping flutters, the warrior broke free from its pit. One of the wings spread out wide, and with a loud whoosh, the warrior spun, slashing and trimming everything in the near vicinity. The great beasts Aragmell and Aramethel couldn't be located, while one of the Xendorian televiewers showed the two doctors hiding under deep vegetation.

The wind from the warrior's flight pushed hard against the baroness. As she now glanced at Patient 00, she saw him looking back at her, no longer with the blank stare. And that made her stomach knot, as she now saw the same look in his eyes that he had right before their rooftop exit.

Venom spewed out from the warrior, and with a sizzle, the vegetation crumpled away. In a matter of seconds, the ground lay bare dozens of meters around the warrior. The warrior's spinning stopped, and with rage, it ravaged thought the vegetation, hunting for its enemies.

The commodore and his fellows engaged in banter and hollered like drunks in Vegas, but she couldn't listen, she couldn't watch her friends die, and she couldn't look at him. She was powerless to help, powerless to intervene, powerless to do. He, however, wasn't powerless to do, and she knew it would cost her. She cursed the Lord for giving him the power she didn't have.

Then she resigned herself to whatever fate would come from Patient 00's leadership. The baroness looked him in the eye, and as he reached out his hand, she brushed it with hers. Patient 00 grabbed firmly onto the baroness's wrist, wrapped his other arm around the Xendorian guard, and pulled them all over the side.

16: To Make One's Bed

There was a mute roar as the commodore's brain registered what he had just witnessed. His physical body raised and his heart sank before he regained enough control to issue orders. "Team lead, protect the objective and secure her exit. I will engage the warrior. All Xendorians to warrior control stations, activate escape gates and containment net." Then the commodore hurled himself into the arena.

A visible net of great electrical power surrounded the arena, and alarms sounded.

The movement of the trio falling had garnered the warrior's attention, and its forelimb speared the Xendorian guard before they could hit the ground. The baroness and Patient 00 bounced with the stabbing of the guard and then fell several feet to the ground. The warrior ripped the head off the Xendorian guard and sucked out his insides before discarding the body.

The commodore lunged at the warrior and landed on its face as it ate his subordinate. The light on the commodore's wrist device blinked as he brought his fist back and planted a devastating blow to the warrior's eye. The commodore darted to avoid the acid that followed the swallowing body. Gripping hard, the commodore activated his wrist device and held on for dear life. The commodore had to concentrate hard on the voice of Commander Lymphod to hear it over the sound of gushing wind. The alien warrior had flapped its wing so as to somersault in the air several rotations at a time. It was the third rotation of the maneuver that cast the commodore off and slammed him into the arena wall. Yet the commodore did manage to hear one part of the commander's report clearly, and it rattled him more than the physical blow: "The humans have defeated our . . ."

The team leader had moved with purpose and captured efficiently. It took him no more than fifteen seconds to have the baroness out of the arena, but he made no attempt to capture Patient 00. Such a failure to protect an objective would not be looked well upon by the emperor. Perhaps, thought the team leader, he might now have another use for her. So he took the baroness quickly down the passageway.

$$\gg$$

Patient 00 ran as fast as he could, yet everything around him seemed to move faster. He chased down the same passage as the baroness but soon lost track. Knowing he would never be able to track them, he decided it best to find someone who would know where they were—and he knew just the alien.

Patient 00 returned to the arena, scanning for any sort of tool or weapon. He felt befuddled by his new reality. Finding no visible cupboards, closets racks, or holders, he ran his hands randomly against the walls, hoping to trigger or move something. His distress heightened as he neared the entrance, when he finally found something to press, and a panel behind it opened.

Without hesitation, he reached in and pulled out the first thing he felt. It didn't look like a gun, yet it had an easily discernible firing direction. Although, figuring out how to activate it might prove tougher. Seconds later, the sound of hurried footsteps manifested into two Xendorian crewmen, probably en route to collect the very weapon Patient 00 had just acquired.

Twisting rapidly, Patient 00 pushed, squeezed, and even pulled as he pointed the weapon. The Xendorians skidded to a halt. The object didn't fire, but it gave them pause. Patient 00 signaled with the weapon for the aliens to move, bluffing as well as he could. For several seconds, it worked, but with the greatest of unfortunate timing, Patient 00 inadvertently twitched and fired the weapon into the corridor ceiling. The shock and surprise on his face gave away his bluff and invited a punishing blow to his chest.

He was knocked backward several feet, in the direction of the weapon cache. The blow knocked him off his balance, and he landed directly below the wall box. A small slit allowed him a line of sight to the weapons. The two aliens spread out in each direction and closed in. Patient 00 raised his weapon toward the slit and fired.

The sound of electrical snaps screamed and echoed throughout the corridors. He felt a strong sting on his hip, and as he moved to crawl away, he noticed a dark scorch mark near where he had sat. Bolts of energy continued to spread wildly. A bolt struck the nearest Xendorian, but the other had taken shelter around the corner. Another bolt knocked the weapon out of Patient 00's hands, and he mouthed a prayer while scurrying as fast as possible.

Patient 00 rose as he reentered the arena. Before he could fully stand, he was in the clutches of the commodore. The commodore had captured his prey on the run and was making sure to stay on the warrior's blind side. Several Xendorians were now engaged with the warrior. They used long, glowing whips to secure the alien insect's legs while group after group attempted to mount it. There was no sign of either of the Annomites or the doctors. Patient 00 hoped they were pursuing the baroness, but it was more likely that they had taken refuge or were fleeing.

The commodore was on a direct course for an exit when he tumbled down and dropped Patient 00 hard on the ground. The commodore attempted to keep hold, but Patient 00's twitching had wiggled him free as they fell. The commodore then screamed out in pain as the little digger creature bit down hard on his ankle area.

It wasn't much, but it gave the opportunity to go on the offensive. Patient 00 snatched a nearby stone of reasonable mass. The little digger Logging yelped as the commodore kicked him away with his free leg, providing Patient 00 enough time to bring the rock down hard on the commodore. There was a cracking noise, and Patient 00 raised the stone for a second blow, but another twitch knocked him off balance, sending the stone to the ground.

Patient 00 was unsure if he had actually caused any injury to the commodore, as he was suddenly back in his clutches and heading for a nearby exit.

$$\sum$$

The baroness thrashed and squirmed, but despite the Xendorian's battle wounds, he still maintained total physical control over her. "Harming you is not my intention. No, you only hold value alive, at least for now. Escaping from my clutches would only get you killed. Your mate, on the other hand, his death would be the icing on my cake and the noose for the commodore."

"Then what is your intention?" The baroness tried to sound unafraid, but she wasn't sure how well she did.

The Xendorian continued to make quick strides down the corridor. "To help myself, Baroness." So far, they hadn't crossed anyone else's path, and the Xendorian team leader seemed to be doing it intentionally. At last, he came to a three-way intersection and put the baroness down, with orders not to flee or she'd be punished. Raising his bad arm as high as the injury would allow, the Xendorian accessed his wrist device and saw an image of Aragmell and Aramethel running down a similar corridor. The alien activated several functions from the wrist device, and then he reached back, grabbed his spear, activated its electrical tips, and got ready.

The baroness's spirits lifted as she saw her two guardians hurrying to her aid. Aramethel sprinted in fast, bent low, and then leaped into the air, but the Xendorian was ready, and its spear rose up from underneath, pinning the young guardian against the ceiling.

It would have been an easy kill for the team leader, but instead, he let the beast fall and rotated the spear so it immediately pressed against Aramethel's back as he lay on the floor. Rising up into a position of dominance, the alien spoke. "Now is not the time, pup." The Xendorian released his hold of the beast and allowed Aramethel to spin over. "You are my prey, and I have captured you. My dominance over you is demonstrated. I offer you a chance to earn your release. Accept or die!"

Aragmell took a warrior stance but made no advance, obviously contemplating the offer. "Speak your terms, Xendorian."

"The commodore has risen above his abilities. It's time for someone with a more appropriate skill set to take the position. In order to rightfully challenge the commodore, he must fail to complete an objective. I offer you and the baroness a chance to escape, but it will cost you."

Aragmell spoke with a reserved tone. "That is a mighty reward. What could we do that would be so valuable to you?"

"Two terms. After your escape, the agreement has expired and I will hunt you down for recapture, and if any mention of this agreement gets out, I will make your capture especially painful, and without the bombast of the commodore."

Aragmell kept the warrior stance. "Agreed, and second?"

The Xendorian almost smiled. "You must kill Prisoner 00."

The baroness's heart flipped as she heard the second demand, but it erupted into anger as she heard Aragmell agree to the terms. Rising from the spot where she had been dropped, the baroness jumped onto the back of the Xendorian and battered the wound as fearsomely as she could.

The alien hissed but held true to his staff while holding Aramethel in check. Rather, the Xendorian turned its head and exposed the telepathic organ, and as it reached out and touched the baroness, she relaxed and fell limply to the floor.

$$\gg$$

Between the bouncing motion of the commodore's grip and the induced twitching, Patient 00 was about to puke. "Put me down, put me down, gonna puke." But in response, the commodore only squeezed harder, drawing out a big mess all over the alien's side. Like a child excited by a bug, the commodore hurled Patient 00 across the corridor and slammed him into the bulkhead.

"What the hell is this, you nasty little creature?" The Xendorian's words were accompanied by a fearsome stomp that broke every bone in Patient 00's hand. Patient 00 yowled, if only for a second. The commodore removed his foot and turned away in order to use his wrist communicator. "Team lead, report."

"Yes, Commodore, I have secured the primary objective and also secured the two Annomites."

"Very good, team leader, meet at the science bay. No more processing delays, I want to inform the emperor of a victory."

17: Science, Schmience

The science bay hummed and buzzed and stirred with the power of electricity, in quantities felt nowhere else on the ship. Large pieces of machinery, beds, tables, and vertical cylinders were scattered about the room like a medical obstacle course. The commodore and Patient 00 arrived at the bay first. Three Xendorians worked the consoles. These Xendorians wore full uniforms, white with blue patches. While their other features were the same, their body size was noticeably smaller.

Once the three had become aware of the commodore, they immediately turned, knelt, and gave the same physical greeting that had been performed in a routine demonstrated before as part an organized military tradition. The commodore returned the salute, and the three rose. "I come bearing gifts of extraordinary scientific importance, as seen by his majesty. Begin your investigation immediately. Upon completion, I wish to take custody of Prisoner 00 for personal oversight of his elimination." The Xendorian unceremoniously laid his captive on the table and turned back toward one of the females.

The commodore, having now finished in his official capacity, moved in a much more graceful manner as he approached one of the scientists. "Lady Imric, it's nice to see you rising in the ranks. Perhaps your skills will be of use in this project."

Imric stepped over to Prisoner 00 and examined his eyes, ears, mouth, and nose before signaling the commodore to place him on another nearby table. A second uniformed Xendorian wheeled over a large circular device with three plates that rotated along an overhead arm and then positioned it above Prisoner 00's head. While nothing formed in the way of words, a strong sense of both disgust and disappointment was tangible from the female Xendorian as it came across from the stone.

The team leader carried the baroness as she lay lifeless in his arms. Close behind followed two Annomite protectors restrained in neon-blue chain assembly. Between the headache and the twitching, it took a moment for Prisoner 00 to register the baroness's condition. "What have you bast—"

Before he could finish the sentence, the commodore put his hand firmly on top of Prisoner 00's face and pushed down hard. Prisoner 00 felt his vision blur, along with a resounding return of his headache.

The baroness was placed on an adjacent table and then given a much more thorough examination. The Xendorian scientists used their telepathic organs to sweep over the baroness before placing her on a mobile table and into a tube that extended deep into the bulkhead. The scientist Imric approached the commodore, moving in close. "Commodore, we all concur that she will make a full recovery without any long-term effects. I shall personally inform you when we have completed our task."

The two Annomites hung their heads low as they stayed shackled in the corner. The Xendorian team leader walked over to the commodore, knelt, and saluted before rising again in a well-rehearsed custom. "The emperor will be most pleased at our victory,

Commodore."

"Hardly worthy of a complete victory. Our losses aboard the Arkapeligo will not go unnoticed by His Excellency. Perhaps if Commander Lymphod is disposed of, I shall make you my new number-two team leader."

"It would be a great honor, Commodore. I would not fail you."

"I am confident you will not. Now come, let us tend to our wounds and make ready for the moment when our prey is free from its scientific captors. We must plan a most egregious death for our Prisoner 00. He has proven entirely too disruptive to be simply eliminated."

The two exited the room, taking with them the overbearing presence of alpha male. The smallest of the Xendorian scientists approached Prisoner 00. "Finally, we can get some real work done. My name is Imric, and I will be conducting your survey. I see you already have a translation stone. Either that or I'm just talking to myself."

Prisoner 00 raised his head so as to look at his new caretaker but found only blurriness and confusion with every movement of his head.

"My, that's a nasty concussion you got yourself, there. Anger the commodore, did we now? Well I hope you learned not to be doing that again. Second lessons are often fatal."

A second scientist activated the circular machine above Prisoner 00. The base spun at a slow, steady speed while the under-plates spun at a much faster rate, with extending and contracting parts. Lights flashed and lasers pulsed, throbbing and pulsating Prisoner 00's body. Cold, slimy hands encased his head while another set held his feet. "You and the commodore seem to be on friendly terms. Has he taken you for a mate?"

Prisoner 00's twitching had become more pronounced yet less frequent, and now his captors were probing and diagnosing as they held him in place. He prayed that they wouldn't find his ace in the hole, his only weapon to fight the Xendorians. Perhaps the pieces were spread out enough, but he was desperate for a distraction, anything—well anything other than what he was about to get.

A tone came across the translation stone with clarity. "What are you saying? I'm here by my own merit, no one else's."

One of the scientists stepped over to Prisoner 00, moving a machine overhead. Imric spoke to her third confederate and then looked at Prisoner 00. "This is going to hurt, immensely."

A pink light emitted from the machine, causing Prisoner 00 to scream and twist his body in an effort to flee the pain. "I meant no implication, Lady Imric. I was simply curious. There is my role in the chain of command to consider, after all."

"Well please keep personal business personal. I have no aims or desire for your position."

"Perhaps that is best, but I must know, if only for personal reasons."

There was no relief, only a transfer from the intellectual fear to physical fear. The machines scanned every inch of his body from head to toe, its lasers burning the hairs off his skin as they tenderized all exposed areas. A visual display of Prisoner 00 appeared on a view screen located on a wall.

"I know not of the commodore's personal affairs. If he had a long-term mate, I doubt he would share that information with me."

"Most distressing, most distressing indeed." The Xendorian scientist operating the machine spoke to her confederates. "Are we sure this is the life supplier to our mystery?"

Imric lifted Prisoner 00's hand and then attached a clip to his wrist. He again shrieked as several needles extended out from the clip and dug their way deep into his skin.

"Yes, Lady Numphia, this subject is indeed the father to our subject. The bloodlines are too close to be anything else."

Looking down into Prisoner 00's eyes, Imric asked, "Are there only two variations of human, male and female?"

Focusing on the conversation helped Prisoner 00 avoid passing out, but it didn't encourage him to cooperate either. "Don't forget about the buttheads."

At first there was an initial flurry of excitement, but the understanding finally sunk in, and the Xendorian scientists looked rather displeased. Pushing a button on the table, Numphia sent an intensely painful burst of electricity surging through Prisoner 00's body. "We will have no more of that attitude. This is a place of learning and exploration. Save your sarcasm for the commodore." Another cycle of the machine started, inducing a crushing pain from some unseen force.

"The commodore is not a man to be tamed. He is a conqueror and will never be anything more. Very poor quality in a mate." Imric sounded annoyed as her quasi boss, Lady Numphia, couldn't seem to drop the subject.

Numphia said, "Strong, rich, powerful, and handsome—yes, those are terrible qualities in a mate. Is that why you have rejected his advances?"

Imric laughed at the forwardness of her compatriot. She grabbed a long, narrow rod while Numphia began removing Prisoner 00's undergarments. He spun and twitched frantically, yelled out, and prayed. Numphia grabbed his genitals, and as she moved them aside, he let out the nervous buildup of air in his lungs and exhaled a whimpering, "Please no." The reprieve didn't last long, as the scientist inserted the rod into its intended orifice.

"Well that and I have a bigger prize in my sights."

It took several torturous and invasive tests before Prisoner 00 was spoken to again.

"This is most distressing. We find no evidence that you possess any relation to the genetic variation at all, yet you are the father of the child in question. I don't understand it. How can an outside genome be added? No race, even the ancient ones, has ever had that technology. Tell me how you conceived the child."

Prisoner 00 twitched as he tried to think through the concussion but found it difficult. "Ya see, the bees shove their pokers into the birds' butts, only to have the birds turn around and eat their lunch."

With an annoyed tone, Numphia spoke to her coworkers. "I have the woman, and she is good enough. I have all the information I will ever need from this. I believe it is time we turn you over to the commodore."

A new voice, powerful and willful, spoke, startling the two. "Again, Numphia, you are wrong on two counts. First, your assessment of the chain of command around here is flat wrong, and second, so is your assumption that you have the ability to understand the unknowable. So no, we will not be turning any of the subjects over to the commodore."

The Xendorian Numphia rose from her perch next to Prisoner 00's table. "Lead Lyndia, so nice of you to pay us a visit, but this project is a special assignment from the commodore himself. I'm afraid you will have to take it up with him. Now out of my lab!"

There was no letdown from Lead Lyndia as she responded. "Who is science lead? Until that changes, all projects are under my purview, so deal with it. This is not your lab. This is my lab, as I am the one wrestling with those war-hungry generals day after day. Without me, your lab would be nothing but a waste-extraction terminal."

Numphia hissed as she and the other Xendorian scientists huddled together and slowly advanced. "Be wary of a commander who cuts you out of the loop. Who knows what else they might cut you out of—or with?"

The two scientists—Numphia, backed by her assistant, Imric—hissed, and the other bounced like a boxer circling the ring. The Xendorian science lead, Lyndia, broke the stalemate with a charge and a howl, sending the clique of Imric and her compatriots backing out the door.

She stood, took a deep breath, looked at the poor group, and spoke loudly. "Now it's time for some real scientists to do some work."

Lyndia shook her hands in fury as they left. Then she turned toward Prisoner 00. He tilted his head to look at the new arrival, but his face was swollen and now somewhat disfigured and misshapen. The Xendorian Lyndia gently rubbed her hand along his face and smiled. "Looks like we have had a few bumps on the head today. Let's just see if I can't get some of those cobwebs out."

The new demeanor and attitude, mixed with the concussion and fatigue, made it easy to trust this new alien. Using a handheld device, Lyndia intensely scanned his eyes and then uploaded the information into a wall computer. Two small devices dropped out of a terminal a few feet off to the side. She placed the devices over Prisoner 00's eyes and smiled. "That should speed up the healing process, but the headaches will be intense and unavoidable. Now that twitching is a mystery, but I'm afraid that my confederate is right. If the commodore is keeping me out of the loop, my position is untenable. So I will have to forgo the examination for now."

The alien then walked over to the wall that the baroness had disappeared into. "Ah, yes, the regeneration chamber has nearly completed its work. Your mate is in excellent health. All of her nutrition, regeneration, and hydration needs have been met." Lyndia accessed a panel on the wall, cycling through different displays assimilating the data as she went with incredible efficiency. "Now that baby is a mystery wrapped in a forbidden cookie jar. I don't understand why we can't determine the sex of the child. Are there only two sexes of human?"

Lyndia didn't wait for an answer but continued to process data. "This truly is a miracle, you know. Never before in the history of everything has there ever been a recorded addition to a genome structure, and with the recorded DNA of both parents, it's truly, truly amazing. Fools like that Numphia can only see this as an anomaly to exploit, a weapon to canonize. I, however, see the grand design and your place within it."

Prisoner 00 could feel the tingling in the back of his head as the optical devices filled his eyes with a magical display of lights and colors. He tilted his head up, but the words failed to come out, yet the alien Lyndia appeared to understand the question just fine.

"Grand design, no, I don't mean that idiot emperor and his thuggish guardians. I'm talking about grand design." Lyndia paused for effect. "A design so simple it works for everything yet so complex there is an illusion of an answer for everything. I believe this to be true of your child as well, but I'm afraid that my beliefs are in the minority—now more so than ever before. The riches that our conquests have brought us are taking us ever farther from the proper path, the path away from the true one."

Prisoner 00 twisted his head to face Lyndia and twitched. "What?"

It was the closest thing to a smile that Prisoner 00 had seen on an alien thus far. "Forgive me, babbling on about politics when time is so preciously short. We have much to discuss and preparations to make. My list of allies was already thinning, and I'm afraid it's only a matter of time for me here."

$$\gg$$

The commodore and the team leader leisurely paced down the hall. At first the commodore spoke joyously as he recounted his battle and self-deemed victory. "Alone I battled the terrible creature. Heroically I saved the objectives and faced the warrior! I lunged straight at the warrior, with total disregard for my own safety. I blinded the creature with one of my most powerful blows!"

The Xendorian team leader listened enthusiastically, as if he wasn't actually there for the events, but having finally gained a foothold to talk, he quickly changed the subject. "Yes, Commodore, it will be a great highlight to your illustrious career, but I beg of you to listen now with unemotional ears. I know how much you despise the prisoner, 00, but I would not make a good XO if I didn't alert my commander to possible dangers, and . . . opportunities."

The commodore stopped walking. "Very well, team lead, as your stock is rising with me, I will grant you your request. I will hear out your plea as to why I should sacrifice an honor most deserving and desired by me, the killing of Prisoner 00."

"My commodore," the team leader spoke softly but confidently, "thanks to the fruitless efforts of our commander, Lymphod, you have been robbed of many levels of victory, but where he failed, you still managed to succeed. This human species, while inferior, is very adept and dangerous when paired with modern technologies. Yet you and your men were able to capture the leader of the spacefaring humans. Let us not portray ourselves as having failed to achieve the highest levels of victory, but as victors over a cutthroat, adaptive, and perhaps even blessed species."

The commodore cringed on the word "blessed." "You know how the emperor hates those words, yet I see some wisdom in your strategy. The species of the Arkapeligo group throwing themselves into kamikaze warfare as they desperately fight to save their unborn blessed savior. Yes, I like the narrative much better."

The team leader stayed close to the commodore. "And, sir, not only have you captured the community's religious idol, but you have in your position the leader of the human resistance, father to the blessed one. Let him not be a passing muse of vengeance but a trophy to give to the emperor."

The commodore stood upright. "Yes, perhaps you are right, unleashing my wrath on such a pitiful creature might make me feel better, but it could make me appear weak. Presenting Prisoner 00 as a trophy might prove enough of a distraction to save face, but the loss of any warriors will come at a price with His Majesty. "

The team leader responded pridefully. "Then perhaps the best strategy is to present a solution before discussing the problem."

The commodore smiled. "You mean for me to announce you as my new commander."

$$\sum y$$

The door to the science bay opened, and in the Xendorian tradition, the two doctors and their tiny furry friend were held high and then lowered in recognition of a comrade. Lyndia rose from her position of examination and spoke joyfully. "Ah, our secondary objectives have arrived. Prudent timing, soldier. I shall now take custody of these beings."

In obedience, the Xendorian placed each subject facedown in a line before Lyndia, about-faced, and left.

"Ah, my friends, please, no more need for formalities. Please rise and make yourselves comfortable, but I must warn you against attempting escape, for it would bring terrible consequences I couldn't lessen."

Dr. Fengie, true to her nature more so than her personality, searched the room for the baroness and immediately rushed to the display along the wall, dragging Dr. Fergie. After filling the room with a cacophony of smells, they seemed satisfied with the baroness's state, and then Dr. Fengie began to gather some equipment. Overall, the doctor seemed well aware of the devices' usages and ably tended to her poor blind partner, Dr. Fergie.

The glasses that had been placed on Prisoner 00 dinged like an oven timer, compacted into two smaller circles, and fell to the floor, were a MOP bot—apparently another shared technology—zoomed in to clean up the litter. Prisoner 00 slowly sat up but cringed his neck in pain as he processed the events from the past few days. He eventually regained his equilibrium. "I'm so confused. Whose side is everybody on? How many sides are there?" He hesitated briefly. "Whose side am I on?"

Dr. Fergie, while being tended to by his wife, broke out in laughter. "Another brilliant question from the father of our mystery child. I am finding your species most interesting, so lacking in skill, knowledge, and ability, yet you manage to simplify the universe around you in such a way that you not only understand it but also shape and design it. Amazing!" There was a short pause before Dr. Fengie nudged her husband. "Of course, another one of my tangents. So to answer your question succinctly, we are on the side of good. There are many sides, and you are able to answer your own question through what you choose and how you pursue it."

Prisoner 00 twitched, slurring his words slightly. "Thanks, doc, that's real clear."

Speaking loudly enough for all to hear, the oddly helpful

yet out of place Xendorian Lyndia gathered the group's attention. "Now that everyone is here, we have but a few minutes to come up with an escape plan. I have a contact on the ark, but their resources are extremely limited. For the moment, the battle on the ark and the planet is consuming the majority of the commodore's fleets' resources, including a large detachment of this ship's personnel. I see three ways off this ship—shuttle craft, escape pod, or with some more difficultly, we could attempt a mini-slip. I am a believer, a scientist, and an officer. I will take charge, but I would prefer to leave the task elsewhere, perhaps guardian Aragmell."

The two Annomite guardians held their restraints close— though now free from their grasp, the facade may be needed quickly. Aragmell still held his head low, raising it only enough to be heard. "The shuttle pod will provide more protection in space but will be harder to acquire. The escape pod would provide easier access off the ship but leave us at the mercy of the enemy fleet. A mini-slip would be immediately recognized, and the crew here would attempt to shut it down, while the reception on the other side might be a blaze of lasers."

"Wise counsel, guardian, but I failed to catch your endorsement, if one was provided." Lyndia waited to see if Aragmell had more to say. "Given the resources available to us, I don't recommend the escape pod—too dangerous a transition to the ark. What say you, Father 00?"

Rubbing his temples, Prisoner 00 was finding it much easier to think clearly, despite it all. "I don't understand a damn thing you guys are talking about. A mini-slip sounds like a piece of women's clothing to me. Second, space? It still boggles my mind that I'm in a spaceship right now. Until you crashed down in Manhattan,

I thought my mother was the only alien I knew." He paused for a laugh that never came. "Here's what is going to happen." There was a longer pause this time. "Ok, so I don't know what is going to happen. I don't know what the best plan is, but I do know what I'm going to do. I'm going to kill the commodore."

18: A Trip in Time

"She mustn't be allowed to get away with this, Commodore. What gives her the right to take away my project and deny you your deserved vengeance?" Numphia howled in anger as she vented toward the commodore.

The bridge teemed with a sense of life that the mostly empty corridors lacked. While most of the crew were Xendorians, other species worked at various positions, but it was the massive amount of vegetation growing along the walls and in planters scattered about that gave the room its feel. The floor seemed to be a more natural substance along the lines of quarried marble or granite.

The commodore sat in a large circular platform in the center. Two work stations were placed nearby in front, while several more were spread out behind. "Lady Numphia, I placed you directly in charge of a project, and I do believe you had some time to accomplish that task, did you not? I shouldn't need to remind you that the Wilde will be here shortly. The Arkapeligo group have nearly completed their transverse gate. I have a botched assault to fix and a planetary conquest to wrap up, and the emperor is demanding answers—answers you failed to provide. So if lead Lyndia wants to relieve you, that's her prerogative. Now, here is my prerogative. I have no need for officers who place politics above duty and no patience for incompetence. Lady Imric, you are now command liaison to the science department. Lady Numphia, you will return to your quarters and await transfer. Now, Lady Numphia, you are dismissed!"

A stunned look of surprise translated across Numphia's alien features, yet after a brief moment, it turned nasty. "I guess secretions blind oneself from their own standards."

"Mind your tongue, lady, or I might assign you as overseer of some backward wasteland, such as Earth."

With a reptilian hiss toward the commodore, Numphia ushered herself out of the bridge, leaving behind a smiling Imric, who once again knelt in military discipline.

"Rise, Lady Imric. I now appoint you command liaison to the science department. Congratulations on becoming a new member of the senior staff. Perhaps later we shall celebrate together, but for now you must prove your worth and discover for me the source of this genetic alteration and find out if it is an isolated incident."

"With pleasure, Commodore. I am happy to report that without further investigation, I can confirm that this was an external alteration, unrelated to either the parent or the species. However, in order to determine the actual source of the manipulation, I request a transit to the surface to examine the site of conception."

"A wise and bold course of action. Excellent start, liaison. Now report back when you have relevant information." The lust on the commodore's face as he spoke translated in all languages.

Lady Imric's voice now lacked the strong tone. "Commodore, in order to achieve this task in prompt order, I will need temporary custody of Prisoner 00."

The commodore's body straightened, and his physical demeanor transformed. "This creature's ability to elude what it's due troubles me greatly. I have even underestimated it myself on more than one occasion. If this be absolutely necessary, I insist that the team leader join you."

The conversation suddenly stopped as Imric and the team leader entered the science bay. Physically, there was nothing out of the ordinary. The two Annomite guardians sat in their corner, shackles fully visible and attached. The two doctors treated one another, and Prisoner 00 lay naked on the table, yet the two approached on full alert of an ambush, as if they could sense it in the air.

Performing the traditional salutatory act, Imric spoke. "Lead Lyndia, I am very happy to report that the commodore has chosen me to replace Lady Numphia. I look forward to working with you on several projects benefitting our great empire. For the moment, however, I would like to take temporary custody of Prisoner 00, as we wish to take him to the surface for evaluation of the conception site."

Lyndia paused in deep thought before making various predetermined, if not slightly odd, gestures. "It is most joyous that the commodore has been so focused on your talents and rewarded you so commensurately to them." Lyndia stood and raised her arm, allowing Imric to stand at ease. "Lady Imric, as to your request,

I would be happy to oblige, and might I say that your vision has already proven wiser than your predecessor's. Perhaps the rotting worm has been plucked from the bushel." Lyndia used careful emphasis as she finished. "My immediate plans do NOT need to be executed. Therefore, you may have your Prisoner 00 now."

"Wait, wait, just wait a second." The normally jolly Dr. Fergie yelled out with urgency as he was still being tended to. "Please, before you separate the two, we must first see their mating ritual and learn how the child was conceived."

The two Xendorian scientists looked at each other, communicated unspoken thoughts, and finally agreed. "Agreed, Prisoner 00, you will perform the mating ritual that produced the child, expediently and urgently."

Dr. Fengie moved toward the tube where the baroness lay unconscious and opened it.

The room stopped and stared as Prisoner 00 stood dumbfounded and red-faced, at a loss for words.

$$\sum\!\!\!\!\!/$$

The shuttle craft was the size of a large room. The equipment seemed to be modular as several MOP bots were busy taking and bringing large workstations and other unknown items. The team leader smashed Prisoner 00 down hard onto an L-shaped piece of furniture and ignited several strands of neon-blue restraints.

The front viewport spanned nearly 160 degrees, and as the craft exited the hangar, a dark night sky filled up with an unbelievable array of stars. He couldn't see anything other than little specks, but HUD displays on the viewport showed locations and allegiances of other alien information. Then the craft turned, and the dark sky filled with the most beautiful blue. The HUD display changed colors to create better contrast with the radiating blue beauty of Earth.

Never in his life had Prisoner 00 ever been ambitious for space travel, but by doing it now, he was filled with regret and remorse. How much time had passed since that night with the baroness on the roof? He wasn't quite sure, but he longed to be there again, in her arms. No sight of beauty could overcome the lovers' longing. The craft, possessing far superior technology, entered the atmosphere with barely a bump. The shuttle HUD pointed out multiple "friendly" craft—support craft for the planetary invasion, he suspected.

As they passed down, through, and into the atmosphere, a huge billow of dark-black smoke rose up from the ground. The ship was moving too fast for Prisoner 00 to find its origin, but as they passed it, another appeared ahead. A strong vibration rocked his chair as the shuttle manipulated its exterior hull to become more aerodynamic. The ship tilted, slowing down to the point where objects on the ground became recognizable. A long formation of humans marched in column lines as two Xendorians flanked their sides.

"It has been some time since the empire has had a good infusion of slave labor." The team leader shifted through various displays and graphs on his console. "Not a very hardy species. My god, how does such a fragile species reach the top of its food chain?"

Lady Imric sighed as she looked outside. "Look at this

planet. It's a paradise. This species was given the gift of dominance, and abundant fertile land and water. And nearly the entire planet is habitable, not even any large predators. Such a shame for what is about to happen."

"They say you have the commodore's ear. Why not, perhaps, have the commodore defer the Wilde attack and claim it as your province? It has a good location, central spiral, yet isolated."

"I detect a sense of fishing in your suggestion. Whatever attention and respect I have garnered from the commodore is due to my performance and abilities as an officer. Should I choose a mate and wish to be endowed with his gifts, this little planet would be far from adequate."

The team leader let out a small squeak. "There are many reasons to go fishing—to satisfy one's own hunger is usually the primary. Hunting a rare catch is my personal favorite."

There was a short pause as the lady interpreted the conversation. "You may come off as gentle, team leader, but you can't hide your intensity from me. Reptiles like you can accomplish great things, but—"

This time, the team leader moved away from Prisoner 00 and closer to the lady. "Intensity is the power to ignite the passions of others. Something the commodore's leadership lacks, at least for the moment." He now stood behind the lady as she piloted the shuttle. "My intensity, my leadership, and my passion will be felt everywhere."

He then leaned back, turned around, and looked at Prisoner 00. "Thanks to our spies aboard the Arkapeligo, we were able to determine the building of consummation." He activated a display, and a video of Prisoner 00 and the baroness jumping off the building played over and over on repeat. "Now you will tell us the exact location of the consummation."

Prisoner 00 looked blankly at the team leader, twitched, and sneezed. "Can't help you there, buddy. I wasn't invited."

"Why do you always insist on this? You know that non-compliance will result in tremendous pain, yet time after time, you continue to annoy, counter, and delay. I will have no more of this. I will search your memories one by one if I have to, and know this, you will die before we leave this system."

The shuttle touched down with a loud screech from the thrusters, followed by a whine and a hiss. The team leader picked up Prisoner 00 by the waist, lifted him like a toy doll, and walked out into the dimming sunlight of a cool New Jersey evening.

The feeling of fresh air and sunlight brought back a sense of life to Prisoner 00. The three approached the baroness's building's main entrance. The streets had been emptied, and only an overturned sedan lay silently—a victim of circumstance. The damage to the back side of the building had been considerable. With the ocean side of the building nearly gone, every room was now exposed. The canopy that once so proudly overhung the entrance to this fine establishment was but a shred of what remained behind, just a damp piece of cloth swaying in the wind.

The team leader raised Prisoner 00 and used his body to open the front entrance. The interior of the building was a mess. The floor was still wet in places, furniture lay strewn about the lobby, and the smell of death was pungent. The team leader put

Prisoner 00 down in the center, took off his neon restraints, and commanded him to lead them. "To the place of the child's conception."

The awkwardness of the situation left Prisoner 00, speechless, and he searched the room with his eyes, hoping for an idea—an idea for what, he wasn't sure. He had no intention of escaping without the baroness, and he actually had no memory of the consummation. Helping these aliens out wasn't on the agenda either. The idea of leading them on a wild goose hunt was appealing, but pointless and trite. So he took a page from his father's book: when all else fails, go with the truth. "I don't know where the consummation occurred."

The two Xendorians closed in around Prisoner 00. Lady Imric spoke first. "We have had enough of your games. If you will not give us the information, we shall take it from you." The middle spire of her head began to twist, exposing the spongy circular organ the commodore had used before. The team leader tripped Prisoner 00, sending him onto his back, and held him down so tightly that it proved difficult to breathe.

Lady Imric placed the organ on his forehead, causing an instant burning sensation all along the front of his brain. His body convulsed as she prodded, searched, and tore apart his memories. Desperate to find a method to push back against the pain and his attacker, he focused and brought up the baroness in his mind. He thought back to that night. He remembered the look she had given him. Focusing hard on the memory, the invading presence had found what it wanted, and the pain narrowed down deep in his brain. Losing control of the memory, he now watched himself as if it were a movie—Big M slicing off his nipple, the baroness patching it, and then there was blackness, followed by agony.

Over and over, the nerves in his brain where probed, prodded, and exposed, each time more intensely than the last. Finally, Lady Imric pulled back, exiting herself from Prisoner 00's brain. "He doesn't know. He truly doesn't know. Can you tell me how that can be?" With an angry thrust, she pushed Prisoner 00 to the ground. "We will examine the bed in which he awoke." The reptile's voice sounded more forced than before, and there was a slight yellowness in her face.

The team leader continued with a sympathetic tone. "Initially, I found the commodore's distaste of this species to be overblown, but the more I am forced to get results out of them, the more frustrating they become. Never before have I encountered a species so unintentionally obstructive. They lack the mental powers to be that many steps ahead of us. They, they lack the physical abilities to be a challenge, and yet they thwart us at what feels like every turn. The commodore and I understand. However, the empire does not. Therefore, I am afraid that all excuses must be muted.

"I have no mind to play political bantering. I am as committed to achieving our objectives as you are. Have you not yourself experienced frustration at these humans' hands? How is that shoulder feeling?"

They started to climb the stairs, with the team leader once again carrying Prisoner 00 like a large doll. "Physical scars are badges of honor. Scientific failure is not."

Prisoner 00 could feel the vibe change dramatically between the two. Body language was apparently universal.

Lady Imric said, "It was on the backs of great scientists that our civilization rose to greatness, and it will be on the backs of warriors that it falls to new depths."

With a new harshness, the team leader hissed his words. "Such rhetoric from someone sucking at the commodore's breast."

"I am an accomplished scientist, proud of my contribution, and I am a female proud of myself. If who I share my bed with bothers you, then perhaps you are misplacing your jealousy."

"Such venom from a subordinate will most certainly poison the well. Count your blessings, for they may soon run dry."

The three now entered what remained of the room where the baroness had mended Prisoner 00's nipple. He skimmed his hand across the rough scab, now covered in ridges from being torn apart and rehealed several times over now. A drop of blood covered his finger, as his sporadic twitching had once again disturbed the wound.

Lady Imric placed a small box in the center of the room, adjusted several elements, stepped toward Prisoner 00, and put her hand on the top of his head. She grabbed hard and pulled out a large swatch of hair. She set the hair in the top of the box. It ignited in a blue light that colored the room, overpowering the dimming evening light and turning Prisoner 00 a glowing neon blue.

She said, "Disgusting, does your entire species mate in this room? It will be very difficult to isolate the prisoner's DNA, much less what I'm looking for."

The team leader grunted with a slight satisfaction. "Another scientist wasting a guardian's time on frivolous dead ends."

Lady Imric sneezed. "Another guardian looking only to destroy that which they don't understand, or is too lazy to."

"Just get it done, scientist."

$$\sum\!\!\!\!\diagdown$$

Her heart palpitated, and her body pulsed with an erotic heat. Waves of wet warmth rushed upward as her mind searched behind closed lids. Blood flowed through her body, draining the extremities. Each wave started as a tickle and grew in intensity with each new crescendo. The baroness felt her body warm and her adrenaline rush. Then, as quickly as they started, they stopped and the baroness lay smiling, lost deep in the void between wake and dream.

She was unable to fight back an initial wave of panic and screaming as she opened her eyes to the smiling orange barrel of one her two doctors. The words came across both verbally and mentally. "Ah, I see our treasure has finally awoken. Tell me, do you know me?"

It took a second, but the baroness regained her conscious awareness. "Dr. Fengie, what's happening?" Immediately grabbing for her pants, she felt reassured that they were still on and, as far as she could tell, in place. She scanned the room as she tried to calm her breath and slow her heart. He wasn't here. It annoyed her greatly that he was the first one she looked for, but her body was calling out for him, longing, deeply and urgently.

A chuckle erupted from Dr. Fergie as he patiently laid down the devices that once covered his eyes. "What a species, not for a moment does she trust in the hands of the universe. The power and sexual dynamics of this species are quite complex, always engaging and manipulating the situations and stimulations. I can only imagine your history is filled with gluttony of wars over power and love."

Dr. Fengie held the baroness's hand and helped her sit up. "How do you feel, my dear?" The doctor ran a tentacle across her forehead and stared into her eyes. "We are still in the clutches of the empire." Dr. Fengie turned to face the Xendorian Lyndia. "No offense, Lady Lyndia, but there are few of your kind in the empire anymore."

Lady Lyndia moved to the side of the baroness, opposite Dr. Fengie, and began speaking to the baroness. "My dear, it is my great honor to meet the mother of a god."

The realization of her pregnancy once again slapped her in her face. The appearance of an alien now calling her child a god brought in a wave of emotion that overcame her.

"Baroness, my name is Lady Lyndia, and I operate as the commodore's chief scientist, but I have pledged my loyalty to an ideal—an ideal that my position has let me pursue with abandon. A privilege few of my kind now enjoy." Lady Lyndia turned around and paced a bit. "My species was once a bastion of scientific insight and discovery, but as our technology made us powerful, it also made us immoral. Species far and wide would call on us for enlightened government, but those days were long before I was born. For I was born into a post-flood empire. Our home world was a very beautiful planet. It was a jewel of the universe. Then came the floods. So great, so intense was the water that it destroyed nearly the whole planet's surface. As our scientists failed to understand the nature of the disaster, we were unable to cease the water from covering the land.

"Unable to save their home world, the Xendorian scientists found themselves well out of favor. The rise of the warrior species hindered all scientific attempts to re-vegetate the plant. The guardians seized the opportunity to take power of the empire and have been running it into the ground ever since."

The baroness was more confused than ever. "What does any of that have to do with my child?"

"Of course, my point, the destruction of my species' home world was an act of superior authority, for only one Xendorian on the planet survived. Cast out as having gone crazy from the destruction, by the populace, he spoke of a message from that authority, and I believe your child is the fruition of that message."

The baroness flung her legs over the table and took several deep breaths. She held her hands over her womb. "Where is he?"

Lyndia naturally assumed the question was for her. "My child, that was before I was born. I'm sure he is long since dead now, but I do hear that the planet of Zentak has a memorial to him."

The baroness shook her head, looked at Dr. Fengie, and asked again, "Where is he?"

Dr. Fengie returned a blank stare, but her blind husband spoke up. "My dear Fengie, listen to the inflection for help in understanding her. Her meaning of 'he' is regarding her mate, not Lady Lyndia's story."

Catching sight of Aragmell, the baroness focused on maintaining her composure, made all the more difficult by the silence about her question. She exploded with as minimal an outburst as possible. "Where is he?"

Lady Lyndia looked around at the group and gently coughed. "As the newcomer to your fellowship, I had hoped to be spared the task of giving you bad news, but I am afraid that your mate has been taken to the surface. It is very likely that once they examine the conception site, they will terminate him."

The baroness tried to stay calm, but her anger was palpable in her voice. "Give me a weapon." Feeling surrounded by aliens only intensified her feelings. "Give me a goddamn weapon, now!" Again the aliens stood motionless, sending the baroness into a near tizzy, with tears streaming down her face. She jumped off the platform and searched the equipment drawers, nooks, and crannies until she came upon a surgical knife.

The group of aliens watched her as she moved, like a group of children watching a terrible magician, unaware—as are the adults—that the trick will end in failure. The baroness, now armed, walked directly toward Aragmell and placed the blade at the creature's throat. "I have seen your true colors, beast. I have no need for a bodyguard who would sacrifice the ones I care for. Follow me not! I see now that I am truly alone, and the only one I can trust is out there in need of me. So I will go to him, even if it costs me our lives."

$$\gtrdot$$

The building was a hollow shell of the magnificence it once was. Prisoner 00 stared longingly at the bed. Memories of the baroness floated across his mind. Lady Imric scanned and examined the room. In total, none of the four devices she had brought had managed to find what she was looking for, and with each new negative result, her frustration grew.

Prisoner 00 walked to the rear of the room, surveying the landscape that was once Manhattan. The black slates had all been removed. The tethers, and now even the greatest city of all, were gone. All that lay behind was a vast empty ocean and a New Jersey beach covered in debris.

The team leader's wrist device beeped, and the commodore's image appeared above it. "Science surface team, report."

Lady Imric pushed a button on her communicator. "My time and resources have been limited, but I have found no indications that would support the external interference theory. I see no signs of non-humans at this site. I am requesting additional time to examine a larger area."

The commodore's reply was swift. "Negative. Wilde are immediately inbound. Last of my soldiers will be off the planet in forty minutes. You two now have four. Expedite return to ship. Team leader, you will take the prisoner to its cell, and then report to my office."

The two Xendorians knelt in a military salute, and the transmission ended. Prisoner 00 took a deep breath and surveyed the area one last time, only this time he was sure he saw a motion. Looking ever closer, he now saw an exposed arm. At first his instinct was to look away from the probably severed limb, but the arm definitely moved. The arm was slowly rising, as if in an unconscious attempt to grab hold of anything. The person was a floor beneath them, covered under the rubble. He turned his head and saw his Xendorian master hurrying over. Out of time, and more appealing options, Prisoner 00 jumped down.

The team leader was no fool and was obviously prepared for his prisoner's attempt to jump. A strong clasp grabbed Prisoner 00 by the chest, and as his feet moved over the edge, he fell only a few feet before being suspended by the grapple that was tearing into him.

"You arrogant fool, so you wish to fall—I can make your wish come true." As the team leader approached the side of the building, he pressed a button, releasing the prisoner to fall several feet before digging into his chest and nipple scar. It burned, and his head became woozy as he fell too far, below the arm.

His hands clasped, holding the crest piece and trying desperately to relieve the pressure and agony. Yet he now floated low enough to grab the limb. With a bite of his lip and a burning in his chest, Prisoner 00 was able to grab a footing on an exposed pipe and use it to twist his body and push off in the direction of the limb.

The voice of Lady Imric came as if an angel were speaking. "Are we done acting like a child? We need to be moving."

Prisoner 00 was getting good at concentrating beyond pain, and as his captor slowly brought him up, he reached out, grabbed the wrist, and held on as best he could. Prisoner 00's shoulders popped with the weight of his body, and his chest felt as if it was about to be ripped off, and suddenly one of the baroness's girls rose out of the debris.

Had there been more time, surely the girl would have been left behind, but with barely a double take, the team leader had secured his prisoner and his newfound slave in one motion. They bounded down the stairs with a grace and speed beyond human capability. Within seconds, they were back inside the shuttle craft, and without delay, the team leader threw the baroness's girl to the side and strapped Prisoner 00 back into his restraining harness.

Prisoner 00 recognized the girl. She was the same one the baroness had pawned off on Big M, but for the moment, his head was too concussed to remember the girl's name. Prisoner 00 fidgeted and wiggled, but he was left helpless as that poor unconscious girl's body bounced around the cabin with the jostling of the flight as the shuttle abruptly lifted and sped off.

19: Tallyho

The doctors nestled close together in the corner, their tentacles dancing and caressing in an odd ballet as each new topic fragranced the room. The furry creature Logging curled up in a ball like a sleeping dog.

Yet the rest of the room stood in stunned submission as the tiny, if not powerful, frame of the baroness held the absolute beast of a warrior Aragmell in a position of mercy. "But, mistress—" Aragmell began to speak, but the baroness roared.

"That's baroness, you murderer!"

"Yes, Baroness." The creature looked as if it was going to beg for forgiveness, but then its face changed again. "I have failed you, my lady. You have the right to take my life. It is yours to do with as you please." Then, taking the baroness's hand, he moved it from his neck to his throat and rotated it so that she could simply push it through.

Rage burned in the baroness's eyes, and for a moment, not only could she see herself pushing the blade through, but she relished the thought. Yet as her resolve tightened, it also faltered. She slowly slid her hand down from the beast's throat, and her body fell against the alien's chest. The baroness, who had always been the strongest person she had ever known, now sobbed and collapsed into the arms of someone she feared, hated, loved, and barely knew.

"How could you, how could you agree to it?" The tears streamed until they turned back into rage, and she beat the beast's chest with her fist. Yet as her energy drained, so did her rage and her wall against the tears.

It took several minutes, but Aragmell knelt down and embraced the girl. "If you wish to save him, we must acquire a shuttle craft and pursue them. The planet's surface will be the easiest place to recover him. The baroness pulled back, wiped away the tears, and nodded in affirmation. She then turned to face the room.

A strange ensemble of faces stared back at her, and her words came out garbled. "I just need you all . . . to know . . ." Her thumb went to her mouth, and she gently bit it. "Thank you." The two doctors had broken away from their corner, and Dr. Fengie now embraced the baroness.

The moment lasted a bit too long before the baroness broke away and came toward Lady Lyndia. "I know I have not known you very long at all. Yet you have gone to great lengths and exposed yourself to risk in order to demonstrate your trust in us. So I ask you now, can you get us to the shuttle craft?"

Lady Lyndia bowed with a smile. "Thank you, your words honor me, and your trust blesses me. I can indeed get us to a shuttle craft, but I am afraid that we must go before the commodore first. Taking a shuttle craft on my own authority during a time of battle could get me killed."

The baroness nodded. "Very well then."

$$\sum y$$

The ship shook with a great intensity. Wave after wave of turbulence pounded against the ship as its engines throttled back, pushing with all their might. There he was, restrained and helpless. Prisoner 00 had saved this girl, only to watch her die. It wasn't love, but he had been intimate with this girl, and that was more than nothing. Guilt filled his thoughts, and grief overcame him.

The ship banked left, and the girl was thrown against the bulkhead. Her body moved without reaction, lifeless of conscious thought. He could see her chest rising and falling, but only slightly. He scanned the room, desperate for a way, desperate to do something, anything. His legs flailed, searching, feeling, hoping to find a way. The baroness gave him strength and confidence, this girl gave him longing and desire, and neither was helpful. For the first time in his life, Prisoner 00 felt truly alone.

⟩⟩

Being carried like a doll was much less comfortable than being carried like a toddler. Once again, the baroness was in the arms of an alien, executing a plan she couldn't believe herself able to execute, nor able to find a way to stop herself.

Retracing the path would be impossible. There didn't seem t be a single straight hallway anywhere in the ship, nor could she easily discern most of the doorways. The walls were covered in vegetation, and the air was hot, humid, and sour. Lady Lyndia and the baroness had discussed what she hoped would happen and a couple of possible alternatives, but to call what they had a "plan" was to embellish greatly.

It was near the destination when Lyndia suddenly took a knee and the baroness felt in control of herself. The tint of Lyndia's skin had a red hue, and the flaps of her skin were waving along her neck. She rested one elbow on her knee, brought the other hand to her head, and rubbed.

"Are you ok?" the baroness asked quietly, as she was uncertain of who was around and might be listening.

Lyndia took a couple of long, deep breaths, and then with a start, she grabbed the baroness and once again marched toward her destination. "You will not speak to me, pitiful human." A much softer voice followed, not audible but only in her head and still quite faint. "No, but we must move forward."

The baroness could feel the burning desire and perseverance coming from her captor, and it brought about sympathy. She knew the cause, but not the how of Lyndia's aliments. Had they mixed the viruses yet? She didn't remember mixing them.

The baroness felt a twist in her stomach as her worry overcame her resolve. No amount of alien company could give her the reassurance he could, and damn if he wasn't just plain wrong, a lot. Yet he had power inside him, and his power was her power— they had become one, with child.

Lyndia leaned against a wall and held the baroness at a more restful position. The words once again came across very weak and shallow, and only in her mind. "Something is wrong. My strength escapes me, and my mind pounds in pain."

The baroness forced her thoughts forward and mentally whispered as best she could. "Please, Lady Lyndia, I must save him. He means more to me than I want him to." The emotional transmissions of the stones were incredible. The baroness could actually feel this alien's sympathy and renewed determination.

Lady Lyndia stood erect once more, manhandled the baroness, and spoke aloud. "You will not speak unless spoken to. Disobedience will merit punishment." The baroness nodded in acknowledgment, and together they stepped from an innocuous hallway and into an amazingly grand command center.

$$\gg$$

The shuttle lurched left, flinging the helpless body of the baroness's girl, Terresa, and smashing her helplessly against a hard-tiled wall surface. A loud eruption of laser blast struck the shuttle, emitting sparks from various junctions. The interior filled with a moist heat, and Prisoner 00's seat burned momentarily as it flared with heat.

The shuttle banked hard right and down, tossing Terresa near Prisoner 00's feet. Still bound to his restraint, Prisoner 00 reached out his foot but only ended up smashing one of her fingers before the shuttle banked left again, sliding Terresa back across the shuttle-bay floor.

Several electronic sounds of varying pitch and intensity sped like bullets around the shuttle. His view of the cockpit window was highly obstructed, so all Prisoner 00 could see was an occasional burst of colored light in a wondrously star-filled sky. The two Xendorian captors piloted their craft in a cooperation he would have thought impossible just moments ago as the two bickered like political rivals.

Twice more, Prisoner 00 felt his seat heat up with a burning intensity as the echoes of laser gallivanted around the interior. Each maneuver that brought Terresa closer was met with an attempt to secure her body, but Prisoner 00 felt helpless. So he called in a new voice, an internal voice that seemed to project out from within him, and with that voice, he asked for help.

Prisoner 00's seat burned his ass and forearms as Lady Imric screamed and the shuttle broke off into a dizzying spin. His stomach churned, and for the first time in a long time, he was glad it had been a while since he last ate. Terresa's body smashed against each wall as the shuttle slowly spun, and she finally landed on top of Prisoner 00's body. He squeezed hard as the poor girl's body flailed haplessly about.

After several dizzying rotations, the shuttle now straightened out, and a bright-blue, magnificent piece of Earth lit up his small view out of the cockpit. The shuttle hummed and crackled in a tumult of electrical cracks and hisses, and mechanical pops and whistles. Terresa's body fell more comfortably onto Prisoner 00, and he was now able to release his firm leg grip as her head gently landed in his lap.

$$\text{\Large\reflectbox{\yen}}$$

"Commander Lymphod, this delay is unacceptable!" The voice of the commodore echoed both inside and outside the baroness's head.

The voice of the commander was barely audible, as it only came across verbally. "My intention was to achieve one hundred percent accuracy. I will expedite the evacuation immediately."

"Fleet command, where is my telsa net?" The commodore turned and paced the room. "Our one and only damn weapon against the Wilde and it isn't even deployed yet! Unacceptable."

Again the replying voice only came verbally. "Redeploying

fleet to engage. Final ship will be in place at estimated time of Wilde arrival."

The commodore barked out several more commands before he finally brought his attention to the baroness. "Ah yes, Lady Lyndia. What news have you to report?" The commodore gave her body a thorough check. "And are you feeling well?"

"Apologies, my commodore, I am fatigued, but I assure you my mission progresses well enough. This creature has revealed the existence of an object that may hold an important clue to our mystery. I request use of a shuttle craft and temporary possession of this creature for extraction of an artifact from the surface."

The commodore and Lady Lyndia exchanged a hard look, but the baroness could sense nothing from the stone. "I am afraid that I must decline your request. New science liaison Imric will be returning shortly from the surface. Meet her in the hangar bay, and inform her of your discovery." Again the two exchanged a hard look before the baroness felt her body rise and then fall as Lyndia performed the customary ceremony, turned, and left. "And, Lady Lyndia, do see that you make your way to sick bay after your meeting."

$$\gtrdot$$

It had been decades since Prisoner 00 was last on a roller coaster, and he now remembered why. Simulated motion was much different on a screen compared to the real world, and he was about to puke. Terresa's body rested unnaturally, but with a few swift maneuvers, the shuttle settled into a smoother course, not to mention Terresa herself.

He gently relaxed his legs, and the girl's body slowly

slid downward. With each unexpected shudder, he clasped hard, squeezing her to a point of discomfort, had she been conscious. Her body finally wiggled down to the point where it relaxed against his lap as her arms dangled loosely to each side.

His nerves tightened and his lip quivered as he waited, waited to see if she had survived. Her face was down and away, in his crotch, her body trapped between his legs. Was that swaying her body or the ship? Was the bouncing her breathing or the ship? Was her skin warm, or was it the ship again?

His feelings were different now. Just days before, he had no more feeling for her than lust. Now he was desperate to protect her, to raise her, to be her father. He was desperate to be the person he couldn't before. He was going to be a father, and for the first time, the truth of the matter sank in, and it was terrifying.

Memories long purposely forgotten now returned, and with no method to vent them with anger, he was forced to face them, and it hurt. It hurt so badly. There is no greater tormentor than one's own self, and to be trapped with himself was agony. The pain of past memories and future fears burst out in a river of tears he would never have admitted to creating.

The shuttle's interior volume decreased as the two pilots no longer faced immediate danger. The sound of the tears was broken as Imric spoke to fleet command and the shuttle was cleared for landing.

$$\cancel{\gg}$$

"Well that went nothing like what we had discussed. What do we do now?" The cadence of Lyndia's steps was different somehow, choppier for sure. The baroness felt herself rising and falling as her alien captor would slowly relax, become aware of it, and quickly correct, only to start the cycle over again.

There was no reply, and the labored breaths of Lyndia were becoming more and more noticeable. While it would be impossible for the baroness to self-navigate this maze of windy corridors, it definitely felt as if they were heading in the same direction as before.

The baroness waited as long as her patience would allow. "What is happening? Are we returning to the others? Is there a new plan? Tell me what you are thinking."

The intensity of the reply was startling, and heard only in her mind. "You will mind yourself, little one! I am the superior being!" The baroness froze in shock, thawed only slightly by the less chilling apology. "Forgive me, but I don't feel well. I was ordered to the shuttle bay, and that is where we are going!"

Again the baroness focused her mind so as not to slip out some stray thought about why Lyndia might be feeling so ill. Even in her weakened state, this alien could easily destroy the baroness in a physical fight, and without her guardians, she had no way to rescue him. The thought of his presence—flawed, unpredictable, and even somehow scary—still managed to fill her with hope. Where there was hope, there was power, and wherever he was, there was hope. That was somehow infuriating to her.

The hallway burst forth in a strong red light, flashing for a second and then relinquishing. Lyndia labored ever onward, faster now with the alarm. The baroness wiggled and squirmed but was unable to free herself. She attempted to protest, but Lyndia squeezed so hard that it forced the air out of her lungs.

The baroness kept her fear for the baby foremost in her mind. She wasn't positive how the stones worked, but she could feel a small release from her captor's pressure when thoughts of the baby entered her mind.

It was some meters before Lyndia finally took a knee. The baroness considered fleeing but thought, the better I know the enemy, the better my chances. Instead, she decided to use some mental pushback. "What is happening? What does that light mean?"

A nasty look crossed Lyndia's face, scolding the baroness with her predatory eyes. "Yes, it is time for some answers."

The baroness attempted to step away but was snatched up. Lyndia's eyes now pierced with the sharp points of a predator. She brought the baroness in close, the foul smell of her breath staining her nose receptors. A red hue exacerbated her viciousness. The baroness tried to escape, but it was futile, and as they neared in proximity to the center tower, Lyndia's mantle began to rotate, exposing a spongy circular tube.

The baroness prepared to scream, but it was too late. Lyndia was inside her mind.

$$\sum$$

The hangar bay located on the side of the ship now slid open as an orchestra of lights and signals guided the ship home. Terresa had yet to make a conscious move, but Prisoner 00 had seen enough death to know when there was still life. He had finally stopped crying, but his heart had been altered, changed in a way that would forever guide his future. The path forward was no more clear than his reality, but with its change of direction, he felt a sense of renewal, hope, and most importantly, longing—a longing for something more substantial, more meaningful, and more emotional. Something to replace the terrible, terrible past.

The ship slid nicely in at first, but a tense outburst from the team leader sent Imric scurrying in haste with the controls. A sudden jolt in the ship coincided with a twitch from the illness, causing Prisoner 00 intense neck pain.

Nervous and urgent chatter filled the cabin, but with all the pain, he wasn't able to hear any of it. When the collision came, it came without warning. It came silently and swiftly, so fast it seemed to be outrunning the accompanying sound. The cabin began compressing, moving without pause or hesitation, as the walls crushed everything in their path.

His body lifted and changed axis, yet still his restraints held. Had there been time, he would have prayed, but it all happened faster than a thought through the brain and slower than gridlock in the eyes. The girl's body moved too, but he was powerless to intervene, and as he felt another shift in his body, he closed his eyes.

There must have been an intense flash of movement, but it was all a blur to him as the shuttle crashed into the hangar bay. In his next conscious moment, he was still seated and alive. Now, if only he could open his eyes and find the girl.

20: The Most Powerful Force in the Universe

They came in random patterns, but for having always been in control, the baroness found it gravely troubling that she couldn't even think her own thoughts now. Her short-lived journey replayed over and over again, each memory being scanned for its emotional content. Her fall down the shaft was examined closely for Aragmell's role in the situation. The ambush in the corridor—again the alien was looking at Aragmell. While the baroness couldn't quite grasp what the alien was after, it was certainly related to her guardians.

A burning sensation, small at first, radiated in the back of her head. With each new movement the alien made in her mind, it furthered the flames. She had to fight back, had to find a way, yet she couldn't think of anything, only what the alien wanted her to remember. With fatigue and frustration, she had almost reached a daydream-like state when she saw a flash. She followed the flash with her mind's eye, and it came again, only this time there was more than a flash—it was an image. The baroness pursued the image, and now she was able to get a good look at it.

It was the commodore, and the grimace on his face was menacing. She slipped back into her own memory, just a hint at first, but the more she focused, the more it came. Pulse after pulse, each new round brought slightly more clarity until, at last, the terror of the newness overcame her. Yet the memories she was experiencing did not match her own. The baroness had no such fear of the commodore in this way, nor had she ever seen such a look on his face. The image moved only a quiver, like pictures, at first. The more she focused, the easier it became, and soon the images were a movie.

The commodore approached a kneeling Xendorian. It was someone special, someone loved, and the baroness could feel the emotional attachment. The baroness's heart beat faster, and terror gripped her deep inside as if she knew what was about to happen. The kneeling Xendorian looked up, its face longing, remorseful, and loving. The commodore slowly moved behind the Xendorian, lightly grabbed her shoulder, and slid his hand down toward the center. Then, with a quick thrust, he killed the kneeling Xendorian.

The connection was lost, but the feeling of loss was over-whelming. A strong lurch by the ship forced Lyndia to release the baroness as she braced herself against the wall. Red lights once again flooded the hallway. The baroness, still overcome by the emotion of another's memory, paused her flight. Was she just attacked? She wanted to run but had no idea where to go.

It took her a few seconds, but Lyndia accessed a panel on a wall, again something that would have been totally invisible to the baroness. "That, was that the truth?"

Lyndia turned from the panel and studied the baroness. "The truth is that the commodore is a very dangerous individual with great skill, great ambition, and no morals. That is why we are going to the hangar bay as ordered. As for that?" Lyndia motioned toward the ceiling. "That was a collision in the hangar bay. No doubt caused by the efforts of your escaped friends."

Feeling that she was neither friend nor foe, the baroness was once again being carried by Lyndia, at amazing speed, around a few corners. She saw some Xendorians working feverishly to extinguish flames, while a herd of small, black robots stampeded past them and into the hangar deck.

$$\gg$$

It was fear that kept Prisoner 00's eyes closed. Physical pain was easy, for his body's signals were easy to ignore. His heart's aches, however, could only be expressed in overwhelming emotions that either erupted out in violence or stained his soul with their truths. He couldn't bear to lose her again. She was so small, so innocent, and so precious, and he had failed her. No, it was too much to face losing her again.

Yet even if it was tiny, there was a chance she was still alive, and if she was still alive, she would need him. With his eyes closed, both were true: she was still alive, and she did need him—and she was already dead, lying there waiting to expose his overt failings. To open them would be to face a possible truth that he had failed, again.

He grasped for control but found none. His emotional wall struggled to hold back the tears, and as he opened his eyes, he couldn't see past them or the memories. His vision cleared slowly, each blink bringing that horrible reality back to truth, and when he finally caught a clear sight, he knew what had happened.

He tried to lash out in anger, and he tried to vent the pain, but there was nowhere for it to go. So he turned his head, unable to look upon his failings anymore.

His tears came so ferociously that they burned, and as he

turned away, no longer able to accept the truth, he saw her—no, them. He saw them, and without intent, without effort, he had repeated the same set of missteps. She was beautiful, magical, and in trouble, and he had to face the truth that she was doomed and it was his fault. How could he protect her? The baroness and her child—he couldn't do it, ever. Now, as he looked at the girl, he realized that he would be forced to face his failure, not once but thrice more. Oh, what cruel fate would force a man to fail those most important to him, over and over again?

"Death, give me death, you cruel bastard. I can take no more." He shouted in a voice not verbal, not internal. Had there been a way, he surely would have killed himself.

𝄞

The alien put the baroness down as she and the other Xendorians rushed to the aid of the pilots. The baroness ran to Prisoner 00's side, his head frantically shaking no, tears pouring like rain from his eyes, his face swollen and red. This misery was on a deep level. All those times she had gazed into his eyes, she knew it was there, but she had no idea how intense it was for him.

Her tears formed in sympathy as he ached. His body twitched, his eyes faded, and his heart broke. Another human body lay several feet to his side, and as the baroness neared him, she recognized the mangled corpse as Terresa. Terresa had been one of his new favorites, but the emotional impact she was having on him hurt her.

Fear crept into her heart. Would he be faithful? Could he love another? Could he really be who she needed him to be? The closer she got to him, the more she wanted to retreat. The new truth of her life was too much. She needed him to be strong, not like this crying fool. Anger burned inside her, frustration set in, and her feet stomped. How could he? He was supposed to be hers, and hers alone. How dare he give his heart to another? How dare he?

The baroness came forth in a rage, but as her hands reached for his throat and his tears washed over her hands, her heart softened. She raised her hands, now placing them on each side of his face. He twisted and squirmed, thrashing in agony, but she had no fear, no more anger, and as her hands made contact with his skin, she could feel the pattern of his breathing change, but the panic remained.

What had she done? A new emotion crept into her heart: guilt. She didn't ask him if he wanted to be a father; she simply chose him. Damn it! Why did she have to choose him? Why did she have to get pregnant? Why did she have to do any of this? It was all her fault. It was all on her, and now that she realized it, it hurt her too.

She sat on his lap and slowly brought his head under her control. As she made eye contact, she saw the sorrow, the pain. It wasn't Terresa—it was something more personal, and she could feel it, even if she didn't know what it was. She peered into his eyes, connecting with his soul, and she said the only thing she wanted to hear. "You are forgiven."

$$\sum$$

Rage, rage had always been the answer. Now that it was taken away, other emotions were proving overwhelmingly painful. Each new emotion, each new fear, and each new realization hit Prisoner 00 harder than any bar drunk, jock, or even alien ever could have. Never before had he wished, begged, or prayed to be freed of his prison with such intensity.

What did she say? The words came out jumbled in tears. "What did you say?"

Again she looked at him, tears coming down from her own eyes. "You are forgiven."

The words shook him. They entered his mind but held no meaning. They entered his heart, and still they found no meaning. But when they entered his soul, his prison evaporated. The pain of failures past came again, but differently. He had failed, he was dead, and while the pain was there, it had been transformed— transformed into something that gave new life to his soul, his heart, and his mind. He was forgiven.

PART 3

21: Girl Time

For several long, heart-breaking outbursts of sobs, Sasha stood there holding her new friend. A troubled and varied array of emotions went through her mind. Even though she knew it not to be true, Sasha blamed herself. She was the one who had suggested getting drunk, she was the one who fought back, and she was the one to blame.

Emilia pulled back, never really having engaged Sasha in an embrace, and let loose several angry kicks into a nearby couch. "Stupid fucking boys, why do they have to ruin everything? Why? Why? Why? Can't there be just one good man in this world? It's always, 'touch this,' 'let me touch that.' Am I nothing more than a vagina?" Emilia released another volley of kicks into the couch before breaking down into tears.

Emilia's comments confused Sasha. Sasha wanted to blame the individuals, including herself, not the sex. To Sasha, boys had always just been around, especially Daddy. She couldn't imme-diately bring up any negative memories of boys. In fact, she had learned many things from boys. After some thought, though, Sasha also realized that she had never had any form of sexual encounter with a boy before, nor had she any desire.

The stream of tears rushing down Emilia's face provoked a strong reaction in Sasha, and a feeling of anger rose again. Sasha wanted to rage—against the perpetrators, against Emilia's tears, and against herself for failing. Normally this level of anger would have provoked an intense round of fog, but things were different around Emilia. She felt more in control, more responsible, and more important. The continued sight of her friend's tears quickly vanquished her rage, turning it into something more human. "Emilia, I can protect you. I can keep you safe. I can love you."

The regret came instantly as that last set of words came out. She had overplayed her hand, exposed more of herself than she should have, and now someone she was starting to care about—someone who was struggling, someone who was afraid and confused—had more put on her.

"Love, love, what the hell do you know about love? There is no fucking love in this world, just debauchery and lust. Love is a fairy tale used to deceive little girls into thinking they have a chance. Consider yourself lucky you're just a weapon. There is no worse fate than being a woman."

The viciousness of the remarks pained Sasha, and no instant regret on Emilia's part would undo the hurt. Sasha stepped back. She had opened herself up more than she had intended, and now her worst fears had come to fruition. She calmed herself, making sure to control any signs of the fog, but she had lost all chemistry with Emilia. Sasha felt her emotional wall rising. She wanted to run. She wanted to take back the words. She wanted to die.

Sasha was wrong. Emilia, being more empathic than other people in Sasha's life, picked up on her rising panic and—with two simple words—released all the tension like a breaking dam. Two words that undid all the hurt, followed by two words that strengthened their chemistry, refreshed Sasha's heart and brought two strangers closer together. "I'm sorry. Thank you."

↩

"Oh, man, I'm high, too high for driving. Holy crap, has it been that long since I last . . ." Considering the car was empty, Captain Drexter was speaking to himself, yet it came across as more of a coaching up. "Concentrate, concentrate, look for an opening, focus on the objective . . . there." The captain had managed to park his vehicle. His head twirled around, and for a few seconds, he enjoyed the last of his high. However, his time was limited, and he needed to come down. He surveyed the surrounding streets, a liquor store, and a couple empty storefronts. Down the street, he saw a coffee shop. Enticed by the prospects of both caffeine and a snack, he double-timed it, making sure to lock the vehicle behind him.

Returning with supplies in hand, he felt reassured that he could now drive safely, and thanks to the preparation work ahead of time, his uniform and gear were inspection ready. The untimely discovery that his keys were not in any of his pockets sent a sudden body-freezing jolt throughout his body. His eyes moved slowly, and his heart sank, for there was nothing worse than missing a military obligation by getting high and locked out of a vehicle.

↩

Sasha felt her heart race. In one night, she had expended more emotional energy than she had in her entire previous life. She no longer wondered why Father had denied her this part of the human experience. It was exhausting. Every phase, every look, every word Emilia made consumed her full concentration and analysis. Yet for all its enormous effort, she craved more, not only more quantity but more intensity too.

Emilia approached and gently hugged Sasha. "I already feel closer to you than some kids I spent an entire year with, after school." A slow tingle crept down Sasha's back, and her body froze. A range of emotions, hormones, and thoughts pulled her in a million directions at once. Sasha restricted the words before they came out and ended up silently mouthing them: "I love you."

Emilia's head tilted as she asked, "What?"

Sasha's heart pounded as she scrambled for a cover, unaware of what she'd done. Again Emilia had brought her to the point of extreme exertion. "I . . . would . . . love . . . to watch a movie with you, is all that I was going to say. I must admit, I am feeling a little tired all of a sudden."

↩

For a brief moment, just until the longer-term consequences could sink in, Drexter wanted to know his near future. Lacking that ability, however, he cursed himself and pulled up wildly on each of the door handles. He looked around. The liquor store had some loose papers on the ground, but nothing useful. Tracing along the empty storefront, he found half a wire, maybe part of a coat hanger. Looking back at the vehicle, he saw a small crack in the passenger window—not big enough to get a finger through, but maybe the wire.

His pulse quickened. He was already pushing it, regarding the time. Sure it was most likely some stupid parade, inspection, or other protocol BS, but he was still more than a couple years away from survivable retirement. A poor showing today might make those years rather unfulfilling. He grabbed for his phone, wanting to locate the nearest locksmith, but was greatly disappointed to realize it was also still in the vehicle.

Desperate, he bent the wire to make a hook and placed it around the window. At first he pulled down, hoping not to break it. It wedged a bit but popped back up when his pressure decreased. He tried again but stuck his wallet in the gap as he pulled down. It lodged in place, so he looked for something bigger and found a rock. He now pulled down on the window and attempted to wedge the rock inside.

A siren blared, startled the major, and rattled his wallet enough to drop it into the vehicle.

His desired mind clearing from the caffeine—and adrenaline, now that two uniformed police officers were aiming weapons at him—had yet to materialize. He froze and his jaw dropped a little, yet no words came out as a midforties officer with a graying mustache approached. "Just what in the hell do you think you're doing?"

There was a long pause, as his brain refused to process the encounter, on the grounds of its unfathomable nature. "All right, rookie, cuff him and search him. I'll keep an eye on him and call it in."

His thoughts ran like a herd past a predator, avoiding capture. His body offered no resistance as an early-twenties Hispanic man advanced, wide-eyed and visibly nervous. The new officer spoke with a mild quiver in his voice. "Any sharp needles, scissors, or blades in any of your pockets?"

The older cop stopped speaking into the radio and came

back. "What, isn't this where you're going to tell us that this is really your car and you just accidently happened to lock your keys in the car?"

His mind searched, but down every path was impending doom. To claim ownership of the car was to admit ownership of the marijuana inside—a potential court-martial, retirement-stealing type of offense, especially for an officer. He could flee, but he was already being handcuffed. Taking a misdemeanor charge meant the chance of vehicle confiscation and eventual discovery, or not.

The younger officer finished handcuffing the major, looked into the vehicle, and weakly spoke. "Eh, Chip, there are keys in the vehicle."

Officer Chip looked annoyed. "Listen, rookie, HQ wants us on post, like, now. Throw him in the back of the car, bag the rock and hanger, take some pictures, and get it done now!"

It was a move based on pure desperation rather than conscious thought, and it was the first time Captain Drexter had ever resorted to something he personally detested—and it would become his second regret of the day. "Discrimination, discrimination!"

Bringing his hand to his forehead, Officer Chip yelled, "Get him in the damn car, rookie!"

While it fell short of fleeing, the captain was in a state of flight as the adrenaline continued to push out the same word, over and over. The junior officer continued to lead his prisoner, but he did so with an underwhelming amount of force, allowing the captain several additional moments outside the car—at least until a sharp pain stabbed his side and brought him to his knees, knocking the junior officer back.

A powerful hand grabbed him by the shoulder and tossed him into the back of the vehicle. His entire body hurt, and his head pounded, but he still heard Officer Chip's lecture through the windows.

"When I say put the perp in the back of the fucking vehicle, I mean put the fucking perp in the back of the goddamn vehicle! I don't mean let him cause a scene. If you want to survive a career out here, kid, you need to grow up real fast."

The young officer shook his wrist as the Taser automatically disengaged itself. He uttered a few words of defense, but the senior officer started up again.

"Do you have any idea how much more fucking paperwork you just caused me? Use your damn head. You know of any military installations around here? You know what the hell is around here? Military surplus. Look at those fuckin' eyes. This dude is so cracked out he can barely even speak. So, rookie, you tell me what's more likely—that a military officer in the middle of bum town accidently locked his keys in the car or that some hobo ripped off surplus, saw a wallet on a car seat in front of a liquor store, and tried to steal it. Now get him secured, get this evidence bagged, and let's get on our damn way."

The captain sat stewing in his own thoughts. He silently cursed "the man," ignoring the fact that some might even consider him "the man." He cursed himself, the police, and the circumstances, but surprisingly he didn't curse the marijuana. Every time he could gather a coherent string of thoughts, they were lost or garbled before they formed on his lips, keeping him a fidgety mess.

This weed seemed particularly strong, and he tried to think back to where he had acquired this batch. Again his thoughts were interrupted as they arrived at the station.

The younger of the two officers led the captain through a maze of obligatory requirements, including pictures and fingerprints. The young man was still on his first week of actual street duty, and his newness, eagerness, and interest in what most officers would consider mundane was quite refreshing. It crossed the captain's mind to try reasoning with the young man, but he figured it was well past the point of no return. In the end, he went into a holding cell with roughly ten others to await his phone call, still unsure about whom to call.

22: Prisoner Lift

The hours passed by, but no one came to give him his phone call. No one came to check on, process, or even transfer a prisoner, and now Captain Drexter was becoming nervous. He thought back to what the senior officer had said during the arrest: "HQ wants us on post, like, now." The thought that his capture had been due to a simple lack of situational awareness was most distressing.

No one had called him in, and no one had ambushed him. He had simply forgotten to look around. Now he lay prisoner, AWOL, surrounded by a few lowlives—drug fiends, by the look of them, a pimp, and an angry man with his head in his hands. A large group of angry men with matching tattoos dominated the cell to one side of them, while a separate group of large, tattooed men were housed in the opposite cell.

The ever-looming nature of his AWOL status now demanded that his first call be to his CO. The base would send out an enlisted MP with a bucketload of paperwork that he and the local sheriff would have to work out together. Then he would be transferred, in handcuffs, back to base, where he would be put in the stockade until a military judge could finally get around to looking at the case and figuring shit out.

Instinctively, he worried less about the procedural consequences than the possible consequences of his absence from Sasha. Never before had he been away for more than a day, and even that was a planned exercise for Sasha, and his last time with a woman. Emilia was a good girl, empathic, smart, and military aware. If there was a single other person suited to help Sasha, he hoped she was the one.

As the day passed, the only person to come through the holding area was a cafeteria worker, who had distributed slightly warm hot dogs in plain buns. Captain Drexter felt sorry for the poor man as he was riddled with a verbal onslaught. The delay and lack of attention had certainly riled up several of the inmates. One man even threw the hot dog back through the bars at the poor fellow.

Captain Drexter had come to the front of the cell and thanked the man as he received his hot dog. To his surprise, the man handed him a second one. Initially believing it to be some kind of gratitude, he was disappointed when the man gestured toward the inmate sitting motionless with his head in his hands.

↩

Something new was happening. It was the fog, but different. This fog had a warm embrace, not like before. Sasha's heart fluttered. Billowy pink and red clouds filled the room. A gentle mist of sweat formed on her skin. Before, the fog had always acted as a clarifying agent, but this was different.

Emilia's hand now lay limply on Sasha's thigh, their arms pressing with ever-increasing tension and rising warmth. An amazing burst of heat and energy rushed through Sasha as Emilia's head fell against her shoulder. The beauty of the clouds overwhelmed her as they pulsed with the caress of Emilia's hair against her back and shoulder. The heat from Emilia's breath blinded and excited her as wave after glorious wave swept across her neck. Lost in a velvety pillow, Sasha's body stilled, paralyzed by excitement. Flooded by hormones, her body exploded with convulsions.

The jostle startled Emilia enough to bring her out of her near sleep. Emilia rubbed her eyes, said good night, and left Sasha a raging mess of energy and emotions as she collapsed where she sat.

↤↦

Captain Drexter was feeling less sympathy toward the food worker, and the hairs on the back of his neck rose with anxiousness. The man he was supposed to share the food with had barely moved all day. The midtwenties man just sat there with his face in his hands. He had a shaved head and wore a slightly torn, plain white shirt and long, baggy shorts.

He could feel the change in his body as his thoughts became more aggressive. Why in the hell did he give the black man food for the white racist? Were they trying to play some sort of game with me? I should just eat the damn bastard's food. He is just a fucking prisoner, after all.

His pulse was galloping now. Scenario after scenario of violence ran through his mind.

As he prepared to approach the distressed prisoner, he took a deep breath and looked down, only to notice that he had squeezed one of the hot dogs so tightly that it actually split in two. The physical acknowledgment of his mental state had triggered something in his brain, a release of some sort. The anger and rage were militarily installed. This was something self-learned.

He took another deep breath and, with clarity, realized that his first step had been very powerful and forceful as a man with a pre-intent mission. Sasha had again entered his mind, and now he understood what change had occurred. He was no longer just an officer. He had become a father.

Nearing the compressed man, he stood taller, loosened to a simply stern look, and spoke loudly, so as not to come across as weak. "Hey, buddy, here is your dog." The man remained motionless. Instead of reevaluating, he tried again. "Hey, man, here is your dinner."

This time, the man reacted swiftly and angrily, slapping one of the hot dogs out of his hand and onto the floor, and he began an angry rant. "Do I look like I want a fucking hot dog, bro! Do you think a fucking hot dog is going to fucking help me, man! Some of us don't fucking need a goddamn hot dog." The man took several aggressive steps forward, close to the captain's face.

His heart drummed with a mighty beat, and his body jumped into fight mode, but he fought it off. Images of himself coaching Sasha down and out of the fog ran through his mind. He refocused his body's surge of energy and brought it back down. He had seen this type of anger before in mess halls and dormitories, and often at home. Throughout most of his life, the man in front of him would have registered as nothing but an immediate threat, but now he was different. "I think you are still worthy of this hot dog. I heard somewhere that all can be forgiven."

The words sounded foreign, even to him, but the result was unmistakable. The man paused as his brain reprocessed the unexpected encounter. He thought the man was going to strike him, but instead, he looked down at the dog, which had been squished into nearly two pieces now. The prisoner acted unsure of himself and then took out the dog part, put it in his mouth, and returned to his former position.

←

The haze, as Sasha was now labeling it, was slow to dissipate. Its warm energy still pulsed through her body, moving like waves across, down, and through her body. The fog reached out, searching for the object of its origin, its desire, and its maker. Emilia had gone, taking with her its purpose but not its energy.

Sasha's hands moved and traced with the waves, but with each outstretch, the fog lost some thickness, and each wave weakened in intensity. A feeling of frustration started to grow, consuming the energy and fog as nourishment.

Soon Sasha found herself lying on her back, knees up, alone in the middle of the floor. An impulse to visit Emilia's room was quickly brushed aside, but Sasha was now far away from sleep, alone, and restless. With her last focused thought of the night, Sasha thanked God there was still plenty of beer.

←

Well that could have gone worse, much worse, Drexter thought to himself. Only now that the incident had ended did he even consider not giving the man his dinner and eating it himself. Perhaps even that was the food man's intention; he was another brother, after all. If the man had wanted a hot dog, he would have at least gotten up for it, as there wasn't anyone in his way. The more he thought about it, the more he regretted his generosity.

Why should he, a man who had spent a lifetime of service, now when he was facing the biggest crisis of his life, not be the one to have two damn hot dogs?

Tossing and turning, he felt his anger slowly rising higher and higher as his thoughts circled and circled. Then, finally, as he neared his boiling point, the lights dimmed and two jailers entered. It was anything but exciting and did nothing to progress the situation, nor was it even amusing, but it was a distraction enough to break the cycle of his thoughts, allowing them now to turn back to Sasha. His blood cooled, but now his stomach churned as he wondered how the hell he was going to explain this one to her.

↩

The world felt like it was spinning. The pounding of her head, the churning of her stomach, and now the bouncing of her couch proved all too much, and Sasha rolled onto her stomach, shifted her head, and puked. She opened her eyes, saw a planter fall off a side table, and closed them again. "Oh, this is awful. I hate this," she moaned. The world spun and spun, and with some more dry heaving, Sasha vowed, "Lord, I'm never going to drink again."

↩

Holy hell, did he ever need a hit right now. By now, the captain was certain that the cell was only supposed to be a temporary staging area, but whatever the hell was going on, it now made his overnight very restless, cold, and uncomfortable. He could just imagine—almost to the point of making it true—that green, stinky smoke tumbling through his lungs, working its way higher and higher, till at last it reached the brain, allowing the body to finally exhale and relax.

His problems were immense and growing more daunting with every passing AWOL moment, with every moment away from Sasha, and with every moment without his old friend. Obviously he had faced many uncomfortable nights in the field, but it had been some years since his last overnight field event. The realization of his situation only amplified his desire for a smoke.

He often took inventory of the other cellmates, and the drug fiends were starting to make him nervous. A high fellow would be easy to manage, while a fellow in withdrawals was a much more worrisome problem. The man involved with the hot dogs still lay motionless with his head in his hands, while each of the adjoining cells appeared to be operating under an organized hierarchy, with men rotating positions and sleep times.

With his final assessment of his current situation, Captain Drexter closed his eyes and spent his last night on Earth tossing and turning over matters that would soon seem absolutely trivial.

23: The Morning

As if the night didn't prove difficult enough to sleep, the morning proved impossible. He wasn't sure quite how long he had actually managed to sleep, but there was now a commotion occurring in the neighboring cell, and as he scanned the room, he found a flurry of activity in his own cell as well.

Several of the inmates in the adjoining cell had gathered around an average-sized man wearing a black T-shirt and jeans, rather nondescript looking. The man had his hands around some tools, which were deep inside the lock. An occasional stir of excitement would build as those close enough to observe coalesced to a uniformity of breathing that built and burst with every failed attempt.

Back in his own cell, a more immediate situation was building. One of the drug fiends was really starting to have problems and was pacing aggressively, twitching, and cursing under his breath. Most of Drexter's experience had been with guys out in the field going through the DT, and that was difficult enough to manage with a whole platoon at his disposal. Alone, or at least alone on his own side, he thought through various fight scenarios.

His own fatigue would be a problem. He was no hand-to-hand warrior, and he wasn't even a combat veteran. For now, he felt it best to stay off the drug fiend's radar, and the best way to do that was to simply lie still and hope he was written off.

It was a good plan, until needing to pee changed the scenario.

He moved cautiously, only when the fiend was facing away. It was a slow process, and he had already waited a while, so the urge to go was growing stronger. He thought he was in the clear as he stood before the urinal, but a raspy, tweaked voice came at him like bullets. "Hey, man, hey, man, hey, hey, whatcha got, whatcha got, whatcha want, whatcha got, whatcha got?"

Greatly hoping to avoid a physical confrontation, Captain Drexter responded with a firm voice. "I don't have anything you want or need, now go."

It wasn't the response he was hoping for, but the fiend came no closer. "So you gots something. Whatcha got? You gots something. Whatcha wants? Whats ya got?"

The captain hesitated, as the adrenaline had overridden the urge to urinate, and ran through a few options before deciding on a calculated show of force, followed by a stern lecture. He reached out, grabbed the collar of the fiend's shirt, twisted it, and brought him closer. "See the uniform?" He pushed the man back and did his best impression of the fiend. "Man, I'm a clean guy, man. I ain't got nothin', man, ain't got nothin', ain't got nothin'. Now scram!"

With a curse, the fiend walked away, toward the other end of the cell, muttering under his breath the whole way. Relieved to have solved that problem, if only temporarily, Drexter moved back to the urinal. The powerful urgency returned, and he unzipped, only to open his eyes and discover, in the adjoining cell, a massive, bald white man who was staring directly at him. "Do you mind?"

To his horror, the man said, "I enjoy watching."

The urge to pee suddenly disappeared again. Luckily, for the moment at least, the group of prisoners broke out in an eruption of cheers as their cell door popped open. Freedom lured away his unwelcome audience, so Captain Drexter was finally able to relieve himself.

Given the coordination and expedience with which the men moved, it was undoubtedly a leader-led effort. One of the largest men, a burly wheelbarrow of a man with a long, slightly gray beard, barked occasional commands. Drexter was familiar with chains of command, and leadership in general, so it was clear as day that this burly fellow neither carried himself nor acted like a leader.

The prisoners had barricaded the door to the front of the station with a large assortment of food carts, chairs, benches, and a gurney flipped upside down. Several of the men tried to fashion weapons out of loose cart handles and chair legs. One of the men started toward their cell but was waved off and signaled elsewhere.

Captain Drexter, now relieved and no longer attracting the fiends, who were desperately seeking the attention of anyone on the outside, could now focus on the strange man sitting with his head in his hands. Had he really not moved all night? This man had a noticeable intensity about him, so much so that not one of the fiends had even approached him. The lack of acknowledgment from the others gave the strong impression of a man facing his own internal prison.

The simple fact that the prisoners had gone unattended for

so long raised the hairs on the back of his neck. These men had broken free, bringing no alarms, no guards, and no reaction at all from the authorities—and that smelled like serious trouble.

The action broke out shortly after a loud whistle rang throughout the room. There was no explosion, no fire, and no sound, but an immense wave of air knocked him on his ass. It was several seconds again before he could even breathe, and the air smelled foul and bitter, but it was joyous on intake.

He lay in front of the bench where he had previously sat. He crawled up, and his hand grabbed hold of a leg, but instead of reacting to his touch, it stayed motionless. One of the fiends was contorted in the cell, his neck crunched at a strange angle against the bars. The second fiend lay wrenching in pain as his arm bent in the wrong direction.

It took a while before he was able to get up again. A loud screeching sound stirred the crowd until it grew into a frenzy when somebody yelled, "Incoming!" and bodies desperately took for cover.

Captain Drexter hid under a bench, but the steadiness of the whistle told him it wasn't incoming. But he sensed an opportunity. "Hey, man, you gotta let us out. If they're bombing us, I can help."

The wheelbarrow of a man coughed several times. "Who the fuck are you?"

"OED, ordinance officer, and that sound is a bunker-buster screw head drilling its way through the wall right now." He had no idea what he was saying, but the allure of freedom was growing. Perhaps the officers hadn't even filed the paperwork and this whole thing could just go away. He could explain his absences somehow.

"Officer, you say, how you end up here?" The man stood like a giant outside the gate.

The first image that came to mind was Emilia. "I didn't ask her age." The man let out a roaring laugh suited to his barrel of a stature.

↩

The smell was awful, and now the noise was unbearable. Sasha opened her eyes but slammed them shut again after what she saw. The room was a disaster of a mess. The floor beside the couch, near her face and on her clothes, was drenched in puke. The smell brought on dry heaves, but her stomach was now empty. She dry heaved as the effort of sitting upright nauseated her.

The loud humming pounded back and forth inside her skull. She couldn't trace its origin, nor could she escape its effects. An agitated and hungover Emilia entered the room with a screech. "What the fuck are you doing? That noise is awful."

Sasha was in no mood to take the blame for this torture, especially after all the frustration Emilia had caused last night. "I was sleeping. You set the goddamn alarm off."

"Well turn it the fuck off, already!"

"You turn it the fuck off, already!"

Emilia covered her ears and moved aggressively but slipped on a puddle of puke and landed on her back. The cold, wet, smelly shock distorted her face to a look of horror.

Initially Sasha felt an impulse to lash out at Emilia, but seeing her in obvious discomfort softened her baseline feeling.

Emilia looked at her hands, processed what exactly the substance was, and—with a gut-wrenching blow to Sasha—asked, "What did you do?"

It was by far the worst Sasha had ever physically felt, but now Emilia made it the worst she had ever emotionally felt too. And once again, Sasha swore to the Lord that she would never drink again.

The wheelbarrow of a man finished his laugh without haste, apparently not bothered by the deafening pitch outside. He then called for the small, nondescript man who had worked the lock earlier to come over. The man knelt beside the door and started working on the lock.

Captain Drexter felt something change in his stomach, which he finally recognized as hope. Lacking any physical way to manifest this new feeling, he used the only power he could think of: he prayed.

A whisper into the wheelbarrow man's ear dashed Drexter's hopes and prayers. "Sorry, T, can't be riskin' psycho there getting out. Soldier boy and his little girlfriends will just have to figure it out themselves. Besides, what good is knowledge of weapons you don't have?" Then the wheelbarrow man turned around and resumed issuing fortification orders.

The pitch and intensity of the noise varied and changed, but nothing ever came. At one point, the group actually took cover, only to the have the noise change into a hum. The group took turns hunting through the room, exploring, destroying, pulling, and prodding, yet they never managed to find a way out. It was as the group began discussions of an assault that the silence came.

↩

Tears came first, but it all came. Emilia, now sitting in puke drowned in a terrible pitched noise, spit up the remains of her stomach. Then she ran out of the room and back toward the bedroom.

Sasha, now frantic with guilt and embarrassment, worked feverishly to clean, but she found it hard to see clearly behind the tears. She had never felt worse, physically or emotionally, and the fog from the night before seemed like a dream more than an actuality.

The tears eventually subsided, and Sasha could hear the water running in the bathroom as Emilia washed up. The endless scenarios of what to do or what to say were maddening, and Sasha almost wished none of this had ever happened.

It wasn't the first time she had felt this way around Emilia, and there was salvation from the last, in the form of hope. Sasha's head pounded as she replayed the stories, actions, and feelings about Emilia. There was something about her that gave Emilia the gift to make things right. So Sasha kept hope, tried to keep the tears back, and tried with conscious effort not to overthink scenario after endless scenario.

Even since before the gruesome party incident that canceled the Sasha program, she had a good stomach for gross-out stuff, and now while cleaning up this puke, she was thankful for it. Now if only Emilia would clean up the mess between them.

↩

The timing of the silence of course brought about a slew of theories as to the authorities' actions, all of which were to be proven wrong, as the sound of rushing water slowly built, rising with a commensurate, if yet unseen, force until it finally drowned out all other noise. The noise crescendoed with an impact against the wall that shook the building with a single mighty jolt and knocked Captain Drexter back off his bench.

While he was far away from an ordinance officer, he had never seen anything in the military that could emulate that first nonexplosion explosion. Nor had he seen any military equipment that could bring to bear so much rushing water so as to nearly topple a building.

For one guiltless second, he actually hoped for a natural disaster and a way to skirt all this. It was short lived, as the worry over Sasha again took hold, and the thought of her loose in a natural disaster zone could be disaster piled on disaster—or worse yet, she could be hurt. Once again, the captain's stomach twisted.

The loud, urgent shouts of some of the freed men drew his attention, as water had started rushing into the room from, of all the worst places, the drainage pipes. He prayed to God that the toilet wasn't backing up sewage water, and his nose told him otherwise, so he and the fiend jumped onto the bench.

Astonishingly, the angry man still trapped in the cell with him still hadn't budged, other than to make minor adjustments. His feet now soaked in slightly foul water, still floater-free as far as the captain could see.

Two of the freed men now turned the gurney right side up and filled it with things older children might think would help it float, while the others mostly climbed. The wheelbarrow man, the nondescript lock picker named "T," and a third man of solid build, with short brown hair, a long nose, and the neck of a man you wouldn't want to face in a fight—but not necessarily someone you would need to cross the street for either—worked diligently, attempting to stop the inflow of water.

↩

With all the emotion Sasha was putting into her cleaning, she nearly forgot about the noise, at least until it started to change pitch. When a noticeable vibration shook the floor, the hair on the back of her neck rose, until the pounding of the hangover regained its hold.

The room went silent, except for Emilia's running water, which quit shortly thereafter. The taste in Sasha's mouth took her to the kitchen in search of some water, but the faucet only spit out air, followed by nothing. Confused and thirsty, she took the cup to the half bath, where that faucet failed as well. However, she could now hear water dripping from somewhere.

The noise led her back toward the elevator shaft, where water was leaking out from under the door. Another leak sprang from the ceiling vent, and then another and another. Soon the intensity of the drips increased. Sasha moved toward the bathroom Emilia occupied and shouted through the door. "Do you have water in there?"

"No, and you're lucky I was already done shampooing. What did you do, anyway? How did you make that alarm stop?"

Sasha was nervous, tired, and now scared. "I didn't do anything, but I do think we have a problem."

"Yeah, I think the steam built up in here, because there is water dripping from the vent. When is your dad getting back, anyway? Shouldn't he have called or something by now?"

As if Emilia's tone alone wasn't annoying enough, now she had given Sasha something else to worry about. "No, it's happening out here too, and from the elevator. We are underground, right, on an island? Do you think we should worry?"

"I think you should worry about that mess you made."

"What is up your butt this morning, Emilia?" She had heard Father use that expression once. Now she kinda reveled in the ability to use it herself.

The door opened, and a crying Emilia revealed herself. "I puked too. It's in the bedroom. I'm so sorry. I just can't go in there." With her face covered in tears, Emilia reached out and hugged Sasha.

The unmistakably human quality of Emilia's reaction softened Sasha's attitude. "Of course, I will take care of it."

24: Shei Yao Yi Bei Shui?

It was a pattern and an unmistakable piece of evidence
that disclaimed a natural phenomenon, but Captain Drexter was
convinced it wasn't the authorities either. The pitching, screaming
sound that seemed to emanate from everywhere returned, with a
decrease in the water flow. The second wave impacted against the
building with a slightly decreased intensity, still strong enough to
shake the foundation, but the bricks of the wall didn't move this
time.

He searched his mind, but only the most improbable
of scenarios fit the available evidence. The authorities, jailers
included, must have been outmanned in handling whatever the
hell was going on out there. He watched the freed prisoners work,
desperately trying to avoid the water, either by floating on it or by
comically trying to stop it. Yet as a distraction, it proved insufficient. The knot in his stomach grew, and so did his time away from
Sasha. He even remembered jokingly praying to God for it to be an
alien invasion—at least then Sasha could make use of herself.

Each new wave brought with it a new surge of water, and
it now almost reached knee high and the top of his bench. As it
became inevitable that he could have to face the filth, Captain
Drexter jumped in and gently tapped the solitary man on the
shoulder. "Join us on the bench, no need to punish yourself like

that, man."

"Mind your own fucking self, dude. What you know of punishment? You think I'm worried about drowning in some shit water? Hell, that's fucking paradise compared to what I've got waitin'. So take your goddamn hands off me, and go play hero some-the-fuck elsewhere."

The comments that only a seemingly short time ago would have sent him into a fury now only brought pity and sorrow to Captain Drexter. "Well I will keep a spot open for you if you'd like to join us."

↩

This must be what it's like being a parent, Sasha thought to herself. Only for Emilia would Sasha willingly and even a tiny bit joyfully clean up this mess. Sasha again liked the way she felt around Emilia—currently, useful and needed.

The flow of water as it steadily dripped from every overhead access made for an easy cleanup along the cement flooring. However, it was starting to back up and puddle along the drains, and that made Sasha very nervous.

After changing clothes, Emilia returned. "What do you think we should do?"

The sight of Emilia's new outfit—only a tank top and short shorts—completely distracted Sasha from her train of thought, causing her to stare stupidly until Emilia asked the question again.

Sasha shook her head slightly. "Should we call someone? My dad?"

Now that Emilia had showered, her mood seemed better, but not quite like the sweet girl from before. "Yes, yes, he at least could contact someone for repairs. That way we won't have to talk to that fucking rapist up there!"

Sasha went into the kitchen, where standing water was now accumulating, to use the phone, but there was no dial tone. "Shit, now what?" She looked at the elevator, slowly walked in front of it, and looked at Emilia. "Don't worry, I kicked their asses once. I can do it again, and they know that now."

Sasha put her hand on Emilia's shoulder and squeezed gently with her palm. Emilia placed her hand on top of Sasha's and smiled. "I know." The two girls looked at the elevator, and then each other, and held their breath. Then Emilia pushed the call button.

↩

This was getting ridiculous. Trapped with victims and the scum of the earth, Drexter was going to die. A lifetime of service—to society, the future, and Sasha—but at the end, he was going to drown an AWOL officer while his daughter was alone in chaos. Captain Drexter had never felt more like a failure.

The freed prisoners had built some scaffolding, and T was now busy at work on an upper window. The group's cohesion was quickly lost, and the once-leader apparently had gone missing, whoever he was.

The water was now waist high, and remarkably the demon man had still yet to move, with water now only a foot below his mouth. Water was obviously filling the other rooms as well, but the last blast barely shook the building, and this time, there was no further return of the noise.

"Is it over?" one of the men yelled out.

"First tell me, what the fuck is it? How the hell should anyone know?"

He didn't bother to keep track of their fighting as he looked around at his cell, pushing, pulling, and hoping to find something loose, anything missing. Escape was becoming more urgent, and he felt his heart rate rise, his shoulders tense, and his stomach churn. How desperately did he ever want a bowl to smoke? That might at least settle his stomach down. Then, as if on a prayer's cue, the water stopped dripping, and bubbles indicated that the air in the pipes had been replaced by the water returning.

Sasha could feel her heartbeat, and her mind was fogging. She gripped tightly to Emilia's hand and focused on its warmth, its heat, and its embrace, and she used that focus to push the fog away. The light hummed as water still crept out from the edges of the door. There was a strong vibration that brought with it the return of the alarm.

The elevator light had gone out. The door had failed to open and left the girls with several tense moments before they once again stood at a loss. "Well shit again." Talking out loud seemed to push out the fog, and Sasha looked around, found a screwdriver in a drawer, and returned to the elevator.

"Good idea," Emilia said with a smile that showed it was a genuine compliment, which warmed Sasha. Sasha held the screwdriver up to the door and paused before inserting it. Emilia laid her hands on top of Sasha's. "Is this what we should be doing?"

Sasha smiled and finally felt confident enough to lead in front of someone she admired so much. "I'm not sure, but I am sure we should be doing it together." The two exchanged glances and inserted the screwdriver.

↩

No field exercise, no deployment, no nasty training event could ever have made Captain Drexter feel so dirty. The water drained at a snail's pace, and the fiend he had already invested first aid into was now feverish from both withdrawals and hypothermia. Resolved to avoid another failure, he held the man close and tight, hoping to keep both warmth and control. His body lacked the energy to sustain this pose indefinitely, but every other avenue his brain traveled down simply led to another worry, fear, or regret.

His body ached, and the fiend trembled and shivered until, in a desperate act that had never crossed the captain's mind, the fiend bit him. With a scream, Captain Drexter pushed the fiend, sending him splashing backward into the water. Horrified by the realizations that he had once again missed the obvious and that he would fail in his task of taking care of this soul, he stood stupidly as the man shivered, barely above water.

With an unexpected swiftness that shocked the captain, the demon man reached out, grabbed the neck of the fiend, pushed him under, and held him there.

↩

It was a nightmare, Sasha's first chance to make a meaning-ful decision in front of Emilia, and she was going to get them both killed. Water rushed out from the door, squirting in every direction as it rushed past the screwdriver. Pulling the screwdriver out of its hole as a natural reaction only made things worse. Water streamed from the opening with a force of power so great the doors themselves bent outward slightly.

Neither girl was injured, but both were sent to the ground, which was now already covered in an inch or more of water. Dumbfounded, Sasha now stared with hatred at the stream of water. She grabbed a cushion from the couch, walked with determination to the door, and attempted to block the flow of water. She pushed her frustrations out onto the cushion, and Emilia started to laugh at her.

The sight of Emilia laughing only further enhanced Sasha's anger, but not the fog. "That's real freaking helpful, Emilia."

Emilia stopped chuckling and stood up. "No, I was just thinking about what kind of sick humor the Lord must have if he finally gave me a friend only at my end."

The comment caught Sasha totally off guard. Emilia wasn't blaming her—she was blaming the Lord. Sasha gave up and threw the cushion off to the side, letting it float away. She walked up to Emilia and hugged her. "This isn't the end."

The moment of silence was followed by another strong vibration shaking the entire building, which burst open the elevator doors, allowing a wall of water into the apartment.

↩

The simple murder of a poor drug fiend weighed more heavily on Drexter's mind than he would have anticipated.

Whether it was the stripped-away humanity, pity for a soul lost
to the power of drugs, or the guilt of pushing a man to his death,
Captain Drexter let a single tear drop. The body floated motionless-
ly on the far side of the cell. The water level was lowering, but it
was still above the bench line and draining entirely too slowly for
comfort.

The noises had stopped, and now that the water wasn't the
most pressing matter, Captain Drexter noticed just how dark it was
becoming. Judging by his internal clock, it still should have been
the middle of the day, but it was noticeably darker, and none of the
interior lighting had activated. Whatever was occurring outside left
these prisoners to their own devices, and possible survival. It was
time for action. It was time to call for help.

↤

The last jolt had obviously burst the dam, for water was
flowing at a river's pace from all directions and rising fast. The two
girls ducked and covered, only to spend several seconds moving
aimlessly, at a loss for action. The guilt Sasha was feeling had
only become more and more amplified, as her mind could focus
on nothing more than the forthcoming sight of Emilia drowning
because of her.

Damn it, Sasha thought to herself, where the hell is the fog?
It was supposed to help her when she didn't know what to do, but
no fog. Emilia had regained composure and first grabbed Sasha by
the wrist and then led her off to the side of the elevator. Sasha's
chest labored with heavy breaths. Her skin became paler, her lips
bluer, and her eyes darted in all directions.

Emilia wrapped her hands around Sasha's bicep and moved

in close. One of Sasha's hands brushed across Emilia's breast, revealing the fact that she wasn't wearing a bra. The sensation calmed Sasha, as her mind was able to rally on a new thought track. "What are we going to do, Sasha?" Emilia's voice carried a tone not of anger or resentment, as Sasha had feared, but of faith and encouragement.

Sasha closed her eyes and took a deep breath. "Swim."

↩

"Hey, T. Hey, T." Thus far, "T" was the only name Drexter had learned, and it didn't seem to be helping him much. He was certain that he was being heard, and he was just as certain that he was being ignored.

Desperate and out of ideas, he didn't feel too far out of place with the drug fiends, who were only a short time ago begging for outside attention and assistance. "Hey, buddy. Hey, pal, come on, man. I'll trade you for some pot. I'll help you guys escape. I'll be a human shield." For what felt like hours, Captain Drexter called and called, only to be rejected and ignored.

Right when he was about to give up, a most distressing option presented itself. The man who had so elegantly declared his desire to watch the captain urinate approached the cell with an offer. "Suck my dick and I will get T to let you out."

For a horrifying half second, he actually considered it. Yet he had already crossed enough lines during this outing, so he decided to try another tactic. "After you let me out, how about I let you suck my dick?"

"Don't play your mind games on me, soldier," the man

said, unzipping his pants. "I get pleasured, then maybe, maybe I give you what you want."

Captain Drexter cringed.

↩

"What the hell do you mean, swim?" Emilia's objection to the plan, while still painful in its infliction, was born out of surprise and a lack of understanding rather than malice or blame.

Sasha said, "Ok, there is only one way in or out of this shelter, the elevator shaft, so we are going to swim up the shaft."

Emilia's face bore the strong look of disbelief mixed with fear. "I'm not that good a swimmer, plus water is coming out of the elevator. How the hell are we supposed to swim up it?"

Sasha took a couple of deep breaths before her mind was able to clarify its own plan. "Ok, when the room fills with water, it will also fill the elevator shaft, creating a water flow we can use to help us up the shaft."

An extreme look of terror stoned Emilia's face. "Are you crazy? After the room fills with water, you might have some superpower to breathe underwater, but I sure don't."

The water level was rising high, waist level, and it was cold and salty. The girls were beginning to shiver, and despite Emilia's initial better composure, her panic level was rising along with the water.

Sasha took a moment to look at Emilia, and it filled her with power. This was the first person she could call a friend, a person she didn't want to let down again, a person she wanted to save. Sasha grabbed hold of Emilia's biceps this time and moved in close. She used one of her hands to brush the wet hair off of Emilia's face. "I will help you, I will protect you, and I will love you." Then she kissed Emilia's forehead, and both girls inhaled a deep breath.

↩

Of all the most disgusting circumstances to encounter a large, burly queer of a homosexual, it would have to be on the one day Drexter most urgently needed the assistance. Yet as hard as he might try, the option was going to have to be shoved off the table. "Listen here, fellow, you might be the one on the outside, but I've got the goods in here, so you want it? Come and get it." Captain Drexter was far from certain he would persevere in a fight, but it was far, far better than the alternatives—nothing, or *that*.

The large homosexual reached in but fell short of being able to grab the captain. Had the captain been a more experience fighter, he might have been able to take advantage of the homosexual man reaching his arm in, but the idea crossed his mind too late.

The homosexual man whistled and shouted a few profanities before promising to wipe the smirk off the captain's face and leaving. The captain scouted his surroundings, only to find that little had changed. One corpse lay floating, trapped under the bench, while another was wedged in the far corner, its shoe in between some bars, and the lone man still sat with his head in his hands.

With no hope of escape, his fears about Sasha abounding, and his career in jeopardy, Captain Drexter had never needed a hit so badly in his life.

↩

The girls stayed close, cuddled together for warmth, but no amount of companionship could ease their journey of death. The rising sense of panic, the darkening room, and the exhaustion from treading water were all waging havoc on Sasha's confidence. There was now only a foot of air spanning between the water level and the ceiling.

"I can't go on, too tired." Emilia's shivering was starting to worry Sasha. "Let's stand on the kitchen counter at least."

It was easy to forget how much stronger and more durable she was than Emilia. For a brief moment, she felt the way a man must feel—a powerful, strong defender, protector, and caregiver. Yet it was fleeting without someone to do them for. A kick from Emilia's leg and a gasp from her mouth signaled the time for action.

"Listen to me, Emilia, we will make it, and we will make it together. We can't go until the water starts pushing hard that way. We want to stay right here because this water will be rushed back up the elevator shaft."

A trembling, exhausted, and scared Emilia never looked so ugly, yet so precious. "Are you sure?"

Only a few breaths remained, and it was too late to respond. Even if Sasha had the air and time to respond, she might not have had the confidence to even speak it out loud. The girls each took their last breath and held each other tightly as they waited for the plan to happen. And they waited, and they waited, and they waited.

25: Cold Dawn

It wasn't going to work. Nothing was happening, and Sasha could barely feel any movement at all in the water. She cursed herself, as she had once again failed. Fearing it was already too late, she hooked her arm in the weakening grip of Emilia's armpit. Sasha thrashed her legs, pushing with as much force and determination as she had ever had in her life. Had they not been submerged, tears would have been streaming down her face.

Sasha had never prayed for a miracle, nor had she ever been inclined to, but at the moment, she felt like she had been granted one. The water grabbed the girls, and with a force much stronger than Sasha, the two were rushed up the elevator shaft at a confusing speed.

It was impossible for Sasha to keep her orientation, breath, or wits. So she did the only thing she could: she held on to Emilia for all her worth. A strong jostle from Emilia only worried her further, as there was no way of knowing what lay in the shaft above or to the sides—until Sasha's left shoulder slammed into a hard surface. The elevator cord kept the rebound to a minimum, but Sasha could feel the hurt.

It would bruise, but Sasha had experienced worse physical pain. Although, she had never found it so easy to power through it before. Despite the soreness of her shoulder, she pounded the ceiling until, at last, a panel moved. Directly above the impact point, something had loosened, so Sasha pounded vehemently until it finally shook free.

Precious oxygen had never seemed so miraculous to Sasha before, and yet so distant for the one she loved. She pulled herself out with one arm, refusing to release Emilia. There was no breath for Emilia, no sudden gasp for lifesaving breath—only a limp, pale body, and Sasha was the cause.

↩

The water continued to sink but left behind a bile grime on everything it had touched. Pacing proved too slippery and nasty a proposition for what it would offer in relief. Drexter's stomach churned with worry, hunger, and disgust, and a dryness began to form all around his mouth. His day was getting worse and worse.

He had faced similar kinds of challenges before. Like any career officer, he couldn't escape the inevitable difficulties the army supplies. This time, however, the stakes seemed almost higher than life and death—it was both personal and spiritual. Only the Lord himself could concoct such a terrible menagerie of events.

For the next several hours, Captain Drexter leaned against the upper part of the back wall, internally cursing a Lord who before had no formal place in his life.

↩

"No, this can't be the end of the miracle." Sasha wondered why she would be forced to face this alone after just being given a chance. She grabbed Emilia's limp, pale arm, laid it against her weeping face, and fell face-first onto Emilia's stomach. It wasn't much, nothing more than a wheeze, but she heard it, and Sasha bolted upright, waved her hands in panic, and continued to cry.

It wasn't the fog, it wasn't a lack of desire, and it wasn't even a lack of knowledge, but the emotions Sasha was feeling were creating a cloud so thick that only panic remained. Her muscles jumped into uncoordinated, purposeless gestures as those emotions drowned out her brain's commands.

An unintentional slam to Emilia's gut made water project out of her mouth. The blunder brought back with it the miracle of hope, and with the hope came a thought, which propelled Sasha immediately into CPR thrusts. Over and over again, she pressed as her tears flowed. Her body was now focused, oriented, and motivated. She stayed strong and steady as she vowed not to let fatigue become a factor. For a hundred thrusts, Sasha kept rhythm and pace, her sweat mixing with the tears, creating an intense stinging in her eyes. Then, as Sasha's count approached two hundred, the miracle ended.

↩

Too tired to stand anymore, Captain Drexter sat next to the man who had been sitting remarkably still throughout the entire ordeal. Truly, he felt at a loss for words, his brain so bogged down in everything going on that he spoke more from his heart. "Misery needs company, and I feel mighty miserable right now." He waited a while before speaking again. "Guess we both got plenty to be upset about, including ourselves. I certainly won't ask anything you don't wanna say, but I'm happy to listen to anything ya got to say. Sometimes it's best to get outside your own head, ya know."

Again the captain waited before carrying on. "There's

something I remember hearing, growing up as a child. 'Until you the reach the end, it's not over.'" He waited once more. "The meaning I take from it changes all the time. Guess its meaning has progressed with me. It may not seem like a gift, but it has been a beneficial part of my life for a long time. Maybe someday it will serve you well too."

As his speech ended, the lights went out, and the prison sat in total darkness.

↩

Sasha wondered which loss would be greater, herself or a loved one. She thanked the Lord that she didn't have to face either one, at least not yet. Emilia was not doing well. An immense amount of water came out of Emilia, her body convulsing, constraining, and wringing itself like a wet towel, until finally that first precious gulp of air entered her lungs. Several hard, wet coughs were chased by more breaths, each one working to restore the lost balance.

Emilia didn't, or couldn't, speak. Her body lay nearly motionless, her chest heaving with labored breaths. Sasha burst out in a new round of tears fueled by joy and worry. She held Emilia's hand close, but it still hung limp.

The artificial yellow of the emergency light inside the elevator tinted everything, and Sasha struggled but managed to realize how cold and pale her friend's entire body was. She ran her hand along Emilia's face and down her neck, and then she ripped off the tank top and the bottoms. She then removed her own clothes and pressed herself against Emilia's shoulder and side, giving her friend as much warmth as she could without causing more harm.

No amount of worry or stress could overcome Sasha's eventual fatigue, and as she lay there warming her friend, her eyes closed, and without permission, she fell asleep.

↩

"Sasha, I must find Sasha!" The words came out in accordance with the dream, but the context fell away as the captain stirred back awake. It would be impossible to tell how much time had passed or how much sleep he got. "My cellmate, my compatriot, maybe even my friend, are you still there?" There was no reply, only the sounds of breathing. "I must get out of here. Sasha, I must find Sasha!" He kicked the bars of his cell with frustration.

Noises in the distance told of stories and injuries as the other prisoners attempted to navigate the dark in an effort to find clean water or food, or even shelter to sleep. Again the captain spoke. "My friend, we can't just sit here, yet I don't have any ideas. Perhaps you have some, or perhaps we could create some." He waited. There was a change in the breathing pattern, to a slightly faster pace. Otherwise, there was no motion or response. "My friend, are you dead?"

This was harder than getting through to a teenage Sasha, who would often break the silence with a snappy remark. So Drexter wasn't surprised at the man's tone, only the content, when he finally spoke with venom. "Do you want to butt fuck me?"

"What, what do you mean?"

"I said, do you want to motherfucking butt fuck me? That would be the only possible reason you would ask if I was still fucking alive."

Once more, Captain Drexter felt surprisingly cool, considering the outburst, more like a father than a prisoner. Perhaps he was becoming more comfortable in that role. "No, no, none of that, my friend. I won't, however, vouch for that man somewhere out there in the dark. No, I was just hoping you might have an idea as to where we might find some drinkable water? Or maybe an idea how to get out. I have a daughter, Sasha. She's out there."

There was the sound of a foot stomping. "I could piss in your fucking mouth. This is just the beginning of our torturous descent into hell. Now piss off, Daddykins, so I can receive God's wrath in peace." This was a man consumed, consumed by a demon.

↵

Emilia just lay there—breathing, yes, but alive, still unknown. Sasha cursed herself for being too slow, too weak, and too stupid. She pounded her hand against her head over and over again. Her eyes hurt with the sting of tears and salty water.

The elevator swayed but held true, never springing a leak and only allowing splashes of water to enter the room. The yellow emergency light taunted Sasha as it repeatedly revealed her failures. Her stomach ached, and her mouth was dry. Had she not been in physical union with Emilia, she would have gotten up and destroyed that light by now, yet her friend still needed her warmth.

Emilia had taken to random bouts of shivering. Each time, Sasha would both rejoice and dread the action. Her breathing had steadied, and despite the difficulty with that damn lighting, Sasha would have sworn Emilia even had some color returning to various parts of her body.

At one point, Sasha laughed at the thought that when she first met Emilia, the idea of being trapped naked in an elevator with her was appealing. It was as if her gentle laugh had burst a dam, for a gust of wind entered the elevator and the water level started to drop, and Sasha smiled.

↩

God's wrath came quickly, encompassing the entirety of his dark universe. It started as tremors, as if multiple great beasts were jumping in unison. Some of the men yelled, others relocated, and one man even screamed, but then everyone buckled.

Every sense told Drexter that the demon man next to him was experiencing the same thing. Gasping breaths spoke out in the dark as gut-wrenching momentum pulled the men down under heavy gravity. No physical presence was touching them, yet its physical touch was unmistakably present.

A gentle lurch in the pull caused one man to puke, someone up higher along the windows maybe, and Captain Drexter might have puked, had his stomach not been empty. The lurch continued to gain in strength, and while he had already been forced to his knees, he now faced the prospect of being toppled onto his side. As his body tilt neared a tipping point, so did the lurch slow and finally begin to move back in the opposite direction.

A swinging arm suggested that the demon man either was trying to fight an invisible enemy or had nearly lost his balance. Either way, the captain was in no position to defend himself, and the lurch was pushing him directly that way. Fearing the violent nature of the demon man, and the fact that no amount of ingratiation would stop his wrath under duress, Captain Drexter dropped facedown on the nastiest floor he had ever smelled.

↤

Sasha's smile didn't last long, and the rocking was getting less and less gentle. The water was receding quickly, and as she now looked down the shaft, it was a ten-foot drop to the water, and who knew how far to the bottom. Sasha now faced another choice. She could jump into the water, hoping it still flowed deep enough to support her. Throwing Emilia down first wouldn't work, and carrying her on Sasha's shoulders wouldn't be any good for someone in Emilia's condition.

Time was running out, as were Sasha's options. She now projected fifteen feet to water level. She figured there would be a ladder in the shaft, but in the dark, it was impossible to find. Her time to make a decision grew short. Fighting off the panic was all Sasha could muster. Again there was no fog, no guiding presence, just a never-ending barrage of terrible thoughts while she watched as her lone friend lay dying.

A strong lurch in the elevator flipped Sasha's stomach. Leaving Emilia wasn't going to be possible, for she knew that guilt and shame would follow her forever. Action was desperately needed, yet her mind was blank.

It was a sign from above that brought the answer, and as the elevator lurched and gravity grew heavy, it smashed down and opened a panel. Sasha whispered under her breath, "Holy shit." The light came crashing down, bringing along a corner of a ceiling panel. This time, Sasha acted without pause. She jumped up and looked around for an idea, an idea that wasn't difficult to find.

She really wished this day would end, and now as she and

her fingers worked bitterly to open clips and pull pins, she was ready to skip the next week too. Darkness covered the elevator as an unseen force pushed down hard upon them. Sasha's stomach protested, but to no avail. A jolt shook the elevator, and a loud snap could be heard.

↩

Oh, God, did it stink. Oh, God, did his stomach hurt. Oh, God, did he ever need a hit. And where the hell was God, anyway? Captain Drexter's mind rambled with curses as he hated every moment of his current existence. Yet he saw no way out of it either.

Suppressing his gag reflex, he built a stronger base with his knee and lifted himself up. However stronger he tried, it only felt as if gravity would countermand his physics and deny the request. Gasps and dry heaves filled his ear as the demon man continued to struggle.

It seemed to go on for ages and ages. Every foul breath coated his lungs, every drop of sweat slickened the floor, and every motivation seemed a goal too distant. Great thunder brought a distraction but no relief. Someone managed to yell, "Incoming!" but there was no sound of any hustle or jostle of movement to accompany it. As his body started to fail in fatigue, the thunder once again roared, piercing his ears and pounding his brain.

Having a handicap was a pretty foreign idea to a soldier. True, many soldiers were taken from the battlefield with handicaps, but it never hit home until it was too late. The silence that followed such an awful sound could only mean he was now deaf. Again he cursed a god who would take away a useful sense while letting his sense of smell nearly bring him to tears.

With the loss of sound came relief as well. His stomach no longer churned, and his body lifted without effort. The cold was an unexpected, yet hellish, twist. And Captain Drexter simply forced his mind to shut down before he gave God any new ideas.

↢

Had Sasha been only a few inches to her left, any body part beyond that line would surely have been severed by the whipping cord. However, it was hard for Sasha to recognize her good fortune while falling down an elevator shaft.

Her heart sank even faster than her body fell. Smoke was pouring out of the elevator and climbing up through the cracks along the side, and in a moment's time, the shaft had filled. Oddly, however, the smoke brought with it cold, deep cold as if the smoke had collected every heat molecule and whisked it away. Then, just as oddly, the elevator seemed to stop falling for a moment. Sasha swore she had actually left the floor, only to have it confirmed with her landing. Her wrist and forearm landed first, but it didn't stop her head from taking a significant blow. The pain blurred her vision, but she was still able to see that Emilia's body had been severely disturbed. Her mind commanded, but her body failed. Smoke filled the elevator, leaving Emilia's body in a hazy, dark shroud. Sasha rolled onto her side, the movement greatly sickening her and temporarily blinding her.

It was like feeling in the dark, but at last her hand made contact. It wasn't a pulse, it wasn't a breath, but it was warm, and it was enough for Sasha to let go as the fog overcame her.

↢

It was the last thing Drexter expected to see, but it was a

most welcome sight. The night sky loomed large and frightening, fought away by only a single light. The rays bounced and filtered throughout the room, gradually fading as they went.

Yet the light's power was unmistakable. One beam spread out for all to find in the dark. Captain Drexter's eyes focused intently on it, feeling its warmth in the sudden cold, rising to his feet under the power of its hold, and again he felt alive.

The demon man next to him was having a similar experience, at least until he simply returned to his position of self-imprisonment and ignored the light. Despite his complaints, the captain felt pity for someone who could carry such guilt as to impose himself into this type of prison.

Hoping to make a joke, the captain moved his finger toward his mouth as if lighting a smoke. "My friend, will you not enjoy a light with me."

"Stop fucking calling me your friend! I don't want to interact with you, I don't want your god, and I don't want your fucking preaching anymore. So take your god and leave it the hell away from me. Damn, dude, take a fucking hint before I fucking kill you!"

The dismissal wasn't unexpected, but the eruption stunned the captain. What the hell did the demon man mean by "your god" and "your preaching"? The captain had much time to contemplate how he, a nonbeliever, could be accused of "preaching."

↩

The fog always, always, always brought about bad things. Unless engaged in combat, the fog was to be considered a threat.

This time around, even the fog couldn't overcome the physical, and Sasha's body could only endure so much while hungover and without food, water, and sleep.

The fog was lifted by a light, a bright light shining directly into Sasha's eye. A man in uniform knelt above her, moving his mouth repeatedly. Yet she was having trouble making sense of it all, as history had taught her that the fog could block out sound. They were in a hallway, the lights were all red, and there was commotion everywhere. Emilia—Sasha began to search for Emilia, but her head was being hindered by something around her neck.

Bodies were in fervent motion in the background, and Sasha tried to focus her search, but the man in uniform kept getting in the way. Another uniformed man, a Hispanic man of small stature, came beside her and laid down a long board. The new man's uniform was different, and it was for Synied security.

The first man moved his face in front of her. This time, however, he brandished a weapon. A needle held up in front of her was all it took for the fog to come back, and when the fog came back, bad things always happened.

26: Round and Round

Time had no meaning in the world of the fog. Its natural rhythm adjusted to the situation even though Sasha had little control. These two men posed no danger and were in the midst of trying to help her, but she had no conscious thought.

Again the blows came swiftly, accurately, and painfully to the two men. Several well-placed kicks knocked them to their knees, and their pleas to stop were only met with fists of fury. Luckily, the fog hadn't interrupted the others from working on Emilia. Although fast, the fog had only appeared for a groggy revival, and it vanished with the sight of her friend.

Emilia lay lifeless, with a tube deep inside her throat, and two different racks held bags of fluid, each dripping into her arms. Pads ran along her bare chest, sending out signals that came in all-too-slow beeps. Emilia had a brace around her neck and was taped down to a board. Sasha exited the now-half-opened elevator door and approached the two uniformed paramedics, a man and a woman, each slender and black. The woman barked out commands as the man either complied or responded with an answer, but it all made no sense to Sasha.

Sasha's own body cried out in stress, fatigue, and dehydration, causing her to collapse into a sitting position. All the discomfort, all the pain, and all the close calls she had with her friend only amplified how Sasha felt about Emilia—that they were soul mates.

↩

The beam of sunlight had given new energy to the other prisoners, as well as a new sense of urgency. Several men, including T and the wheelbarrow man, were working feverishly at a window. "There are people in the streets. I can see people," one of the adjoining men yelled in excitement.

"Motherfucker, it's nighttime, and the power's off. How you going to see shit?" The question came from down below, but Drexter wasn't able to see who had spoken it.

"How the fuck you seein' shit now? I don't fucking know. I can just see what the fuck I can see."

"Well what the hell are they doing?"

"I don't fucking know, standing around in shit. Now you want me to paint you a damn word picture or pick you a damn lock?"

"You're going to fuckin' do both."

Captain Drexter listened as intently to the conversation as a news junkie would a major story, pained by the event but unable to look away from the oncoming emotional train.

Then, with another earthquake-type lurch and twist of the group's stomachs, they saw the most horrifically beautiful image move into their singular view: Earth.

↩

The words came as unconscious whispers, yet they still came over and over again. "Please, God." Had someone brought it to her attention, Sasha probably would have stopped the prayer, but here and now, as she watched her friend lie in limbo, the prayer came over and over.

Slowly the commotion came to a halt. The man kneeling next to Emilia had his hand on her shoulder, while the woman stood on her knees. The room grew silent before Sasha's ears focused on a familiar sound that had already faded into the background. The beeps of the medical machine were gradually rising in pace. Another gentle cough from Emilia was more than enough to jostle the entirety of Sasha. Without thinking, she held her breath in anticipation. When Emilia sputtered her first word, "Sasha," Sasha beamed with the pride of a mother and exhaled her response: "Emilia."

↩

A burst of excitement ushered in a new round of activity. This time, even the demon man looked up from his prison. The brilliant-blue light shined throughout the prison, reaching deep and even illuminating the bodies as they lay soaked, dead, and soon to be smelling. The contrast between Drexter's hellish prison and the heavenly blue of the ocean was stark and terrifying.

"What the holy hell is that?" a voice from above asked.

"Yo, that looks like the fucking Earth from all those movies. What the fuck is going on?"

A deep, thick moment of silence passed as each man worked out the answer for himself. Captain Drexter didn't speak loudly, but in the absence of sound, it traveled well. "We are in outer-fucking space."

A loud commotion of heckles, jeers, and disbelief rained out in response. A shoe then rapped against the bars. Bits of material came out, when Captain Drexter realized why the shoe had become disposable, which simply grossed him out. "You must be a fuckin' grunt, soldier. It's just the sheriff playin' some sort of fuckin' game with us." Again Drexter missed who had spoken. "They just got some sort of projector on a screen, probably some civie watchin' *Forrest Gump* in space, or some shit. No, now is the time to escape. T, you fuckin' done yet?"

"No, I ain't fuckin' done yet. I ain't got no shit for tools."

Captain Drexter turned around, only to find the demon man back in his own prison and two nasty corpses lying just beyond. This place was truly hell, so he retreated to a mental hole, where he sat cursing the Lord he had been accused of preaching for.

↩

"Sasha, I can barely hear you. My eyes won't open. What?" Emilia let loose another volley of sputtering coughs.

"Emilia, I'm here." Sasha moved closer and grabbed her hand. It was warmer than before, but it still felt weak and limp. Tears sprang from her eyes. "Just relax, it takes time. We've been through a lot, and rest will help you." Emotions were hard to control, especially as a teenager, but for Sasha, one of them trumped the rest: love. Love was the only emotion that could make her weak on the outside but strong on the inside, and Sasha's internal processes told her that now was the time to reassure her friend, her love.

After some time, she felt a gentle tap on her shoulder from the black female paramedic. "Miss, for our safety, I'm going to have to please ask you to go ahead and back up now so we can move her to a better location."

Sasha was too deeply involved with Emilia to take offense at the request, nor to accede to it either.

The words echoed, but there were no further physical attempts to communicate. "Miss, miss."

The paramedics and the security guard had grouped together, tending to each other's wounds. The black paramedic raised a can of mace and pointed it without firing.

"Where will you take her?" Sasha could feel the presence of the lady. She had no need to turn her head and look.

The lady paused. "I actually don't know that yet. We don't have access to a medical facility."

"If you don't know where she's going, then I'm not fucking going anywhere."

"Ma'am, this isn't open for discussion. She can't lie here in the hallway, and I can't finish my job while you are present."

"How about I kick your asses again if you don't fix her right this goddamn second?"

"Ma'am, after what you did before, we would choose to take our chances on running for our lives rather than deal with you."

Sasha felt the buildup of fog evaporate with her surprise at the lady's bravery.

"Now, ma'am, if you'll kindly step back, and I mean way the hell back, we would be glad to fix your friend out of the goodness of our hearts, but even Christians believe in self-preservation."

Tears replaced Sasha's anger. "What did you mean, we don't have access to a medical facility?"

There was another long pause before the female paramedic spoke. "Because, honey, we are in outer space now."

She responded before her brain had time to process what was said. "Oh, good, I'm dreaming. I thought this hell was really going on around me."

↩

The prisoners made several attempts to exit, but they were thwarted at every turn. The window's plastic was too strong to smash through, the locks wouldn't budge without tools, and the front door could only be opened from the outside. The group's resourcefulness and creativity were surprisingly advanced for such obviously uneducated individuals.

Captain Drexter spent most of his time pacing, worrying, and fretting. His list of worries was getting longer, but Sasha remained permanently affixed to the top. How or why they ended up in space—or if they really did—was an incredibly big issue, but it took far less precedence than escape, water, or even food.

His conversation with the Lord had led him nowhere but round and round. Scanning his surroundings, he couldn't help but feel that the Lord was right to wipe out the human race, that Jesus was the fool to save it. He was abandoned before a trial, discarded by a society that would rather just lock up black men and leave them to die than hear out their stories. Looking for things to curse and resent was easy, but the captain knew that good wasn't difficult to find either if he looked hard enough.

"Something's happening, yo. All those people, they be running now. They all running this way." T pointed as he spoke.

The voice sounded like it came from the vicinity of the wheelbarrow man, but Drexter still couldn't figure out who was speaking. "What the hell they running from?"

Another man joined a nearby ledge, but T maintained the best viewing platform. "Oh shit. Oh shit, y'all. They fuckin' running from a, from a, from a—"

"Fucking spit it out!" the wheelbarrow man yelled.

"A goddamn alien, yo."

↩

It took some discussion and debate, but it was finally decided that Emilia would be returned back down to the shelter. The floor they currently occupied was a holding area for biologically altered samples, and while it offered medical equipment, it didn't have a doctor and failed to provide any measure of safety.

No stairs occupied the building, and the elevator was out of commission for the midterm, no less. While they didn't suspect any spinal or neck damage, the paramedics weren't physicians, nor did they have access to X-rays, nor could they diagnosis the vision problems she was having. Moving a body up a shaft was a greater challenge than moving one down, so they decided that once a physician could be found, they would have to come here.

Sasha eventually agreed to the paramedics' request, but not until they had chosen a location. She nursed her shoulder and wrist while gracefully and expediently climbing down the ladder in the elevator shaft. The crew worked surprisingly well together. Several times, Sasha had to fight back the impulse to join in, but after a while, she was able to calm down, even agreeing to a saline pack, some bottled water, and military rations that had survived the flood.

It wasn't a moment of serenity, but as Sasha lay back, relieved by her friend's successful journey, she thanked the Lord for getting her this far. She sat next to Emilia and ran her hand through her hair. Emilia's conscious self was back, but her vision still wasn't, and it was getting harder and harder to reassure her friend that she would see again.

It was a new and different role for Sasha. She had always had plenty of attending nurses, doctors, and specialists, but she had never had to care for someone before. Sasha couldn't guess how much time had passed since she first met Emilia, but it felt like she had grown years during it.

↩

The wheelbarrow of a man barked out his reply. "What the hell? You guys been hitting something off of the fiend corpses or what? Talking about being in outer space and aliens walking down the block and shit."

T shouted out a response but was outblasted by the eruption of gunfire.

Everyone in sight ducked, but it was obvious that the bullets were not being fired at them—barely even a ricochet bounced off the exterior walls. It was a peculiar sound for a gunfight. A massive amount of ammunition was being expended, but there was no chorus of attack or moves like an army battle. No, this sounded more like soldiers unloading on an approaching runaway vehicle.

To anyone else, the motion would have seemed abnormal, but fearing an oncoming vehicle, Captain Drexter found the best cover he could: two dead corpses. Round and round he went in his cell, but only they stood out. The thought and the idea that crept into his mind was more dreadful than any he could imagine. Truly, he thought to himself, only a greatly powerful asshole could design so much torment, and how awful a god it must have been to allow it to happen.

Captain Drexter had experienced anger before, but as he moved the first corpse, he felt a rising intensity of anger that bordered on hate. As he moved the second corpse, he moved to a level of hatred so strong it fueled his muscles, bore his pain, and spurred him on to "live." It was a hatred that burned in rage for one thing, the only thing he could imagine putting him in this position: the Lord.

He grabbed the bloating bodies of the dead fiends and stuffed one underneath the bench and against the wall, snuggled up alongside it, and pulled the other close in front. It was a constant battle with the dry heaving, but he was determined to do one thing: live. If there really were aliens, then Sasha was born for this, and she would need her father more than ever. If not, there was an entity in need of some repayment.

27: In the Name Of

It would be too long a wait to keep Emilia immobilized to a board, but they insisted on a neck brace as she lay on a damp couch in the middle of a very soggy, stinky, humid room. The residue left behind from the water suggested that it wasn't entirely clean water, but at least there wasn't any toilet smell.

Ration packs and water bottles had been stuffed into every crevice of cabinet space, and the entire group now mingled and recovered from Emilia's move. Sasha finally found the time to speak with her friend, and she couldn't help but bombard Emilia. "What do you think she meant by 'we are in outer space'? Do you think we can trust these people? How long do you think it has been since my dad left?"

The questions came out in machine-gun fashion. She formulated each next question while still spitting out the last idea. A warm hand placed itself on Sasha's lap, and after she put her hand on top, another covered it. "Sasha." The sound of Emilia's words was so sweet to her ears. "Sweetie, you need to slow down. I don't have any answers to your questions."

Guilty tears streamed down Sasha's face. "I did this to you. I did this to you. I'm so, so, so sorry."

Emilia stared blankly at Sasha. "Sasha, my dear, you saved me. You didn't do anything other than become my hero today."

The words filled Sasha's heart with a sense of relief and desire. "But your eyes, your body."

"My body will heal. I'm alive, and that's more than I expected. I feel like, well I guess I feel like I have been given a gift."

"You're not mad? Angry at what has happened?"

"Who is there to be angry at when, after all, I'm still alive with a will to be done? So I am thankful that you have given so much to protect me, from those boys, from the water and the paramedics, who were actually trying to help me, by the way. I know now that God sent you to be my protector. I am ever so thankful."

Sasha felt a coldness sneak into her heart for a moment as she thought about how naïve and foolish this person was—thankful for an existence that would blind her. Sasha would have had other desires for such a god, if they existed.

↩

The wall shattered, and bricks flew as if they were glass shards. There were no screams, no whistle, and no movement. The bewildered, fatigued, and hungry prisoners stood motionless, too tired to either run or fight. So each one simply sought not to be seen as the huge beast entered the room. It stood tall and daunting, and came toward the center, near the edge of both cells.

A green liquid was oozing out from several sores in the creature's skin, where he had suffered injury in between armor points. At first, the creature moved slowly, observing the environment and its occupants. The prisoners remained still until one man broke out in a full gallop toward the opening in the wall. The alien, who had thus far been slow and meticulous, suddenly moved with incredible speed and agility, captured the man, and lifted him by his legs, high into the air.

The alien grabbed a device from his belt and placed it deep into the man's throat. A red light near the end of the device indicated that the result was negative, and the alien threw his carcass carelessly about like a flimsy doll. The alien moved gradually back toward the cages and scanned the cell intently before grabbing a handful of cell bars and bending them out of the way.

The alien stood in front of the demon man, grabbed him by the neck, and lifted him high as his legs hung motionless. Again the alien grabbed the device from his utility belt, but as he prepared to insert it, he yelped out in pain, looking down. Captain Drexter had taken a short metal rod and, using a brick, smashed it down hard on a break in the alien's foot armor.

The alien dropped the demon man, who coughed vehemently. Tossing him aside, the alien picked up the captain by the neck and prepared to stuff the device down his throat.

↩

He just stood there, the creature who seemed to have appeared from out of nowhere, looking, observing, and planning. He towered seven feet tall, scaly armor covering his reptilian skin. He bore the face of a dinosaur, with three pillars protruding from his skull. The middle pillar appeared to bounce and move with a motion, and unconsciously Sasha had already identified it as a weak point.

There were no screams to announce his arrival, no sounds as he almost seemed to glide across the floor. The smaller black female had been the first to notice him, letting out a ghastly sigh of fear. The motion was startling enough to swing the entire group's attention. After regaining some composure, the paramedics and security stood in a scared yet defensive position around their patient.

Only Sasha dared to step forward, driven not by bravery, not by adolescent arrogance of youth, but by the fog. Cloaked in its safety, guided by its wisdom, Sasha knew now was the time to embrace the fog—if only she knew how. There had been plenty of practice on exiting and avoiding the fog but very little on interacting with it.

No words were exchanged as Sasha stood before the elevator door and the creature stood in the middle of the broken elevator carriage, two warriors silently preparing for battle. There was no need to announce friend or foe, no need to report the stakes, and no need for introductions. The wounds of killing always bore down on a soldier's soul, worn as immobile badges spoken in a language healthy souls could never hear, but Sasha knew the language, a language she could never forget, and the time for conversation was over.

↩

Captain Drexter was held high, like the predator was displaying his catch before consumption. The beast looked into his eyes as a dominant animal would a challenger. The device blinked green as it neared the captain's throat, and the alien's demeanor seemed relieved.

Drexter was lowered to the ground, and although his neck was squeezed, he could still breathe, some. Instincts screamed for him to kick, twist, and squirm, but he was stuck. Ice of the soul chilled his spine, freezing him in place. Surprisingly, the beast let go, so dominant over his prey that even in release, he dare not flee.

The beast bent down and, without physical reaction, removed the small pipe from his foot. Moving as purposefully as a cobra, he examined the pipe, and then with great force and frightening speed, he slammed the pipe directly through Captain Drexter's foot.

It was devastatingly painful yet still unable to wake him from his trance. The captain dropped to his ass, winced in agony, but again failed to flee. The act of domination had been completed, and Captain Drexter awaited his death. Whether it was the ringing in his ears, a mind block from a telepathic alien, or just a plain old concussion, he was oblivious to the new sounds now distracting his captor.

The speeding sounds of bullets whirred by his head again and again. Faint yelling echoed in the back ground. Then a terrible, loud burst picked him up and threw him from his captor's side. All orientation now lost, the feeling and control of his body was now at the will of physics.

Yet he felt motion—not a lifting motion, as before, but a pulling motion—and a growing speed with it. His eyes had been open, but only now as his conscious mind slowly returned did it begin to process. Men, prisoners, were carrying him. To where, he wasn't sure, but he was sure of one thing: the demon man was a strong son of a bitch.

Sasha moved with lightning speed, but it still wasn't enough. The creature countered, dodged, and returned her attack. The fog was present. She could feel its presence guiding, focusing, and even protecting her, yet it wouldn't be enough. This creature had vast physical abilities, military training, and a few centuries of evolution more than Sasha.

The battle was intense, if not short. Sasha landed several blows but barely phased the alien. After taking a forceful kick to his head, the alien grabbed Sasha by the back of hers and threw her across the room. The alien drew a long shaft from his waistband and closed in on the group surrounding Emilia.

Sasha was terrified. Her head hurt, the fog waned, and her body cried out to run and flee in terror. Fear had no hold over love, and no amount of fear was going to stop Sasha. Several bursts of pepper spray from the security guard did more harm to the group than their intruder. The creature approached to within arm's distance of the guard, grabbed him single-handedly, raised him high into the air, and inserted the long shaft down the man's throat. A red light buzzed, and the creature expunged the shaft and threw the man off to the side.

The two female paramedics cowered backward, and the alien came toward Emilia. He stood high above her, examining her from head to toe. The creature raised the shaft and held it next to Emilia's head as if measuring how deep it would skewer her.

Sasha stood ready in a warrior stance. She couldn't see Emilia's face, but she knew the fear that must be in her eyes, and how desperately she would need her help. Sasha called in challenge to the beast. She had no plan, no hope of winning, and not a prayer of physical domination, but she had one advantage. Everything she cared for was at stake, and that made her highly motivated.

28: Blue Dawn

The parking lot smelled like burnt fumes and ash. Holes littered the vehicles along the alien's path. A few bodies lay scattered about, those poor unfortunate or untactical officers who had gotten too close and paid for it with their lives. The city looked different, and not only because of his ass being dragged along the ground. The dark city was basked in a beautiful blue light, and as Captain Drexter's eyes drifted farther upward, there it loomed: Earth.

Their momentum stopped, and the demon man finally dropped to his knees in exhaustion. Captain Drexter, still wobbly from the explosion, was slowly coming around. "What the hell is this place?"

There was a stern look on the demon man's face. "Only interrogators insert answers into the questions they ask."

The comment confused the captain, but training and instincts moved his body as he continued to follow the demon man, who was running quickly. "What's the rush?"

"Gunfire has stopped." He didn't turn his head or seem to care whether the captain was able to keep up or not.

↩

With her lack of a plan also came a lack of response.

Immersed in his task of examining Emilia, the alien paid no mind to Sasha. He made ready to insert the tool. Sasha grabbed some unopened MREs and began hurling them at the creature, but he still paid her no attention.

Frustrated at being ignored and fearful of failing in her task, Sasha charged, extended her leg out, and attempted to kick the back of his head. The creature was too fast, too aware, and too expecting, and easily dodged the assault. It confiscated control of Sasha's body and tossed her aside, just as it had the security guard's corpse.

Sasha landed hard again, but she was spared any broken bones or head trauma. It was clear to her that she couldn't physically harm the beast, couldn't defeat him in battle, and would eventually be killed by this thing, but none of that mattered next to Emilia. Sasha charged again, attacking lower this time. The beast was ready again. He raised his foot in preparation to counter against her and bore down on his leg hard.

The beast wasn't the target this time, and Sasha was ready to dodge the blow. She made contact with her target, grabbing the alien's tool from his clutches. There was no time to stop, only time to pray—pray that the alien would in fact follow her, and hope that she could in fact escape from him.

↩

It didn't take long for the alien to relocate his prey, and in their exhausted state, the captain and the demon man were way too slow to escape. The captain howled in pain as he was lifted by the top of his head and shaken about while the alien closed in on the demon man. The alien showed no outward sign of strain, frustration, or even pain, yet the pockmarks showed that he had been injured repeatedly by gunfire, and he now had an oozing mark on one of his feet.

Once the alien had his prey, he turned around, placed the two downward facing in the middle of an intersection, and released them. Panting hard, the two men looked at each other in fear. They had only a moment to regain their composure as the alien grabbed for his belt device, and an unspoken, undefined plan emerged between the two. The alien held the device high, and in what appeared to be an animalistic display of domination, he turned his back to them and roared victoriously. With a nod of the captain's head, the two spun in different directions and fled as fast as humanly possible.

↩

Sasha felt the alien's presence behind her, but there was no time to stop, no time to look back, and after a few more seconds, no pursuit either. She held the device in her hand. It felt like a cane in size and weight, yet the interface on the top was incomprehensible. Whatever its value, it was certainly less than that of Emilia's, and now Sasha would have to return to face an unbeatable opponent or face a lifetime of guilt. The choice was more difficult than she would have admitted to anybody.

The image of the battle replayed in her mind's eye over and over. The speed, the agility, and the power were all on a level far beyond her own, and no scenario in her head ever played out in a victory. Sasha spun in circles, knowing that she once again faced an unfair and difficult decision. She held the alien's cane and lifted it before her.

Sasha looked up toward the heavens. "Come on, you bastard, give me something, anything." Tears slipped from her eyes, but nothing happened. She prayed, "Come on, you bastard, don't screw me over, after all of this." There was still nothing, just nothing in response. Sasha wasn't sure exactly what she was waiting for, but she knew what the silence meant. She was on her own.

A strong feeling of abandonment crept into her heart, along with anger and rage. But she kept her composure, waiting for a sign. She even dropped down to a knee in hopes of a sign, one that never came, and the longer she waited, the angrier she became. She felt alone and orphaned by a Lord who would smite the innocent of their health, separate children from their parents, and let loose a plague of alien scum to destroy everything she loved and created. No, it was no longer time for prayer; it was time for revenge.

↩

His thighs burned, his head pounded, his throat burned, and his feet barely seemed to move. The captain scanned his surroundings, hoping and praying for help, but none appeared. He rounded a corner and took a second to catch his breath. Surprisingly, this area of the city, 56th and Lexington, looked mostly intact, and while this street was unfamiliar to him, he knew where he needed to go.

Getting there was going to be a problem. Peeking around the corner wasn't what gave his position away, but it was the start of his next round of problems. Seeing that the alien had pursued him, he hoped that the demon man would return with the cavalry, but soon the alien had the captain trapped in his clutches once more.

The captain kicked, twisted, and shouted, but every blow that he landed seemed to be nothing more than a pat on the shoulder to his captor. The alien continued to hold him high while using his free arm to grab the tool from his belt. The captain pleaded in between gasps of air as he flung his legs out wildly. The captain pinched the alien's arms, searching for a miracle, only to find one.

An image appeared from the alien's wrist device, and in rehearsed order, the captain's captor dropped to a knee in some sort of ceremonial tradition. Noises ripped across his ears, but it was all incomprehensible except for the tone. The alien's grip on the captain's throat tightened to near-death levels, the pace of his breathing increased dramatically, and the constant interruption by the other alien gave the strong impression of an employee being scolded. And that led the captain to believe that he may want something to vent on.

After several more seconds, the image disappeared and his captor rose with a howl, stared into the captain's eyes, and then shoved the tool down his throat.

↩

His nasty reptilian body hovered over Emilia like a dirty old man on a desperate prostitute. He rested one of his hands across her face and the other on her stomach. Rage swirled through Sasha's body as her heart primed its engine.

It was Sasha's intent to break the device, but it proved to be sturdily built, and as she slammed the device against the wall, it only rang out with a chime. Never before during any exercise had she ever felt weak, and she only hoped her anger would be enough to overcome it. Overcoming it looked like her only choice, for the alien's attention was once again directly on her.

She could feel the fog's presence, but it lacked focus, unaware of how to protect itself. The alien burst through the air like a swimmer from a wall, and within no time, he held the other half of the tool and stood face-to-face with Sasha. She pushed the fear away with anger—anger that she fueled with the spite of a Lord who didn't prevent shit but instead piled it on, tempting her over and over again, with relief just outside her fingertips. But that fear had no place in a determined mind on a suicide mission.

Sasha could see death's wake on her opponent's soul. Human flesh hung from his teeth, and his breath stung her face. If this was the worst hell could give her, then she would bring down her deliverance. And with that, she sprang.

↩

There it was, a light at the end of a tunnel, no sound, no feeling, only light and dark. Death was much more like the stories than Drexter ever would have imagined. So this is it, he thought to himself, a lifetime of service to my country and Sasha, and this is how I die. His conscious mind flooded with the images of his past few days, the hardships, the anguish, and the simply unfair way he was treated. If that's fucking God, he thought, then fuck God. He felt a seed of anger plant inside his chest.

Falsely arrested, abandoned by the authorities, forgotten, and betrayed, Captain Drexter was getting himself angrier with every reason he could think of. "Where the fuck are God's people? If God was so damn great, then why the hell does this hell exist? If God's going to abandon us and the devil's going to screw us, then it's time to take care of ourselves."

The captain's roar of rage startled a pair of strange men as one of them was shining a light into his eyes. The startle caused one of them to burst out with, "Oh shit," as he fell back. The captain exploded off the ground, took a warrior stance, and began searching. The new group of strangers who had gathered around him didn't register in his mind, as it was singularly focused on battle.

The rage and adrenaline only lasted a few seconds, for after he stood up, his body's physical demands became overbearing, and he fell back down to his knees, dry heaved, and tipped over on his side.

The light returned, but this time, the captain couldn't fight it anymore. Exhausted and confused, he embraced the light, closed his eyes, and slept.

↢↣

Sasha's body lifted through the air like an acrobat launching from a trampoline. Her body spun, rolled, and twirled in the air, making the alien's counterattack look like a wild miss and allowing her to land down hard on his back. Sasha still held on to the device, and with all her might, she pulled it hard, hoping to lodge it in what would have been his neck, but again the alien was too powerful and too agile.

The pullback from the alien ripped the device from her grasp, and as a bronco to an unwanted rider, Sasha was thrown back across the elevator shaft. This time, she felt the injury as her shoulder dislodged from its socket. The pain seized her body as it instinctively curled up into the fetal position.

The alien stood tall over Sasha, grabbed her by the throat, and raised her like a trophy. He unholstered his staff and raised it in preparation for his victory slaying. Misfortune favored Sasha as the alien discovered a malfunction in his tool, rendering it useless. Discouraged by the lack of either progress or success, plus Sasha's repeated interruptions, the alien was having no more of it. Sasha hung desperately as the alien grabbed her right leg and broke it in half before tossing her body into the kitchen.

She shrieked as the alien turned his attention back to Emilia. With his primary tool damaged, he once again assumed the position above Emilia. Sasha crawled up to a sitting position, but her entire body winced in pain, her brow dripped with sweat, and tears fluttered down in between. Desperate and hopeless, Sasha could only watch as the alien bent down closer to Emilia.

↩

A stern slap to the face along with, "Stay with me, Captain," took away the drowsiness, but the pain and fuzziness remained. People he didn't recognize were talking to him in words that he was having trouble understanding. Even the needle poke barely registered through the muddle of information being thrown at his brain. The captain could feel his head bobbing slightly, but where his head was in relation to the world, he couldn't say.

His body rose as if his soul held back on its lift into heaven. Slowly, ever so slowly, the world around him grew in clarity. First the vague outlines of the skyscrapers babbled their way into the heavens, and then came the shapes of uniformed people. Last, as his sound mind snapped back into place, the confusion of his present circumstances returned as, up on one of those skyscrapers, he saw an alien climbing after a man he knew and now shared a bond with.

The demon man was scurrying up a ladder, much slower than the alien was ascending. The alien still had another two flights of straight ladder before he reached the demon man, but it would be no more than a minute before it was too late.

The captain ripped the needle out of his arm as soon as he was laid down in the rear of the ambulance. Surprised, the small Asian man posed little resistance, and the captain soon shoved another paramedic out of the driver seat as he limped in from the rear cabin. His body screamed out in protest with every motion, but the adrenaline and morphine worked well enough to mute it. He had failed Sasha, he had failed his cellmates, and he had failed himself, but he would be damned if he was going to fail again with the demon man.

The captain put on his seat belt and floored the vehicle.

29: Love's Need

Her love needed her, and she needed her love. Sasha cursed herself, this horrible beast, and this or any god who would set such events in motion. She again faced the fear of her weakness, but this time, she lacked the energy to summon enough anger to overcome it. She was weak, powerless, and next in line to be eaten, harvested, or whatever was planned for them.

A chill ran down her body as the alien lowered his head next to Emilia's. His mouth moved ever so close to hers, almost close enough to lick the tears running down. Horrible images ran through Sasha's mind as she could only sit helplessly watching, like witnessing a slow-motion train wreck, unable to look away yet incapable of intervening.

Yet Sasha had a gift, the fog. The alien revealed its tender organ hidden behind an armored skin, reaching out like a sucker feels it path beforehand. The fog blurred the world around it, focusing, tunneling, and narrowing it all down to one target, one chance. Sasha crawled over to the kitchen. With great agony, she pulled herself up, searched for a knife, and once again faced her tormentor.

↩

The airbag struck Drexter's face like a boxer late in the fifth with a clean shot. The rest of his body bounced back and forth a bit

before coming to a slouched rest on a deflating bag. There was no
plan, just rage, and a short moment after the collision, his rage had
vanished with the return of his awareness.

Had the beast landed without injury or with better balance,
the captain would have been an easy kill, but the beast fell on
his back, with a gut-wrenching hiss of pain. The bounce from
the alien's fall shook the vehicle so hard the captain was tossed
hard, back into the seat. Dazed, the captain could only lie still,
lacking the strength and clarity to go on. The cabin of the vehicle
lay motionless as two fatigued warriors each pursued the will and
capacity to carry on.

A stinging round of coughing from the captain finally burst
the bubble of silence, renewing the urgency of purpose between
the two warriors. The captain leaned to his side, attempting to roll
onto the passenger side of the vehicle. Pain signals pinged his brain
in a constant chorus of pulsing, throbbing, and piercing, drummed
out only by the sound of one voice in his head. With the captain's
fire again lit, he crawled, leaned, and dragged his ass over to the
passenger side and opened the door.

Looking back as he exited, he saw the alien down on a
knee, interacting with his wrist. The captain threw his arms out,
bracing himself against the ground as he dragged his body behind.

Emilia's body sent out a scream, a scream that communicated much more than fear. The tone was hollow, like a recording.
The sound came out mechanical, as if synthesized. And the
message was empty, as if her mind had been taken out of the loop.
Sasha pulled herself along, unable to put even the slightest pressure
on her leg. Crawling along the ground made for the quickest form

of motion.

Sasha could only imagine what was happening to Emilia. The beast maintained Emilia's pose as her body twisted, shunted, and pulled in any direction in a futile escape. While he was deeply involved in his process, Sasha was able to close ranks much faster than expected, without drawing the alien's attention. Fast is smooth, and smooth is fast, and Sasha found a rhythm: knee-wrist-toes, knee-wrist-toes. A fully healthy Sasha would have been in striking range.

She moved with a purpose and as if with a guide. The fog prepared her for the dangers, focused her efforts on mission needs, and readied her for the unexpected. Beautiful streams of silver clouds rushed alongside her, urging her to move quicker, faster, and smoother. The alien finished with Emilia and rested her back down, her eyes frozen open, her body stiff. He turned to face Sasha as she closed width, but it was too late. She finally had the advantage, and with that advantage, she plunged a knife down into that alien's tender facial organ.

↤⌐

Hands again greeted the captain's shoulder and dragged him up. Luckily, they were the hands of two uniformed police officers. "Oh shit, Chip, it's that guy from before." The voice was familiar, but he couldn't place it offhand.

A reply came between heavy breaths. "Just carry, rook, just fucking carry."

The captain was being dragged toward a stretcher by the very two officers who had arrested him sometime before. "You assholes left us to fuckin' die in there, not even a sip of clean fuckin' water." The captain spoke an emotion not quite clear. The emotion was not anger, for he had used up all of his anger. It wasn't betrayal, as he didn't feel a specific anger toward these two individuals, and it wasn't hate. It was an emotion higher than instinct. It was overpowering of the need for self-preservation, fear of pain and death, and it was actionable.

The captain's body stood in protest. He would follow his emotion, and he would assert himself by not allowing the assistance of those who would leave him to face such a hell. "I will not be manhandled again by the likes of you two."

The young Hispanic officer stepped back, trying to minimize his sense of awe. The older officer, however, just rolled his eyes and growled at the younger officer. "Listen here, man, a whole hell of a fucking lot of people got left behind, or the royal up-the-ass-fucking treatment. After nearly thirty years of this job, you know what I've learned?" There was a pause only long enough to make effect. "You can only help the people in front of you. Let God deal with the fuckin' rest of the bunch. Now lay the hell down, and let us get you to the med tent. Colonel Major's going to want to speak with you, if you really are military."

With that, the captain basically collapsed into the stretcher they had been carrying him toward.

↩

The fog burned with a yellowish red. Again and again, it told her to thrust the knife deep into its victim. The alien screamed out in a wretched wail that pierced Sasha's ears. His arms flailed up, grasping at his attacker. Sasha wrapped her good leg around the alien's neck while still hacking at the organ.

A terrible-smelling ooze poured out of the wound, and while a powerful hand finally grasped Sasha's leg, it was too late and the strength of the grip dwindled fast. Still with great energy, the alien curled into a semi-fetal position and paused. The smell intensified as the pus began to boil up into big bubbles, bursting forth with the most wretched chemical smell Sasha could have imagined.

A new sound emerged from the alien as he screamed skyward. A powerful shock wave exploded throughout the area, throwing Sasha once again against the elevator-shaft wall. A piece of debris slashed a deep cut in Sasha's side, spewing her blood in a huge mess.

Sasha lay stunned in pain and discomfort, a warm liquid dampened her clothes along her side, her leg bent awkwardly, and her head was getting lighter and lighter.

↩

A barrage of gunfire startled the captain back to awareness. Again a needle lay in his arm, a bag of saline dripping into his veins. He could feel a return of his strength, but every muscle, every joint, called out in protest at the slightest movement.

A wily-looking officer—complete with a flowing white mustache, a pencil-thin figure, a hard crusty nose, and long choppy eyebrows—closed in on the captain. "What in the Sam Hill is going on in my city? Where the hell are the reinforcements, and what the hell is the military going to do about these nasty creatures killing my officers?"

The captain slowly tilted his head back, taking in the funny-looking angry man. More gunfire burst from nearby the tent, jolting the people inside with its proximity. "Fine, just tell me how to kill these bastards!" The colonel shook the captain in frustration before a paramedic pulled him back.

The tent canopy was suddenly pulled back and thrown off as if it had been a blanket covering a table. Light temporarily blinded the group before the alien grabbed the paramedic and shoved his device down his throat. An officer with a silver collar opened fire on the alien, only to draw his attention and be next for the device insertion.

The rest of the group fled, while the captain lay too tired, too hurt to fight anymore. The alien approached and grasped the captain's thigh with one of his feet and then the other. Escape wasn't an option, but the weight of the alien bore less pain and pressure than expected. The captain attempted to throw a punch but was easily rebuked and held in a deep hold, able to move only enough for shallow breathing.

The alien moved his face in close. The droplets of saliva burned the captain's face. The three pillars running the length of his crown began bobbing up and down. The middle pillar moved so as to reveal a new horrible sight, a round grasping tendon. Black and slimy, it oozed its way onto the captain's face, exploding his mind with an overwhelming number of images and senses. The captain yelped in an echo of his voice, his body thrashed, and his head burned to the core of his brain.

⟵⟶

The voice rattled between the edges of Sasha's skull, bouncing, echoing, and rolling aimlessly until captured. Where the voice was coming from, she couldn't tell, but it came again and again. She felt the warmth on her hand, the numbness of her leg, and the lightness of her head, and she felt like it was time to sleep a nice, long sleep. That damn voice kept waking her up—didn't they know how damn tired she was?

A moment of silence finally arrived, and Sasha closed her eyes. This time, something hit her—not a powerful blow, nor did it hurt, but damn, she was never going to get any rest. The sounds rolling around in her head were getting louder and louder, more and more forceful. It seemed the more Sasha protested to sleep, the louder the voice became.

"Sasha! Sasha!" The word took hold but still needed time to round out into a thought. Who the hell was this calling her over and over again? Where the hell was she? The light reignited a throbbing headache as she attempted to open her eyes. The redness was awful. Movement caught her eye, but she had no desire to open her eyes again. She had only desire to sleep.

"Sasha! Sasha! Please, I need you." Again the light punched her brain in the face, but Sasha held strong, and this time, she could see the movement. Emilia was waving her arms. Sasha's heart pumped faster. Her mind was fuzzy, but she had to go, had to move—her love needed her.

↩

Drexter could feel the intruder. Its location pulsed with a throbbing ache, moving, shifting, and searching along his mind's pathways. The images came along, all of them his own memories. Memories he hadn't seen so clearly in years were at the fingertips of this alien bastard.

No matter how hard he tried to exert his will, he could gain no control. His life, his memories, and his feelings were being fast forwarded, rewound, and viewed in search of something. He focused hard on a single thought, trying forcefully to regain control of a front he never imagined fighting on: his own mind.

There was a certain moment when his bond with Sasha became parental in nature, no matter the biology. Her schooling began almost from birth. Being born into the program meant time spent with her biological parents was kept to a bare minimum. Toys and imagination play spurred creativity, while social interaction created dependency. The captain never had a natural paternal side, but a child's love in its purity overpowered his own preconceptions.

It happened by accident. A toy had fallen on the floor, and he simply bent over to pick it up. What happened next was completely unexpected. The voice came sweetly, softly. "What's your name?"

Mistaking the comment as being directed toward him, he paused in confusion.

"My name is Kitty. What's your name?" The movement of the child's toy now led him to comprehension.

In hindsight, he still wasn't sure what made him do it, but it set off a course of events that led him to where he was now. He said, "I'm Bob. Nice to meet you." Words can't express what a child's face can, and when the pure-glow joy lit up Sasha's face, who he would be changed forever.

Now he needed that moment again, and from that moment, he would fight outward, reclaim his mind, and pursue it to the physical, where he would reclaim his daughter.

30: Angels and Demons

The distance was daunting, the pain excruciating, and the will waning. Emilia called for her, but the words were hollow within Sasha's veins. Sasha threw her elbow forward but could no longer pull herself up. Her breaths were labored but shallow as the blood ran thinner and thinner.

The fog came again, but different. There was no aim, no message, just a void. None of her other senses seemed to be working either. Softness filled her body as her pain evaporated away. In the world of the fog, time had no meaning, no relevance. Sasha felt on the verge of sleep, unable and unwilling to wake up.

It was a blissful experience until her conscious mind failed to find a thought. No memories, no ideas, no sensations—it shifted into panic. Sasha thrashed with her mind, grasping wildly, hoping to catch a glance, a reminder, of who and where she was before.

Nothing came. Over and over again, nothing came. The void grew deeper, her body grew number, and her mind grew dimmer.

"Damn you, Lord. Cruelest such a bitch around. You better fucking take me into heaven, or so help me, I will find a damn way in." Sasha's tirade was intensely venomous in its mental delivery. Her mind now burned with a passion. Its fire grew with each new thought as Sasha repeatedly imagined herself coming face-to-face with the Lord.

"Hold your hand here. Put as much pressure as you can."
The words came with a warm sensation, from somewhere out
in the fog. While unfamiliar, the voice came again, stirring her
conscious mind back to life. And again the words came, each one
seeming to take a little bit of the fog with it as it rushed by.

The words came over and over, and as Sasha's mind lost
hold of its hate, an angel appeared.

↩

The images moved fast, tracing people as each memory of
the person was shown in linear order. Despite the home-field advantage, it took every ounce of the captain's strength to refocus on
his chosen memory, with each victory lasting but only a moment
before the alien recaptured control and resumed his search.

Finally the alien narrowed its focus to a single individual,
an individual the captain would hesitate to admit knowing. His
memories slowed down to a watching speed, and he saw himself
walking into her establishment for the first time. He was nervous,
excited, like a teenager in a man's body. She could have taken him
for all he was worth, but she was a woman. Her practiced Southern
charm, her presence, and her softness were all on display. She led
him to a room, sat next to him, and placed her hands along his
wrists. Again he pulled back toward the memory of Sasha, but its
effectiveness was waning, and he had now become erect while
battling in the emotion of the memory.

The captain had still failed to gain the upper hand, but he
had a new strategy to pursue. The alien continued to probe his
memory for her. Again he saw a memory of the baroness sitting

on his lap, her legs squeezing tightly around his waist. The feeling of passion grew, along with his erection, and his capacity to draw back to the memory had faded away. So he drew now on a more recent memory, a memory more connected to his passion and lust—his memory of Emilia.

He forced his mind to remember her legs, the skirt, the waist, and that gorgeous naughty-teen look she carried about her. Again the alien pulled back to his target, and the baroness held him from behind, nibbling on his ear and asking if he had been "satisfied." His erection pulsed to a near climax, when the captain started to worry he might not be able to regain control, and having someone else in his head made it hard to think. Again he retraced his fantasy, from his vehicle after their first meeting—if memories wouldn't work, maybe fantasy would. He came close to Emilia, kissing her neck and touching her breast and ass. He pulled back, and again the face and memory had shifted to the baroness. There she was, whispering so gently it came with a tickle on his ear: "I have someone special for you tonight." Fighting to take control, the captain altered the memory and replaced the girl with Emilia instead.

Yet the battle was lost over and over again. With every attempt, the captain failed to do anything but delay and annoy his invader.

↩

"Angel" was too unflattering a word for such a beautiful creature. Her hair, nasty and matted, floated above her. A brace stiffened her neck and hid her chin. Blood covered a uniform jacket that was much too big for her. Ripped shreds of a bandage hung uselessly underneath.

Had Emilia looked at herself in a mirror, she would have been horrified, but as Sasha lay helpless in her arms, she couldn't imagine a more beautiful sight. Tears streamed down Emilia's face, her hand applying pressure and unable to wipe them away. Sasha tried to speak, but her body failed to respond.

The blurry fog still blotted out most of the world, hiding with it most forms of thought, yet her angel was as clear as day, and as Sasha lay bleeding to death, she was struck by the thought that only a god of good could create something so beautiful out of something so awful.

↩

As the battle waged, the captain would draw away, only to be pulled back again. Each time he had met the baroness was carefully examined, crossed-checked, and rewatched. What the alien was looking for was definitely connected to the woman.

The connection broke, leaving behind a tear in the captain's mind. The pain was excruciating, radiating throughout every nerve in his head. Blackness filled both his eyes and his mind's eye. His body curled into the fetal position, and with a sudden drop, every muscle in his body relaxed.

The alien screeched as the demon man bore down an ax upon the back of his neck. Green blood burst forth from its wound, hissing in the air as it bubbled away. The ax swiveled wildly as the alien writhed in pain. Nearly invisible with its speed, the alien sent the demon man flying through the air with a devastating kick. The alien twisted and twirled as it finally grabbed hold of his splinter of pain.

For only a moment was the alien still, but for Colonel

Major, it was opportunity enough, and his weapon rang out with amazing accuracy. Three shots rang out, each one lodging into the alien's exposed organ. A barrage of bullets blasted across the alien's body as officer after officer emptied their clips into the beast.

The alien sauntered backward and then fell to the ground. In traditional fashion, a dog pile of officers immediately began linking together sets of cuffs to restrain the carcass, should he return to life.

The warmth was amazing, the tickle on the skin exhilarating, and the smell so intoxicating that Sasha was forced to open her eyes. Then she was forced to close them, as her mind refused to process what she had just seen. She decided that she must have been hallucinating. Her body felt warm all over, but there was an extra layer of heat along her leg, a deep penetrating warmth that seemed to massage down to the bone. Again came a most intoxicating smell, as if lavender and hickory exploded out of a chili relleno. Sasha was compelled to reopen her eyes, and again she was immediately compelled to close them.

A squeeze brought back her focus, and a gentle massage soothed her greatly. Sasha focused on sound, but she found none, as if she had gone deaf. The smell made it difficult to keep her eyes closed, and as she opened them for the third time, she was forced to acknowledge the truth of her situation. After her first alien encounter ended up in a battle to her near death, she was now at the mercy of an alien who looked like a scoop of dog food with a bunch of worms sticking out of it, and none too happy about it.

Sasha kept her eyes open, yet she still found it entirely too difficult to see. "How did you find me?" The mute vibrations of her words were the only sound. A stone was slid into the palm of her hand by a tentacle she hadn't even noticed was there.

A voice rang out, but the sound came from within her mind: "My poor dear, we just followed the trail of death and destruction. Now tell me, how do you feel?"

Sasha closed her eyes again. "I'll let you know when I wake up."

↩

A deep, penetrating blackness surrounded the captain. A void filled this thoughts, and a blankness of sensation fell across his body. For several minutes, nothing happened. Then, as if a light switch had been turned on, all of his senses returned. He was overwhelmed by the amount of sensation. The light was intensely bright, the wind intensely cold, the noise deafening, and the pain frightening.

A voice rang out in his head: "Relax, you're in a place of healing now." The voice was clear, but his mind was still unable or unwilling to process the overwhelming amount of sensation he was feeling. There was only one the captain could think of that could speak directly into his brain. "Lord, is that you?"

A chuckle accompanied the voice's response: "Oh my, no, but we are all children of God. I'm a healer. We were sent here to help you recover from the Xendorian attack. Such brutal bastards, they have no respect for lower life."

For a moment, the captain had forgotten it all—the pain,

the alien, the deaths, and even Sasha. "Sasha, where is Sasha?" His body exploded in alertness as his mind finished rebooting. His ears could hear the commotion of background noises ranging from screams of pain to soothing music to beeps and hums of electronics. His nose filled with a barrage of flavors—lavender, melted plastic, laundry detergent. Each smelled distinct yet fluid as they shifted in and out.

The captain opened his eyes again, and there above him was yet another alien.

↩

Sasha opened her eyes—no alien. With relief, she hoped that the whole thing had simply been a dream. The oozing, swirling patch of gel around her leg and ribs suggested otherwise. She tried to move her leg but found it incredibly stiff. In fact, the harder she tried to move the leg, the stiffer it became. After a few failed attempts, she gave up.

Sasha was in a hospital, a human hospital. The room looked like a typical hospital room, with two beds separated by a hanging sheet and a window overlooking another tall building across the street. A beautiful blue light radiated into the room from the outside. The TV was off, and her sense of hearing had returned. While the room itself was pretty quiet, there was a lot of activity going on in the hallways.

She examined her own physical condition and realized that her leg had shifted. This time, she wiggled her leg, only to find it willing to comply. She recognized many of the cords and devices that were hooked up to her. It was not the first time she had woken up from the fog in a hospital.

Sasha traced back her memories. How far back did the dream start? Was Emilia real? Sasha's body was showing the signs of severe bruising, but that wasn't a first either. The gel around her leg made her nervous, very nervous, for she had dreamt that an alien broke her leg in a horrific battle.

She turned to the side, only to find it painful throughout much of her torso. She looked under her hospital gown and found much of her body to be tightly wrapped. She wanted to jump down, wanted to start her search for her father and, if real, Emilia. Yet Sasha's wants had finally been denied by her body, her will no longer forceful enough to overcome the pain and injury. So she lay back down and waited. She would need time to recoup the will, she would need time to adjust to the pain, and she would need time to clear her brain. With much guilt and trepidation, Sasha rested.

↩

Keeping his eyes closed felt like the better option for the moment, yet allowing a delay in finding Sasha wasn't acceptable. "Where is Sasha?"

Again the voice echoed deep from within the captain's own brain: "I'm sorry, I don't know what a Sasha is? Is it a food?"

"It's my daughter, you idiot! Now damn it, get me someone who knows where she is, or get me on my feet so I can find her. Now!"

A new voice, a somewhat familiar voice, rang out from outside his brain. "Those are the words of the father, not a soldier. I'm fearful to make an assumption, then, that you are not part of a larger group sent here to assist us with our alien problem." A warm hand then grabbed hold of his. "It's ok to open your eye now, son.

I promise they work again. These here doctors are more than I ever could have imagined." The words soothed and commanded, spoken by an authority used to handling and de-escalating tense moments.

A kind smile, a curly white mustache, and a badge that read "Major" greeted the captain as he opened his eyes. "It's good to see you still got fight in you, because we are going to need as many good men as we can find before this is over. Now, why don't I get my men to track down your daughter while you come with me? The mayor and Mr. Cook want to see us as soon as possible. So up we go." A gentle yet strong hand wrapped around the captain's wrist, and with a practiced manner, Colonel Major maintained control of the conversation. "Now tell me Sasha's last name and known location."

↩

Oh, God, that snoring was obnoxious. It was completely disruptive to her sleep, and it had to stop. Sasha's body ached, pinched, and squeezed all at the same time, yet she could feel the correction, the sheer amount of healing, that had occurred in just a short nap. Her leg responded gracefully, quickly learning how to move at maximum allowable speed. The bandages across her midsection squeezed her chest, forcing her to make concentrated breaths, and pinged with pain at every little rock underfoot.

Sasha pulled the curtain back, both hoping for and hoping against it being her father or her Emilia. Instead, it was a dark-colored white man. Deep bruises covered the front of his chest, and tubes ran in and out of the man's side. Braces held his head and neck relatively in place, and more tubes ran into and out of his nose. The snoring was vibrating against the tubes and making an awful racket along with it.

After seeing a large burn mark in the shape of a cross, Sasha no longer had the heart to wake the man up, but the noise couldn't continue either. Across the room, she spotted an oscillating fan but had to let it go, as a rib poked out with a punch of protest. Despite her best intentions, the man in the bed—who she was now noticing had two dark-red imprints surrounding his eyes—woke up. "The demons have come. God's wrath is descending upon us! We must flee! We must flee!" The man's body writhed as he pressed to escape his medical and mental prisons. Alarms buzzed and machines beeped as the man continued to struggle. "No mercy for the damned, no mercy for the damned. I must flee! No mercy for me!"

Two humans in white coats rushed into the room and helped restrain the man. A third woman in a blue outfit entered the room with a needle and, with a skilled hand, inserted it into a tube that soon flooded the drugs into the man's body. For several more minutes, the man ranted out gibberish while the three attendants held him in place as best they could. Gradually winding down, the man started to whisper rather than scream, and mutter more than speak.

The whole sight frightened Sasha even more than her dream of fighting the alien. A chill ran through her, and the hair on her arms stood up. The woman in the blue uniform came close. "Sorry about that. I'm glad to see you're feeling well enough to stand and even move around some. I must insist, however, that you get back in bed. You still need plenty of rest after your ordeal. I don't care how miraculous these new doctors are."

The woman's response further dashed Sasha's hopes of it

all being a dream, but she still held on a little longer in fear of it all. "What happened? What's going on?"

The woman let out a snicker. "All I know, my dear, is that a surge of patients came in like a flood. I'd never seen this hospital so overwhelmed before, and the poor victims had the most horrific injuries. We were well past overwhelmed, when all of a sudden, these scary-ass barrel monkeys showed up out of nowhere. At first we shit and pissed ourselves a little bit, but as we all stood there motionless, the monkeys sprang into action. To be honest, my first thought was that they were going to eat the patients, but no, it quickly became apparent that they were saving them, and at record speeds and with incredible accuracy. Now, my dear, how on earth," the lady left an unusual pause, "did you end up here?"

Sasha looked at the woman. Her face was very kind but not very pretty. Sasha searched her mind but found only a headache at the end of each thought. After a hesitation, the woman came back. "My dear, why don't we start with your name?"

It was an embarrassingly long pause, but Sasha was able to finally speak at last. "Sasha, my name is Sasha."

The woman smiled and was about to speak when the man burst out again with renewed vigor despite the drugs. "Sasha, Sasha, I must find Sasha. That's what he said."

"Excuse me, but that's what who said?" Sasha felt her heart flutter as the hope of finding her father grew.

"Mister loony tunes, here. Arrived here just ahead of you." A large smile broke out across the nurse's face. "Oh my, now isn't that a miracle, the two of you ending up together?"

An instant frown broke out across Sasha's face. "But I don't know this man. How could, or why would, he be looking for me?"

The smile on the nurse's face evaporated to embarrassment. "My apologies, honey, I guess it's just coincidental. Now, why don't you just lie back down, and I will see if I can get you some breakfast. I hear they have some MREs now, on two." The nurse took the fan and set it up, all the while watching carefully to make sure that Sasha was able to get into bed.

31: The Briefing

The leg and torso moved without pain, yet he couldn't seem to lose the limp. The elder policeman escorted Captain Drexter with a practiced patience. Barking frequent commands into a headset, he spoke clearly and concisely, yet generally enough to still give his lieutenants flexibility in carrying out their tasks.

From what the captain could glean, while it was bad everywhere, he must have been in one of the worst spots. One, maybe two more alien intruders still roamed and probed the populace. It was a short walk to the command center, but at the captain's limited speed, it felt like it took forever to get there. Luckily, the center was located in the basement, and descending stairs was no trouble at all.

The room was lit, but a severe lack of power still kept most of the monitors dark. The space buzzed with activity, but in the middle, as always, was the politician. A short black man with the most awful haircut—long and slicked back, yet short on the sides—and a well-trimmed mustache sat surrounded by a group of staffers who were talking rapidly. One man sat to the mayor's side, but he looked disinterested as if lost in a daydream or memory.

The colonel led the captain around the ramp and down into the center pit. The mayor waved off his staffer and stood up to shake the colonel's hand as they walked in. The mayor started a round of applause, and the room gradually caught on and joined in. "My friends, the guardians of our city, and defeaters of Goliath. These men have suffered dearly and accomplished a great deal, for which we owe them very much."

After the round of applause had run its course, the mayor sat back down and summoned the two closer. "Captain . . . Drexter, is it? Glad to have you here with us. My name is Mayor Mandainity, but most people just call me Big M. These are very trying times, as you well know. My people have been murdered at the hands of ruthless alien bastards. Obviously they have the capability of blowing our assholes out through China, yet they do not. Why? Can you tell me this, please? Why have they taken this city, and what are they searching for? Please, what can you tell me? I immigrated to this great city when I was just a little boy, and this city took me in, and I became one of its people. Then I became its protector. Now I serve as its leader. This city is me and my people. How can the army simply do nothing?"

The captain unconsciously took a step back. "I wish I knew more. I was on my way to meet with my unit when some of your boys decided to throw me in fucking jail. I was in the jail when all of a sudden the world went bonkers, as if gravity got fucking hammered. Then these big-ass waves slammed against the wall, shit rose up from below, and corpses floated about till the fourth fucking horseman broke down the cell, probing and killing the hell out of people. Now why don't you tell me what the hell I don't know, starting with where the hell my daughter Sasha is?"

The mayor and the colonel exchanged glances before the colonel responded with grace. "It's too premature to say, but there were two teen survivors from the other alien battle sight. I have a unit going over there now, to personally handle it."

Then the mayor said, "So what I am not hearing is that you are part of a larger unit. I'm not hearing that there are federal resources pouring in from—well I wouldn't fucking care where, you know? I am not hearing good news for us, so are you a deserter?"

The captain smiled with the news that she was alive. Of course Sasha would have found her way to the center of the battle, and "two teens" must have meant that Emilia survived also. "No, mayor, I'm a parent. Not only am I a parent—I am a parent of the most miraculous teen to ever grace this earth. I can tell you right now what happened at that other battle sight. Alien met Sasha, Sasha killed alien, and alien got in a lucky last blow."

Big M tucked in his shirt. "Yes, my friend, but let's hope her injuries were nothing more than just a lucky blow. She is being taken care of at the hospital. Now please help me so that you can go to your daughter."

Captain Drexter looked over at the colonel to receive confirmation and reassurance. "Mr. Mayor, I'm not sure what you want from me, but my primary mission in the army is the oversight of that teen girl. My place is by her side."

The mayor started to pace back and forth, his face posed with a serious and stern look. "If my need were not so great, I would not be so insistent. I need a man who understands how a chain of freakin' command works. I need a man who can organize chaos, plan ahead, and follow through. That uniform and rank tells me that you have those skills. My best man, my best friend, was taken by these bastards. But I'm not even sure which bastards took him. My next-best man is a useless lump of shit so caught up in the loss you could throw him off a fucking cliff." Big M flailed his short arms about, gesturing in the direction of the man sitting behind his chair. "My next step would be to take a specialist out of their field and comfort zone. So I am drafting you to be my acting emergency manager. It will be a learn-as-you-go job. Welcome to the team. The colonel here will show you around and get you settled while I ready the transition. Nice meeting you, Captain Drexter." Then, with a direct wave of his hand, he motioned the two men off and returned to his prior briefing.

The colonel started a conversation as they walked down a ramp. Ahead was a faintly lit room full of display monitors. "You will learn to like the mayor. Not for his personality, of course, but for his love of humanity. We ourselves had a rocky start. I found his tone and manners abrasive and insulting, yet every time a complex issue arose, he was loyal, perceptive, and understanding. Don't worry, I think you will learn to like the team. Oh, and your daughter and her friend will be escorted shortly after they receive the final go-ahead from the doctors to be released."

"Colonel, I appreciate the welcome, but I fully intend to tell the mayor that I will not perform his requested actions. My duties are clear, to find and maintain my daughter, Sasha. She could very well be a key to human survival in this new, multi-being universe." Captain Drexter stood as erect as possible, almost at attention. "I have no other responsibility, nor can I accept any. My plate is full."

The colonel smiled. "Yeah, go ahead and tell him that and see how things go."

↩

The room was amazing, half sci-fi tech lab and half WWII

bunker. Many of the consoles were blank, and only a simple screen display of statistics appeared on what the colonel referred to as RUDY. On it was a count of officers, with numbers displaying active, injured, on rest, and unaccounted for. At the moment, the last column had the largest number in it. Below was also a list for fire and medic staff along with transportation administration, customs and federal agents, reserves, and recruits. Below that was an inventory of goods.

The colonel gave a rundown of what the total capabilities of the room were, but at minimal power, it was about as good as an early 2000s cell phone. He then moved into the current communication system, as installed by the captain's predecessor. Each building was to select three people to act as communication runners and another five to act as general labor, and they were to identify any special skills or equipment within their building.

"Currently we have the general-labor pool working with Commander Thomas over at a downed building. Damn tidal wave knocked the entire son of a bitch down. Don't believe there was a single survivor from inside that place. God rest their souls. Today is a dark day, and my men need to be out there in the thick of it, and right now they're out there doing without me. Now, my XO is a good man, but they need me, and you're here to replace me." The colonel pressed the keyboard below the screen and brought up a street map of the island.

Pointing to each location as he spoke, he moved fast, obviously ready to get to a new task. "Here is where your battle area was. Here is where your daughter's battle area was. Here is where—"

The captain interrupted and touched the same locations

on the map. "And where are we now?" The colonel pointed, but before he could speak, the captain again interrupted him and took over the conversation. "Now where is my daughter? Because you seem to be making many assumptions about what I am willing and able to do. My one priority is Sasha. After I know what state she is in, I can then contribute to solving your problems—depending, of course, on her status."

The colonel took a big smell of the air and sized up the captain long and hard. "Your persistence will serve you well in this office. I think you will make a fine addition around here, and trust me, we are shorthanded." The colonel spoke again, into his shoulder mic, and after a few exchanges, a nervous look crossed his face. "Well it, uh, seems that your daughter is quite a handful, and she is refusing to leave the hospital until she see her father, Captain Drexter."

Captain Drexter couldn't hold back the smile that now beamed across his face. He had never known a woman's love, other than Sasha's. He felt that a woman's touch could be bought and paid for, but a woman's love could only be earned. Sometimes he could sense it, feel it, from her—the baroness. She had a way a looking deep into his soul and fishing out the best of it. Never once did he ever mention Sasha, but she knew. Whether it was intuition, psychic powers, or something else, she knew how to make a heart feel cared for, if only briefly.

Drexter signaled for the walkie-talkie, and the colonel handed it over. "Sasha, Sasha, it's me. Can you hear me, Sasha?"

There was a long pause before the radio returned with chatter. "Are you?"

The sound wasn't enough to be convincing, but the captain pressed the button, waited a second, and then continued. "Sasha, IS THERE ANY FOG THERE?"

Again there was a long pause, but what came back was decidedly the sound of a teenage girl, as a hint of attitude was unmistakable. "I'm fine, Dad, thanks for asking. Now, where are you? And how does this man I'm with know who I am? How could you leave us alone with those rapist bastards?"

The attitude was reassuring, but the captain still felt his heart jump as she finished. He spoke in a heightened tone, even before firmly pressing the button. "What rapist? What man? Sasha, what MAN? What has he done to you?"

Again came the long pause. "It was the Synied security guards. They attacked me. I fought them off. There is a man here who keeps screaming out my name, some guy in the hospital room with me. Who is he? How does he know who I am?"

"Security? Where are you? Are you ok?"

There was another pause. "That was six questions. Six questions before you asked if I'm all right."

The father in him couldn't help but respond. "No, it was the sixth question, not six before."

"You know what, I think I want to stay here some more. I've suddenly developed a headache."

The captain's frustration boiled over, and he shook the radio vehemently. Calmer now, he spoke in a softer and smoother tone. "Sasha, I'm very glad you're ok. Now will you please join the policeman and come here? Later we can figure out what to do about security and who that hospital guy is."

Again came the pause. "NO."

He shook the radio again, almost slamming it down on the ground. Having been down this road in the past, he knew all too well that he had annoyed her and she was looking for a fight. It was time to change tactics, and he had a new strategy in mind. "Sasha, how is Emilia?"

The dramatic change in tone was unexpected and worrisome. With great emotion and sobs, the long silence was broken: "n't know. I don't knowwwww."

The colonel, being a competent man, had already acquired another radio and was simultaneously hunting down Emilia. It wasn't long before he had a room number of a likely candidate and relayed it to the captain.

Drexter spoke into his radio. "Sasha, calm down and take some deep breaths. Control the fog, first and foremost. I have good news for you, Sasha. Emilia is fine. She is in room 802A. Now will you please come here?"

By now, the two had become accustomed to the long pause, but this one stretched on and on before, finally, a man's voice came across. "Hello, hello. Captain, Colonel, Sasha has dropped the radio and bolted out of here. I will attempt to follow her."

Placing his head in his hands, Captain Drexter shook his head. "Now you see how full my plate is."

The colonel smiled big. "Children, I have four. Now back to the briefing."

"Wait a second, Colonel. Not to nitpick, but could any of your children single-handedly kill one of those aliens, or every man in this room, including me? While I appreciate the sentiment, my child is also a weapon of mass destruction."

←⌐

While no one stood at attention, the room came to a sudden halt as if all the air had been sucked out when the mayor walked in. He strode confidently for his small stature. A cache of assistants and position holders spread out, surrounding the machine known as RUDY. The colonel nudged the captain to the appropriate seat, and the group sat in near unison with the mayor.

"Just to make sure we are all on the same damn page here, Earth is in the fucking sky. How it got there, I don't fucking know. Aliens are rampaging our streets, probing and killing my, our, people. Anyone disagree that our number-one priority should be fortifying the fuck out of this city?" The mayor looked around the table, locking eyes with each person. "Colonel, something to say?"

The colonel coughed and cleared his throat. "If I pull my men away from the food supplies, we could face two huge hurdles. One, it simply won't be enough and the effort will be futile. Two, the second we pull away from the supplies, those with the guns are going to take them, and that will mean a strong, organized crime element, and we could lose what, at the moment, is our mandate to lead—the food and water."

The mayor slammed his fist down on the table. "Damn it, man, you're right. Keep your men where they are. That, however, doesn't mean we can't or shouldn't do anything. Transit authority, security guards, fucking militia volunteers need to be organized.

Who wants to run that fucking show . . . Drexter? You have already protested to the assignment. Make your choice now, office job or field job."

The captain was at a loss. He felt confident Sasha was ok, but he didn't care about these people, didn't care about this city or its problems. "Mr. Mayor, I decline both. My mission is more important than whatever you think can be accomplished here. I will give you what advice I might have, but this isn't my show or my story. Sasha is all I care about and the only thing I want to focus on."

The mayor rolled his hands together and then wiggled his fingers before standing. He seemed quite composed and cool, yet he climbed onto the table. He strolled down the center of it, looking each person in the eye as he passed. Finally, he stood tall by the captain. "What the fuck kind of man are you?"

The captain wasn't normally a man to be intimidated, but the mayor's smallish stature somehow had a demanding and commanding presence.

"Captain Drexter here thinks he is too fucking important to help. Too goddamn important. He has to baby his baby, maybe suckle that teet and all."

Expecting an assault, the captain raised his hand and edged forward in his seat, but the assault still came unexpectedly as the mayor fell down, off the table, and into the captain's lap. The mayor feminized his voice as he continued. "Awww, Daddy, I'm so glad we survived the apocalypse. But, Daddy, where are my friends? Why are we the only ones alive? Why do you keep sticking that thing in me?" The mayor batted his eyes and then slapped the captain before rolling back onto the table.

"This man is obviously too pussy to lead men into combat, Colonel. Leave your man in charge of the police. You are taking command of all unassigned personnel. Captain, when you are ready to clean that sand out of your clit, I need you to take charge of coordinating operations here."

The mayor returned to the head of the table, turned around to face the staff, and casually jumped back off the table and calmly sat down again. The captain was frozen with embarrassment and stunned with anger. He felt like both laughing and attacking. The colonel shot the captain a look that said, if nothing else, "I told you so."

The mayor, obviously having some experience dressing down assertive men, took no time to let the situation linger. Instead, he broke out and continued the meeting as if nothing had happened. "Moving on, I need a clear rundown of what resources I have available. Mr. Anderson, I need to know what the hell is going on with our equipment."

One of the men sitting along the far side of the table shuffled some papers, and after a hesitant start and a look of apology to the captain, he finally answered. "Well, yes, um. Mostly bad news, I am afraid. Whatever has happened has completely detached us from the power grid. There is the mothballed Edison compound, but we would need to do some work to get that up and running, and let's just say that it's going to be dirty and we are going to need a lot of coal. Currently there are forty known build-ings with positive power supplies from their own internal sources.

"As for our equipment here, we are still working on getting

our primary generator turned on. Our secondary generator is only equipped to last a day or two, so our time is running short.

"All vehicles, public and civilian, have somehow been disabled. The mechanics are optimistic they might be able to get a pre-computer vehicle up and running.

"Food—all designated storage and food venders have been declared positive control, but as expected, it didn't take long before several, if not all, of the smaller outlets got raided.

"Radios and batteries are currently enough to last, but once they start running out of juice, we have no way of recharging them. Luckily, Mr. Hashmore implemented the runner system before he left, so we can still communicate with the others, but we have no idea of the total losses yet.

"The hospitals have enough reserves to last out a week, but as of right now, we are basically looking at a return to the damn Stone Age."

"Hold the commentary, damn it. Focus on getting what good fuel we have in reserves to the places that need it." The mayor moved on to his next assistant before the news could even sink in "Ms. Stevens, you're next on the bad-news stand. Tell me what you got."

Ms. Stevens, a middle-aged woman with a nice body and youngish face, spoke clearly but without making eye contact. "Uh, yes, I do have some good news. Thanks in large part to Mr. Hashmore, our supply of water is actually pretty good. The bad news is that, without power, we have no way of filtering or distributing it."

The mayor cursed under his breath, moved his hands in a cross, and looked aloft. "Captain, simply do your best. I hired the best, so don't worry about matching his shoes—simply try to fill them." The mayor hunted the faces of those around the table before he called on his next assistant.

"Mr. Drexter. The colonel's men here will continue oversight of the food and public order. At your request, the colonel himself will organize and lead the defense force. Your mission, then, is to organize the rest of fucking society. That means the building collapse, hospitals, and transit are now your responsibility. Additionally, you must come up with a food-and-water distribution system. Ms. Stevens and Mr. Anderson will assist you on that end as well. Mr. Anderson's first priority is to work with the utilities to get them up and running. Your job, Mr. Hashmore, is to make sure they have what they need in terms of supplies and protection and proper priorities. And last, Mr. Hashmore . . . excuse me, Captain Drexter, we will need lists of both the living and the dead."

Again the mayor stood up, but not on the table this time. "These are trying times, my friends, but we are fated to meet this task. Each of us must work outside our comfort zone, with consequences we wish weren't so. Now, take a look around the room and know this. This is our team. There are no secrets, only weaknesses to overcome." With that, the mayor clapped and headed out of the room.

↩

The room collapsed into their chairs, exhaling in a collective breath. They spent the next few seconds looking at each other, trying to decide which emotion they should be feeling, of the many that man had brought out in such a short time. The colonel, having worked with the mayor the longest, was the first to stand and push in his chair. The motion snapped the rest of the group from their trances, and the room suddenly burst into activity.

Captain Drexter followed after the colonel, tapped him on the shoulder, and tried not to look nervous. The colonel turned around and smiled his "I told you so" smile. He didn't say anything, just raised his eyebrows in response.

The captain started off with his hand in his hair, but by the end, he was nearly standing at attention. "Colonel, I, um, well I'm not really . . . you know, um, trained, yes, I'm not trained. Not trained for this job and my daughter. The army, you know, they never trained me for this type of work. I do not have the proper training to properly execute this job and request reassignment."

The colonel lowered one eyebrow. "Are you asking me to switch roles?" He paused as if expecting a response and then burst out. "Too late, Romeo. The mayor gave you a chance in there, and you failed to take it. Now the sick, unfortunate, and whiny are your problem. I don't even have the power to reassign. Go ask the mayor. If you didn't notice, he is the boss around here. Even if he is as loony as a tune."

Captain Drexter still lacked the proper brainpower to keep up and move forward with the dramatic changes recently occurring in his life.

The colonel spoke again. "If you want my advice, trust your gut and your heart. The mayor might seem bat-shit crazy, but there is a good heart buried in there somewhere. I can tell he's worried about Maria too. She may be a whore of wife, but that man loves her, and he won't be quite the same until she is back." The

colonel slapped the captain on his back and strode off, leaving a
cache of assistants all looking at him for guidance.

"Oh, Lord." The captain spoke under his breath. "Oh, Lord,
what the hell have you gotten me into?" He raised his eyes to the
sky. Had there not been a building in the way, he'd have been
looking directly at Earth.

↩

The situation was ever changing, but with focus and little
thought power, the captain was able to move into the job easier
than expected. Strange people kept approaching him and identi-
fying themselves as belonging to either this department or that
organization, or hell, even X building. The rules of the old world
had been thrown out, and he was being relied upon to help form
the rules of the new.

At many younger points in his lifetime, the captain would
have enjoyed such a challenge, such an impactful position. Yet
now all he could do was constantly bug the police for updates on
his daughter. He wouldn't feel the same until she was physically
here. Oh, how he longed for the energy and persistence of youth.
In fact, this whole ordeal had left him feeling dog tired, anxious,
and now even a little depressed—all symptoms a nice sativa smoke
could cure, but there was a very real possibility he would never be
able to smoke again.

Sasha was still refusing to come to the center, but she was
with Emilia, and her actions and attitude suggested that she still
had control over the fog. Emilia was in rough shape, and even with
the alien doctors' advanced knowledge, there was still a chance of
her passing, even if remote. Sasha had developed fast feelings for

her new friend Emilia, and it brought a strange knot to his stomach.

It would continue to be a long day for the captain. Building lines of communication was easier than expected, with much of the infrastructure put in place by his predecessor, but the hard part was getting the correct message to its desired destination. The computer proved adept at inventory and personnel control, but he had to assign a full-time person to the task of keeping it all organized.

In truth, for all the pressure put on him, he found most of his job to be simply matching needs and abilities. This group needed this and had X capability, while that group over there needed that and could do this. It was really very military-like, just non-combat missions, debris removal, equipment transportation, personnel location, and such.

It was all starting to smooth out when, once again, things just went to hell.

32: Omens and Comas

Sasha sat next to Emilia, unable to pry the smile off her face. Her friend was not only going to be fine but looked as beautiful as ever. Emilia frowned at the tears, but that didn't stop them, so she herself burst forth with another round of crying. The two had been together for several minutes now, but neither had yet been able to speak. They sat holding hands, sharing a mental rewind of horrors they had just been through together.

These strange alien doctors were actually very good, and they smelled wonderful. They were nothing scary like the beast in the dungeon. In fact, they were kinda cute, Sasha thought, like the squid who made a suit out of a wheelbarrow and was exploring the land, using a tentacle on each side.

Getting used to their voices in her head would never happen, or at least it felt that way. Their words would echo loudly in her skull but never enter her ears. It was disconcerting and uncomfortable, even if what they spoke was gentle and kind. The medicine they had, however, was some powerful stuff, but it lacked the fun part of her normal drugs. She called it the "groggy," as opposed to the foggy. The daze that came from the base tech's drugs could be fun, make all her father's words silly, relax her whole body, and let time melt away.

Her father—the thought of him shocked her, just because

of how long she had gone without thinking of him. She had never been this far away for so long before, and she felt a tinge of guilt for not missing him more. Emilia consumed most of Sasha's idle thoughts, pushing her father further and further into the background.

The doctors—Emilia's was named Maggana, and Sasha's was named Maggieno—were a cute couple. They would often waddle side by side, their top tentacles intertwined in an action both chemical and affectionate.

Maggieno removed all of the slime restraints, allowing bold new sensations to a skin that had grown accustomed to its surroundings. Sasha had been given a clean bill of health but had to perform a litany of nonsensical tests to prove it to the human doctor. Emilia, on the other hand, had been told that she suffered some internal damage, including organs. While her prognosis was good, she would have to stay in the hospital for a few days of observation.

Sasha was torn between wanting to be with Emilia, who consumed her every thought, and being with her father, who needed her. A verbal fight had broken out, as Emilia seemed less than interested. This was her father—could she just so willingly leave this place and seek him out? Emilia's encouragement to leave was getting annoying. She was told to stay put, so why was she pushing? After some unpleasantly exchanged words, Sasha became agitated and stood up to finally follow the policeman waiting at the door.

↩

It was Emilia who made the decision, and if she was upset

about it, then that was fine with Sasha. Sasha fidgeted and wiggled as she sat brooding in the back of the makeshift police cruiser. Over and over again, the words came, each time the message's tone becoming harsher and harsher until Sasha had twisted it into the worst possible interpretation: "I DON'T want YOU to worry about MEEEEE. GO! GO! And see your father, go take CARE of HIM."

Sasha rewound the episode repeatedly. What did Emilia mean? Did she really want her to go away, to go anywhere else? Don't worry about meeee—what does she think, I'm not good enough for her to "worry about"? Worry about him? What, doesn't she want me to care for her? What a bitch!

Damn clouds, can't even tell where the annoying blue light is coming from. Little extreme on the building's neon lights, jerks. I bet Emilia would love it, simple bitch that she is. Who the hell does she think she is? She's not too good for me. I will show that hussy who is the top shit around here.

What is with the fucking clouds? They're just above the building. Don't make me come up and kick your ass, clouds.

↩

Emilia closed her eyes and rested. The silence was enjoyable for the moment. The stress, pain, and emotional strain of the past few days had been more than exhausting. She had been through some difficult spells and sleepless nights, but nothing before had even come close to this. Her body melted, and the soft ripples of nose breathing fell into a rhythm as she sank into the bed.

In the purgatory of in between wake and sleep, time had no meaning, no sense, and her thoughts faded into the subconscious—

at least until a madman screaming, "Sasha, Sasha," was wheeled on a bed, sorely needing mending, into the room across the hall.

Emilia tried to ignore it and return to her body melting. It was uncomfortable enough while hinting for Sasha to leave. How could she return this quickly to interrupt her sleep? When the noise and bustle of the nurse and staff subsided, Emilia could again hear the moaning of the man across the hall: "Sasha, Sasha. Sasha, Sasha."

Emilia ripped her sheets off in an initial outburst of frustration. She stomped across the hall, the noised muffled by her hospital socks. Anger projected from her face, but as the door opened, her irritation went away and she missed her new dear friend.

The man was restrained to the bed with the same green slime that had been used to brace her wounds. Yet despite the obvious care and treatment he was receiving, his body was riddled with scars and bruises. A burn mark in the shape of a cross had been made across his chest, aged several years now, but still, it was as clear as a tattoo.

He fidgeted and fretted, turning left, "Sasha," turning right, "Sasha." Emilia watched the man for several minutes before stepping into the room. After some debate, she finally spoke. "I know a Sasha. Who is she?"

The man changed from crazy insane to scary insane with the twitch of an eye, his piercing stares now squarely on Emilia. She stopped. Frozen in terror by a man restrained in a bed, Emilia dared go no further.

The patrol car—a very loose definition of "patrol car"—awaited Sasha as the patrolman escorted her down to the first floor. A pedal cart with a glass divider and mounted restraints in the back was going to be her ride. Having just finished a fight with Emilia, Sasha's mood was bad enough, and this travesty of a vehicle only soured her mood more.

The officer, obviously used to people in bad moods on bad days, acted professionally, without speaking or actively engaging with Sasha. She sat down hard and shook the cart, and the two left unnoticed and unmissed.

The ride progressed slowly. Each block looked like an endless display of blue storefronts as the radiant Earth now sailed like a moon across the sky. The road was bumpy, sure enough, with plenty of obstacles to go around, but most of the discomfort and extra strain came from Sasha. The girl harrumphed down to one side, nearly tilting the cart, only to become fidgety and harrumph down on the other side.

Each thought that came seemed to be a variation of the last, all repeating the same theme. It was not long before the anger over Emilia's callousness had pushed Sasha into a tizzy. The bike fell as she jostled too much in the back. The officer tried to recover but ended up falling completely off the bike. The moment he took to regain his awareness was more than enough for the fog to lead Sasha away.

↩

There was nothing to be found—no blood, no ripped clothes, no signs of impact on the "vehicle." Nothing, it was as if the girl had just vanished. Seriously confused, the patrolman extended his search pattern and spent another ten minutes before finally calling anything in. "Base, this is officer 1211. I'm sorry, just now, the girl known as Sasha is gone. There was a tip over in the cab, and now she is just gone."

↩

Jobs, relationships, and of course parenting all go in cycles, but nothing could ever have prepared the captain for bad news about his daughter. When the words came across the radio, his body felt stuck in place while his mind moved in fast forward. "She is just gone. Gone." The most horrifying words he could possibly have heard. Now he again faced a decision about abandoning a job he didn't ask for or enjoy, but it also meant abandoning its resources too—resources that made him able to do things he never could as an individual out in the field.

For hours now, things had been calm. No more aliens scouring the city and probing its innocent citizens, treating them like pawns in a game too big for them to understand. No more gravity disruptions upchucking everyone's food rations. No more tidal waves power washing the city. The damage was immense. The entire coastline of the city, from all angles and blockings inward, had received damage. Only a few select buildings were able to power a minimal amount of equipment.

The alien doctors, whom they still had no formal contact with, seemed confined to the hospital by their own choice. The major had stationed his XO outside the hospital to monitor their movements, but none had come or gone. Captain Drexter was now reassigning these men to help assist in finding Sasha. Each district commander had set up a comm link with the captain at his desk, through which he would find equipment and resources, edit mission objectives and perimeters, and coordinate civil services as they were able and available.

All of this felt so pointless. Who the hell cared if District 3 needed more body bags and gloves? Who cared if civil-service sections, such as sanitation, had entirely walked off the job? No, the only thing he should have been doing at this moment was the one thing he wasn't: looking for his daughter.

Captain Drexter ripped off the headset, threw it on the desk, and turned to storm out. Not two full steps into his walk did he face, once more, the small brick statue of Big M. "You are needed here, my new friend. Now sit down and let me explain it to you."

↩

Guilt and a low threshold for self-preservation kept Emilia from turning around and running out of the room—guilt about shooing her friend away, about being a burden to her friend, and about needing her friend now. Courage was never a factor in the equation, as Emilia was driven by emotions, not reason—and who needed courage without the awareness of danger?

The words started with a squeak, but Emilia soon composed herself. "Sasha, um . . . Sasha, who is she?"

The man's stare pierced her soul, chilling her deep inside. "She is the one he is looking for. The one who saves."

Emilia took a defensive stance without realizing it. "So he wants to save her."

A gentle hiss preceded his words. "He didn't say."

Emilia swallowed hard. "So what do you want?"

The man changed the axis of his head. "Only to obey."

"Obey what?"

"My orders."

"Which are what?"

"Given as needed."

"By who?"

"By those who give the orders."

"Who gives the orders?"

"The order givers."

"Who are . . . ?"

"The ones I obey."

"Am I an order giver?"

"You have not given any orders."

"Would you obey my orders?"

"I obey my orders."

"Would you obey *my* orders?"

"I obey my orders."

↤

The only thing small about the mayor was his physical size. The man possessed an aura and presence that dominated the room, and being alone in a sparsely decorated closet-sized room with such a man was intimidating. Sasha was lost; he had to act. Over and over, the captain repeated the phrase in his head, trying to keep the fire of his passion hot.

Biggo pulled out one of the two chairs on the far side of the table and then walked back around to the front side, turned a chair backward, and sat. The captain hesitated, deciding whether or not to bolt out of the room and begin a frantic search. The indecision lingered long enough for the mayor to turn his head back around and eye the captain.

The captain begrudgingly sat upright and formal in his chair. Biggo pulled out a cigarette, lit it, and offered an open pack to the captain. The captain declined with a wave of his hand, only to have the mayor return the gesture with a shake of the box. Again the captain began to raise his hand in decline, when he noticed that the pack had two types of cigarettes, one being green and hand rolled.

"Your daughter is missing. You are compelled to chase out of here, run after her, like a wild man screaming her name in the wind. She needs you here, now. Go ahead and smoke that, you're already very anxious and wound up. I need you cool and calm. Go ahead, my brother, we can smoke it together while we discuss how to save your daughter."

The captain smiled back at the mayor and, compelled by the smoker's logic, grabbed hold and felt that wonderful sensation as it spread out into his lungs, up his spine, and with a burst of smoke, blurred out all conscious thought and worry.

↩

The man's voice was intense, but Emilia wasn't frightened by it. She was driven by guilt, longing, and anger. The past few days had done much to strengthen her resolve but had failed to mature her on a similar scale. This man may have had information—information she needed, would need, or would need to give to Sasha.

Emilia approached the man, turned a chair around, and sat. His piercing stare had not altered more than a blink, and now she returned the stare. The longer it went on, the more irrelevant she deemed it to be. She wasn't going to win any staring contests.

She tried a second tactic. "Perhaps if you follow my orders, you will be rewarded." Her voice gained confidence farther into the sentence.

The man double blinked and tilted his head the other direction. "What reward does the master offer?"

Emilia looked around the room for ideas. She could offer this man his freedom, but the hair on the back of her neck stood upright at the thought of that. The room was sparsely decorated: a reclining chair to one side and under a window, a TV mounted in the corner, and an empty counter with a stool beneath it. "I can offer you the reward of entertainment. Tell me what I want to know and I will turn it on for you."

The man blinked twice more. "You idiot, we aren't even on Earth anymore. There isn't going to be any TV. Stupid girl." His eyes bulged as he pushed out the second syllable of "stupid."

"Do you know for certain?" Emilia didn't have much on hand, so she pressed with what little she had. "Perhaps, but there are plenty of generators and news towers in this city. Maybe they could be trying to broadcast. These alien doctors have seen our technology. Perhaps they can now communicate with us on TV. Or maybe we are still really close to Earth and will just be getting a delayed signal. I guess we will never know." She slid the stool out and leaned against it, making herself semi-comfortable.

"Master is a good negotiator but a poor judge of character, for I care not for my fellow man."

"Then why care at all about Sasha?"

"Sasha is the one he was looking for."

"Then why does he matter?"

"He is the exception."

"The exception to what?"

"To us all."

"What do you mean?"

"He is the only one too . . ."

Emilia nodded to get the man to say more.

The words came out twisted, with a different tone. "Righteous. God will punish. Avoid, evade . . ." Again the man's eyes opened wide as he struggled to speak. "Heeelp."

↩

Oh, man, did it ever feel good to smoke again. The captain could feel his internal chemistry returning to calm, his mind floating from subject to subject. His lungs filled with the wondrous smoke, time and time again, until it felt no different than a Friday night on the couch. The two men sat idly in the room, watching it gradually empty of smoke as it wisped about, rising to the vents.

Whatever conversation there had been was fairly general, idle, random thoughts focused on Sasha. That haphazard conversation led to a moment of retrospection and silence—both men, for the first time, taking the time to reflect. They were emotionally dampened, yet the overall effect was still mind-blowing. Aliens were real, they were in space, and most of those they knew were now dead.

The room dropped in energy, and the silence spoke to the great losses and great changes that had occurred. That silence was broken with a jolt to two brains so lost in thought that the world snuck up on them, when three loud, thunderous knocks rocked the door. The disruption was so big even the smoke zigzagged in fright.

Straightening, the two men now looked at each other, ever so slowly returning to the world around them. The captain, his body and mind working out of sync, attempted to rise but instead jumped forward and slammed his crotch into the table, causing intense discomfort.

The mayor, never nervous about the repercussions of smoking, showed far less panic over the noise. He let out a chuckle after the initial startle, as if laughing it off, but neither man rose to answer the door. Instead, the two locked eyes and laughed, and the captain walked it off in a couple of quick circles.

"No more children for you, eh?" The mayor cackled a little too intensely, unable to physically lift himself out of the chair.

After a few circles, the captain sat down again, as he couldn't remember what he was supposed to be doing.

Again the chamber rattled with three thunderous knocks on

the door. This time, the captain covered his ears while the mayor dug up the will to stand and walk to the door. The mayor took a deep breath before pulling on the chain and opening the door to a small herd of assistants and attendants. One voice clearly rose above the others as he opened the door.

"A new kind of alien is attacking the hospital."

The smoke cleared, and the sense of urgency returned. The captain had to save his daughter.

↩

The single, small LED light shined directly on this unnamed man standing in front of Emilia. His face both snarled and smiled. His eyes penetrated, and his ears tracked. This man was dangerous, but she wouldn't let herself be deterred from her task. She was fueled by emotional guilt, youthful innocence, and a strong desire to believe. So when the screams began and the light flickered, Emilia had to make a scary choice.

In the hallway, nurses banged on doors and screamed for anyone who could move to get the hell out. Then, as quickly as it had started, the light died and the noises faded. Emilia paused in shock and then moved toward the man. He lay motionless in the dark. Only a blue glow filled the room as the faintest of lights crept in from under the door.

Emilia tried to speak, but her voice floundered. "I, I, I will save you. Um, conditionally. You must acknowledge me as a master, or you, you ,you will stay here in the dark." She tried to compose herself, but her heart was beating a million times a second. Her blood flowed everywhere but her brain. She had seen how to release the restraints, and she was confident that she could do it in the dark too.

The man cocked his head at a new angle before speaking slowly. "You would save me? To what end?"

"You must help me protect her."

The implications and idea seemed to surprise the man. His stare went blank, and his ears appeared to fold back some, toward his head. "Sasha?"

Emilia nodded. "Sasha."

"Again, master is a good negotiator. I accept."

↩

The captain composed himself just in time not to laugh at the "new kind" part of the man's warning. The meaning of what was just said to him would need reinforcing before it stuck. The mayor and the captain both looked stern, but neither said anything in response. Probably expecting his boss to lead the conversation, the man waited and then stuttered as he spoke. "This alien appears to, um, be much bigger than the last. The police are all too afraid to engage it. So far, it appears to be destroying the corners of buildings and trying to capture the people inside."

The man again paused to see if either the mayor or the captain would respond. "Colonel Major thus far has been trying to evacuate some of the nearby buildings, but he says we desperately need stronger firepower."

The two men looked at each other and exchanged a smile with their eyes as their brains spun the wheels, trying to catch up. It was the mayor who spoke first. "What the hell does he expect?

Tanks? Tell him I can get him dynamite. Blow down a building right down on fucking top of it."

The man at the door waited a moment. "That will be plan A. Is there a plan B?"

The captain responded this time, having a great deal of experience both giving and getting lectures. "Hey, you just worry the hell about getting plan A to work. You let us worry about plan B and getting that to work. Got it, kid?" The captain waved his hand to reinforce his message, and the man retreated to execute what little he had been given.

The mayor pulled out a small bottle of eye drops, used it, and passed it along to the captain. "Now you'll see how much less emotionally you will be thinking now." A quirky smile crossed the mayor's face as he repeated the same word. "Now. Now back to the adventure."

↢

The floor vibrated, and the building swayed. Screams from indiscernible places echoed down the hallways, under the doors, and into Emilia's room. She moved another foot closer to the man as she steadied herself. His face began to change in its appearance. He now had a most "sad puppy eyes" look. Emilia evaluated the man's body. Heavily scarred and tattooed, it was obvious that this man was no stranger to pain.

A great "T" had been burned onto the man's chest, taking up most of the torso. Bullet holes, dog bites, and long cuts were all visible despite the massive tattoo's attempt to cover them up. He spoke gently and softly. "Please." The building returned to normal, and Emilia stood even closer to the man as she reached an arm out to brace herself against the bed's railing.

She felt conflicted. The only thing that did make sense to her was that this man wanted to protect and help Sasha. That, Emilia thought, would make them at the least uneasy teammates. She hesitantly put her fingers into the green blob of a restraint, moved her fingers into position, and released the clamp. Initially believing there to be two clamps, she was surprised at how quickly the man was able to wiggle himself free of the restraints.

Emilia backed away and was now next to the door when the man stood erect. He was taller than expected, thicker too, his presence formidable. She half turned to open the door, keeping an eye on her new friend, when to her horror, Emilia discovered that the door wouldn't open. The handle jiggled, but nothing happened, and the door wouldn't budge.

The man's piercing stare returned, and Emilia didn't like the way he was looking at her. Guilt was an inappropriate feeling, yet she was stricken by it. The man staggered toward her, his tongue running across his lips and his eyes moving up and down her body. Emilia wanted so much, so badly not to have done what she just did.

The man reached out and grasped her hand on the door. He also yanked the handle, confirming that it wouldn't open. Then he moved his body around Emilia's and pinned her against the wall. She looked down and squeaked like a mouse. "Please, stop. I don't want this. Please."

33: I Say Hello, You Say Goodbye

The operations center buzzed and hummed as more computers now worked and more people flowed around the room. The noise level was high, but these were professional and diligent workers. Luckily or unfortunately, public service is a cruel mistress that far too often breaks families apart. Most of these people were there because they had no family remaining, or had no family to begin with.

Several aides rushed toward the mayor, each one shoving him a notepad of information to address. The mayor waved his hand, brushing them off, and then leaped up onto a table and called for everyone's attention. "Eyes up fucking here, right fucking now, on me." He loosened his collar and walked across the table so as to address as many as possible.

"Today is more than a day of infamy. It is our day of reckoning. Today we must decide our own fate, our own course, and our own destiny. The people out there, they are counting on us back here to support, enhance, and encourage our dying brothers out there. We cannot lead from the front, so we must push from the rear. Right now our brothers and sisters have tasked me, and now I task you. They cannot destroy this enemy—they need weapons. We need to find and deploy those weapons. This is our only task, our only goal. It is one we must now all, every fucking one of us, concentrate on before we can go back to those other vital tasks we so urgently need done."

The mayor finished his 360 lap around the room, making eye-to-eye contact with as many as possible as he went. "Now, who has a weapon or knows where to find a weapon other than dynamite?"

Random suggestions rang out from the crowd: "Synied office . . . organized crime . . . terror cells."

A few other, though less probable, suggestions were shouted out before the mayor thanked everyone and called together a select few. The mayor, with the captain by his side, made arrangements for all avenues to be pursued and then dismissed the group.

The captain stood still, torn by a newfound loyalty to this crazy bastard of a man, but he knew what had to be done. "Mayor, it's time for me to go. I have a weapon for you to use, but only I can deploy it, and first I need to find her."

The mayor gave a baffled looked. "You would risk your life to save a girl you want to attack a giant alien. And they say my marriage is confusing." The mayor chuckled before slapping the captain on the back. "I know it must be true, so go and follow your crazy notion. I can no longer stop you or convince you to stay. Perhaps this might just come in handy along the way." He handed the captain three small stacks of dynamite.

↩

Emilia felt his hand on her inner thigh. His breath fouled her nostrils with an awful smell so strong she could taste it. His body blocked her escape. His hand held hers firmly in place, the

other on the door. The angle of his body bending over hers made
her feel powerless. His hand moved to grasp her wrist, and he
forced her hand down onto his throbbing member, through the
trousers. Emilia closed her eyes and prayed. She prayed like she
had never prayed before, continuously whispering, "Oh, Lord,
please, no. Please, Lord, no."

The man released Emilia's hand, but her body had locked
up and she lacked the bravery to move. The man unzipped his
trousers and exposed himself into her hand. He moved his face
onto her neck and began kissing it. She squeaked again, in protest,
but felt like she was outside of herself, as if viewing this tragedy
from another perspective. Inch by inch, he moved closer until their
bodies were fully compressed together.

Emilia turned her head away from him and the door, only
to hear it open. She always considered herself athletic, but she was
nowhere near as fast as this man, and before she could even flip
her head back, he had the nurse under his control. The man twisted
the woman's arm high up into her back and slammed her into the
bed, bent over. He grabbed a tube from the medical equipment and
strangled this poor nurse who was only trying to find survivors.

The man smiled a hideous smile as he looked down on the
nurse's lifeless body. The woman was of average build and looks,
early forties most likely. Having satisfied his bloodlust, his carnal
lust returned, and the man rotated back in Emilia's direction, but
she'd left him behind with an empty room and an open door.

↩

The streets were empty except for the apocalypse of cars.
Captain Drexter knew from the map that the hospital was about

eight blocks away, six blocks west to south, but he couldn't tell where the hell he was. Disoriented, he spun around, and then around again. He closed his eyes and began to brainstorm ideas, when he heard someone yelling, "Soldier . . . hey, soldier, over here." The captain turned to see some people at the front door of a lobby, waving him in.

The captain neared the group. Too pressed for time, he felt no shame in asking for directions. "Where is the hospital?"

The two people looked at each other and then backward, as if toward a crowd. "What's going on out there? We were told to stay inside, but we don't know why. We want to come out."

The man started to say more, but the captain stopped him. "Answer my question first!"

The man pointed in a direction, and the captain began moving as he shouted back. "Command center's over there. Ask them yourselves."

As the captain moved, so did the street numbers. They were labeled "East" and getting smaller, so he must have been heading west. After a four-block near sprint, he heard not only screaming but shattering glass and construction noises. Attributing his slow-down to the noise and not fatigue, the captain put his hands over his head and walked. He hadn't located the hospital yet, but he spotted something awful, something he feared even Sasha couldn't face.

He felt a pain in his heart and prayed that Sasha would never have to confront such a creature—yet here he was, searching for someone he loved so much, just to ask her to risk it all. The captain had reached the corner and would now be in view of the thing once he started to cross. The alien was literally tearing down an apartment building while foraging inside for the inhabitants.

The creature was massive, two stories high. Built like a praying mantis, its skin looked to be armor tough. Its long, barbed extremities scraped away at the building, sending mounts of concrete, wire, and brick to the ground. Then its jagged edge would rotate and dexterous, small limbs would scavenge inside.

Yelling again caught the captain's ear as he heard a familiar voice. "Take aim. Fire!" A crackle of fire burst out of an upper story in the building across from him. Smoke billowed out the windows as if on fire, but the alien barely noticed as hundreds of shells pounded down the middle of its back torso. The volley ended, and after a round of cursing, the captain heard the colonel's voice: "Fall back."

The captain, initially consumed with finding his daughter, now reevaluated his next course of action.

↩

Emilia ran. She ran and ran until she couldn't run anymore. Upstairs, down hallways, down, down, down all the stairs, and through numerous sets of doors, Emilia ran until she was not only lost but surrounded by death. She was in a long, dark room. Blue light shined in from a few scattered high-ceiling, small windows. Bodies were stacked in rows, piles and piles of them spanning the entire length of the room.

The foulest smell on earth entered her nostrils, staining her memory and warping her mind. The bodies were haphazard as they lay, each one suffering a fate seemingly as cruel as the previous and as awful as the next. Emilia walled off her emotions as best she could. Her breathing was too loud. He would hear her breathing. Why couldn't she stop breathing so loud? He'd heard it too, the man at Synied. Damn it, she thought, why can't I breathe quieter? I'm going to die.

She felt the pit of her stomach churn and ache, but a noise terrified the puke back down. Someone had come through the outer double doors. Emilia stood out. As the lone one standing, she would be noticed immediately—that is if he didn't hear her first, with all the damn breathing. Then the doors to the room opened, and Emilia fell to the ground.

Nothing was said. Whoever had entered had done so without speaking. Emilia curled herself up into the fetal position. "Don't breathe, don't breathe," was the mantra she repeated in her head. The person walked without notice of haste or stealth. Then a new sound brought relief, the sound of a cart. The wheel banged in a rhythm as it glided across the tile floor.

Why would that man have a cart? This was probably just an unfortunate morgue operator. Feeling confident, Emilia stood back up, totally catching the man off guard. The two looked at each other, one befuddled and one terrified.

After a second, the man's sinister smile returned. "Seems I am being rewarded handsomely today. So you will too. It has been some time since I last shared my wonderment. I have enough saved up to share some with you too. NOW!"

Emilia screamed and ran as fast as she could to the far side of the morgue. The closer she got, the more she realized there was no exit and he was in pursuit.

↩

Planning and executing an attack from the rear was a complicated and onerous task, and now the captain saw a way to almost single-handedly execute the mayor's scheme. He could see the group diligently plotting every detail they could think of. Who would get the dynamite to the colonel? Did the colonel have personnel trained in how to take down a building? How would they choose a building? How would they lure it to that building? How would they evacuate that building?

It all seemed so immense—so much to decide, with so little information. However, as he stood there now, in what used to be the world, he saw his destiny, his call to action, his purpose in life. Sasha had a new ally in her battle against the fog. Emilia had already proven her worth in that department, by the fact that she was still alive and interconnected with Sasha. No, thought the captain, he had done his bit for king and country, and now it was time to do his bit for his daughter. He would never be able to spare Sasha of hardships in life, but he could eliminate this foul, hideous beast.

He had failed to follow through before, and it nearly got the two most precious females in the world, to him, raped. Now he would not let anything stop him, not a call to duty, not an obligation to the rest of humanity. The captain squeezed and felt the power of the dynamite in his hands and knew his only obligation was to save Sasha from this trial, and bringing down a building would be a hell of a way to go.

↩

Emilia pushed her thighs harder and harder, shoving off with as much speed as possible on each step. It was a futile effort, and her brain both recognized and avoided that fact. The cart was no longer making noise, but his footsteps against the concrete flooring came in an awful pattern, each one ringing horror deeper into Emilia's psyche.

At last, she reached the wall. Her hands hit first but for only a moment, as she spun and braced for his attack. She could almost feel his hands on her. The unwanted groping, the unwanted affection, the unwanted breathing—it all paralyzed her heart as she raised her emotional wall.

Emilia was fast, and the man was still seconds away. She had enough time to look left and right, but she only saw open space and piles of bodies. The helplessness had already gripped her body, but the delay gave her body time to think, time to remember.

She felt the man from Synied's hand on her again. She remembered how she couldn't move, but then Sasha did. Sasha moved, and moved fast. There had been no conscious thought behind the act, simply a progression of thought after breaking through the paralysis of shock.

Emilia raised her leg hard and stiff, slamming it into the man as he reached her.

He cringed and fell to the side. Emilia ran again—no thought, no pain, she ran harder than she ever had before.

↩

Timing would be important, and it would be out of his control. The captain knew where the colonel was and what course of action he would be taking, but the colonel wouldn't tell him if it meant the front-door exit, within sight of the beast exiting stage left, or a back-door fall-straight-back maneuver. Unfortunately, plan B was pretty much the same as plan A, minus the distraction. The captain held three large sticks of dynamite and identified three targets, the beast's hind leg and the two small inlets on each side of the nearby foundation. Would it be enough to bring down the building? He doubted it, but many of the buildings had already been structurally weakened.

The captain hid behind the corner, but his time was winding down. What few souls were still alive in the building would soon be devoured, and the alien would move on. The captain's breath returned, the benefit of a military career. He ducked down into a runner's starting pose and waited until he thought he could wait no longer.

The windows were all empty, the door was stuck shut, and by now, the officers must have left out the back, so it was on to plan B. The captain had seldom contemplated the afterlife, believing the majority of religion to be tomfoolery, the greatest institutionalized lie of all time. Yet as he looked out at his immediate fate, he found his conviction to that belief faltering and hoped that something more would be on his side for this one. Stopping short of conscious prayer, the captain wished and went.

↩

Emilia willed herself to jump, skip, and run as fast and as high as she could. The building's tilt and the motion of the stairs, none of it rang true to her. She was being hunted, the prey in flight. She had no destination, no plan, no course, only a desire to live and the will to run.

Her lungs would burn as soon as her body returned to normal, but for now, as she reached the top of the stairwell, they puffed. They expanded her chest and exploded in exhale. The noise burst from her lips, and her muscles protested. Hope carried her body forward. She had reached the top, and hope lay on the other side of the door.

Hope stayed on that side of the door, too, as Emilia reached for the handle and pulled on a locked door. Three, four, five pulls and it still wasn't enough for her to believe she was once again trapped and waiting to be raped. The man's words echoed up through the stairwell. "SWEETIE, where are you going, my sweet? I love these games we play, but I grow weary of foreplay. Luckily, I already got my excitement out, so I can take my time and enjoy you, my sweet, sweet reward."

The words only rang in horror, without meaning to Emilia. Tears cascaded down her face, and her hand pounded constantly against the door. "Please, somebody, anybody. Please." Her voice descended into a crying whisper as the target of her words changed. "Help me."

↩

Beyond being in the zone, beyond intensity, and beyond self-preservation came a point where his force of will simply executed. The captain may have been in full sprint, but he willed the top of the dynamite off, exposing its fuse. He slid the lid down along the fuse and sparked it to life as he neared the alien's hind leg.

The target was a small gap that exposed itself as the alien above constantly shifted its weight to and fro. Smoke and dust were so thick he could feel it in his mouth and on his skin. So far, the alien had failed to notice him, but it would only take a second for the captain to go from noticed to dead.

The skin stretched, and the opening exposed itself, allowing the captain to deposit his lit explosive while still in motion. Screams echoed out from the building's open front—a woman was in the alien's clutches. She went into the alien's mouth headfirst, her head bitten off and discarded as the alien began sucking out the poor woman's insides.

Sliding as if into home plate, the captain lit his second explosive and exited out from under the alien and settled next to the building. The motion was smooth and the execution flawless, but the task faulty and the errand impossible.

The captain had been spotted. It was the remaining physical presence of the building that saved him from the alien's slashing extremity, and the explosions from his own arsenal nearly killed him. The way forward had been blocked by the alien's limb, so the only way for the captain to go was back, back toward his second explosion, and he was still holding an explosive.

It was total blackness and, for a second, totally painless. The captain heard more than felt the crunching of his body, and he lost control of his final explosive. The concrete and plaster of the building's wall had locally collapsed, dropping some of it down onto him. Lying motionless where he landed, the captain had just begun to regain consciousness when the second explosion went off.

↩

Help never arrived, no hero burst through the door, no Sasha bounded up the stairs, and no nurses would come looking for her here. Emilia curled up into the fetal position as tears poured down her face and air blasted into and out of her lungs. The man closed in on her, stopped, and looked down. "Now, now, we can't have one of the masters in such a state. You may want to start down there, but I want to start up here." He reached out his powerful arm, snatched Emilia by the neck, and pulled her up to a standing position.

The man wiped a few tears off Emilia's face. "I know, baby, I know it's a wonderful thing. I'm about to cry with joy myself." He moved in close to kiss her. A rumble wobbled the building, and the two shifted back to the railing. The building had now tilted so much that there was a larger-than-normal space between the wall and the railing.

Emilia now leaned her weight against the man, and had she been able to fight, this would have been her opportunity. But her mind remained in a state of total emotional eclipse, and she was ready for the trauma. The man pulled her even closer, embracing her lips with his.

The second rumble was much more intense, sending more than a gentle sway through the building, and the two were struck off balance. Emilia reacted this time, pushing hard. The man, however, was strong enough and prepared enough to hold on. He grabbed her by the wrists. While he was able to maintain his grip, Emilia was able to gain a solid footing. She pulled and pulled, and as the man's momentum grew, she prepared to push him down the stairwell.

Emilia's hope was once again dashed by the brute strength of her attacker. She now faced her assailant in an awkward stance. She hadn't the position of power to force the man off, and she didn't want to let him recover for another advance, so Emilia made the only move she could see. She slid her feet off the railing and threw her entire body weight downward.

The man quickly lost grasp of one of her wrists, and his body was pulled to the ground, yet he still held on. Emilia screamed as her shoulder dislocated and her body swung in a clumsy motion. The man held on tight, very tight, but his grip was slipping, and he had little power while lying on his stomach. Emilia dangled in pain and disbelief as her wrist slipped away and a large gap several stories deep awaited her.

↩

The world lay black and barren before him, around him, and behind him. It took several minutes for his mind to find his head, and several more to find his neck. The weight was immense, and any push or lift of his head only resulted in pain. The captain wasn't sure he was even breathing until the coughing started. There was air around him, but in the pitch black, it was impossible to say how much.

The captain felt his mind start to reboot, yet there seemed to be a flaw in the system. He could feel his mind reaching out. Pulse after pulse, his brain searched for its parts, trying to account for all of them, one by one. He realized that he didn't know what position his body was in. Were his legs extended? Raised to the chest? Where were his hands? Were they near his body or out and about?

Terror crept in with each pulse that went unanswered, and his unconscious self was already screaming. A moment of relief came as his mind finally found his ears. They rang and hurt, but they worked. The noises were unintelligible but comforting—he was not alone.

Patient, calm, and focused on the positive, the captain was forced to either accept that he had already succumbed to a fate worse than death or believe that he still had a chance to recover. He focused hard on his ears, putting full concentration on deciphering garbled noises into sounds—garbled and jumbled. He closed his eyes and concentrated. Screaming, yes there was screaming. Weapons fire, yes he could hear weapons fire.

He couldn't see it, but the captain felt the wind in his hair, chased by rocks hitting his face. The noises changed too, became clearer, and the air fresher and the weight on his neck gone. He sat upright using his stomach muscles. His brain swirled inside his skull, and his stomach wrenched in pain. Had he not smoked recently, the captain was sure he would have puked.

He spent a few minutes getting reacquainted with several new muscles, including his tongue and lips. The breeze returned, followed by another round of falling and splashing rocks. The captain refocused on his hearing, and a man's voice kept repeating, "Fall back, fall back. Retreat." Loud, thunderous jolts vibrated farther and farther away. Screaming again, the sound of screaming turned his attention toward the other direction.

The screams were loud and intense, a true call for help, and they were heading in the same direction as the alien. The captain tried to stand, but he couldn't find his legs. He pressed on, harder this time. He had to help. Those screams would etch terror into anyone within earshot, and as the swirling in his brain slowed, he recognized those screams. Those were screams from Emilia. His emotions took control, raising his torso. His vision failed him, his legs abandoned him, but as long as he still had life, he still had to help.

34: When Doves Eat

Emilia slipped and fell, her body cascading down the hole between the wall and the railing. Her chest slammed into the railing of a passing floor as she wrestled for control. The back of her thighs collided with the next flight of stairs, and she finally came to a rest on the next flight down.

Neither Emilia nor the man moved for several minutes, assessing what had just happened, like a lifting fog clearing the view for all on the battlefield. Then the man's feet slammed as he started his descent in pursuit and jostled Emilia back into flight. Her chest gasped for air, her legs pulsed in pain, and her heart felt as if it was going to burst.

"Enough of this, I need you NOW!" His voice once again rattled terror into her heart. Emilia could listen no more. The clanging of the stairs, the torturous voice of the man—it was all too much for her. She screamed as her legs propelled her down, down, down, and finally out onto the street.

←↵

The world of the fog wasn't linear, understandable, or avoidable. Sasha's mind had been programmed with far more than it could ever actively incorporate or use, and the fog was her mind's way of narrowing the focus. She never had any memory of what happened in the fog, but her awakening from this episode would be unforgettable.

There was so much that her brain had filtered out that when it all flooded in, it was overwhelming. Orientation, situational awareness, and self-control are all things most people have control of all the time, but not Sasha, and not in the world of the fog.

The most surprising aspect of Sasha's abrupt exit from the fog was how quickly she recognized the source of transition. Exiting the world of the fog was still a fairly unique experience, as was each visit to the world of the fog. Yet coming out the fog was an inconsistent endeavor, sometimes by a trigger source, as was the case this time. Other times, there seemed to be no trigger, leaving Sasha either like a skydiver clearing a layer of clouds or like a driver slowly clearing the dense mist.

Her eyes were drawn directly to them. There was no mystery as to why their presence triggered an exit from the fog. Together they were her entire emotional existence. Now they were in danger, in fear, and in pain. Sasha now knew why she existed, why she had been bred, and why she needed to be dangerous.

↩

He could feel her panic as she grasped him so tightly that he felt her heart beating against his own chest. Emilia's screams belted and echoed deep into the captain's skull, reigniting the tremendous pain pulsing through his brain. He found his hands and wrapped them tightly back around her as she now straddled him. The baroness had sat like this before, only in an entirely different context.

The captain again tried to will his eyes open but could find no receptors. Danger was imminent, but he could find no power, no will to move. The vibrations from the alien suggested an awkward march back in their direction, but they still had some time, maybe. Without sight, he wasn't quite sure.

Emilia's last belt of screaming stopped with a sudden and abrupt blow. The captain could almost hear the wind being knocked out of her. The equilibrium of his ears was returning, for he could now feel their bodies being tilted and lifted. A strong grunt accompanied the lift, but without his vision, the captain failed to recognize its owner.

Emilia finally let in a wheezing breath followed by a few coughs. The two bounced for several meters as they were carried away like babies. The man finally reached exhaustion and had to set them down. The alien's vibrations had become very erratic, with multiple steps or missteps making it difficult to actually locate them.

An alien noise screeched across the street, shattering glass and sending small debris across the captain and Emilia. The vibrations grew intense, smashing, as if only mere feet away from them. Debris constantly showered down and around as screams of an alien battle ravaged down, around and near them.

↩

The alien's neck was between Sasha's thighs. Deep, oozing wounds had been burrowed into each side, about where Sasha's feet rested. She held a long, stringy tentacle in each hand. It wasn't telepathy, but it communicated more than just physical gestures.

Sasha willed the beast toward her father and her love. The alien refused, perhaps sensing the loss of fog, and attempted to reassert its control. Sasha was unrelenting as she dug her feet down into the creature. It hissed in protest, jolting her as wildly as a bucking horse. Sasha met the protest with force, this time not only digging in but also yanking, hard.

The alien screeched in pain and slowed down, as if biding its time. Sasha showed no patience as she unleashed another volley of discipline. The first alien had lost interest in the building and was now bearing down fast. She would be too late. Again she kicked out in frustration, with tears forming in her eyes. She started to curse—herself, her alien captor, and what others would call "the Lord."

Her relief at the sight of a man carrying her father and Emilia did not lessen her anger, only renewed her determination and hope. Sasha echoed out with her mind for the beast to attack. It protested, shook violently, and nearly tossed Sasha off her perch. She noticed a piece of rebar sticking out of the beast, right behind where she was sitting.

Unaware of whether she'd caused that injury, Sasha grabbed it now as the alien began to spread its wings. The area below the wing appeared to have only a layer of skin over it, making it vulnerable to attack. Sasha pulled out the bar, but instead of attacking the new skin, she pierced a hole into the expanding wing. She then ripped the bar downward, tearing the wing as it went.

The alien screamed and jerked Sasha, but with her mind, she commanded it to attack its kin. This time, the alien accepted the order, and none too late as it struck a blow to its fellow on the injured foot, from the captain's explosion. The other aliens went wild yet barely missed her family.

The alien beast turned, and the two now faced off, with Sasha forcing a battle between a reluctant combatant and an injured opponent. The two aliens hissed at each other, perhaps communicating in their own language, Sasha couldn't tell. She knew time was of the essence, and the clouds closing in forewarned of danger.

Emilia had taken as much as she could handle. Her mind had shut down, and her instincts acted alone. No longer trusting itself, her mind refused to accept new input. Her body was now locked in a death squeeze. It was the last and only action she was capable of. After the latest shower of debris and angry alien screams, the captain and Emilia were once again being carried.

It felt like a long distance to carry two people. This man was obviously very strong and very determined. The captain cursed himself for not being able to do more, for being so weak and so stupid, and for failing. He had risked and lost so much. He had failed at his task. The alien beast had not been disabled by his attack, only the captain. Now, instead of assisting his daughter, he would only become another burden to her.

The captain would not allow thoughts of failure to supersede his parental love. It wasn't much, but holding Emilia in her moment of panic gave him enough to know he still wanted to live and still wanted to help. The man was now climbing a flight of stairs, an incredible feat bringing about a strong respiratory response and a stink of foul breath.

It took more than one try, but the captain was finally able to find his tongue and voice. "Where are you taking us?"

The words were mumbled but the man seemed to understand well enough. "We will take the one to safety. Then we will take the other as our reward."

The words and the passage of time had allowed the captain to finally match the voice to the face, and it disturbed him. Twice now, this crazy son of a bitch had saved him, and he felt like there would be a significant cost this time. As his mind finally started to process the words, it became clear that the cost had already been set—it was Emilia.

Emilia barely moved, squeezing as if her life depended on it. She made no sound other than breathing. The captain felt a surge of panic ripple through what he could still feel of his body. He hoped Emilia wouldn't pick up on it, but he was at a loss for what to do.

It wasn't a drop, but the two were set down swiftly. The captain was actually disappointed and scared by how little it hurt. Emilia squeezed even tighter and screamed even louder than the captain thought possible. He could feel her being pulled off by the man. She held on with everything she had, but they all knew it wasn't going to be enough.

"What are you doing? Stop that. She is not for you!" The last statement brought about a noticeable change in Emilia's pull, indicating that the man had dropped her.

After a moment of silence, the man kneeled next to the captain and the shaking Emilia. "Who are you to speak to me like this? I have saved your life twice now. You are in my debt, and you can't even walk. I will have my reward."

A strong, painful slug wasn't enough to interrupt the captain's thought—how does he know I can't walk? Two more powerful slugs and the captain and Emilia had been separated. Emilia thrashed and flailed, hollering the whole time.

By this point, pain was irrelevant to the captain. It was more a matter of finding the actual ability to move that challenged him. The captain rolled himself, throwing out one of his arms. Luck finally showed her hand as the captain managed to grasp skin, the man's shin. The man tried to kick him away. Emilia pulled the other way, fleeing his grasp.

The man had had enough of the captain and now bent down and picked him up by the throat. "You were supposed to be the one, the guide, the master. You saved me in the prison, just as the voices told me you would, but you are not who the voices said you were. You are deceitful, unworthy scum of this earth."

The captain forced the words past the man's hold on his throat. "She is not for you!"

"I have earned what I like, and I shall take it. You have no authority over me!" The man eyes bulged and burned red.

"She is not for you!" The captain saw his imminent death even without his vision. He could feel the man shifting his body, readying the final blow. The captain raised his arm first, hoping to deflect the blow but instead finding the man's face. Then his hands scrambled down to the man's neck and squeezed.

↩

Sasha had a plan, and her alien captor probably knew it too. So she had to think of a new plan, without thinking. Emotion would be the key, the only thing that could outsmart an enemy who knew what she was thinking. Sasha needed to be pissed off. Anger would be the most actionable emotion.

She grinded and pulled hard on the alien's tentacles, lashing out with each thought. "Fucking God, put my fucking family in danger, fuck you. Jesus fucking who? I don't see any fucking messiahs here to help me. How could I have fallen for that shit! Stupid fucking idiot!"

At last the time had come, and Sasha let go. Whether it was conscious communication or situational recognition, it didn't matter. Her plan had been anticipated precisely as she had imagined it. Luckily, she was too damn angry to execute her plan to jump off the beast, as its comrade attacked. Instead, she bore down hard on the beast, dropping it to the ground. She now plunged the rebar up hard into the soft, exposed skin and held on as she swung down to ground level.

The alien beast let out a wrenching squeal as its leg failed to respond when ordered to rise. Sasha scaled the two beasts as they struggled to untangle themselves, overcome by their injuries. She regained her position of command but cringed as she saw her weapon lying on the ground.

Sasha kicked and kicked, but it had no effect. This alien was able to spread its wings. The alien took two massive strokes with its wings, rushing the wind past Sasha with hurricane force. The alien tilted a wing, and Sasha was soon spinning at a high rotational speed. A foul smell added to her growing nausea, and she was now fighting on two fronts.

At last, the alien stopped spinning and landed back down on its comrade. The alien's body sizzled, as did the entire ground and building. The building Emilia had run out from was now moaning, and glass from above started to shatter and fall as the windows burst. The ground floor moaned even more, and Sasha lay on the back of an alien, watching as this great tower leaned farther over and downward. Then she wished for another emotion.

←↵

Never play chicken with a dying man, unless of course, dying is your goal, thought the captain. He had nothing much to lose and only one thing to do: squeeze. Air had long since stopped traveling through his throat, but he willed his muscles ever onward, ever stronger. It was hard to say who won, for the captain could feel his body dropping but not the sensations from the body itself.

It was impossible to tell whether he was dropped, let go, or released. Without vision, he could only use his hands to see. Keeping track of anything much else other than his hands was proving impossible. His head lay on its side. He could feel the cool of the metal against his face, but his neck failed to respond, and he was still looking for his feet.

A foul smell, acidic in nature, entered his nose, clearing his mind a bit. He found his hands and brought them to his neck. His throat raw and painful, the breaths rumbled and snorted as they tried to resume. The captain felt his body tilting, yet he wasn't sure how it was happening. A new sensation started across the back of his head, a hand slowly and gently moving into a position of support. His neck raised, and he soon felt a nice heat surround him. He closed his eyes and rested. Not even the howls of the moon, nor the crumbling of the walls, could tear the captain from his perch full of warmth and comfort, so soothing.

Another sensation took hold, warming his body and

soothing his worries, and he located another body part as Emilia pressed her lips against his.

↩

Is the fog a miracle, an abstraction, or an evolution? Sasha wondered to herself. She felt the beast below her strut as it attempted to free its leg from the corpse below, but with injury and fatigue, it was no use. Sasha lay on her backside on the beast as she watched. It had a Hollywood beauty about it. First came the small bits—glass shards, cement pebbles, sand—and yet falling right behind in slow motion were larger pieces, like brick chunks that used to be the wall, cement blocks, and an elevator.

Sasha wished for a life-flashing phenomenon. She wished to revise her night with her friend, Emilia. She wished to see her father again, to feel his warmth as they embraced like family. But she was sorely disappointed. All see got instead was a loud chorus of howling.

The howling continued and fluctuated, and it was ruining what would otherwise have been an acceptable ending to Sasha. Not only did the howls begin to intrude on her last moments, but they began to physically move her as well. The fog didn't object, and Sasha felt her body relax in the arms of a stranger—the comfort of its fur, the tickle of its touch, the cool breeze from its speed.

Sasha rolled up into the fetal position, her legs nearing her chest, and the beast's arms wrapped around her ass and legs. She reopened her eyes and gasped in amazement. This furry beast launched from platform to platform whether it was a fire extinguisher, car, or other surface not covered by the alien's burning acid. This alien was grace under fire.

At last, the animal with the face of a dog came to a halt. In no more than four leaps, the critter had cleared a city block. Slowly and carefully, the animal laid Sasha down, her back gently resting against a brick wall adjacent to a stairway to the building entrance. Flowers misted the air with the scent of lavender, relaxing Sasha even more.

The first group of humans to arrive on the scene was a squad of armed and armored police officers led by the beautiful mustache of Colonel Major. The group executed as precisely as a military unit, each man taking a corridor of responsibility and positioning themselves correctly.

The animal suddenly stood back from Sasha. A loud chorus of howls echoed down and around the buildings as, one by one, four more of the dog-like creatures appeared into a similarly proficient formation themselves. Large electric spears zapped the sky with powerful bolts of energy.

The animal pulled something from a pouch in his stomach, gave a smile of some sort, and then tended to various parts of his body that were smoking and burning. The intensity of the situation had allowed the critter's injuries to go unnoticed, except by the colonel, who lowered his weapon and ordered the others to do the same. They followed his lead, as he inspired trust and confidence in those below them.

In response and without orders, the dog-like animals turned off their electric tips and stood at a more formal position. One of the animals in the rear of the formation threw a staff to his mate, the one who had saved Sasha. He took position at the head of the formation, bent to a knee, and attached a medium-sized rock to the top of the staff. As he rose, the rest of the animals knelt down in a sign of respect.

"I am Archimius. We belong to the Dognosis clan. I can speak on behalf of the Arkapeligo, and we are here to pay homage and respect to the human guardian." The group rose, pounded their chests in a ceremonial ritual, and returned to their kneeling positions. "Rarely before have we witnessed such an act of bravery, and we shall create songs and rejoice in your victory here today!" Again the group stood up and pounded their chests, this time howling as they did so. "Even if this is the pinnacle of strength for your species, we have surely gained a most powerful ally here today."

One of the aliens from the hospital approached from the side. Moving within sight of Archimius and allowing itself to be seen, it interjected without speaking. "Now, please, if you have no doctors, allow us to heal your Guardian. I assure you that we are very kind and knowledgeable."

The colonel blinked, dumbfounded, and after a moment, the alien doctor came to Sasha and began its examination.

PART 4

35: My Soul, My Soul, an Eternity for My Soul

The meeting ended, and the group disembarked focused and coordinated. These people were worthy of respect, a notable accomplishment for a leader of such strange and abrasive leadership techniques. The colonel was the only one to stay behind. As chief of police, his position was one of the most critical, and he needed to stay in lockstep with Hashmore.

The two men looked out over the conference room's view of the city. The ocean lay only a few blocks away, mostly obstructed by the litany of skyscrapers. The sky had darkened and looked nasty. Gray pillows of clouds were advancing. The two men were drawn from their conversation as the outside environment shifted. It started as a hum but grew louder and louder.

The two covered their ears against the hammering sound. It crescendoed, and through the break in the skyline, a large plume of water rose into the air.

The high pitch of the falling tethers was replaced by the seductive roar of ocean waves. A high wall of water raced through the skyline, aimed seemingly directly at the two men. Later Hashmore would describe his actions as knowledge based, but in truth his body was powerless. He was no Moses, yet here he stood with a wall of rushing water descending upon him.

The colonel tugged and then pulled, but Hashmore was

anchored and unable to look away. The wall of water was coming fast, yelling with its mighty cap waters. For a moment, just for a moment, Hashmore could see the terror in the colonel's eyes, but he felt nothing—not fear, not disbelief, and certainly not the Holy Spirit.

The colonel closed in briefly. "By God, it's a miracle." The wave of water had run out of substance, and as it flooded into the open plazas and parks, it parted. Hashmore relaxed his stance, but he could not relax his soul. Deep inside, he felt a great loss, a great emptiness.

The colonel jumped up and down a time or two before looking at Hashmore. "Can you believe that? Whooooo, if that doesn't reassure you that God is on your side, nothing will, my friend." A gentle pat on the back dislodged Hashmore from his stance. "Come on, Mr. Hashmore, there is a great deal of work to be done, and we need you to lead us through it."

Something was wrong, and no, he wasn't referring to the end of society. Assigning tasks, delegating responsibility, implementing God's will—this was his calling, this was supposed to be his time to shine, but it all felt so hollow. Hashmore had always imagined himself being paraded down the street after saving so many from whatever such disaster. He always knew it would be God's will, but God was nowhere to be found in this disaster. His will was feeling absent in the center of his soul.

A new voice called out, and every new voice brought yet another new problem to solve, meaning more stretching of the resources and less productivity. RUDY hummed with activity. The room was fully manned now, with multiple dispatchers now operating out of the same central location, the major staff all working in conjunction, literally trapped in the same room together, and of course the mayor was roaming around somewhere.

The list of problems was endless—people trapped in darkened buildings, schools without running water, and a workforce mostly still out of communication. "Mr. Hashmore, Mr. Hashmore, you have to help us, you have to." The petite man came running into the room, wearing the uniform of a subway engineer. Hashmore sighed as he turned to face the man, a sad and depressed look strung across his face.

"It's the substation just south of here. There are people trapped down there. I know they're alive, hundreds of them. You have to do something, now!"

Linda, the secretary, came trotting up behind the engineer. "Sorry, Mr. Hashmore, I couldn't stop him. He said it was life or death."

The high heels were a more likely cause of her inability to stop the man, he thought to himself. A quick examination of the man revealed that he was indeed panting hard, as if he had traveled some distance. His feet and trousers were wet, but only a sparse drip now fell to the floor.

Hashmore rubbed his forehead. "What can you tell me about who is alive, where they are, and what we need to rescue them?"

The man caught his breath and his face relaxed, slightly reassuring Hashmore that the man was indeed getting what he wanted. "I tried to save them, but the waters were too much. The lady with the baby, my god, my god! She was pushed down. She lost her baby. My god."

The man was obviously reliving a horrible moment, in fact the most horrible because it was the moment when reality hit home and could never be dismissed again by the logical brain.

Colonel Major was quick to rush in, placing both his hands on the man's shoulders and closing in near his face. "Move on, man. What happened next? You're safe now. Let's get those others safe now too."

The panicked man nodded his head as he mimicked the colonel's head movement until his mind had control again. With a stutter, he continued. "In the train cars, the people were trapped. Water was leaking in through the door. They couldn't open it. Something was wrong."

Hashmore spun around and cursed under his breath. "Oh, Lord, why have you forsaken me this day, so that I should have to wash up the wake of your wrath?" Then he began searching RUDY for somebody who could go check out not only this man's subway station but all of them. That meant having to deal with Cook. Hashmore bit his lip as he pushed the call button, summoning Mr. Cook.

Their rivalry had started decades ago. The mayor would say that Cook beat Hashmore to the punch, but Cook had actually stolen a tip and a career case away from Hashmore. He rode that bust all the way to first-offer retirement. Why the mayor was so enamored with him, Hashmore could only venture to guess. Logic would suggest that Cook had some dirt on the mayor, but it was only speculation. Even Cook's walk was annoying, with its bouncy cadence, and then add his perfectly cut hair and manicured suit—get over yourself, already.

Cook answered with an arrogance that drove Hashmore crazy. "Hey, Hashy, looks like you have a real job to do today. I will forgo the unusual pleasantries so we can go save some lives, hoorah."

The man's voice alone gave Hashmore a headache. "I have a witness reporting people trapped in the sub cars. What can you tell me?"

Hashmore expected some smart-aleck response, but Cook stayed more professional than expected. "It's true, I currently have two water-rescue units in operation, but honestly, I lost contact with a great many of my people who were working the docks. I have most of my active units concentrating there."

Hashmore sighed, hating the fact that this man might be his superior in ways that, though less important in the grand scheme, were still easy to envy at times. "There will be many hard decisions today. Many people will be lost and many lives changed forever. I'm turning the department-of-corrections personnel over to you in order to assist you in evacuation of the subway system."

"But, Hashy, these guys have no training, no knowledge of our chain of command. How do you expect me to deploy them?"

Cook's incompetence drove Hashmore crazy, but he was resigned not to show it outwardly. "Ok, here is a suggestion. Take one of your rescue teams and separate it out so that each man takes leadership of a corrections detail. They can then attend to more situations at once rather than one by one, still leaving one team intact for the most technical rescue efforts."

Cook paused. "What about the prisoners?"

Hashmore chuckled at the questions. How could a non-Christian question his morality? "Maybe they should have thought of that before they betrayed society and got themselves thrown in jail. Let God deal with those lot." Hashmore meant it too. In his mind, it was only a matter of time before God brought his full wrath down upon those most wicked.

⚏/

Communications were always a problem during times of crisis, only making matters worse. If the power went out but the phone still worked, it was a problem. If the phone went out, who the hell cared if there was power? The grosser details were giving a feeling of law and order over the whole city, but the backlog of minor calls was growing.

The colonel was proving much more effective at getting his men up to full strength, while Commander Thomas's crews were still struggling to catch up. Word had come in from the pier, and Cook had indeed lost a lot of his personnel in the flood. As expected, the department-of-corrections officers were more than willing to abandon their gloomy surroundings in order to play hero, so Hashmore ordered them down into the subways to save any and all possible souls.

It's a cruel Lord who takes support away in times of such need, Hashmore thought. The falling of the tethers was only the bomb that stopped the convoy; it was the secondary one that caused the most harm. The noises had started again, but while isolated in their safe room, Hashmore and the others were unaware of it, and as he ordered hundreds of heroes down into the depths of the subways, another larger, more voluminous wave headed inbound.

Rafters and huge slices of material were pummeling deep down into the ocean and land around each side of the island. As soon as one would settle, another would drop down and splash into the ocean, sending wave after wave far into the city.

Hashmore and a few others watched as monitor after monitor went blank with the passing of the waves. Unit after unit lost contact, their markers disappearing like hope in the night, leaving behind only a dark board and a vacant computer display. Hashmore's emotions turned to despair.

This level of failure isn't possible, he told himself. God destined me for this. How could I have failed my Lord so miserably? Or did my Lord fail me miserably?

⚶

He just couldn't explain it. Hashmore watched the unfolding of God's wrath, but he was preoccupied with a bigger problem, a problem of faith. When gentiles can feel God's love, why could he only feel empty? Hashmore studied his computer terminal. It was in power-saver mode, and barely usable. Perhaps, he thought to himself, he had outlasted God's usefulness too. Maybe he was God's scapegoat. Could the God he worshiped for all this time betray him like that?

While Hashmore's outward appearance may have been appropriate for the circumstances, the internal reasonings were far different. He decided to do what he had predominately done in the past during moments of crisis and march on to higher ground before looking around. A moment of panic, a moment of uncertainty, was no reason to abandon ship alone, yet there was a nagging feeling he just couldn't shake either.

Without RUDY, this room was nothing more than a shelter, and in his current state of mind, seeking shelter wasn't going to cut it. So using his phone as a light, Hashmore walked up the three flights of stairs, passed through security despite giving some of the guards quite a startle, and walked outside.

It should have been daytime, but it was dusky, and it wasn't hard to see why. The aliens were dropping rafter after rafter, creating a wall around the city, a wall so tall that it had blocked out the sky. The ground began shaking, like a purr at first but soon more like a washing machine. A flock of birds flew chaotically amidst the conflicting nature of the elements. People littered the streets, sloshing through the standing water, pointing, and screaming at the sky.

Hashmore was still toward the center of the island and couldn't see any ocean from his current standpoint. The intensity of the pitched noises was fading with the light, along with his faith. How could the pinnacle of his existence feel so hollow? The darkness crept in, and it only seemed fitting that it should end like this, in the dark, alone.

Several bright lights shined directly on Hashmore from above. The light broke off into three and began circling him from above. A new red light appeared from out of the darkness, in the middle, bringing a slightly burning, warm glow with it. The beam focused in on his headset and handset. The red light disappeared just before a wet, nasty-smelling substance sprayed him like a skunk.

Hashmore coughed and felt some initial burning in his nose and lungs, but the more he breathed, the easier it became, and his moment of panic was soon over. The encounter was over just as quickly, for the lights vanished into the sky, leaving him with yet another piece of evidence to support the existence of God's nonexistent aliens.

Again the outside ambient noise changed dramatically, increasing the shaking of the island. It now felt like a significant earthquake. The ground rumbled and hummed with the pulse of a mechanical drill. It swayed, but only enough to notice, and as Hashmore looked up, he could see the sway in the buildings as well. People in an adjacent building had started flooding out onto the streets, fearing the tumbling of the buildings.

Creeks and moans accompanied the swaying of the buildings, but to his great relief, none appeared ready to topple, and the noise level seemed to be dropping. The crowd gathered around him, the people moving forward as they constantly adjusted their angle with the ground.

He heard the sounds of puking and, as the wind shifted, even smelled it. Hashmore's mind was relativity clear and calm, on par for his given talents. Yet the difference was his internal self. Before, his belief in the Lord actually gave him power to move forward, to carry on the banter and torch of the Lord, but if the Lord didn't exist, what was the point?

Hashmore felt his gut drop as he and everyone else in the crowd fell to their knees. The harsh sounds of a building finally giving way echoed down the skyline—the crumbling of cement, the tearing of steel, the screams of those lost. The lift was intense. The downward pressure was nearly unbearable, and Hashmore was forced onto his chest, his face now down on the street. He felt dampness on his forehead and smelled salt on the pavement. As he lay there, helpless to move, he wondered why the rapture and ascent into heaven all felt so humanlike and devoid of the godly presence. Maybe, he thought, there is no God and all those jerks, for all those years, just might have been right.

⚡/

Hashmore lay facedown in the cold darkness. The earth-quake-like vibrations had ceased, but the force of gravity made any movement very difficult, and he was certain that the sudden drop in temperature was going to be a bad thing. His breath formed in white vapors, and he felt a sting in his lungs and throat from the cold, when a new sound engaged.

hifting his eye upward, he saw that the rafters were spreading out and expanding. Like great planks of metal, a clear bubble started to fill the space in between, forming large squares in the sky above. Black sky filled in as the shape of the dome began to form. A strong, cold wind blew down from directly above, freezing a tiny ice puddle on the street just inches away from Hashmore's face.

The downward pull of gravity had changed its mind and begun to spin with an amazing amount of acceleration. Hashmore moved onto his backside and looked up at one of the most incredible sights he had ever witnessed, and one of the most disturbing.

A huge blue sphere rose across the new dome's horizon.

⚡/

Hashmore was again dumbfounded, at a loss for how his

faith could explain this. Its beauty was unmistakable, with its vast lush oceans, deep-green forests, and broad swaths of light brown— it was truly Eden. Even if horrific in its implications, it was magnificent in its grandeur. The crowd around him, now visible in the light, had started to take survey of themselves and their situations. He heard tears in tandem with comments like "Oh my god" and "What the hell?"

Once more, Hashmore was in the position of knowing what should be done and how to do it, without the passion to do so. His whole life was leading up to a great event for the Lord, yet this event had done nothing but disprove his most fundamental beliefs about the Lord. Hashmore was caught in a mental paradox between believing despite all that he saw around him and acknowledging that he was wrong at the core, and therefore unfit to serve.

The group started to splinter and break up, with each conversation taking a different twist, each requiring a different set of actions to be taken. Hashmore took a deep breath and prepped himself like a fat man getting ready for a workout. He looked around for something to stand on, found a nearby hydrant, stood up, steadied himself, studied the crowd, and began. "Everyone, everyone. My name is Hashmore, and I am the emergency manager for the city of Manhattan."

え╱

Dispersing the crowd was a relatively easy job. The nervous, scared people needed to stay busy and be productive to avoid panic. By organizing the group into sets of three, Hashmore instructed them on how each group was to make contact with a building, take inventory, and establish communications via the runner system with headquarters at RUDY.

Eager to engage in their new assignments, the majority of the crowd scattered. A few people stayed behind. Some of them were the pukers, now taking the time to clean and right themselves. Some older and younger people stayed behind in their respective fetal positions, distraught over the course of events and loss of it all. There would be no way to know who was actually doing what, but if some of them followed his instructions, Hashmore believed he could get things settled down.

One small group stayed behind, and while Hashmore couldn't quite hear the conversation, it was getting very heated. He took a moment to observe the group. Some of its members were speaking passionately. It took him by surprise that someone could still have this much fervor for anything. He again recognized that he was feeling completely empty inside.

The juxtaposition made him feel uncomfortable, and he considered walking away, when the group approached him. "Hey, you there . . . yeah, you, Mashbore. I got a fucking bone to pick with you." A man wearing a slick suit and an expensive watch, with a terrible haircut, came over. "Just what in the hell do you think you are doing? Are these people your employees? I don't fucking think so, because they're my fucking employees."

In the past, this man would have infuriated Hashmore, but right now, he felt too empty to care. Truthfully, he really didn't care if anyone followed his instructions. But he didn't know what else to do other than execute what he thought was God's destiny for him. In a long diatribe, the man continued talking about how damn important he was. For Hashmore, this was simply what he was doing at this moment. For him, it could have been any task. The depression of losing his Lord was setting in, deeper and deeper.

It was the mayor who ended the conversation. A clean, straight-on jab to the man's nose sent him reeling back, a tear in his eye. The mayor looked at Hashmore. "Politics is fucking over. Now it's time for leadership. Now look at you, man, this is your time, your time to be that superstar, but you look like a man who can't get it up anymore. I don't know what's going on in that mind of yours, but we need you here and now. So get your ass downstairs and tell us what the fuck we should be doing."

Hashmore smiled. He seldom liked the way his friend and boss spoke, but he always seemed to love the message. Hashmore smiled again. If not whole inside again, at least he felt human.

36: To Pray or Not to Pray

For all his years in police work, Hashmore still found the actual collar to be the most stressful and least fun part of the job. Examining the evidence, hunting down the details, retracing the cover-up—those were the parts of the job he enjoyed. Shaking guys down, staking out perps, and chasing and fighting people were not the enjoyable parts of the job. That's why Hashmore and Biggo Mandainity made such a good team—Big M loved every part of the job he hated, and vice versa.

So when the aliens only took Hashmore, it was a source of great discomfort and stress. With the return of the warmth in the air and the stabilizing of the ground came the alien craft's return, hovering right above Hashmore. The undercarriage opened, and a light illuminated the spray like a fluorescent marker, clearly distinguishing Hashmore from the other humans. A pink light surrounded the two men and slowly closed in. Hashmore felt nothing, but the mayor cringed in pain as he was forced to back away. He didn't appear to have suffered any significant injury, but it made Hashmore all the more nervous.

Hashmore looked at the ground as he smelled burning, only to notice that all vegetation sprouting out of the sidewalk was shriveling up. A burst of foul, stale air and fog rushed forth and filled the light-contained barrier. Hashmore held his breath, but each little slip sent a burning sensation down into his lungs. After several long seconds, he heard a sparking noise, and the fog and wind ceased.

Sparks and sounds of distortions brought Hashmore's attention beyond the barrier. The mayor had taken to throwing rocks at the field. As he continued to watch, Colonel Major now approached with his weapon drawn. Able to breathe freely again, Hashmore lost the sense of panic, but only briefly. The colonel and the mayor were having a heated discussion as the colonel prepared to open fire on the alien ship.

While the outside world seemed very concerned, Hashmore felt relieved. If his God didn't exist, maybe these aliens could give him some answers.

⚏/

Answers were what Hashmore was seeking, but what were the questions, and what could he expect aliens to know of the Lord, anyway? Could aliens have a relationship with Jesus? What did their existence do to his relationship with the Lord? Would they have their own version of a savior? Would Jesus be universal or a human endeavor?

Panic slowly grew inside him, like a high school student learning about an exam after ditching the previous class. Any excitement was overshadowed by the implications of the answers. What if the moral foundation from which he had based his whole life was a farce? Could he find redemption in a new system?

Following his train of thought, Hashmore was overwhelmed by guilt. If he was about to be judged, he suddenly hoped for some instant extra credit to cash in on, like the time he helped an old lady cross the street or gave money to a hobo. Alas, there was only a purple light separating him from his world—it held like a solid, reacted like a gel, and now that the fog had vanished, breathed like a screen.

The mayor had prevented the colonel from firing his weapon, and the group had joined him in throwing stones. To what effect, Hashmore wasn't sure, but it was a touching gesture, and for the first time in a long time, he felt a tinge of happiness. His comrades cared, and it was nice to feel like someone cared. It could be hard to feel God's love at times, but then again, it could be hard to feel others' love most of the time.

Again the temperature dropped, and Hashmore's breath steamed in the cold. A strong wind brought with it an icy chill, and with a sudden change in pressure, Hashmore felt himself being gently pulled upward with even greater force. A strong *whoop* sound echoed in his ears as Hashmore was propelled by the hands of the wind, as if God himself were reaching down and lifting him up. With that, he ascended into darkness.

⚖/

Lord, are you there? It's so cold, so very, very cold. Lord, are you calling me? I can't hear you? Lord, are you there? All I want is for your will to be done. All you have to do is tell me what to do, and I shall go to the far end of the world. I will challenge demons. I will do all that you ask. Just please, please give me warmth. I'm so very, very cold. I can't hear myself think over the chattering of my teeth. I can't find the light. Where do I go? Oh, Lord, show me the light so I may enter your kingdom.

Lord, are you there? Why do you not reach out to me? Why do I stand to suffer here in the cold and dark? Have I not carried out your will as I understood it? Did I not do enough good? Lord, if my time is now, why do you not judge me? Why do you not reach out to me? What do I have to do to get through to you? How many of your enemies' demons slayed is enough? How many of your children have I protected? I risked my life every day for you, and in my time of need, this is how I am repaid? To be spit out and flung into the cold and dark, no more than a speck of food to be spit out, not even worth its own in nutrition. Perhaps, Lord, it is elsewhere I should look for enlightenment. Perhaps, Lord, I was wrong.

Lord, are you there? It's so cold, so very, very cold. My heart grows cold too, my Lord. I feel the need for anger to heat my body, for I fail to feel your warmth. I try to stay my mind, but the evidence mounts against you, my Lord. If others, nonbelievers, can feel your warmth but I cannot, does that not say that maybe it is human creation, something that we can conjure within our thoughts and emotions? Victims are real. You can see and smell their corpses. The emotions that create those victims are real too—a jealous lover, a terrorist fighting a devil, and a greedy banker pulling an inside job were all fueled by emotions that they could strongly feel. I, Lord, I can't feel you anymore. Lord, why don't you answer me? Lord, why is it so cold?

Lord, are you there? It's me, Luke, and I'm so very, very cold.

The physical act may have been similar to a child exiting a waterslide, but it felt more like a baby being born into a completely unfamiliar and frightening world. Thank the Lord, it was warm. Not only warm—hot. The liquid, not quite hot enough to scald, immersed his body. Every nook, every crevice, was infused with unbelievable warmth. Hashmore dared not open his eyes or his mouth but lay motionless, enjoying the salvation of its warmth.

He feared opening his eyes, but a desperate need for oxygen forced the issue. The liquid appeared to be nothing more than water, but he was encased in the shell of his prison not more than a few inches from his face. Oh, how cruel to be saved from the cold just to die in the water. God, he wondered, must have a strange sense of humor, or maybe he doesn't exist at all.

Twice now he had faced imminent death, nary a glance of the afterlife, nary a word from his Lord, and nary a vision of understanding or enlightenment. Death sucks, Hashmore thought to himself. Yet the drive for life continued, and he soon pounded ruthlessly on the shell, desperate to escape.

"Calm yourself." A voice came, a voice not from the outside but from within. Maybe he was finally receiving a prayer come true.

He cried out to the voice, using his loudest prayer voice. "I'm here, my Lord. I will obey. Please tell me what to do." There was a long pause, and as it continued, Hashmore found his thoughts running again—maybe it wasn't anything, maybe just my imagination. As his stress level rose, he became conscious of his need to breathe and again thrashed at the shell.

Again the voice came, still from within. Only the Lord could have such a voice. "Calm yourself. Breathe normally." Hashmore's instincts were powerful, and he continued to press against the shell, if not thrash. "Calm yourself. Breathe normally."

Hashmore responded, still in his prayer voice. "My Lord, I

can't breathe underwater."

The voice responded again. "Breathe normally."

Fear gripped Hashmore from several angles, and he was again forced to believe in a miracle as he slowly exhaled through his nose and felt the bubbles rush past his face. He opened his mouth, expecting a rush of water to fill it, but he only felt air— precious, live-giving miracle air filled his lungs.

"At last," Hashmore cried out in his prayer voice, "Lord, you have delivered me a miracle. Thank you! Thank you! Thank you! Oh, Lord, speak to me again. My Lord, please speak to me again."

Nothing happened, but Hashmore was not deterred, for he had heard the voice of his Lord, and no alien could ever take that away from his faith. And perhaps, Hashmore thought, maybe humans were not the only children of God.

$$\overline{\underline{\mathcal{F}}}/$$

With the return of warmth, air, and his faith, Hashmore felt more relaxed than he could remember in recent years. As a young man, his faith had seemed so real, so internalized, but as he got older, the harder it became to hold on to that emotional connection. With so many numerous personal failures occurring over the years, and so many sad and evil occurrences witnessed, Hashmore just ignored the numbness, attributing it to the harsh realities of society. He never noticed the numbness that had started to accompany his faith as well.

Resting his eyes in the moment, Hashmore felt the voice again inside his head. "Can you hear me?"

Excitement rose within him as he felt the excitement of a puppy whose master has returned home after a long day away. Hashmore cried out again in his prayer voice. "Yes, my Lord, I can hear you. Oh, blessed am I, Lord. Please tell me what to do."

While he could understood the words in his mind, they seemed distant. "What's going on? Why are his vitals changing so rapidly?" The voice thundered in his head. "Calm yourself. Relax. Can you hear me?"

Like a teen girl at a boy-band concert, Hashmore screamed out in his prayer voice. "Oh yes, Lord, I can hear you. I am ready. I can hear you."

There was a long pause while nothing happened. Hashmore continued to pray but heeded the request of his Lord and lowered his voice. Calm returned to him as he recited the Lord's Prayer over and over again. It was several recitals before the voice came back. "Can you hear me? If so, please uncross your hands."

The request confused him. Why was his God still asking if he could hear him? Why did God want him to unfold his hands? Hashmore got that sickening feeling in his stomach, but he complied and pressed his hands flat together.

Again there was a long pause as nothing happened. Hashmore pushed away the doubt and focused on the miracle of his still being alive—after whatever it was that he had just been through—and recited another few rounds of the Lord's Prayer.

The words from his Lord came with a crushing blow. "We don't understand your gesture. Perhaps you could communicate verbally?"

Hashmore erupted in tears behind his closed eyes, now

more afraid than ever to open them. "Oh, Lord, why do you not hear my prayers?" He continued the sobs as they staggered his speech. "Who is 'we,' Lord? Is that Jesus?"

The voice took a short pause. "Would you kindly open your eyes so we can finish our exam and open your tube?"

Hashmore took several seconds and said a short prayer to reconfirm that there was in fact no voice of his Lord in his head, just some damn alien. The voice began to speak in order to hurry the process but backed off after Luke opened his eyes and moved. Red light instantly filled his vision, and a string of pulsing, piercing, and popping noises started to give him a headache.

The discomfort didn't last long, and soon the water was drained away, and the door to the tube opened. There, as his vision cleared, Hashmore saw the physical body of the voice in his head and two other, completely different aliens standing in a line as if to greet him.

His conscious mind drove him to take a defensive stance, but his emotions took control and manifested themselves into a pile of puke that was his vending-machine dinner. The bodies of the aliens adjusted but didn't move as they seemed to be at a loss for protocol.

Yet another alien, this time a wheelbarrow full of tentacles and puffing antennae, came forward and placed one of its tentacles around Hashmore. At first he interpreted it as an aggressive move, but the tentacle moved to stabilize his body as another round of puke made its way out of his system and back into the world.

37: Ascent of the Faithful

The alien proved its true intent by completely lowering its guard. Being aware of the aliens surrounding him only enhanced Hashmore's feeling of helplessness. Defecating, climaxing, and yes, puking all felt like pretty defenseless positions in which to be introduced to potentially dangerous beings, yet they appeared disinclined to attack. One even seemed inclined to comfort.

One of the aliens slid forward a few feet. It had a hunchback form of a humanoid with five limbs, one possibly being a tail. Short reddish-brown hair covered its front side, while a long, darker brown covered the sides and rear. Long whiskers reached out of the fur on its back. It had the face of a fox but moved more like a monkey. Its narrow eyes trained on Hashmore like a bird hunting its prey.

Hashmore was able to regain some composure, but he still instinctually took a flight stance as he attempted to restore his breath. Loud caws echoed out from the animal, its head bobbing back with each crow. The sounds pounded violently in his head, and while loud and intimidating, the beast didn't seem to be posing any sort of threat or challenge.

The wheelbarrow alien attempted to wrap its tentacle around Hashmore, but this time, he had the strength to fight it off. The alien didn't put up much of a fight after realizing its actions weren't wanted. Each time Hashmore moved, the aliens would follow, yet they never came too close or moved farther away, with limited variation.

A strange smell began puffing out of the wheelbarrow creature in great quantities, fumigating his nostrils with its pleasant lavender, hickory, and charcoal. Hashmore slowed down in mind and body. The intensity rose quickly, and the effects were remarkably familiar. It wasn't long before he felt numb, just like before, just like the pills.

The wheelbarrow creature again approached to within tentacles' reach, but Hashmore was stiffened by the amazing numbness. The alien tilted Hashmore's head and, extending a tentacle high into the air, placed something deep inside his ear.

The bird-like alien crowed with the same intensity, but this time, the words echoed clearly in English within his mind. "We welcome you to the Arkapeligo, the civilized universe's last symbol of life, a phoenix in a dying universe, a cradle of civilizations, and above all else, a hope for a future. We welcome you and apologize for the less-than-comfortable ride here. My name is Mardoxx, and I am an emissary for the Tilotin people and their leader, Mother Titlion."

Relaxing his posture, Hashmore then dropped down to a knee, more for physical reasons than political. He wiped his nose and spoke a little prayer. "Lord, give me the strength."

Conversation erupted among the aliens standing behind Mardoxx, but it was very hushed, and only the impression that they were discussing him came across.

Wiping his nose and spitting out the last remnants of his puke, Hashmore rose and spoke verbally. "My name is Hashmore, and I am the emergency manager, subordinate only to the mayor.

What have you done, and why?"

After his response, the conversation between the aliens ceased, and they focused with a diplomatic courtesy. Again Mardoxx crowed a tiresomely piercing noise as the words echoed, the way he thought the Lord's had, deep in his brain. "Yes, of course, forgive my terseness, but the local situation requires us to forgo many of the normal pleasantries, forcing us to tube you through the vacuum of space." There was a short pause as the being gave Hashmore a moment to interject, if necessary. Hashmore did not, and Mardoxx continued. "You and your local brethren are now aboard the spaceship Arkapeligo—a spaceship of immense history, culture, life, and power, whose mission it is to save as many species as possible from the threat of the Wilde. The Wilde are the most ancient of all species, but they betrayed the creator and broke the bounds of his laws. For which they went mad, crazy, and hateful. Now their only purpose is to destroy all that was made by the creator."

He took another short break before continuing. "This ship houses the last remnants of thirteen species. Your species will now hopefully become the fourteenth. We races cohabitate as equally as possible, but if outside decision-making is required, we defer it to the Tilotin people as residing caretakers." Again Mardoxx paused, almost surprised at Hashmore's lack of interruptions.

This time, however, Hashmore interjected with only a nod of endorsement. Mardoxx, while having only been introduced, seemed as easy to read as a human. The smile and impressed nature communicated clearly across the alien's face. "Thank you for your attention. I know it must be a lot to absorb, and I'm afraid the local situation requires you to have yet more extensive knowledge so that you may return to your people and lead them appropriately. There are no imprisoned races on this ship, and each race has a specialty that they share with the collective, as rent." Waving with an extended wing, he stepped aside as one of the rear aliens stepped forward.

It was repulsive, with its numerous eyes protruding out of a furry sack that could change the direction it was viewing, much like a turtle if it could rotate inside its shell. It had the body of a spider, with several limbs that towered over its shell, doubling its height to almost five feet. Soon the shell vibrated, and a beautiful symphony of sounds, whistles, hums, and swirls varied its level of pleasantness. With the sounds, soon returned the words inside Hashmore's head. "I am known in other tongues as Hummington. My species is the Pergenese, and we are proud members of the Arkapeligo. We were the fifth species to join in this great venture. Our home world fell victim to the Wilde. We were the last major stronghold against our rivals, who would take advantage of our great loss. Our enemies were numerous, and the ark lost several defenders in our rescue. For the loss of those who would save us, we now live to save and defend the ark as its pilots, crewmen, and citizens. May, too, your species be judged worthy to join the ark, for it is not only salvation but home." The being stood erect for several seconds and then moved back toward its companions and its place in line.

The third creature in formation now stepped forward. The alien also only stood, at most, four feet tall. It had brown skin like the bark of a pine tree. It had leaf-green hair running along its back, arms, and legs. The alien stepped forward, spun around, and collapsed into what looked very much like a furry shrub. After a brief moment, the creature spun around again and presented itself. Of all the aliens so far, this creature's voice sounded familiar, like a near-eastern language.

"Dulax is how you will address me. My people, the Collinary, are proud members of the Arkapeligo. We proudly serve as providers of nourishment and nutrition for the majority of the species here in the ark. Our world of Atania is no longer a great pearl of civilization, as the Wilde stumbled upon our world early in their madness, the worst of their madness. To only the accord of mercy do they now terminate, yet at that time, they did unspeakable things to my people. We were a farming colony, the finest in the quadrant. The ark offered us refuge, but in our arrogance and abundance of a scarce product, we sought out to rebuild what had been taken. Yet with so many resources, so many willing mates, and so few to answer to, we became decadent and failed to build anything of value."

An almost human display of remorse came across in body language despite the dramatic physical difference. "Again the Wilde returned. All of us fled. So few of us lived. Those who did banded together at a lesser colony and launched an expedition to find the ark. After a journey of much hardship and loss, we were finally reunited with the Arkapeligo. Now we pay homage to the ark and its caretakers, the Tilotin, and we devote our existence to supplying the ark with the nutrition it needs to undertake its vital mission." The alien Dulax made a gesture and returned to Hummington's side.

Hashmore finally interjected, eager to fill in some blanks. "Who were the creators of this ark, and what happened to them? What the hell has gone Wilde? Judged? How will I be judged, and by whom? What do you mean by 'local situation'?" Hashmore struggled to remember them all, instantly forgetting each as soon as it was out, for the next question required all concentration.

Whispers and impressions came across his mind, but Hashmore was at a loss for what the four aliens were discussing. Waves of emotions such as doubt, worry, and apprehension came across as he concentrated on their discussion, but alas, nothing substantive. Mardoxx turned back around to face Hashmore, and again the annoying crows came across as the words spoken in his head. "We will, in time, answer all your questions in more detail, but for now, all you need to know is that the Wilde are a grave danger to all of us, every living thing. So grave, in fact, that many of your people have been unfortunately lost as we rush to depart for the local solar system as soon as possible. As to your other questions, you are not the one being judged. Some of your brethren will be. As for your last question, the empire believes that your race has something valuable to collect, and they intend to do that before the Wilde arrive and destroy everything."

Another new alien entered the room from around the corner. This alien was intense in its presence and power. It stood seven feet tall, on two powerful legs. Its front arms seemed to have extra elbows, and a spiky tail waved catlike behind it. Its face was dog-like, and its eyes were narrow. It held a long staff with a bulb of electricity at each end. It waved its paw as Mardoxx continued with the loud crows. "This is a member of the Dognosis species, obviously a very powerful and intimidating race, which is why we don't include them in first introductions. As I'm sure you have already determined, the Dognosis serve as security aboard the ark. I say 'security' because their numbers are again too few to make an army. Not that it takes many, mind you." Mardoxx moved like a chicken across the floor, looking like nothing more than a pet to the huge creature as he stood before the Dognosis alien. Again he crowed, but this time at the alien. The words were still clearly in Hashmore's mind. "Aragnaught, proud warrior of the Dognosis, will you honor your service to the ark by vowing to protect Mr. Hashmore in his quest?"

The alien changed stature, barked loudly, and pounded the electric spear across his chest.

The furry little beast let out a visible chuckle before uncomfortably moving on and back toward Hashmore. "Alas, the last great power in this galaxy is known as the Huban Imperial Empire. A most gifted and powerful race, they once ruled with a Midas touch, but now they control with ruthless abandon, all consumed with the task of saving their empire from the Wilde. Slaves they make out of worlds in days. Now they have come here. Leaked out from within . . . still to be determined, but alas here is where we find ourselves now. The empire is coming for you and your people, the Wilde are coming for your world, and we are all that stand in their way, well at least for the near term." The creature paused, waiting to see how much Hashmore had assimilated.

There was a noticeable pause before Hashmore realized that a response was necessary, and another as he reviewed the last few words. Several questions rose to the top, but as he was about to begin, the creature crowed again. "Time is of the essence, and there will be many more questions. There is one more task we must complete before we can return you to your people."

To his amazement, the creature opened wide, powerful wings, now braced by the large whiskers that protruded out of its back. The creature again crowed as it clucked like a chicken and approached Hashmore. "The judging has commenced, and your race's fate shall be determined by the time we arrive at our destination."

Hashmore reached out his arms in a defensive position as

the smaller creature jumped, grabbed him around the chest, and lifted them both up with its massively powerful wings.

Oh, Lord, are you there? Please tell me, what does this all mean? Whom shall I spite for you, my Lord? This is all so different, so strange. I don't like it, Lord. I feel so scared, so weak, so deprived of faith. Oh, Lord, will you give me the faith? Give me the knowledge? Lord, I am your warrior. I have slain many demons for you. Will you not grant me my peace?

Oh, Lord, are you there? Have you not always shown me the way? Have you not always led me to the wolf as a sheep? Yet this time, Lord, I fear I cannot do what you ask of me. Everyone here is a monster, a threat to your existence. How much more can you ask of me? How much more can I give? Have the battles I waged in your name not been enough? How many more demons must I slay to earn a place at your table? How many more works must I produce to prove my faith?

Oh, Lord, are you there? Please tell me what to do next. Please tell me how much more. My spirit well is running dry, my body aches and pains with age, and yet you continue to ask, continue to order. Oh, Lord, where shall I get the strength? When shall I persevere? When shall I rest?

Oh, Lord, I'm so tired. Will you not renew me, renew my dwindling belief, renew my failing conviction? Oh, Lord, I beg of you, renew my faith. I can go on no longer.

38: Flight of the Faithful

With two powerful strokes, Mardoxx lifted Hashmore high above the room, which had a dome shape, with four entry pods in the center and supporting equipment on the periphery. Mardoxx had altered Hashmore's position and now held him by the arms, around his waist, and under his shoulders. Together they moved toward a large hole in the top of the dome. With a great flurry, Mardoxx thrust his wing to cover them and, with a strong current, began to suck them up the vent.

They were moving fast for three, maybe four stories, Hashmore guessed. Then they burst forward into a greater expanse. It was amazing. It was beautiful. It was scary. For nearly the full distance of his vision, the ship stretched in each direction. Shaped like a cylinder, the expanse was interlaced with large, circular junction points. Some of these junctions seemed to have active transportation systems with vehicles moving in and out frequently. Other junctions were large, dark spots in a vast stretch of correlating, lit buildings and open fields of strange vegetation.

There was no up, no down, maybe even no left or right. Hashmore had never felt so much like a foreigner. Mardoxx again crowed, but slower and weaker as he struggled to maintain his breath. "This is the heart of the ark. We call it the city of eternity, the city of the blessed, and the city of a forever hope, Xeanna. Those residents are the engineers, craftsmen, and trade smiths that keep the actual ark working. They are usually the offspring of the mixed-blood families that can occur, usually outside the boundaries of one or both of the civilizations. There are even a few descendants of the first ones, still alive and working down there, somewhere."

A few powered vehicles passed by. Several large transportation systems seemed to be in operation all at once. Speedier, longer vessels zoomed by more centrally as they fled down the center pathways. Larger, bulkier vessels traveled much more slowly in a separate layer farther out from center. Several vessels of various shapes and sizes zipped up and down to the surface at select intervals. Mardoxx flew higher, staying about five hundred meters above the surface as they proceeded in a flight pattern that Hashmore was sure he couldn't duplicate.

"Why don't we just take a vehicle?" Hashmore yelled louder than was necessary while using the stones, but Mardoxx didn't appear to mind.

"Because those vehicles aren't allowed where we are going."

"And where is that?" Hashmore asked.

"To see the Great Mother."

So far, most of what Hashmore had seen looked and felt more like a city than a military or political organization. Yet as they approached a circular junction point, that look changed dramatically as both Tilotins flew in an inner-circle defense perimeter while small craft with intimidating hardware circled the perimeter.

Stationed at the entry points were Dognosis, checking the visitors as they queued for entry.

The defenders spread out and opened a pathway that led to another vent, which appeared to be their destination. Once again, Mardoxx gave a big thrust and covered the two with his wings as they were sucked up a tube at an incredible speed. They burst forth into another expanse. This time, a huge dome reached high above a tall, vertical spire of a mountain. The landscape was littered with smaller mounds, creating a labyrinth surrounding the great spire.

It was beautiful, if not sparse. Each mound appeared to reach two or three stories high, and on closer inspection, some of the mounds had vegetation growing between them. As Mardoxx descended, Hashmore felt another repositioning, this time much less comfortable. Mardoxx now held Hashmore horizontally and was moving him toward his rear end. "I need nourishment if I am to have the strength to carry us to Mother. I apologize for the discomfort. This should only take a couple of minutes."

With two loud crows, Mardoxx circled back around and dove in low. It took some adjustment, but Hashmore was finally able to attain a forward view, only to discover it was terrifying. The two raced down deep into the foliage at terrifying speed. Suddenly Mardoxx jerked hard right, straining Hashmore's neck as he struggled to maintain position. Then the bird dove down hard for several feet, jerked back, twisted left, and juked down and right. It was a dizzying and painful experience as the bird was most agile in avoiding the vegetation, but the constant jerking was awful. Hashmore felt something wet and sticky smack him in the face, and as the two broke skyward again, he saw several other aliens shaking the vegetation behind them.

It took several thrusts of Mardoxx's wings before Hashmore finally returned to his original position. "Who is Mother? And what will she want from me?" Hashmore again yelled needlessly, as the stones translated directly into another's head regardless of volume.

Mardoxx's response came across very choppy, as if he was still eating. "Mother is the wisest and fairest of all the Tilotin egg layers. She will evaluate and give her final judgment as to your worthiness as a species and report that to the ark council. I will not, nor will Aragnaught, be allowed to join you. This will be an interaction of your own doing, your own free will—and of course Mother."

Hashmore thought for a second, noticing how high they now soared. He cinched tighter as they rose ever higher, toward the great peak. "I don't understand what you just said. Just don't drop me, for God's sake. I'm scared of this height."

"You will face greater, scarier, and more daunting challenges than overcoming a fear of heights on the next few trails. I suggest you shut down that part of your brain for the short term. Fear will not serve you well here." Mardoxx brought Hashmore in tighter, and as they approached the spire, a burst of wind took hold. With a whoosh of his stomach, Hashmore felt them rising even higher, faster than ever.

⚖/

Oh, Lord, protect me now, lead me now, and save me now. What does it all mean, my Lord? What are these creatures doing in your universe? Are humans not the chosen race of Jesus? Did my Lord's son not take my form and save my kind? I don't understand any of this, Lord. Lord, I beg you, reveal yourself to me so that I may once again believe. Oh, my Lord, have I not been faithful enough? Decent enough? Have I failed to vanquish enough of your enemies?

Lord, are these aliens your next task for me? Do you wish for me to bear your vengeance down on these foul creatures? I remember many days, Lord, when you gave me the strength to capture your enemies. Let me feel that strength again so that I can execute your will. I remember that son of a bitch who touched those girls. We brought vengeance down on that demon, did we not, Lord? What of the demon who betrayed its own? Did we not bear vengeance down with our mark of the cross against its sinful body? Yes, my Lord, thank you. I can remember the power of your grace, the strength it gave me. I can feel it starting to flow through me again, my Lord. Yes, my Lord, I can understand your message. Mother—you want me to use this strength against Mother. Yes, my Lord, I can execute your will.

My Lord, fill me with newfound strength, fill me with newfound purpose. I thank you for saving me. I, I thank you for saving those you did. Lord, I thank you for giving me my many gifts. I thank you for this mission. I thank you for everything, my Father. My Lord, please lead me so I may be in your grace at the end. Please give me the strength to bear down your vengeance.

My Lord, why do I need to bear vengeance down on these creatures? Before, the mandate was so clear, so holy. Now I wonder, Lord, is their existence an affront to you? These creatures have not shown ill will toward me, Lord. My Lord, I don't understand. My Lord, I have so many questions, so many fears. What is this all about? What am I praying for? Who am I praying to? Lord, why is all this happening, and where are you in all of this, my Lord?

⚡/

Hashmore's feet touched down gently just outside a large doorway as Mardoxx released him. They stood on a wide ledge, and Hashmore remarked on the beauty of the landscape, calming his nerves and slowing his breath. Mardoxx landed a few feet away. "Did you say something? Did the translation stone fall out during the flight?"

"No, I still understand you." Hashmore stepped back, trying to take in the strange yet beautiful environment. A beautiful blue light bathed the city in its evening-rich hues.

The doors were massive, and the height of the mountain still raised another three stories. They were covered in elaborate carvings, some images and some abstract. Hashmore wondered how he would open the doors, but they opened upon his approach. Inside, the brilliance of the design's beauty was incredible, with large spires of diamond, gold, platinum, and more rising throughout the cathedral like a forest. The branches veered off, revealing an immaculately carved ceiling. Hundreds of thousands of Tilotins were individually enshrined together as one. In the wider view, it was clear that they formed a cross.

Along the wall, hundreds of green-laced perches spread equal distance throughout gave it a feeling of both uniformity and life. The smell of the gem forest permeated his nose and mixed with a warm gentle breeze, giving the cavern a most majestic feel.

Light crowing summoned Hashmore as a soothing voice again spoke in his head. "Come in, my brother. Please don't be nervous. Please call me Mother Titlion. I am the current holder of this house. Under my leadership, I have granted four races the privilege of earning their place here in the ark. Perhaps I may also grant your race that privilege, but that is still to be determined."

Mardoxx bowed and closed the door behind him as the Great Mother stepped out.

Mother Titlion bounced as softly as a bird—not the same as Mardoxx, but Hashmore concluded that it might be a symptom of her age. As she came closer, the frailness of her skin and body became more apparent. "The test has been administered, and your race has demonstrated an ability to feel compassion. And even if it's not to our liking, it was agreed upon that your moral code is designed more for good than for evil. Yet that alone doesn't guarantee acceptance, and the report came with a warning. So tell me, should I fear you?"

Hashmore cursed a little under his breath. "Oh, God. I am not your enemy, nor do I wish to conflict with any of your ark's species, but this new world is still very strange to us, with much for us to learn. My people are strong and capable. We will use force to defend ourselves. From my answer, you may choose for yourself the appropriate answer to your question."

Hashmore always hated politics, but he had been around enough of it to know it when he saw it. Mother Titlion's facial expression gave away the deep thought before her next response. "And what of your race's history? We have seen the scares of many wars on your planet. Are you not an aggressive, territorial race who will surely return to old habits after your adjustments to your new world?"

Again Hashmore spoke under his breath, cursing politics. "My people have an immense capacity for both evil and good. But given the truth and information, we always choose good. The problems with our history come from the corruptions of our societies, through lies from its own leaders' greed and deception, failing to properly distribute resources. Yet a mass of an informed group of humans is to have a powerful and versatile ally for what we would define as good, for I can make no judgments as to knowing your sense of morality."

"You speak like a politician except for one thing—your words have meaning." The body of the Great Mother shook gently as she laughed at her own joke. "I know our time presses against us urgently, but I hope that we can now put down our shields and speak not as politicians but as people. Will you now join me for a short sip of tea? I believe that is what your people call it. It's amazing how universal this drink is. Nearly every world in the ark has a drink born out of warm water and plant life." The Great Mother hopped gently before expanding her wings and taking flight.

She flew gracefully, taking as few strokes as possible, gliding with the unseen currents of this massive hall, and landed in the center, on a pillar unnoticed until now. A lighted walkway extended its way toward Mr. Hashmore. From the heights of the walkway, it became clear that the cavern reached dozens of stories deep into the mountain. Each spire began to branch out as it neared the ceiling. Each knob of the spire was decorated with the most intricate weaving and sculpting of diamonds, platinum, gold, silver, and some unknown materials of amazing beauty.

Hashmore approached the Great Mother as she rested near

a simple plot of dirt. A small table hovered nearby, with steam rising from two small cups. "How many races are there in your ark? Do any of them pose a threat to us? You were the one to bring the subject up, after all."

The Great Mother grabbed one cup off the hovering table and, with a swipe of her hand, sent it scurrying over to Hashmore with the other. "Yes, there are thirteen races left on the Arkapeligo. I'm not sure of the total number of races that have spent time aboard the ark, but its history is vast. We are a unified society in this sense. Each race will have autonomy but must provide economic, technical, or military support to the ark as rent. They may not develop any military gear outside the ark's oversight. There are no contracts. So if we encounter a planet that you wish to inhabit, you may do so provided no senior race wants the planet. We are all committed to the mission of the ark, so posing a threat to another race within the ranks would be counterproductive."

"And just what is the mission of this ark?"

The Great Mother's smile was unmistakable. "To save life from the darkness. Our mandate is not to cure the universe of disease, war, or poverty. It is only to save life so that it may have a chance to prosper."

Hashmore could feel the genuine nature of the Great Mother as both her words and feelings were translated into his mind. "What is the darkness you speak of?"

The Great Mother sipped her tea before speaking again in her gentle crows. "Darkness is physical in what is commonly known as the Wilde. Yet darkness is more than just a physical foe—it is a most destructive force that corrupts from within, unseen. We call it . . ."

Hashmore could feel the back part of his brain warm slightly as the stone searched his mind.

"Sin."

For all the magnificence of this cathedral, it was clear that the central focus was solely along this point. Inside the dirt was a simple symbol, one that he recognized very well. Hashmore felt his heart lighten and his mind rejoice at the symbol. "This symbol is of great meaning to me, and to many of my people. Please tell me, what meaning does it hold for your people?"

"Please sit down." As if on cue, a chair now hovered up and landed on the outside of the dirt patch still several feet away. "Please remain seated. There are a few security systems in place. I'm sure you understand. This is the most important place in all of the ark. Each race considers it a privilege to be alive in the ark, and each race has lost a huge majority of its heritage. Historical achievement, religious wonder, beauties of the natural world, all of them gone, so we realize just how amazing it was for us to have our most sacred sight saved with us.

"The contrast of this plot serves as a reminder to all of my kind. That the greatest of feats is possible with the power of the Lord, but the humblest of prayers is his greatest gift. Here on this spot is where our Lord made his covenant with the Tilotin people. Tilotins are by our very nature a pragmatic and cautious people. Some would say that it comes from our prey background, but most Tilotins believe that it is our Lord who has provided us with relative safety. True, we lost our home world, but the ark, the Lord's people, came and saved not only us but our covenant too.

We worship a Lord who is both powerful and just. By doing our best to honor the covenant our Lord has laid down before us, we find ourselves here, alive and safe. Now I wish to know of your people's Lord."

The words of the Great Mother came as both a big surprise and a huge relief to Hashmore, and he couldn't help but smile some. "I'm afraid I can't answer that question. I can only tell you of my Lord, for my people hotly contest both the message and the messengers of the Lord. I spoke earlier of the corrupt nature of our leaders causing wars, but I would be remiss if I didn't say that our history was full of wars over both doctrine and substance of a religious nature."

The Great Mother and her tiny, frail body shook again in laughter. "Well thank you for the honest answer. Perhaps you will find that your history is not so unique in these matters. How is it that for so many beings, a message so simple becomes twisted and distorted for evil? Perhaps, then, we were fortunate that our Lord made a most simple covenant—'Find God, find good, be good.'"

Hashmore thought it sounded like a marketing slogan, not the words of an impenitent being. His face gave away more than he had intended, and the Great Mother elaborated. Tracing with her hand, she spoke with a new level of authority "The pillar of height tells us that the foundation of good is never out of balance. The cross of solidarity, only together with our Lord can we raise the cross to the top. Together they form the symbol for the God of good."

Hashmore said, "We believe the Lord created a limited universe, infinite to our perspective but limited by boundaries you might know as physics, biology, and chemistry—all to test each individual's free will for morality and intent. We believe in a God who knows all the possible choices and consequences but relinquished the right to choose. So it was with this intention that our Lord made us our covenant and with this intention that we work to save life and pursue the moral choice as best we can.

"For me, this symbol is also used to represent a covenant our Lord made with my people, but for us, it represents a great sacrifice. Our Lord had grown tired of our wicked ways, and instead of destroying his creation, he rescued it with a miracle. His greatest angel, his family relation, took our form and became the son of the Lord. It was on that cross that we tortured and killed him. But his love for his torturers was his biggest victory, and through his death, our Lord forgave our wicked ways and allowed us to continue and even join him in his kingdom."

The Great Mother's jaw dropped, and the expression was unmistakable despite the physical differences. "Am I to understand that your people have actually met the son of the Lord? Am I to understand that your race is God's chosen people? The stories of the Lord's son are known throughout the galaxy, but to meet the race that bore his death and were responsible for his torture, that is more than I can bear."

Hashmore asked, "Please tell me, what of the Lord's son have you heard? I desperately desire to know if the same Lord I've worshiped my whole life is the same God as yours."

The Great Mother turned and coughed. When she returned, she looked significantly older. "Please don't tell that story to any of the other races, yet. Your people are extremely hated by most of the universe. As for your inquiry, there would be a great deal to discuss." The Great Mother took another sip of tea and patted her lips. "Let me just say that God was displeased with many of his children. So the Lord bore unto the most impoverished, decadent, and disgraceful of his children the greatest of his miracles, an incarnation of perfection."

Hashmore started to feel more and more uncomfortable. His faith had never felt stronger, but his self-image and worth were taking a hit.

The Great Mother continued. "Of course, many will understand that it wasn't your generation personally that did this awful thing, yet there will be several whose anger will be mighty. There must be a way to verify this is true."

It was the first time that Hashmore could sense any emotion from the Great Mother. Until now, she had been very calm, yet now a strong sense of worry was washing over him, as did her words on his brain. "You claim that your world was inhabited by the messiah. Do you have any proof of this claim? Is it possible to get a DNA sample? What have your people done to memorialize the events? Are there only two kinds of humans? Is there prophecy of further prophets to come?" The Great Mother flapped her wings and closed in toward Hashmore.

The near proximity of the Great Mother, plus the order not to leave the chair, put Hashmore in a most uncomfortable position, as if he was suddenly the one being interrogated after the crime. "We, eh, eh, um, we are not exactly sure where. We have guessed, but our Lord came to us at a time before we had the written word. Most of our text comes from generations later. The story goes that after his death, Jesus's body was placed in a nearby cave. Three days later, he appeared again, alive, out of that cave."

The Great Mother hopped back, and suddenly a flying, buzzing machine approached and transformed as she grabbed hold of it. It was an interface pad, and the Great Mother was feverishly interacting with it. Suddenly the area surrounding the covenant turned into a view screen, and while it was black, the edges were clearly visible.

The view screen now displayed a 2-D map of Earth. "No need to stand, please point to the area where the cave might be found." Hashmore found it fairly intuitive. A laser point now beamed from his finger, despite an absence of visible equipment. He pointed to the Middle East, and the map zoomed in further and further until the greater Jerusalem was on display. The Great Mother looked over Hashmore to confirm that this was as close as he was going to get it. Then she began filtering through various overlays. The information it was able to display was incredible. An entire labyrinth of aged cities buried on top of each other. Cycling through the overlays, the Great Mother again turned her attention to her interface pad.

After a few gestures, she threw the pad off to the side, and as it fell, it transformed back into its buzzing form and flew off. The view screen now displayed yet another alien. This one was very reptilian yet with a mix of dinosaur, like a mixed-blood child. Three pillars were etched on the crown of its head. Sparely yet elaborately dressed, this alien was clearly of some importance.

The alien hissed with its tongue as it spoke. "Why, Great Mother, how regrettable it is that we must speak again. What have you come for this time? Or am I to assume that this is purely a political call?"

The Great Mother sounded aged, as the previous fire

appeared to have been extinguished. "My dear emperor, I see you have continued to pursue your quest never to mature. This is a matter of immediate urgency, so I used a channel I knew you would respond to—your great monogamizer. You must call off your dogs and defend this planet. I believe this planet could be the garden home to our worship. You must defend it from the Wilde."

The alien slid to his left and walked across a large, lavish dressing room. "My, how you have aged, time has not been your friend. You are slow now, Great Mother, well behind my wealth of knowledge gathered from the greatest of beings throughout the universe. But no, I have no intention of saving this planet. Your backwater religion has no place in reality. The loss of this planet and any of its relevance will never be noticed."

A wave of frustration and anger poured out from the Great Mother as she spoke between grinding teeth. "My dear emperor, for your amazing wealth of knowledge, you lack vision. This isn't some ruse, isn't a game. This could be the planet of our messiah."

A venomous response came back. "Messiah, I am my own messiah. There is no Lord. There is no Jesus. I am the ultimate power in this universe! Entire species bow down at my command. That is real, not this fantasy about some all-powerful being. I am well aware of this story, but it has no meaning in this universe, and I will make no effort to save it, nor its people. These pathetic creatures are barely worthy of salves. Your faith hasn't served you very well yet, nor will it ever."

With that, the view screen cut off, and the Great Mother spun around so Hashmore was unable to view her face. While the words were unintelligible, the emotion they carried came across clearly to him. After a moment, the Great Mother composed herself and returned to the conversation. "My apologies, if we'd had more time, this would have been conducted in private, but our time grows short, and our mandate grows ever larger. The emperor's soldiers will not permit us to openly search for the cave. This poses a great challenge, one that I must meet, not only for our people now, but for our Lord, for yes, I do now believe that we worship the same God, for he is a universal God, a singular God, a God of good. There is one more all-important question you must answer. Are there only two kinds of humans?"

39: An Angel's Choice

For the immense power and magnificence of the room, it had felt very ancient until now, as the Great Mother was being swamped with an overwhelming amount of data. The full screen displayed a map with various objects moving at different speeds and in different directions, each one undertaking its own mission. How she kept track of it all was beyond Hashmore's technical reach.

Despite the chaotic nature of what was happening, Hashmore was able to ascertain that she was delegating a lot. The use of the stones had given him a good feel for the Great Mother's mood and strength, but it didn't come across clearly enough to be verbalized. One advisor after another would pop up on the view screen and then be sent on their way as soon as the information or orders had been transmitted.

After a slew of attendants, advisors, and associates had been attended to, the screen finally came to a pause. Several minutes later, the activity came to a lull and the Great Mother turned back to Mr. Hashmore. She released a heavy sigh and then hopped back to her tea and perch.

A large octopus in a barrel filled half the screen, while an image of a woman filled the rest. The Great Mother looked at Hashmore and again asked the question, "Are there only two kinds of humans?" As she spoke, the image of the woman shifted and zoomed into an internal image of the woman's uterus.

Hashmore gave only a stunned look in response, for he knew the women on display and it was not a proud relationship. The Great Mother paused before turning toward the alien on the screen. "Doctor, what more can you tell me about our mystery?"

"Great Mother, our previous scans can get us no new information. At present, there are too many genetic markers to indicate which type of human this child will be. Our last update from the medical ship was intercepted by the empire, and we no longer have her in our custody.

"These are trying times, and I have fallen behind. For as much as he postures, I know the emperor is fearful. Only would he take such a personal interest if the ramifications could be great. No, I'm afraid that the empire has chosen the hard route, leaving us with only difficult choices."

The Great Mother took a long sip and stared into the distance. "I'm afraid that the empire has chosen to unleash one of its most powerful weapons, one that even our Dognosis friends cannot easily defeat. They simply call them warriors, but that label is misleading. The Xendorians are the most gifted species in the universe. They have speed, strength, and intelligence, so when I suggest that even they can be hunted, I want you to know that it is no warrior—it is the devil's own brood that hunts them."

Hashmore felt like he had been patient enough, and now it was time to lead the conversation. "Look, Great Mother, I am inclined to believe that being abducted by your species is the best of the options, but honestly, I don't really know what the hell you are talking about. Our Lord Jesus came to save humanity. How could the other races even know of him? Not even every human knows and believes in him. I don't know what you want from me or even what I'm supposed to be doing here. If you have come to evaluate whether we pose a threat to you, then the answer is no. We are trapped in a city in the dark, on a spaceship we don't have any control over. I was hoping to get many of my questions answered, but all I have now are more questions and more confusion."

The Great Mother clearly felt the emotional distress in Mr. Hashmore's words despite the calmness in his voice. "Quite right you are, Mr. Hashmore. Let me see if I can't simply and clarify for you." Again she took a long sip. "This ship is on a mission to save the last of each species it encounters. Our mission is born out of the necessity caused by the devastation brought about by the Wilde, a race so powerful they destroy entire worlds. Your world is next on their list. While we are trying to save your race, another species known as the Huban Imperial Empire has come to claim your planet's riches, of relics. The emperor might have played it cool, but he fears the power of the Lord more than even the Wilde. He will not, as he stated before, abandon this world entirely, but he will let it be destroyed. In order to satisfy himself that the home of the universe's greatest hero will never pose a threat to him, he will first loot and plunder anything that might be useful, including the mother of our mystery child."

Again she stopped for a long sip. "This leaves me in the position of having to choose. Do we fight a superior power in hopes of protecting some of the Lord's treasures and people, or do we allow them to be taken by the nonbelievers and defend the last of their kind? Last and most tempting, we could attempt to rescue the mother and mystery child. Any way I choose, the cost will be devastating. Any mission we attempt is uncertain in outcome. If we flee, will there be repentance for our fear? I'm afraid I waited too long to retire, and now these trying times are mine."

Hashmore felt his heart lighten with a reassurance of faith. "No, I think you are wrong, Great Mother." He now sipped too. "The power of the Lord lies not in the treasure of his church, the hallowed ground he walks on, or even the miracles he brings into this universe. No, the power of the Lord lies in the story of his redeeming son. A story that lives on in its believers."

The Great Mother fluttered as she chuckled. "How wonderful to meet such a believer, a man of true faith. Yes, you are right, we must protect life. I will order the Dognosis to assist in the defense of mankind. May God protect you and save your souls."

The lights in the cavern grew brighter, the screen vanished, and Hashmore floated away in his chair. The chair hovered a few feet away, leaving him squirming in his seat and hoping not to fall. He watched the Great Mother open her wings and gracefully lift off and soar elegantly through the currents. There was a momentary pause before his chair tipped over and sent Hashmore free-falling through the cavern.

⚡/

Dear Lord, my Father, who art in heaven, hallowed be thy name. Thy kingdom come. Thy will be done. Give us this day our daily bread. And forgive our transgressions as we forgive those who have transgressed against us. Lead us not into temptation, but deliver us from evil.[1]

Oh, Lord, save me, save me once again, SAVE ME, oh,

---

[1] Based on Matthew 6:9–13 (KJV).

Lord?

Again I come to you, ashamed of my lack of conviction and faith in your great plan. Oh, Lord, why have you chosen me? What am I to do? What will of yours am I to fulfill? Why, Lord, must you choose to speak so opaquely? Will you not lead me as I am to lead your people? To what end?

To what should I believe, concerning these alien creatures? Are they also your children? To what end am I supposed to support? Lord, I have never been more confused about my faith, about how I am to be. Why don't you answer me, Lord? Why do you throw me off a ledge only to pull me back from the brink?

Why, oh, Lord, do you threaten my life over and over again? Save me, Lord, save me! Let me not die now. Save me again, my great master. Once again, will you not use your infinite power to protect me? Save me, who so diligently tried to follow you. Lord, use your power.

Lord, if your power is so mighty, why not destroy your enemies and be done with it? Why, oh, Lord, must you make your people struggle through this awful life? Why am I fearful of failing you? Will you not give me the strength? The heart? I am terrified both that I will die now and that I will live. Please, Lord, can there not be a third choice? I am scared, Lord. Will you please save me?

I have no strength to fight such fierce enemies, I have no courage to face these aliens, and I have no conviction to follow you. I have only you, Lord. Why can't I feel that is enough?

Dear Lord, my Father, who art in heaven . . .

A giant breeze slowed his descent near the bottom of the mile-plus-long cavern. A second current spun him in a gentle circle, only slightly nauseating him as he once again entered a black hole at the bottom of cavern.

$$\overline{\underline{\mathcal{L}}}_{/}$$

A burst of white light flashed across his vision as Hashmore half-heartedly welcomed God's answer for his safety. Hashmore stayed in prayer as Mardoxx's cold, hard grasp twisted him around, and together they reclaimed a less nauseating position. Waiting out the last of the bumps in the flight, Hashmore finally opened his eyes to find they were not alone. Several other Tilotins, some even carrying equipment, had joined in formation, each with a look of reverence on its face.

It was a very short flight to the nearest landing site, which he thought Mardoxx had referred to as Xeanna. The two landed, and within moments, dozens of aliens had formed a group surrounding Hashmore. This was more than just citizens welcoming a newcomer. They watched in amazement.

The group stared in silence, awaiting some unknown trigger to burst out in either excitement or anger. Hashmore stood back, not sure if they were expecting a speech or what, but he was feeling more uncomfortable.

At last, Mardoxx moved to the center and waved his arms in a gesture whose meaning was lost on Hashmore. Feeling the adrenaline from the crowd, Hashmore half expected an attack, but instead, Mardoxx came forward and bowed. Following suit, the rest of the crowd bowed too. Confusion set in even deeper, as he was now sure that they expected a speech or something from him.

He waited several long minutes, in hopes that Mardoxx would give him some clue, and then he finally walked up to Mardoxx and tapped him on his shoulder area. Mardoxx finally looked up and read Hashmore's face. Then he rose and turned to face the crowd.

"My friends, my comrades, and my fellow believers, today we have yet further proof of our Lord's greatness. The nonbelievers would say it's a problem with the stones, a problem with transmission or even translation, but we know the truth. For eons, we have worshipped our Lord through his son, never being able to directly communicate with our Lord. Oh, how have we longed to speak with our creator? How many of us have perished in our quest to find the Lord and his true nature? How many treasures have we squandered in the hopes of finding our Lord? How many methods have we tried to communicate with our Lord? Now we have found an answer, an answer only the Lord could provide.

"This lowly creature, blessed without physical, mental, or any other significant advantages, has been given the greatest of all gifts. I believe that God has chosen the meekest of species to have the most powerful gift of all. Only a God of true compassion, true love, would bless these lowly creatures with this beautiful gift. Perhaps now, before we go into battle, we can savor this gift just once."

Mardoxx turned back toward Hashmore and bowed. Confused beyond understanding, Hashmore looked stupidly at the crowd, totally unaware of what "gift" he had been granted.

Mardoxx, slow to read Hashmore's body language, eventually got up. "Mr. Hashmore, you have been given a truly unique gift, and we would greatly appreciate it if you would share it with us before we face certain death. You have the power of the silenced, the power to speak beyond the stones. You have the power to speak to the Lord himself. Please, will you not lead us in a prayer, so that even if it's just this once, we may have a personal blessing, not from the Lord's son but from the Lord himself?"

Hashmore knew it was easy to believe when facing evil, but it was harder when he had to lead others who also believed. Exacting God's vengeance on a demon was why he loved being a cop, but pastor was the last job he would ever apply for. This was now a new way to test his faith. It was a challenge he now had to decide if he could meet.

His heart thumped, his skin sweat, and his mouth dried to a point his words evaporated. The strange crowd of aliens grew bigger, with even stranger beings joining. Several drones and other creatures swarmed the air with buzzing and humming equipment. It was the most attention he had ever received. When one leads from their own authority, they lead from their own confidence, but where does one's confidence come from when they lead with another's authority?

Mardoxx finished his request and returned to his previous position, again kneeling. It was clear that "no" was an unacceptable answer under these circumstances, but Hashmore was damned if he knew what to do. A strong throat clearing from Mardoxx finally broke his lapse. Sputtering and stammering, Hashmore spoke the only thing that came to mind.

"Dear Lord, my Father, who art in heaven, hallowed be thy name. Thy kingdom come. Thy will be done. Give us this day our daily bread. And forgive our transgressions as we forgive those who have transgressed against us. Lead us not into temptation, but deliver us from evil."[2] Hashmore paused, only now reading his audience. He was reassured and finished the Lord's Prayer.

There was another awkward pause before Mardoxx rose to face the hub of the gathered. "Arkapeligians. We are blessed! Let us now go forth and execute God's will." The crowd erupted into loud cheers, and music burst forth as the crowd dispersed, singing in unison. Mardoxx turned and took flight, looping around and grabbing Hashmore. Mardoxx's words and tone came across very clearly: "Our intelligence was wrong—you are not a politician."

$$\overline{\underline{\angle \underline{\cdot}}}/$$

"What happens now?" Hashmore hoped his nervousness wasn't transmitted as clearly as Mardoxx's disappointment and anger.

Mardoxx waited nearly two full strokes of his wings before responding. "We will go to see Baronious, dog lord of the Dognosis."

Hashmore hoped for more conversation, but the tension was lessening and Mardoxx was calming himself down. They quickly came to another entry port into a new civilization center. The same arched entryway slowly curved with gravity so as to turn those passing along it onto a new axis, leading down into a cave that opened like a mouth. Unlike that last entry port, which was limited to personnel and small equipment, this opening was large enough for cargo craft to enter and exit at the same time.

Several small hovercraft joined in escort while a clear pathway formed as large dog-like aliens stopped all movement to

2   Based on Matthew 6:9–13 (KJV).

clear the way for Mardoxx and him. Never before had he felt so empowered and yet so afraid. Time had become so meaningless during recent events. Hashmore felt a strong headache building in the back of his head. It hadn't exploded yet, but when it did, history had taught him that it would be a doozy.

Mardoxx flew directly into the cavern and burst forth into a wondrous new landscape, bringing a miracle to Hashmore's eyes and slightly terrifying his soul.

40: You Are What "What You Eat" Eats

Seven great spires rose gallantly to the roof of the dome. Between them ran long stretches of cable, with cars flowing between the two. On the ground, a created river—dammed on both sides—held in familiar vegetation that grew between the dam walls and the slope up to the level of each side. A familiar creature flew along the banks, swooping down into the vegetation. Then, coming up alongside Mardoxx, and similar in physical appearance, were a flock of Tilotins. Yet Hashmore could tell something was different. Maybe it was the stones projecting Mardoxx's feelings to him, or maybe it was the more instinctive way the other Tilotins were flying.

The longer the Tilotins stayed next to them, the more anxious Mardoxx acted. After realizing that their journey would take them some time, Hashmore broke the ice, hoping to distract his pilot from the emotions. "Not a friend of yours? Who lives here? Where are we going now? Who will I have to talk to next?" Hashmore made sure to wait between questions, but Mardoxx seemed to be in no mood to pander or humor.

"You know, Mardoxx, there is quite a bit about this place that reminds me of your species' dome. Do you guys have two? See those plants around the river there, very similar to some in your place. Tall spires, even the humidity and temperature are similar." Hashmore felt the detective inside coming out as flashbacks of working perps ran through his mind. "So what's up with the other birds? Are they flying like you guys, back home? This place feels more like a city. I can see transportation, housing, commerce, and dare I say, even some farming? So what? How come your place was so old and sad feeling, and this place feels more alive, more energetic? What the hell is wrong with you? What, my prayer not good enough for you? What? Am I not proving worthy of this so-called ark?"

Mardoxx had finally had enough. "Will you just knock it off, already! Your incessantness is driving me crazy. Can't you just sit there until we arrive? Please, let Baronious answer your questions."

"Ah, but, buddy, you just started to answer mine. Why don't both of you tell me so I can get a clear picture? Baronious is who?"

Mardoxx let out a sigh. "Will you just let me fly in misery? I dread visiting the Dognosis habitat, much less His Great Assship, the undisputed leader of the clan."

Hashmore felt the thrill of the case building as his excitement grew about his new surroundings as well. "So not a personal friend, got that pretty clearly. Those guys are like you, and they don't seem to mind it here."

Mardoxx snapped more than expected "Don't compare me to those mindless flockers. I am nobody's prey."

"I have not known you long, Mardoxx, but this place obviously bothers you. Your entire demeanor has changed since you arrived."

"I really don't feel like a history lesson right now. Can't you just wait patiently? We shall arrive shortly."

"How is that fair to me?" Hashmore started to feel that zone again, making him nostalgic for the days when Big M and he would shake some perp down and catch and fish. "Here I am, searching for some truth, trying not to jump to any conclusions, but if I don't have all the information, how am I not going to do that?"

Mardoxx's mental sigh was quite audible as the alien adjusted his hold on Hashmore. Hashmore was now in more of sitting position, thus far the most comfortable.

Mardoxx finally spoke. "We don't have much time before we arrive, and I will not deviate for your lesson's sake. Many centuries ago, two species were caught in an eternal struggle of hunter and prey. Each time the prey would develop new methods of protection, the hunters would develop new ways of killing. Prey initially finds safety in numbers, communications, tactics, and tools, and in this fashion, the two species were locked in a perpetual battle of survival and a race to escape, first to the other habitats and continents, and then even to the stars. Only after separation— not only of life from nature, but prey from predator—did the two find an uneasy truce."

"Sounds pretty intense. How are things now? I know how hard race relations have been on my world. I couldn't imagine interspecies relations, much less having one sentient species preying on another sentient species."

Mardoxx let out another mental sigh. "Hence the non-sentient version you see flying here. These Tilotins are the great sacrifice of my kind. You see, as we fled to the stars, a grand

bargain was struck. Hoping to prevent the Dognosis from perpetu-
ally following us, each Tilotin was given a test. If they passed, they
fled with the group. If they failed, they stayed and became lunch."

"No wonder the animosity is as thick as butter. How did
you both end up on the ark? How did the Tilotins wind up in
charge? How did—"

Mardoxx interrupted. "Those questions are best answered
by His Ass-ship, Baronious, and as we have arrived at the front
door, this is where I will be leaving you."

"But where do I go? Who do I see?"

"This is not my domain. Ask your guardian, Aragnaught.
They will contact me when you are finished, and I shall return
then." Mardoxx opened his wings and took flight.

Hashmore turned, and with impressive stealth, a large
dog-like creature stood over him, running his eyes up and down his
body.

Hashmore stood in the center of a great plaza. A slow river
curled around it, rushing off just before finishing the encircle-
ment. Aragnaught pounded his chest in the traditional Dognosis
ceremony and then stood erect. When he spoke, it thundered. "I,
Aragnaught, am sworn to and gladly protect the chosen. However,
this is my domain, and you will not deviate from my commands
here. Understood?"

Hashmore was awestruck by the beauty of his surroundings, but his half-hearted, "Yeah, yeah," was found to be insufficient to his guardian. Again Hashmore's daydreaming was inter-

rupted, by the sight of his guardian demanding a firmer answer.

Then Aragnaught began his introduction. "This is Coronation Square. Before we joined the ark, this was the launching pad for the great hunts." The large dog-faced creature whipped its tail, cracking it with a burst of sound.

"Those ancient days of past are considered the golden age for our kind. Now we wallow in the shadow of our prey in the name of a Lord we have never met."

Hashmore felt his brain firing as he continued on with the interrogation. "Have I not seen your covenant? Was I not in the holy place of your Lord?"

Aragnaught guffawed. "Baronious would claim that it is nothing more than a dusty piece of rock they keep in their so-called cathedral. Baronious would ask, what kind of Lord would only make a covenant for one of his children? What kind of Lord would sacrifice his most beloved for scum? No, he laughs at their petty notion of one all-powerful being. He scoffs at the belief that there is anything more than what science can understand someday. The prey, the prey is weak, always hoping for something to save them. That is why they seek out more powerful life-forms."

Hashmore thought and started to respond, "Why do you say he," but was interrupted by the shaking of the platform. Aragnaught grabbed Hashmore by the shoulder, placed him directly behind him, and then showed him how to walk. The two practiced for a few feet, and then they stopped to watch.

The display was quite impressive. Hundreds of Dognosis marched in unison, each one expertly wielding an electric-tipped staff. The vibrations made the ground, a hard rock-like material, bounce like a small trampoline. Column after column marched into formation in the square, each one more impressive than the last. After the troops had assembled, an unseen voice roared out a command, snapping each Dognosis into a new position of attention.

A sharply dressed Dognosis approached one edge of the center and, with the same voice as before, barked out a command, this time sending each Dognosis down to a knee, in a semi-bowing position. Unseen before, several of the Dognosis had moved, and a clear pathway now opened from one end to the other. A loud instrument blurted out in announcement, and a supremely large Dognosis slowly rose higher and higher as he neared the square and stood at its highest point. "Warriors of Atoll, welcome our undisputed leader. His Royal Ass-ship, Baronious!"

The great beast strutted casually across the square, examining others as he moved along. Behind him in a two-by-two formation were four elegantly dressed Dognosis, two males and two females, as far as Hashmore could tell. After crossing the square from the far side to near Hashmore, Baronious the beast turned around, sending the four to make a half circle in front of him. Then each held high a long stick with an elegant stone attached to it.

"To hunt is to live!" The beast bellowed. "Rise, warriors of Atoll, and let the universe tremble at our skill!"

Again the ground set about shaking as a deafening roar of the crowd burst out into cheers. Hashmore's ears hurt despite his covering them with his hands.

"We remember the day, we remember the hour, and we remember the feeling when our prey returned from the dead." The crowd erupted into a sorrowful howl until the leader quieted them down. "We are hunters, warriors, and protectors. We are not murderers!" Spiteful growls came in protest from the group. "When on that day our prey could no longer be denied its place in the realm of life, we made a vow only to hunt nature's bounty and protect the chosen."

This time, the soldiers banged their chests in the traditional fashion and went to a knee. "This is our burden to bear, and it will be our children's burden to bear, as well as their children's." The group in unison pounded their spears into the ground, making a rhythmic sound. "The sins of our forebears can never be forgotten, repaid, or undone. Yet as they harvested life to the grave, back it came with only one message." The crowd hushed, bent down to both knees, and bowed. Baronious moved forward and turned to face the same direction as the soldiers. "You are forgiven."

Hashmore tried to follow along as best he could, but he was awestruck by the Dognosis story and could feel his mind changing from detective mode to contemplative mode. A long, gentle hush filled the air, and echoes of nearly silent words built up slowly to a crescendo in his mind.

Baronious stood and faced the crowd. "And on that fateful day, our prey, risen from its grave, took of its flesh and said, 'Take and eat of my brethren. They are given with forgiveness for you to nourish and support, but eat not of your brethren, for the Father loves all his children.'" The soldiers stood and pounded their staffs in unison.

Baronious raised his hands. "We are here today to receive that nourishment so that we may fulfill our directive. A directive we hold dear, a directive we hold proud." The pounding of the staffs grew in intensity. "A directive we honor with our lives!" The soldiers in unison pounded their chests and then howled. "And till our last breaths, we hold true, we fight strong, and we defend the universe!" Another round of howling rang out.

"Warriors of Atoll. I now deem you guardians of the galaxy!" Great bursts of electric energy exploded like lightning up from the ground, an outburst of energy and emotion from the soldiers. The power of the square was palpable, and Hashmore thanked the Lord these guys weren't going to kill him—at least he didn't think so.

For a while, the atmosphere was so full of noise it was suffocating. Then, right as the crowd began to settle down, the sky started falling. Hundreds upon hundreds of Tilotins dropped from the sky, and the crowd of soldiers broke out into an orgy of gluttony.

Aragnaught finished off two Tilotins before ushering Hashmore down a stairwell, heading toward the river and underneath the great square. Hashmore took one last look at his surroundings and remarked on how natural the landscape looked despite the obvious infrastructure. The river flowed gracefully yet swiftly, and the green vegetation gave way to a bloom of flowers.

A strange, wonderful mix of hickory, lavender, and pine opened his nostrils and strained his memory. An odd feeling ran through Hashmore's body, numbing his thoughts and lowering his speed of motion. Fatigue started to set in, and Hashmore now had to concentrate just to take each step.

The stairs led down to a guarded and heavily shielded door

a few meters above the stream. Aragnaught completed a series of identity-confirmation processes before allowing him to pass. The guard then ordered Hashmore to come forward, yet the harder he tried to move, the more difficult it became. Aragnaught returned to escort Hashmore by the underarm, nearly carrying the entirety of his weight. They stopped for the guard to administer an eye test, but after a second of red light, Hashmore was blinded and no longer felt in control of his own body. Vague, blurry images followed, but Hashmore could make no sense of anything, as if he had lost the ability to think at all. The last thing he could identify was a second arm now holding him under the other armpit, allowing him to completely black out.

Dear Lord, what is happening? Why don't I understand what you want from me? Dear Lord, I'm so confused and lost in this new life. Why? Why? Why do I have so little knowledge and still so few questions? Why can't I just go home, Lord? All I want to do is crawl in bed, to feel safe, to know your comfort. I can't do this, Lord, whatever it is you are asking of me. No, I can't do it.

No, Lord, I won't do it. What will you do, have a giant whale come and eat me? I think not! Will you exile me to a land of heathens? Will you strike me down in wrath? I have seen enough of your universe, Lord, to know your wrath will not come. Lest you forget, Lord, I was your bringer of wrath! No, Lord, I have seen enough of your universe to know that it will be the less fortunate who will suffer your wrath. Those who need not suffer, yet they do. Those who struggle are left without. Godless and hopeless, they suffer the worst you can give them, and yet they persist. What kind of wrath is that? Cruelty! Damn it, Lord! Why do you have to be so cruel?

How can so many suffer terrible fates, with so few opportunities? Opportunities to grow, develop, and even give. Opportunities to give, to help, to care. Why are these so damn hard, Lord? Why am I to be given this fate? Why do I have to be called to suffer this fate? Can you not just give me a dose of wrath, Lord? Punish me so that I can be relieved of my responsibilities. I cannot carry your cross. I cannot proclaim your victory. I am scared, Lord! Please just punish me so that I can move on from your assigned responsibilities. Please show me mercy, Lord! I can't, I simply can't do it.

My Father, who art in heaven, hallowed be thy name. Thy kingdom come. Thy will be done, on earth, in this universe, as it is in heaven. Give me this day my daily bread. And forgive me for my transgressions. Lead me not into temptation, but deliver me from evil. For thine is the kingdom, the power, and the glory, forever and ever. Amen.[1]

---

1   Based on Matthew 6:9–13 (KJV).

41: March to Victory

The words were not directed at Hashmore, yet they came across very clearly. "A flower, this pathetic creature was nearly destroyed by a simple flower. Now, Great Mother, this is too much. How can we protect a species so fragile?"

A familiar and calming voice replied. "Fragility is not a matter of concern, only relevance to the situation and the future, and this species is of the utmost importance. I have no idea why the Lord has chosen this race, but that is not for me to know, only to obey."

"WAAAAA, there you go again with that spiritual nonsense. Your religion is nothing but a runaway imagination based on ancient translation errors. If we are to risk our lives, is there not more you can give me than this malarkey?"

"Your Royal Ass-ship, the decision has been made. The results will speak for themselves. Now time is of the essence. The Wilde will arrive imminently. The empire is already invading the planet, and we are behind the ball. Now do you see the new class of Imperial spacecraft? It appears to have gone adrift, and there are now support vehicles approaching. What is your tactical assessment of this development?"

Hashmore tilted his head and found himself in a large command center. Story-high display screens towered overhead, and consoles were scattered about like desks in a classroom. He was currently in a far corner, and as he tipped his head, he saw a Dognosis in strange apparel interacting with a screen while he sat in a chair.

The conversation between Baronious and the Great Mother was being broadcast on the largest of the screens, and the conversation must have been piped throughout the room. "At first glance, I would say that the empire's new toy has broken down, but as I examine the approaching support craft, I am pondering another scenario." An image of an alien craft now appeared on the other large monitors. "That is a troop transport craft. Highly suspicious that they would divert that many soldiers away from a planetary invasion and their assault on the human habitat." Baronious paused as he stared in deep concentration. "Perhaps, Great Mother, they have lost control of their new ship and are now engaging in recovery operations."

A noticeable smile overcame the Great Mother. "Your Royal Ass-ship, that is a most exciting prospect, and I believe we should pursue it. Has the human recovered enough to join the decision-making process?"

Immediately the strangely clad Dognosis was above Hashmore, lifting him up like a sleeping doll and placing him upright next to Baronious. Not a moment had passed for Hashmore to clear away any cobwebs, nor allow fear to resurface, when he was faced with two imposing aliens looking at him for the answer to an unasked question.

Hashmore shook his head and blinked as the two aliens continued to stare.

"Perhaps this creature's brainpower only matches its physical powers. Then we are surely doomed."

"Then we are doomed together. I declare the human unfit for decision-making duties, Your Royal Ass-ship. Under my authority, I ask you to attack and claim that disabled Imperial starship. I also ask you to send a small detachment to assist the humans in their habitat as they fight for their lives."

The mighty beast Baronious pounded his chest in the traditional fashion and then ended the transmission to Great Mother. He manipulated the controls, and an image of a Dognosis now replaced that of the Great Mother. The Dognosis stood at a position of attention and remained motionless despite the Tilotin blood dripping down from above his eye. Baronious spoke without much formality. "Archimius, you and your squad, get down here, orders." The Dognosis began the chest pound, but the image transferred to the square, where it appeared the gluttony had wound down. Baronious howled loudly, bringing in a chorus from every Dognosis assembled.

Baronious turned, picked up Hashmore like a cat with its own kitten, and placed Hashmore beside him. "Now, my pathetic friend, you shall feel the power and glory of those of us who use our power for righteousness."

Baronious walked to the center of the room, his image being recast above on the ceiling, and called for an electric attack stick. He flung the stick high into the air like a baton and then unleashed an impressive display of showmanship and skill as he wielded the object with great precision. Last, he slammed the electric tip down onto the floor, sending a forceful charge through Hashmore's body, raising the hair on his arms, legs, and neck.

"Warriors of Atoll, war is upon us!" Baronious unleashed another volley of howling. "Today, yet again, we face an old foe, a dangerous and ruthless species, a species that claims the galaxy as their own—a species that boasts physical supremacy, mental acuity, and longevity." He paused with a childlike smile on his face. "And they are a species that fears our name!" This brought another wild burst of howling. "Once again, my friends, we are being called upon to protect the innocent, defend the weak, and secure the future of good. And in these tasks, we shall not fail!" This time, the soldiers did not howl but pounded their sticks into the ground, each vibration in perfect timing with the others as they moved back into formation and his image on the ceiling disappeared.

The room above Hashmore shook with a fearful force, as if the world itself was quaking at their might. Baronious stood next to Hashmore as he steadied himself against the vibrations from the group above. "Now, my weak friend, what do you say to that? I love it!" Then Baronious slapped Hashmore on the back and again carried him like a kitten, off to a side room.

Hashmore was seated in a chair that was more comfortable than expected, next to a desk. Baronious sat next to him, and soon after, five Dognosis entered the room, gave a salute, and then sat down. An image of the long spaceship—a very long cylinder in space, with large bubbles attached in a pattern around its periphery—floated like a ghost above the table.

"Archimius, my brother and my rival, successor to Aragmell and current champion, I am here to present to you a challenge, a challenge of extreme difficulty—a challenge so great no one would question your passing on it."

One of the Dognosis stood. "Your Royal Ass-ship, your words both honor and insult me. You are foolish to believe there is no undertaking too great a challenge for me, so prove to me the worthiness, and I shall carry any burden, no matter how great."

Interacting with the Great Mother was much easier, Hashmore thought to himself. He was lost in thought, uninterested and uninvolved in whatever the hell they were doing. He was being treated like a pet, and acting like one in return. He fidgeted and scanned the room, unaware of the importance of the things going on around him. A short pause in the conversation drew his attention, only it was too late. He had been late to respond, and Baronious now grabbed Hashmore and threw him onto the center of the table.

"This creature and his species have been deemed acceptable for entry into the ark. This creature's species has also been tagged by the empire for conquest and workers. Yet beyond that, this species has garnered an extreme amount of interest, from multiple circles as well. The Adrinoleen declare this species to have some genetic miracle, the Great Mother believes this species to be special to their Lord, and the empire has committed extremely high amounts of resources to this undertaking. I, however, find them to be useless, weak, and inferior. Unworthy of our ark's great mission and unworthy of our lives. I bring you this challenge, not of our hearts but out of protocol. Shall you accept such risk to your own lives so as to protect this lot?"

Archimius reached out and grabbed Hashmore, bringing him close. Hashmore tried to fight back, but the alien was obviously much stronger. Archimius twisted and rotated Hashmore as if he were examining a doll. After several rotations, Hashmore was seated on the table, facing toward Archimius. "What is it about you and your kind that has everyone so worked up? Well I care not for politics, and I care not for religion, so tell me, my pathetic little friend, why should I risk the lives of my men and myself on you and your kind?"

They again stared at Hashmore, waiting for an answer. He looked around, his brain unable to process anything fast enough to respond.

"It does at least have the ability to speak, does it not?" Archimius asked no one in particular.

Hashmore's brain finally caught up. Now he only needed to justify his race's existence. Frustration showed on his audience's faces, yet he was still unable to communicate.

At last, the Dognosis Archimius grabbed him by the collar and pulled him face-to-face. The creature's breath was foul with blood. The smell of death surrounded him, and the death of a thousand lives showed deep in his eyes. The creature seemed about to throw Hashmore back onto the table, when at last, a squeak finally broke through. "Help. We need help."

Having turned halfway around, the creature returned and pulled Hashmore close. Archimius took a long smell of Hashmore, from his feet to his face. Hashmore couldn't help but recoil at the encounter. He was again dropped onto the table, relieved that air was now allowed to flow into his lungs.

Archimius stood at attention. "Archimius will answer the call for those in need. To protect the weak is the greatest honor of the strong, and I shall answer the call of those in need. Baronious, you are my greatest rival. I thank you for a mission that will allow me to prove my superiority over you." With that, the creature and the one beside him gave the traditional chest-pound salute and left the room.

The vibrations had stopped, and Hashmore was on his knees on the table in an empty room, as Baronious had exited toward the main center.

Oh, Lord. What does all this mean? Are you real? Oh, Lord, why don't you answer me? Why am I stripped of all my power, all my knowledge, all my experience? Oh, Lord, why am I so weak?

Oh, Lord, how can you ask this of me? Have I not met my quota? Have I not been good enough? How much more do you ask of me, my Lord? Lord, why must it be this way? Why must I be alone? Why do I reach out to an empty voice? Oh, Lord, why have you forsaken me?

Is my path near its end? Why can't you answer me, oh, Lord? Why do you speak in opaque tongues, with messages so easily confused? Why am I to believe in something I cannot touch, I cannot smell, nor can I taste? Is that feeling I feel really you, Lord? Is it my imagination? How do I live in service to that which cannot be proven? How do I believe?

Look at this place. This is no aftermath of the Garden of Eden. If these are your children, Lord, then why do they throw you away? Are these creatures still not moral? Do they not still care and protect others? Do they not do this despite a lack of your leadership? Humans? Aliens? Demons, angels? Is one's moral character not defined by one's existence? How are we to judge, my

Lord? How am I to know friend from foe, when they all claim to be righteous?

Oh, Lord, why do you not answer me? Why am I left only with clues and riddles, stranded from over the ages, when in front of me is a universe I can study, learn, and understand? What am I to believe, Lord? This universe is too complex, too difficult to be created from one being. To what end would that being have in creating such chaos? To test free will? To test each one's moral character? To separate the wanted from the not?

No, Lord, I refuse to believe. I make my own decision. I make my own choices! I have done enough, Lord. I have done enough. My calling has been fulfilled. Your favors have me exhausted. NO, my Lord, it is time I stood up for myself. I will no longer let you sap me of my strength. I will no longer let you guide me to who I should be. I will decide for myself. And I am a man who has had enough! Send me home, Lord, I shall do no more of your bidding!

☲/

Hashmore looked around and examined the room he was in. It was a normal room, as far as he could tell, with a desk surrounded by—although foreign, still nonetheless—chairs. He spent a few minutes on the table, finishing his prayer, before he stood up and looked for an exit. It took a second to even find the lips of the wall of the door where he'd come in. Masterly crafted, these doors were smooth and would not be the easiest to recognize as a door.

Hashmore walked the room, trying to find another exit, but he found none, nor did he have any idea how to open the other one. He would have to try to exit the same way as the others. He mulled over a few options and then decided that it would be best to just walk out like he knew what he was doing.

He approached the door, only to find a buzzing in rejection. He backed away and approached again, only to be rejected by the buzzing. He had only two choices to believe in—either he was locked in or he just didn't know how to use the door. For scenario B, he decided that, should the aliens notice that he had trouble exiting, he would feign anger and demand to be returned to the Tilotins—at least they were not so scary. The plan for being locked in was still to be determined.

Hashmore went to each side of the door, looking for some sort of interface, whether it be a lever, a button, or whatever, but he was unable to locate anything. The buzzing insulted him each time he walked by.

He moved back to the table and leaned against it. The door finally opened, and in walked Baronious, a Dognosis standing next to him, and another one of the barrel-type doctor creatures. At first Hashmore wasn't concerned, but as the group neared, the hair on his arms rose and a shiver ran down his spine.

A little black robot pulled a cart along with it as well—medical equipment from the room next door, as far as Hashmore could tell. The group moved with a purpose, as if orders had been assigned and there was a mission to accomplish. Hashmore was surrounded and looking up at Baronious's face. He was sapped of his strength, his heart rushing with fear. Yet a few words managed to mumble out. "What's going on?"

Baronious grabbed Hashmore by both arms, squeezing him tightly and lifting him off the ground, raising him to eye level. A sharp edge slowly slid across Hashmore's neck as Baronious's tail curled around his neck. "Now, my little friend, you will tell me all I want to know, or you will see how far I am willing to go."

Hashmore controlled his bladder and prayed under his breath. "Oh, Lord, please protect me."

The table transformed, and Baronious inserted Hashmore into a piece of equipment. A foul-smelling liquid started covering every inch of Hashmore's body from the neck down. He tried to move but was the fly on the paper. "So-so-so, what do-do-do you want?" Hashmore put no effort into covering his fear. Being an interrogator had taught him that an emotional answer tends to be an honest answer.

The Dognosis in strange gear started setting up some equipment brought in by the little black MOP robots. The Annomite doctor worked with a set of tools, bringing one up toward its head and secreting something out of one or more tentacles, and then moving on to the next. The room's entire lighting dimmed, and a hundred memories from the other side of the interrogation table flipped through his mind.

First, Hashmore thought, will come the pleasantries, a tool useful in determining much more than one might imagine. Back talking with insults and answering with a nervous inflection were two of the easiest signs of a successful interrogation. Cold silence and immediate capitulation were signs of a much more difficult interrogation. The most difficult subjects, other than those who were just bat-shit crazy, tended to start off the friendliest.

Hashmore was in no mood for pain, so he allowed himself to feel the fear of the moment. His body recessed its efforts to escape, a waste of energy that could be very useful later. Baronious sat at the table and rotated it so that they were almost face-to-face. "I," he started, paused, and continued, "I have a problem, and you are going to be the answer, or you are going to be gone. My children have been asked to go into battle, and for a cause I don't believe in and a species I don't respect."

"You are a nasty, pathetic race, and that absurdity about your species being blessed by some greater being makes me want to rip your head off. So now it is my job to confirm what I already know to be false."

Hashmore felt the panic of immobility, defenselessness, and fear—all tools he determined to create an emotional response. At the time of occurrence, emotional lies are transparent, while emotional truths are genuine. A pinprick drew his attention as the Dognosis dressed in garb administered one of the syringes the Annomite had been busy filling.

"Now, how does one accomplish such a thing as disproving the unprovable? Well let me tell you." Baronious smiled before he answered his own question. "Confession."

Dear Lord, my Father in heaven above, I'm sorry, I'm sorry, I'm sorry. I don't want this. I don't want this. Oh, Lord, save me from this and I will never forget, I swear. Can't you just one more time? I'm sorry I doubted. I'm sorry I sinned. Oh, Lord, just save me again!

A strange look crossed Baronious's face, if only for a

second. "The Great Mother failed to get the information my children need. So I am forced to get it myself. Let us begin with the easy questions. Are there only two types of humans?" Baronious pulled back and sat staring patiently.

Hashmore tried to determine the purpose of the interrogation—knowledge of tactics is much less useful than knowledge of purpose. Confused and scared, he answered with his gut, hoping only to placate his interrogators. "Only men and women? Is that what you mean?"

Baronious slammed his fist into the table, executing an intense jolt of pain that entered and exited Hashmore's body. "I ask the questions here! Are there only two types of humans?"

Again the jolts ripped through Hashmore's body. "Yes, yes, yes." Each answer weakened as Hashmore endured the pain as best he could.

"Do humans mate with other species?" Baronious readied his fist.

Hashmore winced at the question and paused, trying to decide how to give the most acceptable answer, but the pause was intolerable, and once again Hashmore felt pain. One jolt entered through a wrist and exited from his foot, leaving behind a sting that only slowly faded. "I don't . . . know. I don't know. I didn't know aliens existed." Tears dripped down his face.

"Do humans have gene technology?" Baronious readied his fist.

Hashmore felt betrayed by the questions. How the hell should he know any of this stuff? "Uh, we can read it."

"Lie." Baronious executed another round of misery, this time through the neck and out his right toe, burning along his spine.

"No, no lie. Please."

"How many Imperial agents rule your world?"

Again Hashmore felt betrayed and worried. He had no defense against a pointless interrogation. "I don't know what you mean. Please, I just work in the mayor's office."

Hashmore's body tried to convulse, but it was held stiffly and painfully in place. Blackouts started to drain his vision, and his mind became fuzzy like he'd had a couple of shots.

Lord, oh, Lord. What? What do you want from me? Why do you, I mean, why do I suffer so? Where am I going? Lord, yes, Lord, what is happening?

The look on Baronious's face turned to that of puzzlement and confusion. "How do you speak beyond the stones? It's a farce, a trick somehow!" Hashmore felt his head being turned roughly as Baronious confirmed he did still have the stone lodged in his ear.

Like forgotten children now demanding attention, the two accompanying Baronious now sprang into action. One injected a second vial of secretion into Hashmore as the other attached sticky green gel pads onto his chest. Hashmore's eyes floated aimlessly in his head, and the beeping of the machine now roared in alert.

The crescendo was not far away, and soon the roar lowered

to a protest, then a beep, and then nothing. Hashmore's eyes closed as his brain began to reset. Sleep was about to overcome him when a third vial was added to his already-cocktailed blood.

Hashmore sprang back awake and thrashed forcefully until his breath had escaped him and all of the chemical impairment had been burned off. Baronious stared into his eyes until cognitive contact was made. "At last, forgive the haste of the interrogation, but time is precious and you are much too skilled an interrogator to be reliable otherwise."

Baronious made eye contact with the doctors, confirming that the desired state had been achieved. "Now, let us begin again, but this time, let's have only the truth."

42: Who Dares to Question the Lord?

His stomach ached, and nausea soon followed. The universe spun slowly as Hashmore kept readjusting his eyes to its motion. His body felt tired, sore, and ready for sleep, yet his brain pulsed with an artificial sense of excitement. The fatigue alert cycle made it difficult to keep track of his situational awareness.

"You have no idea how much I miss the historical times." Baronious stood and paced. "Long before the days of separation, before the days the Wilde drove us from our home world, and before the Great Mother took her place. No, we were revered then, honored, and accorded appropriate privileges, no need for Annomite overseers."

Hashmore saw Baronious give a menacing glance at the barrel squid alien, but if it generated a response, he was unable to interpret it. "Yes, it was then that my predecessor himself stood on the Arkapeligo council. You see, we were saved first. Had it not been for us, the ark never would have even known of the Tilotins' . . ." Baronious coughed a laugh, "sentience."

"How, you might ask, if your brain was not swimming so deep in the chemicals, did the Tilotins repay us?" Baronious paused and then burst out with anger as he spoke. "By chaining us like dogs!" His fist slammed against the table, but to Hashmore's relief, it did not trigger another round of pain. "Our words, our intuition used to be enough. No questions, just getting the job done was all they cared about. And we did it. We did their bidding and cleared out the mutineers, and it cost us a great many warriors."

"Parades, parties, admirational rewards, these are just hollow glorifications for the subservient. We proved our worth, we proved our loyalty, and for our trouble, we were relegated to the doghouse! Respect, responsibility, power, that is how you reward the able."

Baronious sighed and took a few deep breaths. "So that is how we came to be here, no longer able to extract the information we need in a timely manner. So we must use less aggressive tactics. If you were to ask an Annomite, an act we will not do, they would say that there is nothing that can't be solved chemically. Now, our doctor here, under the supervision of the Octabarrell there, has given you enough chemical, and enough time has passed that your brain is now my plaything. So let's start with the easy— what is your designation?"

Hashmore felt dizzy and found it difficult to concentrate, yet his body gave an answer all on its own. "I am Luke Hashmore. I work for the mayor of New York, running the department of emergency management."

"Good, now tell me, how does your species measure life span, and where are you in that cycle?"

Hashmore could hear himself answer the question, but he felt more like a viewer than a participant. "We measure age in planet cycles around the sun. I am now in the last third of my life." Hashmore was insulted by that last comment, even if he was the one making it.

"Good, I see the stone is now working properly. My children are boarding transports now, as we speak. Our ships are preparing for war, and our home is preparing to flee. The Great Mother offers us an immense challenge, a challenge so immense it requires an outcome worthy of its cost." Baronious ended his pacing and returned to a close proximity, examining Hashmore's face.

"My children will die today, and I want to know why. Who is the human Lord?"

Again Hashmore felt his body answering the question rather than his mind. "There is no human god, only the one true God." The answer felt joyful as he heard it.

"Is your God the same God as the Great Mother's?"

"Yes."

"How do you know this God?"

"I do not."

"Is your God real?"

"My God is not physical."

"Does your God protect you?"

"Yes."

"How?"

"I do not know."

"Does your God reward you?"

"Yes."

"How, does your God give your race special abilities?"

"No."

"Does your God intervene when you face danger?"

"No."

Baronious's voiced raised with the next question. "Does your God smite your enemies?"

"No."

"Does your God fill your stomachs with food and drink? Does your God lead you to safety? Does your God warn of you danger?"

"No."

"And what does such a magnificent God ask of you in return?"

"Everything."

A loud laugh burst out before Baronious continued. "So you believe in a God you haven't met, felt, or seen. A God who fails to protect you. A God who demands so much in return. And this is the God the Great Mother wants my children to die in defense of?" Baronious turned back around and took a few steps toward the exit before asking his last question. "So what does your Lord give back in return?"

Hashmore cringed at the question. His brain failed to produce an answer, but his mouth did not, and Hashmore could only hear himself answer. "Love and forgiveness."

A gentle grunt came out before Baronious spoke. "Forgiveness for what?"

"Anything we ask."

Baronious left without speaking, but the sticky material holding Hashmore in place now drained out of the bottom, and he was soon free, if not filthy. The Annomite alien dropped some towels down on the ground, walked to the wall, indicated that it could be activated by inserting his arm into the wall, and demonstrated how to scroll through the options before leaving.

It took some time before the door opened and Aragnaught appeared. While the chemicals were wearing off, Hashmore still had difficulty navigating his body, as if his brain would transmit a series of images only to have it stall along the way and need to be reinterpreted by his blind body.

His mission of cleaning up finally complete, Hashmore lay idly wondering his next thought while listening to the echo of his last. He wanted to ask himself so much. Never before had he had such a genuine response to religious matters. In fact, he quite often avoided any public discussion of religion. Church was for those who needed to find the Lord. He just needed to try to live it. Now he had the opportunity to truly explore the ocean of his own beliefs, yet his own mind was drowning, too busy to look around.

"Are you in prayer now? Please tell me, does our Lord speak back?" Aragnaught spoke softly and with true interest.

"A good father listens to all of his children. My voice is no louder than yours, and I fail to understand what power it is that you think I have."

"Would not an eldest or favorite son's voice be heard the clearest?"

"That's the human superpower?" Hashmore couldn't help but let out a little laugh as he asked the question. "We are God's favorite children? That sounds ridiculous. Seems to me, we might more likely be God's naughtiest children. Do they not also draw the attention of a good father?"

Aragnaught paused in thought. "Is your race evil?"

"No, just individuals among us would be called evil. The rest I would call sinful."

"Then it is good that we have a God who forgives, is it not?"

"We—but Baronious is very much against my God. Please tell me, who is your God?"

"We all have the same God. It's all a matter of interpreting his message. I have heard the Great Mother speak. I have listened to their sermons, and I believe. So please, now tell me. How do you interact with the Lord? Your message is carried beyond the stone. No race before has ever been able to do such a thing."

"Interact with the Lord? No, one follows the Lord, or one denies the Lord. There are no other choices."

Aragnaught smiled, something Hashmore couldn't remember seeing in this species before. "I do believe you would be a very interesting partner to discuss the matter with further, but I have been ordered by His Royal Ass-ship to take you to Mardoxx, who will escort you to mission control."

Having returned to a less stressful environment, and a reduction in the chemical swimming, Hashmore now felt more able to interact normally. "His title sounds so strange. Is the stone translating it correctly?"

Aragnaught snickered. "The stone translates it in a different way to each species. May I presume that the title comes across as derogatory?"

"Well yeah, I would say it sounds unflattering at the least."

"It is another victory over our prey. Yes, they originated the word as an insult, a curse, something designed to make our blood boil in fury." Aragnaught's voice rose with emotion momentarily. "But prey has no power over us! Baronious has taken their most evil of words for us and made a title of honor and glory. This is how we remind the prey that they hold no true power over us, simply title. "

Hashmore finally rose, slowly, with fatigue and anxiousness of what was next to come. There was certainly no loss of passion and diversity with these aliens, but all the same, he wished for nothing other than to be home in his bed, to maybe pop a pill or two and escape into a world of the pre-sentient man—dreams. Life, however, never gave an inch, and Hashmore was once again being ushered off into the unknown.

⚶

Aragnaught led Hashmore through a series of corridors, passed a few security checkpoints, rode an elevator, and finally arrived at a massive platform. Two Dognosis agents stood at each side of the door, but they paid them no mind, their duties set on keeping others out. The platform stretched for nearly a quarter mile, with transport lines stacked multiple stories high.

Large crowds of aliens shuffled about, to and fro, most of them Dognosis, but other alien types were mixed in. Hashmore kept looking around, only to fall behind and need to rush to keep up, much like a child following a parent on a mission. While every placard, sign, or posting was unintelligible, the loudspeaker still echoed its words clearly inside his brain.

The two boarded a series of transports, each ride lasting between three and five minutes. Each exchange increased the variety and differences of aliens, yet its purpose as a transport was unmistakable. Aragnaught took great joy in introducing some of the stops and announcing which species was most likely to be going where, but to Hashmore, it was all just a wash of newness.

Aragnaught took great efforts to make Hashmore feel engaged, and despite his military background, he really didn't come across as the soldier type. Aragnaught signaled Hashmore that they had arrived, but he paused for a moment in dramatic fashion before exiting the transport. "Welcome, my friend. This is the heart of the ark. We call it the city of eternity, the city of the blessed, and the city of a forever hope, Xeanna."

Hashmore felt his breath leave him as his eyes scanned the enormity of where he was. The general shape of the ship was cylindrical, with the vast city sprawling out and covering most of the inner surface. His eyes were drawn to the middle of the ship. Suspended in the exact middle were three spheres, each one inside another. A center sphere, a perfect ball, appeared to be full of water. Hashmore could see motion inside but was unable to identify it. A second sphere surrounded the water sphere and was occupied by several small platforms, all empty at the moment. Last was a rotating exterior ring, large but empty except for a circular hole that moved about.

"We call it Blazerball, and it turns out that some of the new arrivals are naturals at it." Aragnaught walked up to a wall and activated a view screen, otherwise invisible. Soon Aragnaught had a close-up image on the screen, and Hashmore was amazed to see dolphins. "We were mistakenly informed that these creatures were sentient, and while they are close, we have had to find a useful purpose for them, or else eat them."

"Glad to see it turned out for the former." Hashmore felt like a child. He had no comments, no ideas, just stunned exploration. Dozens of various species walked by, none seeming to notice or care about the arrival of yet another new species. The platform was again awash with life, hustle and bustle, and from here, Hashmore wouldn't have known a thing about what was going on in the world outside this city, had he not been a part of it.

A few screens running along a wall displayed various cultural oddities—some dancing aliens, an alien engaged in music creation, a highlight of a Blazerball score, and then two humans jumping off a building. The two fell fast. One landed on top of a vehicle flying in their direction, while the other human—a man, from the appearance of it—continued plummeting.

"Ah, yes, here he comes now, Mardoxx!" Aragnaught signaled high into the sky, toward the quickly approaching Tilotin. Mardoxx landed quite brazenly next to the two. The tension between them was much less than Hashmore had expected, allowing him to relax some. They greeted each other as close acquaintances, but Hashmore was unable to participate, for as much as he wanted to, his eyes kept drifting back to the display.

Once again, he was dumbfounded and amazed. For all the size of the universe, it proved to be small enough, for on the display was now a woman—a woman he knew, and a woman he didn't really care to know.

Hashmore's memory drifted back. Oh, how he did love her brothel. Most brothels felt dirty and used. She, however, the lady on the display, was the most remarkable pimp he had ever met. The mayor frequented her establishment, and most of his dealings with her had been damage control, yet she made a customer out of him too. She was a woman of silence, confidence, a master of the subtle control, and a leader of people—in short, she was a woman a man could fall in love with.

Mardoxx and Aragnaught came up to Hashmore from behind, saying nothing and only thinking curious thoughts, transmitted softly by the stones. Hashmore felt his cognitive functions returning from their state of amazement. "Who is she, and why is she on display here?"

The two aliens looked at each other, deciding who should answer, when Aragnaught smiled and spoke. "That is one of the two humans who have been chosen for the test." The next question must have been empathically transmitted across, for Hashmore never even heard the words. "Yes, a test to determine a species' moral assessment and ability to display compassion. We are a very diverse group here. It is important that we weed out those species unable to make proper moral judgments."

Mardoxx spoke next. "The ark itself does not have a criminal code, so we can only accept those sentient beings capable of making moral decisions, expressing a defense of their actions, and accepting others' judgment in areas of dispute. This woman here was one of two to be judged in determining whether your species meets our moral requirements."

Hashmore unconsciously swallowed, nervous that the entirety of his species' morality was being determined by a pimp whore. "When will she be judged?"

Aragnaught responded with a slight sense of excitement in his voice. "Oh no, she has already passed the test. Otherwise, you never would have made it this far."

Mardoxx continued. "We have already granted you an audience with two of our most influential leaders. We would never have allowed such meetings to occur had your species, and you personally, not met our standards."

"Where is she? Is she here on the ark? Can I meet her? Now?" Hashmore's voice rose slightly in nervous excitement.

Aragnaught and Mardoxx looked at each other again, only this time Mardoxx spoke first. "She is the center of everything. It could only have been divine intervention that brought her to us, and the power of sin to have her taken away. No, maybe you do not yet understand. That woman is carrying God's child, and we have lost her, so we must now ask others to risk everything in order to get her back."

Aragnaught pounded his chest in ceremonial tradition. "A challenge and cause the Dognosis clan is happy to accept. My brethren, faithful to the cross or to the clan, will not accept failure, even if it costs us our lives."

Mardoxx turned to Hashmore. "Our time grows ever shorter, and the battle has begun. We must assume our places in mission control as soon as possible. Come, I will answer your questions as we travel." Hashmore was once again in the arms of an alien, being whisked away, farther into a situation beyond his comfort or comprehension.

Oh, Lord, why does your message never come clearly? How can these beings be your children? Oh, Lord, why am I tested this way? Before, the answers were also so clear—see evil, destroy evil. Now, Lord, I see evil in the good around me. I see monsters using me as a political pawn. I see good in the evil around me as these monsters risk their lives, yet, Lord, they risk their lives on the sins of my past. Oh, Lord, how could you choose such a woman as her to be your incubator? Oh, Lord, what am I to do in all of this? Oh, Lord, if you can hear us clearly, why do we not hear you? How are we, such simple fragile beings, supposed to carry out your will in a universe where we are so weak?

"How can the baroness be at the center of all this? What does that mean? You said she was only going to be tested."

Mardoxx flapped his wings and worked himself into a rhythm so as to speak only on his exhales. "True. She was only . . . to be tested. Fate, however, delivered . . . her to us. Yet we were too . . . careless. We let the knowledge es . . . cape, and the empire came."

"I still don't understand, knowledge of what?"

"A promise fulfilled."

"Damn it, that doesn't mean anything. Tell me something I

can understand."

"Our Lord only speaks . . . in parables. We have never met . . . our Lord. We must find our . . . proof in the . . . universe around us. Miracles and enlightenment . . . are our guide. The brood your . . . baroness holds . . . is a miracle."

"That vaguely answers my question." The realization that a woman he had nearly completely forgotten about was pregnant by another man stoked a fire of jealousy he didn't anticipate.

Mardoxx rose dramatically, and once again, the two were being escorted as they approached another hole-shaped entrance. This entry point was different, however. Heavily secured and guarded, there was no adjoining habitat attached to the other side. Hashmore thought that this just might be the very front of the ship.

An alarm echoed, and lights buzzed throughout the great ship. "The Wilde have arrived. The Wilde have arrived."

43: Fight or Flight

Once more, Hashmore was sucked through a hole and placed in a new one. This time, the sky of the universe expanded out in every direction, except down—or back, depending on how he looked at it. An immensely beautiful blue filled the quadrant to his left, and a dampened sun still shone brightly as its rays crossed from his right, racing toward Earth.

Hashmore craned his neck up high, and a big HUD enlarged the image of a circular object under construction. Dozens of small craft zipped about as sparks and cranes danced in a hurried fashion. Suddenly, bolts of light spread across the screen, more and more, until a barrage of them was in sight. One of the small craft imploded, sending chunks of debris everywhere.

Just as suddenly, new streams of light appeared, heading in the other direction. The camera zoomed out, and Hashmore was able to recognize that a space battle was underway. Dozens of craft scurried about, seen as red and green highlights with alien symbols next to them as they chased their pinned object around the map.

This room was very open. A window to space spanned the ceiling. A small seating area arranged in church-pew fashion stood in the middle. A lone alien, a new species, stood next to an inter-face, leaving the rest of the room barren. The alien standing alone had a face made of eyes, dozens and dozens of them. His central core was oval, but it had several extremities protruding from nearly every side of it.

Mardoxx whispered as he gently hopped in lead of Hashmore, toward the seating area. "That is General Pigmy. He has been designated mission leader, and he now holds final authority in all matters until the battle is over." As the two crossed an invisible line, a visual alarm activated on one of Pigmy's screens, bringing a small MOP bot scurrying hurriedly toward them.

A voice echoed in Hashmore's head as the small bot threw up a small staff with a light attached and turned around, indicating that it should be followed. "Human representative, your input is deemed required by mission command. You will proceed immediately."

Mardoxx used his little arms to wave Hashmore forward, and he hesitantly followed this small robotic wonder. Hashmore was led to a podium in front of the seating area, where a circular light indicated where he was to stand. The enormity of the situation that was unfolding in front of him was overwhelming. Luckily, the voices in his head were powerful and straightforward.

"Time has grown very short. Your planet will be destroyed any moment. I no longer have time to both execute an assault and recover my men. Two humans are attempting to take control of the Imperial warship. I need to know from you, what are their intentions?"

A picture of a man Hashmore had never seen before appeared magically in front of him. The picture shrank, and a picture of the baroness replaced it. After a moment, her picture shrank as well. "There is no time for delays. What are their intentions?"

Hashmore could feel a million eyes, all on him, most of them the commanders. He spoke verbally, still unsure of how to use thoughts in conjunction with the stones. "This man, I do not know. This woman, this woman is a strong, independent leader. She will take what is given to her and will do the best she can with it. To what ends, I cannot say."

A new image appeared on the screen in front of him. This time, it was of a young black woman. "The human guardian, what role does she play in your society?"

The comment struck Hashmore like an extra-loud gong hit. "Guardian, what do you mean? The human race has no guardian. I have never seen her before. I don't know if she plays any specific roles in our society."

The questions came fast, impressing upon him the urgency of the situation. "This uniform has what significance, and who is this man?"

A picture of a black army officer now appeared on the screen. Hashmore examined it for a second, as if he might be familiar, but it was too far gone to be recalled. "This man is an officer in the army, a local . . . guardian organization. I doubt many, if any, others in his organization are aboard this ship."

"The empire has removed hundreds of thousands of your species, and several artifacts. Please identify and indicate their level of importance." Several objects appeared. Some had English translations, while most did not. "A large boulder" was labeled underneath a picture of a massive stone nearly the size of a small room. It had no context, so Hashmore moved on to the next, noticing that each picture had a series of indicators ranging from high to low as it scrolled downward. Moving on to the next picture, the theme quickly became apparent—a chalice, two stone tablets with 10 items listed, a ripped white robe, a copper-tipped spear, and two pieces of wood in the shape of a cross. Reacting on instinct, Hashmore immediately labeled each one as highest priority.

"Clarification required. Will the nature of your worship be impaired by the loss of these artifacts?"

"No, I guess not."

"Clarification required. Will your relationship with your Lord be altered by the loss of these artifacts?"

"No, I guess not."

"Clarification required. Will the structure or cohesion of your society be altered by the loss of these artifacts?"

"No, I guess not."

"Clarification required. State nature of the importance of these artifacts."

Hashmore paused. Before, he had reacted on emotion. Now his mind searched for a reason to hold on to something he had forgotten he had. It took another moment, but he lowered the importance setting on each object to medium.

The light above Hashmore darkened, the little MOP bot once again summoned his attention, and he was led back to the seating area, next to Mardoxx and the Great Mother. Hashmore sat beside Mardoxx, who stared with an unreadable gaze as he entered but then returned to normal.

Hashmore whispered as Mardoxx returned his focus back toward the general. "What just happened? What is going on?"

Mardoxx sighed. Then he wrapped his wing around him and responded most softly, bringing even the voice in his head to a mouse whisper. "The die has been cast. The general has chosen to protect the ark. Only a select few will be sent. Now, after your responses, it includes the human guardian and her caretakers."

Mardoxx began to pull back, when Hashmore quickly asked another question. "Where are they going?"

Mardoxx held up a finger over Hashmore's mouth. "Into the Lord's hands."

Hashmore's face protested the vague answer, but he stayed quiet and tried not to pout via the stones. A brilliant flow of light engulfed the room, and as he looked up, the circular object under construction now held a beautiful bed of white light. A flurry of lights filled the surrounding sky as wave after wave of fighters cleared out the opposing side, but to be honest, Hashmore wasn't entirely sure who was who.

The blistering barrages of lights came to an end as, just as quickly, a new image appeared on the HUD, and as its display moved, Hashmore saw that it was a countdown—a countdown to what, he wasn't sure.

The image zoomed in on a hangar bay. A dozen ships, two of which were noticeably larger, exited the bay. They grouped up in a formation. Then the image changed to that of a mammoth portal. Bright white light blazed across its opening.

✍/

Oh, Lord, why have you chosen me? Have I not given enough for you, Lord? How do you ask me to be more? I'm an old man. I can't learn the skills you need me to. I want to retire, Lord. I want to rest. Lord, why do you call on me still? To what quota do you now ask of me? Is not faith alone enough? Why must I live it out? Oh, Lord, it's just too much to be a good Christian. I can't meet the standard. I can't be your servant.

I was a good enough boy. I didn't chase the girls too much. I always tried to be a good neighbor. I have spoken your name in the face of evil. I have smitten your enemies. I have not lived a greedy or slothful life. Lord, why isn't that enough? You ask too much of me, Lord. Let this be the end of my role.

Did I not sacrifice enough, Lord? Did you not already take my beloved? Did you not already outcast me from my home? Did I not follow you then? Now, Lord, again you have taken everything that is important to me. For what? I serve no useful purpose here. I am a pawn, nothing more. Will you not let me retire, my Lord? Please give me rest.

"Transverse gate open. Departure in ten . . . nine . . . eight . . . seven . . ."

Oh, Lord, what now? Please protect me. My Father, who art in heaven.

✍/

The sensation was more than unique. It was trippy. Space, time, matter, substance—all seemed to merge together as if everything was being compacted together. Then, just as suddenly, it reversed and everything returned to normal. Only now, a brilliant-red planet now lay off in the distance as a small blue sun raced across the command center's sky. Everyone, minus Hashmore, in the pews now stood up and executed a series of movements before assuming a bowed position, facing General Pigmy.

The general returned the same series of movements, as if it was some kind of salute, stood in front of the pews, and spoke both verbally and telepathically. "As leader of the Battle of Sol, I am now prepared to give my report to the council." The group in the pews now stood, and the Great Mother took one step forward, one step to the right, and then she hopped forward and assumed a position to the rear of the general.

Mardoxx added the commentary this time, without prompting. "The Great Mother was the one to choose the general, so it is now her place to either lead the interrogation or assume a supporting role, which she has done this time."

"Are there any who wish to question me concerning the battle?" The general almost smiled, until Baronious stepped forward.

"I will question. I will question the courage of our commander. We finally acquire what could potentially be the most important discovery in recent history, and we cowardly run at the first sign of danger! Tell me, General, how much more time would you have needed to recover the child?"

The general took a short moment to compose himself. "The time allotted to execute and plan, and the actual amount of time it takes to do it, are often very different. I don't accept your premise."

"I was there. We were all there, General. There was no immediate danger. You should have stayed. How do you defend your cowardliness?"

"I am not a coward. I acted in the best interests of this ship and its mission. Acting like a hothead and taking unnecessary risks are not the actions of a responsible leader. Ensuring today is not a priority we can lose."

"Ha, destroying tomorrow is all that you have accomplished here today. If the empire ends up with such a mighty weapon, even I will be powerless to impede them. Sentencing us to a slow death is all that was achieved today." Baronious spun around and stormed out of the command center.

Hashmore looked at Mardoxx, who, for lack of a better description, shrugged his shoulders and stood up. "Come, we have one more task for you to complete before we can return you to your people."

PART 5

44: The Final Battle

Alarms blazed, smoke clouded the room, and a startled and shorthanded crew battled in chaos, but none of it mattered. Only he mattered now. Prisoner 00's tears brought forth great compassion in the baroness. She had wronged him, and it was going to cost him, or her, or both for the rest of their lives. The baroness, after some exanimation, was able to release his restraints. He moved slowly, much slower than normal. First, it was the breathing. A heavy, quick-paced rhythm had overtaken the wild, frantic, emotional breathing, and as he focused harder, it decelerated to a gentle breeze.

The baroness rose, taking him by the hand. He stood and gazed ever so longingly into her eyes. He looked like a scolded puppy hoping for a chance to play. She began to turn, when he pulled her back. He moved in close and kissed her. Hundreds of times had she been kissed, hundreds of men had she been intimate with, yet only now did she know what passion truly was.

An immense sense of guilt clouded her happiness. She tried to pull away, fueled by her guilt and self-disgust, but he wouldn't let her. Again and again she tried, but each time, she was brought back to face him. Oh, how did she want to love him back? She wanted to give in, to be his, but after everything, how could she? No, the baroness thought to herself, she had set herself up for failure yet again.

After she finally stopped trying to pull away, he moved in close and whispered, "You are forgiven. You are my love, and we are now one."

Lady Imric and Lady Lyndia tended feverishly to their comrades. Several support personnel had arrived to combat the fire and chaos. A small collection of MOP bots had taken up positions along the far edge of the hangar visible to space. The robots used an accessory tool to open small holes in the shield venting the smoke out into space. The flames were rapidly extinguished, and soon the two humans were surrounded by a small contingent of Xendorians.

Undisturbed by the events around them, the two embraced as lovers lost in their own universe. The far door to the hangar opened, with the sound of electric spears striking out in combat. A Xendorian ran backward, off balance, nearly falling as he entered the room. The wonderful face of Aragmell quickly finished off the alien, and he was followed by Aramethel, the two doctors, and Logging.

The group that had surrounded the humans broke off, forming a new rank against the intruders. Aragmell and Aramethel rushed through, terminating each of the guards as if they were on a higher level of abilities altogether.

The two doctors hurried to the humans. Embracing them tightly, Dr. Fengie spoke. "Oh my, oh my. What a joyous happenstance. Please tell me, are you two all right?" The baroness nodded, while Prisoner 00 just responded with a stern head twitch. The doctor placed a tentacle on his forehead and frowned. "We must get you to the medical bay and administer the antidote."

All action around the two Xendorian ladies had ceased as they stood back, having failed in their efforts to save their comrade. The ladies faced each other, shared unspoken words, and then faced the group. An awkward silence filled the room as they sized each other up, neither trusting the other.

The MOP bots had finished their venting and were now tending to the debris. Otherwise, the room was motionless, still, and tense. Aragmell moved forward, with gel-like green patches covering his scars. He stood in a warrior's stance, before the two Xendorians and his human protectorates.

A gentle rhythm started to shake the room. Lady Imric slid back, an uneasy smile crossing her face. The rhythm changed into a storm of crackles and sparks as line after line of Xendorian soldiers now entered the room. Professional and trained, and in uniform, they quickly and effectively filled the shuttle bay in a military formation. They stood at attention, completely dismissing any threat that might have come from the two guardians.

With some unspoken command, the assembled group parted away and knelt down, spears vertical. The commodore moved slowly, more purposefully than normal. A reddish hue emanated from his body. He approached the group, looking specifically at the two Xendorian scientists as if to size up their loyalty.

With some embarrassment, the two knelt and turned their eyes away. "Lady Lyndia, for failure to produce the results demanded from you and your position, you are to be terminated. The empire does not accept such failure from those in leadership positions." The commodore turned slightly, masking great discomfort, and spoke again. "Lady Imric, I will banter no more. You will take my bed, or I will take your head. What is your decision?"

An unmistakable look of terror crossed Imric's face. She took a deep breath. Confidence flashed across her face before a garbled mess of words came from her mouth. Then, like a scolded dog, she hung her head and started toward the commodore. Lady Lyndia reached out, grabbed her comrade by the shoulder, and gave a look of reassurance. The act soured the commodore's mood as Lady Imric returned to her kneeling position.

"Very well, with much regret, I, too, must sentence you, Lady Imric, to death for insubordination." He spun around and began to exit the room.

Another Xendorian came forward and called the group to attention. "Who here wants the chance to earn a supreme victory?" Every Xendorian raised their spear up high and emitted sparks and cheers.

"Very well, today's honor shall belong to Sergeant Xendor." The commander returned to his last position, and a Xendorian from the back made his way forward. Average in build compared to his mates, Sergeant Xendor twirled and flung his electric spear in a graceful display. He stepped toward the group of non-Xendorians, knelt in ceremony, and charged at the two guardians.

Sparks erupted, sending shower after shower of electric bolts through the air. The sergeant attacked aggressively and intelligently. Each time one of the guardians made a move to get behind, the sergeant attacked the flank and sent them back. It was a beautiful show of the mastery each of them had acquired. The conclusion of the second round of attacks without death brought out cheers from the assembled soldiers.

Sweat poured down the guardians' heads, while flaps opened and closed in a hurried attempt to cool the reptile's body. A third volley of attacks nearly allowed the sergeant to break free and make a run for the humans, but a quick slice from Aramethel's tail ended the thought and forced him back on the defensive.

The action came to a natural lull as the three stood at the ready, trying to physically recover for next volley, when the Xendorian from earlier once again returned to the front. "Sergeant Xendor, you have failed to achieve a supreme, or even total, victory. Return to your place."

With that, the Xendorian repeated the ceremonial action and returned to his place. Bringing the Xendorian soldiers to attention, the leader now turned, ignited his own staff, and yelled, "Attack!"

It was all over. Death was imminent. The two guardians took a knee, faced each other, and embraced foreheads, their long snouts running parallel. The doctors and the ladies had backed up against the far wall and were awaiting death. The hissing, jeers, and electric crackles all emanated in a wave at once as the soldiers started their assault.

Ripples of heat rushed through the shuttle bay. Laser lights flashed with a near-blinding power. Bolt after bolt sent row after row of Xendorians flying back, their corpses piling up as an obstacle for those behind them.

A new sound entered the bay as guardian after guardian

howled in excitement as they charged down the ramps of the landing ships. The bolts of lasers stopped as two small crafts entered the bay and landed. Commotion and chaos once again exploded as individual battles commenced throughout the bay.

Wave after wave of Dognosis charged at and engaged battle with each Imperial Xendorian. Electricity filled the air as spears collided and sometimes struck their targets. Howls of pain and hisses of death filled the bay. Guardians banded together, coordinating their attacks in order to simply overwhelm the Imperial defenders. Yet the defenders proved their might and wouldn't go down easily. Many guardians were pierced and dead as they laid down their lives, allowing others to press the attack.

This battle would have no winners, only death, as some of the universe's greatest warriors fought hard and viciously for their lives. The losses for each side mounted. Untrained reinforcements were insufficient in turning the tide for the Xendorians, and as their numbers dwindled, fatigue started to take the last of them.

The last Xendorian fell at Aragmell's hand. Standing taller than ever, sweaty and dirty, the guardian displayed no signs of the absolute fatigue he must have been feeling. Aramethel gathered up the last of the guardians, and together they formed a circle around him and howled like dogs toward the moon. For several gratifying minutes, the group enjoyed their victory.

Even the two Xendorian ladies finally expressed relief, yet they held their distance in the corner and had procured two staffs for themselves. The doctors scurried about, trying to save life where they could. Little black robots carried body after body out of the room as they pursued their programmed mission without regard for what was going on around them.

Again the rhythm of the situation came to a natural lull when one last Xendorian entered the shuttle bay: the commodore.

⇒⟩

The commodore's face blazed red with fury. His body stood ready, and his mind eyed the room as if he was determining the fate of each one there. The guardians formed a line, squaring up against the commodore. He stood fast, sizing up the situation, planning, anticipating, and preparing.

The lights in the hangar bay went out, and with almost instant reaction time, the commodore struck. He was impossibly fast in the dark, and barely a sound could be heard as the first guardian fell dead to the floor. Another screamed as his body flew across the hangar. A third yelped out in pain, and with the first burst of his spear, the body of a fourth guardian flew into the air.

Finally, bright lights activated from the shuttle craft, illuminating the commodore as he began to square off with Aragmell and Aramethel. Yet the commodore only used the distraction to his advantage as he quickly charged at the young apprentice. Aramethel dodged the attack but was sent flying back off balance. Aragmell lunged forward but had his own momentum used against him, and he was sent flying across the room.

The commodore squared off and faced his two human prisoners. First the right foot thrusted off the ground and then the left, and as the commodore raised his weapon to kill Prisoner 00, he felt a strong blow push him sideways.

While not strong enough to injure, it was enough to sidestep the commodore's attack. Spinning around, the commodore now came face-to-face with a well-toned, if not petite, black girl.

Sasha held her baton firmly. Her body twitched in energetic and nervous bounces. The fog blurred her opponent. His size was massive, his speed dangerous, and his strength dominating. Sasha felt no fear, no worries, and no remorse, for she had the fog. This was what Sasha was made for. This was her calling. She was made for demon slaying.

Sasha charged the fog. It had cleared around her enemy's waist, and as it did, she saw his counter. She ducked low and jumped high. She extended her body as long as it would go, and she cleared the commodore's blow easily as he struck low. Sasha's foot hit the ground, and with a single step, she jumped up against the bulkhead and flew once again over the commodore, who now slung with his baton at her feet as he turned around.

The running-man maneuver worked, and as Sasha landed, she thrust her baton forward and struck the commodore hard on his left buttock. The sparks crackled, and the smell of burning flesh filled the room. But the commodore was an experienced fighter, and absorbing the pain, he flew his body backward and crashed down on top of Sasha.

The air left her body as her back hit flat against the ground. The commodore was on her in an instant. His heavy body weighed down forcefully on hers, staying locked in place. His strength bent Sasha to his will.

Aramethel had now regained his control and had to divert his baton in order to avoid killing Sasha as she was raised up like a shield. The commodore followed Aramethel as he stumbled forward, smashing Sasha down onto the young apprentice's back, and then kicked the two of them hard into the wall.

Aragmell now came forward, his body no longer the towering presence it once was. A fatigue slumped his shoulders, a delay in his reactions spelled disaster, and a sense of failure clouded over him. He moved patiently, defensively, and purposefully. The commodore struck with hard, powerful blows. Aragmell's counterattacks lacked the energy and power of before.

The two circled each other. Fatigue, sweat, and determination poured from their bodies. There would only be enough for one round of attacks, and each side was at its limit. It was commodore's mind that moved first. He struck at Aragmell's waist, but the move was a fake, and as the guardian moved to intercept, the commodore struck with his full weight and power.

The baton struck powerfully, deep into the guardian's side. His flesh burned, and his body wailed. The strike didn't cut the guardian in half like the commodore had hoped, but it still might have been a fatal blow. With the last of his enemies vanquished, the commodore surveyed his surroundings and focused on his prey, his objective, and just maybe his redemption in the eyes of the emperor.

45: Rise of Captain Zeros

Prisoner 00 stood in fear, unable to move as the commodore charged with great speed, each thrust of the legs pushing him forward like a gazelle. Yet with each stride came a grimace. Each motion proved more and more cumbersome, and while the gap was closing swiftly, it still felt like a mile. The commodore raised his baton and took aim as he closed the distance. Prisoner 00 wanted to close his eyes but was locked in place.

The commodore was meters away when he bounded into a last lunge. Prisoner 00 made no big motion, no effort to dodge the attack, but the baton flew clear off to the right, and instead, the commodore's enormous body came crashing down on top of him.

The two collided with force, their limbs and bodies tussling about as they slid across the floor. The commodore's heavy, labored breaths spewed across Prisoner 00's face, but there was nothing more. With the shock of the moment now past, his body remembered with great difficulty and protest how to move. The commodore was alive, but his condition was not good, and if it was fatigue, time was critical, as fatigue wouldn't last long.

Pushing with all his remaining strength, Prisoner 00 rolled the commodore's body off of him. He stood and placed his hand on his hips, raised his foot high, and slammed it down onto the commodore.

"Power and the powerful are irrelevant. Only those with something greater can survive in all times." Prisoner 00 bent over, grabbed the commodore by the towers of his mantle, and brought him eye to eye. "You, you don't have that something." Then he shoved the commodore's face down and stomped his foot on him once more.

It took a while for the realization of what had happened to sink in. The doctors were tending to Sasha and Aramethel, while Aragmell restrained the commodore. Yet the rest gathered in awe as they exited from their hiding place inside the ship. There were more aliens inside than expected. The baroness was the first to clap, and although the others may not have seen the gesture before, they quickly understood and emulated, and the group was soon in full applause.

Prisoner 00 just stood there, dumbfounded and embarrassed, secretly enjoying it a bit too much, until the baroness came beside him and gave him a hug.

Lady Imric made a surprising move, kneeling next to Prisoner 00. "I pledge my loyalty to you, Captain Zeros and Lady Baroness." Then, one by one, the entire room went down to a knee.

The baroness pulled on his shirt and whispered into his ear. "Now is when you give your little speech, not before, now." She kissed him on the cheek and stood back.

Suddenly the joy of the situation had been taken out of it. All attention was on him, even if some of their eyes were not. A shiver of nervous energy ran down his spine, and with a twitch, he started. "Thank you, all. Never at any point in my life did I imagine that I would be in this position, in this place, or be this relevant." He had no idea what he wanted to say, no idea what to say, but he felt relaxed and spoke the words as they came to him. "Yet no matter how low I, us, we, have fallen, we can find renewal. We can find redemption. We can find a way forward. So please stand up and feel the spirit of renewal wash upon us.

"We are a community now, a fellowship of brethren. Our covenant will not be to each other, to our community, or to ourselves. This community now only serves one purpose, one goal, and one shared destiny. Together we must find a way to protect and raise a child. A child coveted by the powerful, targeted by the evil, and as someone once said to me, a child who is a hope for the future.

"Without all of you, I am nothing, but with you, I am something. Something so great even the empire's prized commodore can't stop. This I say to you, we will not only find our destiny—we are going to kick its ass! So come now, let's finish what has begun, and let's take this ship as our own!"

The group stood up and gave a quick cheer. The baroness spoke to Aragmell, who broke out into barking commands loud enough to organize and assemble teams and objectives. Within a few chaotic minutes, the group was amassed, reordered, and sent out with orders to secure the empire's new weapons for themselves.

Only a select few stayed behind: the doctors, who had assembled a triage station; their patients, including the young fighter, Sasha; and the Xendorian team leader.

As the room finally started to settle, a beautiful young Asian girl escorted in a blind army officer in a wheelchair. When they came to a rest, the girl placed her hand on the man's shoulder and whispered something into his ear. "That was a fine speech there, Captain. Only wish I could have seen it for myself."

"These new alien docs are quite the outfit. Can't they give you your sight back?" Being in a position of authority was unfamiliar and unsettling to the new captain, and he was feeling awkward with every interaction.

"No, I'm afraid that even technology can't eliminate the need for miracles. New eyes wouldn't do me any good without a brain that can see. Speaking of miracles, by the way, that is what I have to offer you. You have witnessed Sasha save your life once. Best to keep someone like that around, wouldn't you say? What we ask for in return is a safe place to stay, food, and water while I work with my doctors, who I am told are around here somewhere."

"Yes, sir, the doctors are still tending to Sasha now. Looks like she took quite a blow." Emilia's voice sang in the captain's ears, and he felt a strange mix of both parental and sensual emotions toward her.

"What? You didn't say she was hurt. Take me to her." Captain Drexter was very much in love with Sasha, like any parent, and the gut reaction to the news was unmaskable to Captain 00.

"Look," Emilia sounded natural before her long hesitation, "she is breathing into some sort of bag right now. She is fine." The sad drop in the girl's voice seemed very revealing to Captain 00, but his head hurt too much to figure out what it meant.

What the hell was he supposed to do, anyway? Offer them food, water, and shelter? Oh, the realization that he might just be able to do that was confounding. He looked around. The baroness held on to him but looked examiningly at the man in the wheel-chair and a woman who was now bound to him. He took another moment to look further around, and again he was astounded to find that he held a role in this place. An alien swore to protect him was issuing orders to other aliens. A high-ranking enemy commander lay at his feet, and a spaceship at his command, while not more than just a few days ago, he was nothing more than a loser john, Mr. "No Tip." While he wasn't sure exactly how or why it had happened, he had changed too. He no longer feared a repeat of his past failure. Instead he felt renewed, reborn, and forgiven.

He said, "Well, sir, I will say that you do have quite the fighter in your corner, and the more fighters the better. Yet before you sign on, I want to know something."

"What's that?"

"You ever touch her?"

What did this son of a bitch just say? The words only ma-terialized in Captain Drexter's brain, as his were lips too stunned to move and his anger too great to speak. If he'd had the ability to see, he surely would have laid this bastard out. Who the hell was this guy to accuse him of mistreating his own daughter? His anger finally burned out enough for his brain to process it.

"Look, mister, I don't know who the hell you think you are, but I am a good man, and if I could see you, you never would have been brave enough to ask that question." The reminder that he was actually blind and handicapped hit home hard. Anger morphed into pity, pity into self-doubt, and self-doubt into self-loathing. The fact that he could no longer follow through like he once could have wasn't going to be easy to live with.

"A middle-aged man shows up with two teenage girls, where there is obviously an emotional attachment. So yeah, I'm the one asking the question because if you're going to serve in this community, we won't be having it."

Anger again overtook his pity, and Captain Drexter was torn between hatred and admiration for this Captain 00. A long moment passed as Captain Drexter waited to see if he would say more. When he didn't, Captain Drexter simply said, "I'm a father, nothing more, nothing less."

This time, it was Captain 00's turn to ease back and absorb. "Yes, I do believe I agree. Now, sir, will you please tell me some more about your daughters? How would you like to be addressed? As you are the last soldier in the universe, I am uncertain what assumption to take in regard to your rank."

Nothing could improve his mood more than praising his own child, so despite his own mournful outlook, Captain Drexter's spirits rose as he spoke about Sasha. "Sasha is the greatest athlete, the most agile and dexterous person you will ever meet. Her brain can process information faster, smoother, and more correctly than anyone else. She was designed, trained, and made to be only one thing, an assassin. As for me, well I'm the caretaker of the most powerful weapon ever created by man. Call me Father Drex."

"Well her skill set was on display a few minutes ago. Does your other daughter possess the same skills?"

"Um, Emilia is under my care, or maybe rather reversed now. Emilia is . . . pure joy, but she lacks the superhuman abilities of Sasha. I am to take it we have a deal, Captain Zeros, is it?"

The baroness reached out, grabbed Emilia's hand, and moved in closer. "My dear, you have the mostly striking features. You are a natural beauty, has anyone ever told you that?"

Emilia blushed and gently shook the baroness's hand. Unconsciously, the baroness stroked Emilia's forearm, taking her hand away only to move the hair from Emilia's face. "Emilia, is it? Why don't we take the captain over to the doctors and Sasha? I'm sure Captain Zeros has a mission to finish." Then the baroness sent the captain over next to Aragmell, who was issuing orders via a wrist communicator, while the rest walked over to the doctors and Sasha. A tarp had been laid over the Xendorian team leader, and the commodore was bound and jumbled in his restraints.

When the three neared the others, Emilia placed her hand on the captain's shoulder and whispered something into his ear.

"Sasha, attention!" Captain Drexter barked the command more out of habit than enthusiasm and let a moment pass, and the awkwardness again reinforced his blindness. "Report!" He tried to sound the same, but he wasn't. He couldn't even tell if she was at attention or lying down.

Sasha stood at attention, but the look on her face was mournful. "I engaged the alien attacker but was defeated. Aragmell and Aramethel came to my aid, but again we were defeated. I am unable to report how Captain Zeros was able to defeat the alien. I was too incapacitated at the time to recon, sir."

Captain Drexter's lip quivered, betraying the emotion

behind his words, and he no longer sounded like an army officer but like the man he truly was, a father. "Sasha . . . I'm just so glad you are ok." He wanted so desperately to give her a hug, but he couldn't speak the words, and he couldn't move toward her. It was heartbreaking.

Emilia's hand landed on top of his shoulder, and he used the distraction to try to calm himself. As she walked around him, she brought up her other hand and embraced, hugging him from behind. Sure, they had hugged before, but this had a different level of emotion attached to it, and James Drexter no longer cared to hold back the tears.

It wasn't fair. The vapor both burned and soothed as Sasha's new doctors administered some sort of medicine to heal her lungs, they said. It just wasn't fair. These crazy alien doctors seemed able to cure anything that happened to her, so why couldn't they fix him? It just wasn't fair.

Her father was unconscious when she learned the news. Two officers—Chip and the rookie—had found them as her father lay half dead at the bottom of a stairwell, the building crumbling down around them, but they did it wrong. "Stupid assholes, just grabbed and pulled him. You don't just grab and pull a spinally injured person. Fucking idiot!" Her thoughts tortured her, yet her conscious mind kept them at bay, trying to bat them away each time they came back.

Sasha's mood changed color but not intensity as she saw them coming. Guilt and sorrow took over her brain as she cursed herself for not doing more. Why hadn't she been the one to save him? Why did she have to be the one to let him down? Why did it always have to be her fault when something bad happened?

Her guilt intensified when she saw Emilia, as beautiful as ever. Sasha found it hard to look at her. Would she eventually fail her too? She felt a wall rise up around her heart as they neared. Her father barked the orders as he always did, but she could feel the currents of his emotions washing over her with his words: "Sasha, report." The training had taken over, and Sasha was able to conduct herself appropriately.

It wasn't the first time Sasha had to report a failure, and had she allowed herself to feel the emotion with it, she surely would have cried. Yet the wall held, and her heart was safely secure. Even the quivering in his voice couldn't break down Sasha's voice, and she did what she thought she should: she stayed at attention.

Emilia, however, had different plans, and as she moved to engage Sasha, Sasha felt her wall come tumbling down. It was more than just her raw beauty. It was the gracefulness of her eyes, the calming balm of her aura, and her enormous heart that gave control of Sasha over to Emilia. As Emilia grabbed Sasha's hand, the wall was taken down, and together the three of them embraced like a family. Sasha cried like she never had before, and once again her purpose was clarified. She wasn't an assassin. She was a guardian, and she wouldn't fail again.

⊸⟋

Aragmell led the way for Captain 00 and the baroness, followed by some small dog-like creatures who sparked as they walked, a crazy multi-eyed man-sized fly, a couple of walking cornstalks, and a herd of small, black robots. A few scattered corpses of alien crew members littered the way. The baroness walked up close to Captain 00, and she felt his presence carry over onto her.

The baroness's mind spun, as so much had just happened. Was she really pregnant? Was all this actually some part of a dream? Was she still living the same life? Compared to where she was only a few days ago, her new existence was unimaginable. Only one thing had transferred over from her old life to her new one, and it was him. She ran her eyes up and down him again, bringing his attention and his hand onto her.

Never would she have chosen this, being pregnant and trapped with him. Yet now that it had happened, it didn't feel quite so bad. He wasn't a remarkable man, nor was he a skilled man, but he had something that she couldn't identify. It was what her high school coach would have simply called "it," what her mother would have called "predestination," but to the baroness, it was simply comforting.

Together they walked in silence, the unformed thoughts slipping from her mind to his. They had created a bond, more so than simply being the last two humans alive. They were mates, bound not at the hip but by the soul. At last they came to a large door. The Xendorian vegetation ran along the walls, outlining the door's dimensions.

The baroness took a deep breath and prayed for the best as they came forward. Aragmell stepped ahead and off to the side, waiting to open the door as they approached, but then he stopped and turned back around. "My Lady Baroness and her Captain Zeros, how do you wished to be announced?"

The baroness paused, a look of slight befuddlement crossing her face.

"How about His and Her Excellency?"

The baroness shot him a look of disapproval.

"The Indelible Baroness and Incomparable Captain Zeros?"

She shook her head. "Do you even know what those words mean?"

"The pretty lady and her kick-ass man?"

The baroness breathed out her disappointment, looked over her man, and nodded. It's easy to love perfection, but love isn't perfect, she realized. The baroness placed her head against his shoulder, and they walked forward.

He could feel it building, more exciting than the brothel, more real than his life just a few days ago, and more intense than even his greatest fantasy. When Captain 00 walked onto the bridge, a strange medley of aliens rose in salutations and greetings. He had a beautiful woman who loved him at his side and a renewed sense of spirit and life filling his soul. There would be time for reflection and admittance later, but for now, he simply enjoyed it.

"Please rise for the Lady Baroness and her kick-ass man, Captain Zeros." Aragmell kept a very straight face.

The fly-like creature was the first to speak. "Captain, there are multiple Xendorian warships bearing down on our positions. They have already launched their assault craft."

Panic briefly struck away his golden glow, as he felt clueless once more. "Failure," the word itself, creeped into his mind as a bad omen, and all of his newfound confidence was wiped away, just like that. He looked around at the faces staring at him, waiting, longing, and demanding. Besides the panic, he felt her eyes and even her unsaid words. Failure, he told himself, is not the end but a new beginning. "What's your name and species again?"

"I'm Navigator Flynn. I am a member of the Pergenese species. What are your orders, sir?"

He swallowed hard and spoke while thinking. "Well, Mr. Flynn, take us straight at them, full speed ahead." Ha, it worked again, he thought, the less I think, the better I do.

One of the tall stalk-like creatures spoke next, from one of the consoles running along the side of the bridge. "Preparing for slip-gate activation and transit."

He could just feel it—this was home. No, he was wrong. She was home, and that recognition brought a smile to his face even as three large ships lashed out with their weapons of light as they flew by on the view screen. The doctors approached the couple as three beams of light projected out in front of their ship. A vortex opened as the beams converged and the ship slipped inside its bubble. A vast blackness opened around them, only slowly filling back in with the lights from the stars.

Flynn once again took the initiative. "Captain, I have found a class A nebula only two jumps away. I would say a good hiding place for the near term, if the captain so desires."

The doctors almost seemed to nod in agreement with Flynn as they beckoned the couple back out away from the bridge. "The captain does so desire, Mr. Flynn. I leave the conn in your hands until I return."

"The conn, sir?"

"You know, you're in charge until I get back." With that, the doctors led the still-twitching captain and the baroness to the medical bay.

The baroness held on to Zeros, guiding him as they sauntered down the humid, damp hallway. He looked down at her and smiled. "So I have a question. I'm the father, right?"

She returned his smile. "Yes you are, and no, no you don't have a question."

He gave a stern glance. "No, I really do have a question."

She returned his sternness. "No, no you don't."

This time, he moved in close to her and spoke confidently. "I'm very certain I have a question."

Before he could say more, the baroness moved in closer, let her eyes roll into her head as she thought for a second, and then kissed him. "Don't worry, you were good. Very satisfying." She kissed him again and then pulled away and caught up to Dr. Fengie.

Mardoxx and Aragnaught led Hashmore through a series of hallways and corridors that finally ended in a most unremarkable office. It held a regular human-style desk with a formal, black, squared chair behind it. Nothing sat on top of the desk, which was left of center in the middle of the room. The two escorts motioned for Hashmore to sit. Mardoxx hopped up onto the table while Aragnaught quickly started up small talk, but he found no audience, as Mardoxx was being less than responsive and Hashmore was too tired to care anymore.

Fatigue and age had finally caught up with Hashmore, who'd had about enough. His body ached, his head throbbed, and he felt faint of conviction. Aragnaught managed to find a topic of interest to Mardoxx as the two discussed a game called Blazerball.

Aragnaught's occasional interjections were annoying enough, and now that the two started chatting, each new syllable took Hashmore up another rung on the bad-mood ladder. On and on and on it went. Why was he even here? What were they waiting for? Would they let him go?

The thought of standing up and leaving nearly overcame him, but as his physical body stood, his resolve sank, with no idea where to go or how to get there. The two escorts looked strangely at Hashmore, their alien features still familiar enough to give away their thoughts. The silence was glorious, and Hashmore relished in the moment. But again Aragnaught broke in with needless drudgery, only this time Hashmore's temper overcame his resolve.

Cursing and blasphemy were not staples of his behavior, but he was human. A time would come when his outburst would bring him shame, but for now Hashmore was pissed off and venting. Neither fatigue nor exhalation of air would disarm his temper, but a familiar voice brought comfort and revitalization.

"I know what your mother would do with that mouth, and I would rather choose a bar of soap. Now why don't you stop feeling all sorry for yourself and get to where I can see you and give me a report?"

The intense red of his face softened to an embarrassed hue as his eyes and head searched around for his friend, partner, and boss. "Biggie-OOO," he spoke as his eyes finally found the face of his friend. A view screen behind him, in the corridor from which he came, now softened and calmed Hashmore as he once again felt connected to humanity and his best friend. "It's good to see you, my friend."

"Yes, yes it is very good to see you, my friend. Are you well?"

"Better now, but this isn't the retirement job you said it was going to be."

"That's 'cause you're out of fucking line. I hired you to manage all this shit while I go gallivanting around with the aliens. What the hell, Hashmore?"

"Glad to see you missed me. Any word on Maria?"

Big M's tone softened, and behind the veneer of masculinity, it was sad. "No, that tramp said she was going shopping, so who the hell knows where she went." A short pause allowed Big M to recompose himself. "Haven't completed the head count yet, but it's bad. We had a rough go of it down here." He paused again. "Now tell me, what the hell is going on up there? Some of these alien bastards are trying to rip our fucking heads off while these barrel squids put them back on. Tell me you know what the hell is going on."

"To summarize, sir, we are now part of a spacefaring civilization known as the Arkapeligo—those would be the squids in a barrel, the walking dogs, the man-sized flies, and a few others. A separate civilization entity known as the Xendorians have attacked and raided our world in a search—those would be the guys ripping people's heads off. While yet another species known as the Wilde have apparently destroyed Earth, or so I'm told. We fled before any actual attack by the Wilde got underway."

"If I hadn't seen what I've fucking seen with my own two damn eyes, I would swear you were back on the pills. So what the hell were they searching for that required them to pull people's fucking heads off?"

"A child."

"A child?"

"A child, who has some kind of special gene. In fact, some of these aliens believe we have a special power."

"Don't change the damn subject. Where is the child? Are they coming back here to look again?"

"Where, I couldn't tell you, but I can tell you that we sent a ship full of aliens, a blind man, and two teen girls out to save them before we left."

"Jesus, please tell me you are not in charge up there. I'm questing your sobriety again, and it does leave me in the position of asking you, what happens next?"

Hashmore opened his mouth, but his brain produced no answer. It was Mardoxx who entered the conversation with an answer. "Yes, the Great Mother will give a formal address to the entire Arkapeligo. Then, Mr. Hashmore, you will be returned to your people, and your chosen representative will work here, in this office."

Hashmore motioned with his arm. "See, under control. Now, as to my retirement."

"Retirement?" Big M crossed his arms and mean mugged Hashmore before speaking. "Very well, you're fired. You are no longer the emergency manager. You were doing a shitty job anyway."

Hashmore was caught off guard. Having known his friend for so long a time, he shouldn't have been, but it still gave him pause—enough pause for Big M to continue the conversation. "As of now, you are whatever the hell the person working in that office's title is. At least you were doing a competent job at that."

Hashmore smiled. There was just something in the way his friend managed to order people around that was kind of rewarding. A protest formed in his mind, but with his friend's presence reinvigorating his energy, it found no backing and thus could not form. Retirement had once again been diverted.

The Great Mother stood proudly, perched atop an intricately carved wooden swing. Behind her image was the planet they were now orbiting. Immaculate and formal, she looked more like a leader now than the old woman Hashmore had met in the cavern.

View screens across the ark, all invisible before now, formed seemingly everywhere. In the sky above Manhattan, a bright-red planet filled the sky, and in front of the planet was the Great Mother.

"Citizens of the Arkapeligo, it is once again my great

privilege and honor to be addressing you as head of council, priest of the faith, and fellow citizen. The Battle of Sol has ended, and the costs have been high. Many of our citizens have been asked to make the ultimate sacrifice. Let us never forget the great honor they have bestowed upon us. Let us never forget the honor it is for us to have been saved, not only by our brethren but by this ship of life. Let us never shame those gifts.

"It has been my greatest pleasure and accomplishment to be welcoming my fourth race to the ark. To have saved so many sentient beings from extinction is an achievement to be most proud of. Today we welcome the human race to our collective."

Images of the baroness and Captain 00 now replaced the one of the Great Mother.

"Yet it is also my greatest disappointment that my time of leadership should include so much death, loss, and destruction. Darkness attacks from every side. Allies long forged have been swept away into shadow. Points of refuge grow thin. Friendly ports to call upon are fewer and fewer. And while we have accomplished so much, hope of success feels so far away. For so long, we have saved so little in comparison to what has been lost. For so long, we have been longing for, searching for, and praying for a weapon, a catalyst, a savior. For so long, we have held on to a fading hope.

"Yet the hope is real. This ship is real. This ship is a light against the encroaching darkness. This ship can shine. And now, my citizens, we have hope again to fuel our light. For what seems like so long, we have looked out into that darkness and seen nothing but an onslaught of darkness, yet today something is different. Today we have seen something new in the darkness. A shimmer, a shine, maybe even a ray of light, but that light can be nurtured, grown, to release a new era of light.

"Our mission will never change, to protect life. However, now we have another mandate, another task. We must seek out this light, nurture it, and unleash it.

"Much has been lost, much has been sacrificed, and now more is asked. It may feel overwhelming, overburdening, and asking us to achieve the impossible. Yet the hope is real, and if we use our camaraderie, faith, and perseverance, I truly believe we can accomplish these greatest of achievements.

"Thank you, and God bless."

The three sat idle. Personal effects of the Xendorian who had previously inhabited the room were still scattered about. This, they were told, this would be their new home. What they would be called to do and what would come of their future would be anybody's guess.

Father Drex sat slumped in something resembling a chair. Sasha departed the room in search of a shower, or another form of hygiene, and Emilia sat next to the former army officer. "I'm scared too."

Father Drex sighed and held out his hand, waiting for her to grab it. "Emilia, I feel so fortunate to have found you. Sasha has a connection to you, a connection that even I don't have with her. While I may be blind, I can hear it, I can sense it. Emilia, Sasha is in love with you."

An emotional tinge came across in Emilia's voice. "I know, but I don't know what to do about it. I can't love her back."

Before the blindness, he still harbored a sinful hope, but now depression and handicap had taken that hope away, and the captain knew Emilia wasn't for him, wasn't his *yuanfen*. Yet she could be what he and Sasha needed. "Emilia, I know it won't be easy for you, but you must let Sasha have these feelings for you. She will need them, she will be called upon to risk much, and she will need an anchor to come back to. If you can't love her as a love, you must love her as her friend, because she will need more than I can be for her."

"What if she wants to love me?"

Father Drex gulped. "Be brave, my dear. I will do what I can for you."

The door slid open, and Sasha entered with a big smile on her face. She ran up to Emilia, grabbed her friend's hands, and bounced as she spoke. "Oh my god, we shower in a freakin' waterfall. It's so beautiful. I can't wait for you to see it." Sasha bounced around and then saw her father.

She sat next to him and gave him a hug. "Thank you. I'm so, so, so sorry you can't see this. Please come with us. I'm sure I can find someone to help you."

Father Drex let out a depressed sigh as he once again felt the weight of his burden upon others. After a long moment, he lifted his head and looked in her general direction. "Go ahead, I need some time to think."

Sasha exchanged a worried glance with Emilia, and after a nonverbal debate, they decided to leave. Sasha gave him another long hug and hurried to get her shower gear. Emilia came close to Father Drex, kissed him on his forehead, and whispered. "Sasha still needs a father. I still need a father. I still need you."

The girls left on their excursion, and the father sat alone in the darkness of his future. The weight of this new burden was immense. It was too much for him, so he dropped to his knees and prayed. "Dear Lord, please, I need your help."

⌣⟩

The machines hummed and vibrated, and the doctors' needles hurt and stung, but they assured Captain 00 that the twitching would eventually stop. While he would experience muscle spasms, they would eventually pass. Nothing about his surroundings was familiar. It would be impossible for him to even find the bridge again. Many of his new comrades were still very unfamiliar, and in some ways frightening.

As unprofound as his life before may have been, it was at least predictable and carefree. Now he faced an entirely new future, one of responsibility and unpredictability. Running, fleeing should have been his inclination, yet there was no place he wanted to be more. There was joy to be found here, and with her.

The doctors worked diligently. Dr. Fergie and his mate, Dr. Fengie, examined, diagnosed, and cured. Again and again they repeated the cycle. And his body slowly returned to something closer to normal. The pain and suffering of this ordeal began to set in. Never before had he felt so awful, yet his body was sprite with spirit and will.

⌣⟩

A buzzer sounded, drawing the attention of the group.

"What is it?" the baroness asked as her monitor flashed with a red light.

Dr. Fergie laughed one of his jolly laughs and smiled wide. "Why, my dear, nature has once again proven that the most complicated problems have the simplest solutions. In this case, that little bundle of mystery you are growing down there."

"What does that mean?" she asked.

Dr. Fengie answered for her husband. "Why, my dear, it means that you are having twins. Both a boy and a girl. And it looks like only one of them has our mystery gene."

"Which child?"

"Why, the proper one of course, my dear."

THE END

Made in the USA
Coppell, TX
15 January 2020

14558844R00307